"Please help me."

Gently, Jaxon cradled Libby tight against his heaving chest, feeling every heartbeat her body took, fighting the overwhelming urge to protect and soothe.

It was a losing battle, and he knew it.

Jaxon Castille, jaguar warrior, felled by someone like Libby Jamieson.

He cursed the irony.

Libby.

He had dreamed of ways to make her pay. He had lain awake so many nights, fighting the desire that ravaged his body at just the thought of her. Rage fed the cat, enticing it into a frenzy that drove him, day after day, fueling the hunt.

And look where that got him.

Here he stood, quivering with need, holding onto the woman who'd shredded his life into slices of want, need, and emptiness.

By Juliana Stone

HIS DARKEST HUNGER

Coming Soon

HIS DARKEST EMBRACE

Juliana Stone

His Darkest
HUNGER

AVON

An Imprint of HarperCollinsPublishers

This is a work of fiction. Names, characters, places, and incidents are products of the author's imagination or are used fictitiously and are not to be construed as real. Any resemblance to actual events, locales, organizations, or persons, living or dead, is entirely coincidental.

AVON BOOKS
An Imprint of HarperCollins*Publishers*
10 East 53rd Street
New York, New York 10022-5299

Copyright © 2010 by Juliana Stone
ISBN 978-0-06-180877-7
www.avonromance.com

First Avon Books paperback printing: April 2010

Avon Trademark Reg. U.S. Pat. Off. and in Other Countries, Marca Registrada, Hecho en U.S.A.
HarperCollins® is a registered trademark of HarperCollins Publishers.

Printed in the U.S.A.

10 9 8 7 6 5 4 3 2 1

His Darkest
HUNGER

Chapter 1

It did not bode well that Jaxon Castille was working.

In his particular area of expertise it meant that someone was going to die.

It wouldn't be pretty. Death never was, but it would be an act full of stealth, precision, and deadly accuracy, performed by the best that there was.

Jaxon threw his satchel to the ground as his eyes fell to the semifrozen earth at his feet. The coolness of late spring lingered there, and his quivering nostrils inhaled a fresh, crisp shot of air, blowing out a fine mist of warmth in return. He was well over six feet in height and moved with a sinuous grace at odds with someone his size. His features were dark, a true reflection of both his Spanish heritage and the emotions at war inside his body.

He was tense, and took a few seconds to calm his spirit, his black eyes quickly scanning the small knoll where he stood. The slope was steady and crested down into the valley, where it rushed up against the outskirts of the small town of Winterhaven.

A muscle worked its way sharply across Jaxon's cheek, and he clenched his teeth in an effort to maintain control. Off into the distance the last lingering rays of sun painted a vibrant picture of reds, oranges, and yellows in the sky. Dusk was rapidly approaching and nervous energy clawed at his insides, as thoughts of his forthcoming mission slammed into him.

It was time to put old ghosts to rest and move on. *It was time for her to die.*

Steely resolve flickered across handsome features that at the moment were obscured by cold fury. *That* particular emotion had taken up a permanent residence, ever since he'd received intel on his target several days earlier.

Intel that he had been waiting three long years for.

A picture rushed into his mind, and he growled low, deep in his belly, as visions of entangled limbs, long blond hair, and violet eyes assaulted him. The pressure along his jaw increased tenfold as his face darkened at the memories.

Traitorous bitch.

His skin began to burn, and his eyesight blurred as his heart rate increased. He was close to the edge and could feel the beast clawing just under the surface.

With superhuman effort Jaxon pushed all thoughts but the deadly mission from his mind. He began to methodically examine the terrain around him, automatically finding the precise spot to set up his sniper gear.

His eyes swept back to town, and as evening fast approached, one after one, lights began to flicker on in various homes and businesses.

He was only interested in one, and, using his binoculars, his eyes hardened at the sight of several patrons inside the small diner.

She hadn't shown up yet.

But she would. His intel had indicated that she always reported for work at five o'clock sharp. He would be waiting for her tonight.

And it would be her last.

A bitter smile exposed even white teeth as he made preparations for the coming hour. He turned in a circle and scented the wind. Satisfied that no creature, human or other, was near, Jaxon reached for the large satchel and with great care unpacked his M40.

The large rifle had been modified at Quantico, but his team further enhanced the weapon. It was now cutting edge. He could take out a target at well over one thousand feet. His little bag of goodies contained several variations of nasty little bullets: silver for lycans, anticharm for magicks, and extra special ones for vamps. These were dipped in holy water and engraved with etchings and symbols of a large sacred cross.

Tonight, he knew he would need none of those. His target was human.

She would never know what hit her.

Something slithered through his brain then, and for the first time in days a shred of emotion other than hatred grabbed him. It was fleeting, gone as quickly as it had come. But it gave him pause nonetheless.

Was it his conscience? Was something trying to tell him that eliminating her was a bit extreme, even for him?

Angrily, he checked and rechecked his weapon, anchored it on its tripod and settled in to wait. He glanced down to his timepiece, noting his target would be in range within the next five minutes.

His target.

Funny that.

She had a name, one that when spoken used to make his body tight with desire. It was a name that had not crossed his lips in a very long time, and now it had come to this.

She was a target. *His* target. His smile slashed through the gloom and he snarled savagely.

He sure as hell had thought of her every day, picturing all kinds of ways to exact revenge. Truthfully, a quick bullet between the eyes was probably more than the bitch deserved. If he had his way, she'd suffer, just as Diego had.

On the day she'd betrayed the entire unit.

Movement inside the diner caught his eye and Jaxon felt the world slip away as he brought the binoculars to his eyes again and focused on the brightly lit interior. There were several patrons inside enjoying a greasy meal of Americana, and several kitchen staff could be seen scurrying about further inside. He noticed two new staff members and felt a slice of impatience stab him.

She was nowhere to be seen.

A flicker of annoyance rushed through Jaxon but was quickly put to rest. He was used to waiting. Patience was a virtue, and in his line of work it usually meant the difference between life and death.

He lay there quiet, focused and with deadly intent.

When a flash of blond hair moved from the kitchen and into the main dining area, he almost missed it. Jaxon bit his tongue, tasting the coppery scent of his own blood.

The world did indeed stop then. Everything faded into a swirl of fog as he expanded the amplification to give him a close-up of the face that had haunted him nightly.

He hissed sharply as the lens focused, feeling a keen sense of frustration run through him as her back was presented to the window. He could take her out now. One bullet straight to the back of the head and she'd be dead before she hit the ground.

Instead he held his breath, willing her body to turn so he could lay eyes upon her one more time.

Her body was hunched over slightly, and as he took a second to clinically look her over, he was surprised to note the drastic weight loss. The seam of her spine was plainly visible against the white cotton shirt she wore. She also seemed to be favoring her left side, her posture suggesting weakness there.

Her long blond hair thrown up into a careless ponytail had darkened somewhat, as if she'd been too long from the warmth of the sun. A few of the strands had fallen free, and he watched the arc of her hand as she attempted to push the tendril from where it tickled the side of her neck.

His eyes homed in on the pale expanse of skin there, and once more visuals he cared never to visit again darkened his mind. Angrily he beat them away, welcoming the fresh rush of emotion that infused his spirit as hatred again encircled his heart.

He was done. It was time.

He carefully placed the binoculars to his left and leaned in low, setting his eye to the telescopic lens attached to his weapon.

Within seconds he had a clear view, his fingers grasping the trigger as he eyed his target with determination.

He just needed her to move slightly to the left and the civilian would be out of the picture. Then he would have a clear shot.

She bent toward the patron before pausing, and once more he noted the stiffness of her movements.

Without warning she turned quickly, and the flicker of pain that crossed her features startled him. But Jaxon was even less prepared for the face that peered out into the night.

As if she knew he was there.

The expressive violet eyes seemed to be too large for her face. There were dark circles ringed beneath them. Her pallor was startling and her cheeks shrunken. Her generous lips were without color, and as his eyes focused on her once more, Jaxon felt a sharp pang of . . . *something.*

Her eyes were wary, pained. He could see from several hundred feet out that, as she peered into the early evening gloom, she was scared shitless.

He laughed harshly under his breath. She *should* be scared out of her mind.

A thought rushed through him, so out of character that he dismissed it right away. But as he watched her slowly turn from the window and walk toward the kitchen, his mind was already made up.

In his entire career he'd never once broken protocol. But tonight was different. He would let emotion take the lead, and maybe he'd get some sort of closure.

Maybe he would find out why she'd betrayed the unit, or better yet, why she'd betrayed *him*.

The cold part of his heart roared to life as he jumped to his feet and grabbed his satchel. Quickly, he dismantled his weapon, hitching the large bag around his shoulders before making his way stealthily down the embankment toward town.

Yeah, it was time to make things right.

Before she took her last breath and felt the heat of his vengeance, Libby Jamieson would know who her executioner was.

Deep inside his soul, the cat roared with pleasure, and Jaxon quickened his pace in answer to its call.

"Libby, does table seven want mashed or fries with his steak?"

The line cook waited expectantly, and Libby felt a moment of panic as she grabbed her notepad, her eyes scanning the pages furiously. She felt her heart speed up as the blank pages flashed by, the beginning of a panic attack well in the making.

Tears began to form at the corner of her eyes, and blackness tickled at the shattered pieces of her brain.

Pete, the owner and resident head cook, noted her pallor and flew from behind his roost, taking the pad away from her gently.

"Libby, calm down. It's all right."

His slow drawl washed through her, and the feel of his fingers massaging the tense muscles in her hands provided a token bit of relief.

Frustrated, she shoved the pad of paper at him, her voice catching on a sob.

"What's wrong with me, Pete? Why can't I just get it right?" She turned from him, trying to count. Sometimes it worked. Sometimes it didn't. "I was doing fine. I told him the specials, and he told me he wanted his steak medium rare with steamed veggies, and then . . . then I got distracted. Something was outside."

Pete winced at the anguish that colored her delicate features. How he wished he could make it all go away. He was an old man, a widower with no children. His life was the diner, and when this little slip of woman drifted into town a few months ago, he knew she needed special care to mend her broken spirit.

And he had tried. *Good lord how he'd tried.* But wherever she came from had been nothing short of hell, and it took time to get her to trust him. She'd only been able to work and interact with his staff and the patrons over the last few weeks.

She'd not had an incident in a day or so, and damned if he was gonna let her get all out of sorts because she'd forgotten if a customer wanted mashed or fries.

"Take a deep breath, darlin'. You said he ordered steamed veggies, and . . . just think, sweetling, it'll come."

Libby fought the blackness with all her might, and was rewarded with a sense of calm that loosened her tight muscles and allowed her to breathe. She closed her eyes and concentrated.

It was only a few seconds before they flew open and a rare smile washed over her mouth.

"He wanted fries . . . and gravy, with a side dish of mayo!"

Pete patted her softly on her shoulders, "See, darlin'? It's not that hard to do."

Libby watched as the burly cook turned and shouted down the line, "Libby says the gentleman wants fries with gravy and a side of mayo. Get to it!"

The silly grin didn't leave her face for a few more moments. Pete moved back behind the grill and flashed a smile of encouragement. "You did good."

Inside, nestled against the emptiness of her soul, warmth flushed through her system. It was one more battle she'd been able to win. One more challenge overcome.

Her hand went to the left side of her rib cage and she massaged the sore area under her heart. Pete had taken her to a local doctor, and she was informed that her ribs had been broken at one time, but they had not healed properly. She'd had pain as long as she could remember; which by most standards wasn't long at all. She had no memory whatsoever of life before coming to Winterhaven. She knew her name and that was about it.

The discomfort was something she'd gotten used to, along with all of the rest.

"Libby, we just sat a new customer in your section. I gave him a menu and told him you'd be with him shortly."

Libby glanced at the tall brunette who stood in the doorway. Maxine didn't much care for her. That was obvious.

"Unless you don't think you can handle it," she added, " 'cause I sure as hell wouldn't mind serving him. He's smokin' hot; all tall, dark, and sexy."

Libby felt a headache begin to finger its way sneakily into her head. At the moment, she wanted nothing more than to leave, to just go up to her little apartment atop the restaurant and try to forget everything; the nightmares, aches, and pains . . . all of it.

But she knew she couldn't do that. Pete hadn't taken any money for rent, and she could no longer accept his charity. It was time she started contributing and paying her way.

"No, that's fine, Maxine. I'll be out in a second."

She counted to ten, ignoring the smile that graced Pete's face, and marched herself back out into the diner.

Mr. Steak and Fries smiled when she walked by, indicating with a nod of his head that his drink needed refreshing. She quickly complied, bringing him a fresh pint of beer.

The customer at table three had his back to her, but she could see that he was perusing the menu, and knew she should go and check on him. Her feet shuffled slowly along until she was but a foot or two away.

He was large, muscular, and she could see he was tall, even seated. His hair was blue-black and closely cropped, but the texture was thick and it spiked in different directions atop his head.

The arms that rested on the table were darkly tanned, as if he spent a fair bit of time out in the sun. The left arm had a series of intricate tattoos that disappeared beneath the sleeve of this shirt. She shook her head at the sight of them, so strange yet beautiful. As he flexed the muscles in his arms, the tattoos seemed to move, as if alive. His legs were long and stretched out before him. They were covered in khaki pants that did nothing to hide the powerful limbs that seemed to be anything but relaxed.

Libby felt a hint of unease waft through her, but she angrily shoved it aside. She was sick and tired of being sick, tired, and scared. Enough was enough.

Inhaling deeply, she drew in a calming breath and took two more steps until she was level with him. Keeping her eyes averted, she looked at the specials written on her pad and read them off quickly. Her voice was so soft she was afraid he wouldn't be able to understand her and she'd have to start all over again.

When she was done, she waited patiently for him to tell her his order. Moments ticked by and no words were forthcoming. Quickly, her eyes flickered to the table, and she became mesmerized by the tapping fingers that pounded out a staccato beat against the brown grain tabletop. They were long, lean, and incredibly male.

She felt a small flush of heat make its way up from her belly, spreading warmth over her flesh until her pale cheeks began to color.

"Would you like to order something, sir?"

She was about to try again, feeling like a fool at the continued silence that stretched between them. But then, when he finally spoke, she jumped, startled at both the timber and the effect he had on her.

"I'd like you to look at me."

His voice was low and rough, with an edge of steel to it that sent her defenses crashing into red alert. Her first instinct was to flee, to rush through the door of the diner and never look back.

She fought it. She fought it hard, and inside felt a

sense of wonder that she was able to mumble a few words instead of run.

"I'm sorry, what would you like to order?"

She turned slightly, angled her head and exhaled softly as she looked into midnight eyes that were staring at her with lethal hardness.

Her tummy took a nose dive and she almost stumbled as the intensity of his glare washed over her. The man was on edge and clearly pissed off. Danger clung to him, caressing his shoulders and surrounding his body like an invisible force.

She could feel it, deep inside; he was not to be messed with. He was the kind of man who would eat someone like her for lunch.

He was the kind of man that haunted her nightmares.

Libby broke into a sweat as her body heated up, full of anxiety. Her breath was coming fast and hard, and she could feel the blackness, once more skirting the edge of madness.

A small sob escaped her as she fought for control, trying to tame the emotions that ran rampant through her frail body. Her side began to ache from the pressure, and instinctively her hand went to it, massaging it slowly.

The man's eyes followed this movement, and when they once more locked onto hers, a tingling awareness rushed through her. Her head was pounding now and she thought she was literally going to come apart.

His eyes still held hers, but something in them had changed. A flicker of emotion colored the blackness that was there, and she swayed, her hand grabbing his shoulder.

"I'm sorry, I . . . don't feel well."

He shrugged away violently from her touch, and Libby withdrew her hand, feeling as if she'd been scorched. She staggered back, her eyes never leaving his, trapped by the bitterness that she now saw.

"Libby, do you need some help?" Maxine asked from behind, the tone sarcastic and gleeful at the same time.

"Please, I . . ." An intense jolt of pain ripped through her brain, and Libby's hands automatically went to cradle her head as she saw stars. Her eyes tried to focus as she watched the notepad fall to her feet. But she couldn't. The world seemed to be heaving underfoot, and she swayed as the darkness that had been cloying around the edges of her mind erupted violently.

A moment later her body fell forward and she would have smashed face first into the hard tiles if not for the large arms that grabbed her.

At the same time, glass shattered to their right and a spray of bullets rained down, punching the empty air where they'd both been.

 Chapter 2

The world stopped completely for Jaxon Castille.
Bullets flying everywhere, screams and shouts ripping through the air in terror; all of it faded into nothing but white noise. He could hear his heart beating steadily inside his body, and as he inhaled air deep into his lungs, the whooshing sound it made echoed eerily in his head.

Everything slowed and came to a halt.

Everything but Libby.

His vision focused into a narrow beam that encircled her body and nothing else.

Her legs had collapsed as she pitched forward. Instinct took over and his arms snaked out, grabbing her around the waist, and he went with her, cushioning the fall with the hardness of his body. He covered her face with his hands and turned as shattered glass blew out and rained down on them.

Her scent instantly went deep, and the animal that lived inside of him quivered excitedly, wanting . . . craving the female it had long been denied.

With great effort Jaxon pushed the beast back, his eyes quickly scanning the face he had never forgotten. She was so incredibly pale, a shallow ghost of her former self, and the feel of her frailty hit him hard in the gut.

The look in her eyes when she finally had the courage to meet his own had stunned him. They were full of horror and utter confusion.

In that instant he knew. Libby Jamieson had no idea who the hell he was. No one, not even Jodie Foster, could have faked such a performance.

What the hell had happened to her? And where in the hell had she disappeared to these last three years?

An even more pressing matter occurred to him as the scent of blood drifted through his nasal passages. His heart leapt into his throat as he turned her face in his hands, before they quickly ran down the length of her body.

He didn't realize he'd been holding his breath until he was satisfied the blood wasn't coming from her, and he let it out heavily.

Quickly he turned, still cradling her close to his body, and spied the other waitress, Maxine. She was lying in a pool of blood, while a few other staff members were crouched low around her. Within a few seconds Jaxon was able to ascertain that the unfortunate woman was the only casualty.

One of the waitresses was giving her mouth to mouth, but he knew that her life force had already seeped from her limp body, mingling with the pool of blood that was slowly growing larger.

The door from the kitchen flew open and two men charged into the melee of screaming, frightened people. The older gentleman ran to the downed waitress and touched his fingers to her throat before shaking his head sadly. A fresh hail of whimpers sprang from the waitress who had been frantically trying to resuscitate, and she collapsed onto her friend as she cried out in anguish.

The older man patted her head in sorrow before springing to his feet. His eyes searched wildly, and when he rested them on Jaxon, his face went white and his legs almost buckled.

Libby meant something to this man. Jaxon growled and held her possessively as he approached. The beast began to clamor loudly, wanting to make an appearance, and he leapt to his feet quickly, ducking behind a wall, using it as a buffer between him and the sniper who was still out there.

A sniper that had come for both Libby and himself.

Rage, all consuming and black, flushed his face, and the older man halted. It was only concern and fear for Libby that pushed him forward. "Is she . . . ?" His voice was hoarse and tears thickened his tongue.

Jaxon shook his head, answering in a clipped voice. "No. She just fainted."

"Thank God. I'm Pete, what the hell happened here? It looks like a war zone. I've already called 911. The police should be here any minute."

Pete looked back to the dead waitress and his voice broke. "I just don't understand how this could happen. I don't understand . . . any of this."

"Can you take Libby?"

Jaxon's voice cut through Pete's confusion and he carefully placed Libby in his arms. "I'll be back. Make sure no harm comes to her."

He grabbed his bag and strode toward the door, barely contained fury humming along behind him.

"But you can't just leave. The police are going to want to talk to you."

Jaxon didn't bother turning around, but his voice drifted back toward Pete as the door closed behind him. "Just keep her safe. She belongs to me."

Off in the distance, the wail of sirens signaled the arrival of local law enforcement. Jaxon quickly slipped into the alley behind the diner and reached into his pocket to retrieve a cell phone. He hit number one on his speed dial.

"Yeah, Dec here."

"Declan, it's me."

He heard a long static-filled pause in his ear as he waited for his former weapons specialist to get over the shock of hearing his voice. After their unit was ambushed three years earlier, the team had been dismantled, and they were all been reassigned after the debriefing. He tried to keep in touch, but had not bothered with either Declan or Ana in well over a year.

"How did you get this number? You need a level five clearance before it's given out."

Jaxon gritted his teeth, trying to hold the beast down and keep his composure. Declan O'Hara wanted to have a pissing contest, but he had no time for that kind of shit. "I'm in a small town called Winterhaven. It's located in northern Michigan. I found Libby."

There was a pause once more as his former teammate took a few moments.

"And she's still alive?" The voice was harsh, deadly cold.

It was Jaxon's turn to pause as a host of emotions washed over him. "I came here specifically to put a bullet between her eyes, but yeah, she's still alive."

"And the reason for that is?" Declan's manner had wintered even more as the barely concealed contempt they all felt for Libby rose to the surface.

"Something's not right here. I was sent this intel on a secure channel. I didn't take the time to check it out, so I can't even tell you where the hell it came from. What I *can* tell you . . . is that things are not what they seem. She has no clue who the hell I am, and someone just tried to take the both of us out."

Jaxon paused, tight-lipped with anger at the audacity of the unknown assassin. His voice became harsh and he growled into the cell phone. "I need you to find out where that intel came from. This was a setup. It's not about Libby. It's about me. Someone wants me dead, and I aim to find the bastard before he gets another shot at my ass."

"And what about Libby?"

Jaxon paused before barking into the phone, "Leave her to me. She has a lot to answer for, and trust me, she will pay for her complicity in Diego's murder."

"Right, *sure*. So where we gonna run this investigation? I'm assuming you want to keep it on the down low."

"Meet me at the loft in twenty-four hours. Call

ahead and let Cracker know you're coming. You still in touch with Ana?"

"Yeah, she freelances with us every now and again. I can't promise, though. Not sure she's even in the country."

"Call her. I'll expect to see the both of you tomorrow night."

Jaxon clicked the cell and shoved it back into his pocket. He listened briefly as the sound of police and emergency response teams intermingled with the shrieks and cries of the scared patrons inside the diner.

The lonely wail of a wolf lit the night sky, and suddenly the beast inside him became painfully agitated.

Jaxon took off at a run, climbing the fire escape until he was on top of the roof. He crouched down low, senses quivering in the cold night air. Reaching into his bag, he retrieved a small pair of night vision goggles and began a scan of the area along the embankment, where he'd set his sniper gear up less than an hour ago.

No movement could be discerned. Whoever took the shots had probably disappeared as soon as they'd been fired. He would have known his aim had failed, his cover blown, and retreated.

Savagely, Jaxon snarled as his body hummed in anticipation. It had been far too long since he'd hunted. Running to the far side of the building, he leapt over the side and landed over twenty feet below. He paused, scented the air, then broke into a run.

The heavy satchel slung from his shoulders was not a concern, as his long legs quickly carried him down the small valley and up onto the high ridge that followed the western side of Winterhaven. Once on top, he turned back toward town, ignoring the chaos that he could see inside the diner, and began to calculate distance and angles.

Once he was satisfied, he picked up the pace and found himself close to the area he had chosen earlier that night.

He dropped to his knees, his eyes searching the ground for clues. There was nothing there. This indicated a professional. Anger rode him hard; anger at himself. He'd put his own life in jeopardy because his entire psyche had been torn into knots at the thought of seeing Libby again.

At the thought of killing her.

He inhaled deeply. The scent of the sniper filled his nostrils, and he growled loudly as the lingering odor left a trail he could follow easily.

Jaxon's skin began to burn once more, and this time the energy would not be denied.

With a mighty roar, he grabbed his satchel and quickly found the safe cache he'd carved out of the ground several hours earlier. Throwing his gear inside, he stripped his body of clothes and boots, tossing them in along with the rest.

A large moon hung low in the sky, its soft glow caressing the hard lines of his body, the only witness as the change came over him.

Long fingers of mist swirled and clung to his limbs as bones popped and muscles elongated. His skin rippled and fell away, leaving a thick coat of glossy black fur in its place. When the mist cleared, a large jaguar barked a warning, his cry echoing loudly in the quiet night air.

The beast shook out his powerful limbs and quickly ran to the area where the sniper had been. He inhaled his enemy's scent deep into its lungs. The stink of a human male filtered through his nasal cavity, and the great beast took off, running hard.

The scent was still fresh in the air and on the ground, and he followed it easily. The sniper had packed up quickly and was already on the move. The cat knew he needed to cut him off before he reached his vehicle.

Adrenaline pumped through his body, and Jaxon gathered as much power as he could, his four legs propelling him as he followed the scent to a small outcrop of tall conifer trees. He entered the green forest silently, and his ears twitched anxiously as he picked up the sounds of heavy breathing.

His enemy had pushed hard, taxing his physical capabilities to the limit.

Slowly, the black jaguar picked his way down a steep incline, until he sighted his enemy fifty paces to his right.

He froze, his nostrils twitching in anticipation of a kill.

The human part of his brain exerted a bit more pressure to contain the beast that so desperately wanted to destroy.

Instead, the cat hunkered down, low to the ground, its belly touching the earth floor as he slowly, with care and stealth, approached the large male.

The man had stowed his weapons and just settled onto the back of an all terrain vehicle when a soft beeping alerted him to a cell phone call.

The cat watched as the man flipped the cell open

and paused before answering. He cleared his throat loudly and spoke into the device.

"It's me."

The animal strained to hear a voice, or even a whisper of the person on the other end, for surely it was the bastard that had ordered an attempt on his life.

"That's a negative. There were complications. Look, I said I'd get the job done and I will. He's found the girl and he didn't kill her. Trust me, he'll take her and run, and I'll be following closely. When the time is right, I'll take them both out."

The animal trembled as he continued to watch the male. The man threw the cell phone into a compartment and started the all terrain vehicle. Its loud rumble vibrated through the earth, and the jaguar's great paws jumped at the sensation.

He gathered his power, and with a mighty roar leapt from his place of hiding. He jumped with full force and successfully knocked the man to the ground. His huge paws swiped hard and satisfaction filtered into his system as the scent of blood rose into the air.

The man screamed, twisting his body in an attempt to get away, but the beast was too heavy and much too powerful.

Jaxon roared his anger as his body straddled that of his enemy, his muzzle baring deadly canines. The man's body let loose and the smell of urine mingled with the red blood that flowed freely from his damaged face.

Jaxon called the mist to him, using the weight of his powerful limbs to hold his enemy in place as the change overcame him quickly.

The man yelped, confused and scared out of his mind.

Jaxon snorted in disgust. This piece of shit thought to take him out? Savagely, he grabbed the man's neck and brought the trembling form close to him. Fear lay heavy in the air, and his voice cut through the thickness of it as he threw his words at the enemy.

"Who gave the order for the hit?"

The idiot's eyes had widened, and the pupils dilated as if he were in shock. He opened his mouth to speak, and after Jaxon loosened his grip around his throat, he croaked out a response.

"What are you?"

"That's not the answer I was looking for. I'll only ask one more time—who gave the order for the hit?"

The man seemed to regain a bit of his composure, and he studied Jaxon in silence. He seemed resigned and exhaled softly. "So, you are real. I thought they were full of shit." His eyes turned pleading then, a last ditch effort, so to speak. "Look, I don't know who's giving the orders. You know the way these things work. It's nothing personal . . . it's just a job."

Jaxon snarled loudly, his hands grasping the neck tighter. He leaned down, whispering quietly into the man's ears, "That was the wrong answer, and don't take this *personally*. I'm just doing *my* job."

With a quick twist, the man's neck snapped. Jaxon threw his lifeless body to the side as he jumped to his feet. He grabbed the cell phone the man had used earlier and pressed the redial button.

The phone rang twice, before an automated voice announced that the number was no longer in service. He cursed and tossed the phone back into the compartment. A sense of urgency stole over him, and he quickly set to work. After searching the body for ID and finding none, he dragged it down to a large pond and over to the remains of a beaver's dam.

Wading into the water, he carried the body and shoved it deep inside the dam. He then drew more branches across the opening. Quickly, he ran back to the vehicle and drove it hard at the water, jumping off as it sailed into the dark depths, the engine carrying it all the way to the bottom.

After clearing all signs of struggle from the earth floor, his body once again claimed his jaguar form, and he took off, back toward Winterhaven.

Once he retrieved his clothes, Jaxon made his way back to the diner. He climbed up to the roof and down the fire escape that ran into the back alley. He stole through an open second floor window and took a moment to gather his senses to him. There were still police and investigators inside. He knew they'd be there for hours reconstructing the scene.

He needed to avoid them. He had no time to get involved in a shooting investigation. He had to leave this place immediately.

And he wasn't going alone.

Jaxon looked around and realized he was in a bedroom. Not Libby's. The scent that lingered on the tousled sheets was male and unwashed.

He quickly left the room, his footfalls soft and undetected by the young man who sat on a couch watching television while speaking to a friend on the phone. "Yeah, a freaking shooting, if you can believe it. That chick Maxine is dead and everyone else has been told to stay in their rooms. Guess the cops will be asking me questions later. I won't be able to make poker night."

The young kid's voice droned on, and faded into the distance as Jaxon left through the front door, passing within inches of him.

Once he was out in the hall, he noted that there were only two more apartments. The first one to his left smelled stale and empty, so he continued down the hall. He paused at the last door on his right, his fingers touching the handle, caressing the large brass knob softly.

He brought his fingers up to his nose, and the smell of Libby fell over and through him. His knees felt weak, for just a second, and he angrily kicked those particular feelings to the curb. She deserved nothing from him, and she'd get even less.

She had bought a few extra days on this earth. Until he knew what the hell was going on, the status quo would remain in effect.

His fingers reached for the handle, and he was surprised to find it turn sweetly as the door opened to him.

Yeah, he might as well make good use of those few extra days that he would allow her to breathe and live.

A few extra days Diego had never been given.

A few extra days to make her pay.

Chapter 3

The door opened silently, swinging inward, and stopped just shy of hitting the wall.

Inside this space that she called home, Libby was everywhere, and nowhere. Her scent lingered in the air, tantalizing his nose, spreading dark emotions through his system as he slowly made his way into the tiny apartment. There was nothing here that appeared to belong to her.

She was a woman with less than nothing, and as he looked around the bleak living area, a picture of her was beginning to emerge that was far from the hellcat he remembered.

One more piece of the puzzle to figure out.

He moved deeper into the main room. It was narrow and the walls were gray, bare of pictures, with not one living plant to be seen. *Ferns.* She used to love ferns and huge blue hydrangeas.

A small tingle of *something* slithered through him

as his eyes continued to take in the depressing little room. The place she called home.

Alarm bells were beginning to clamor in his head, and a feeling of unease continued to gnaw at his belly. A hardcover book caught his eye. It had been thrown carelessly onto the threadbare sofa, which was literally the only piece of furniture in the room. His fingers trailed over the worn volume before he picked it up.

Unlocking the Mysteries of the Mind.

The woman from *his* past loved reading gossip magazines and articles on home décor. Anything light to offset the grim reality of her job. Looking around once more, he shook his head as his body tensed. He wasn't the only one who had changed in the last three years.

He moved toward a hall that led to the back of the apartment. He could smell her there. Her soft feminine scent was the one thing that hadn't changed, and it became the singular constant in an otherwise bizarre evening.

Jaxon slipped into the room, silent and deadly, like the predator he was. His eyes automatically found her on the bed, where she lay, deathly pale, in a state of agitated sleep. She was faceup, her right arm curled to the side of her neck, the long graceful fingers entwined deep into the heavy blond waves that haloed her head. The other hand cradled her left side.

She looked like a fucking angel.

He quickly crossed to her side and leaned in close, sniffing her face and wrinkling his nose as a medicinal scent wafted toward him.

Fuck. She'd been drugged. What the hell had she taken?

As he continued to study her, he wanted to feel nothing. He wanted to be able to look at Libby as if she were nothing more than another target. But even he, cold bastard that he was, could not deny how shocked he was at finding her here, amidst this filth and in such a wasted condition.

Jaxon rubbed his temples, feeling a nasty headache begin to pull at his brain.

What comes around goes around.

Yeah, Libby had found some bad karma for sure, and as an image of Diego's battered and bloody corpse lashed through his mind, he clenched his lips tightly together.

There was still a whole hell of a lot more to come her way, and he'd be the one dishing it out.

His timepiece beeped then, and with a start he realized he needed to get the hell out of Winterhaven. Within the next few hours the sniper he'd killed would be missed. And a secondary team would be sent to find him.

It would be a logical assumption that they'd start here. It was the first place he would look.

He needed to leave immediately.

His black eyes swept the bedroom, looking for anything he might need to bring along.

But even here he saw nothing. He searched the drawers in the rickety dresser, pulling out a few pieces of clothing and shoving it in a bag that lay on the floor near the window. Everything was in rough shape. In fact he'd hazard a guess that all of the clothes she owned were used. From what he could see, most were too large and well worn.

He glanced back at Libby, a frown sliding across his lips. She had been an incredibly beautiful, strong, and assertive woman. When she entered a room, she wanted every single eye to be drawn to her. And they usually were, both male and female.

It used to drive him fucking crazy.

She moaned softly, her limbs twitching as she shifted position. The flash of pain that gripped her features had him crossing to her quickly, and his hand automatically went to smooth the thick mess of hair from her face.

"Don't you dare lay a finger on her."

Jaxon froze, his eyes slowly rising until they met the intense blue ones of Pete.

The old man was now brandishing a gun, and at the moment it was aimed straight at his heart.

"You have some explaining to do. Starting with, who the hell are you, and how did you know Libby's name? She can barely stand to talk to a customer, let alone have a heart-to-heart with a total stranger."

Jaxon kept his composure. Pete might be old, and from the way he held the gun, not much of a hunter, but a gun was dangerous no matter who held it. "Put your weapon down, Pete. I'm not the enemy here. I came to save Libby."

The lie slipped easily from his tongue, but left a bitter taste nonetheless. "This was no random shooting," he went on. "Most definitely there was a gun for hire out there. He was a professional, I'd say military caliber, and there will be another to take his place before this night is done."

The older gentleman held his own, refusing to lower the gun. He moved closer to Libby, and Jaxon felt his patience slipping. Time was running out. He needed to leave. But he remained calm and kept his anger in check. Now wouldn't be a good time to rattle the old man. He was much too close to Libby.

"Who are you?" Pete asked. "And how do you know Libby?"

"My name's not important, but I can tell you I used to work with her, a long time ago. I haven't seen her in almost three years."

Pete held Jaxon's gaze, his eyes narrowing. Clearly, the old man didn't trust him. "You're gonna have to do better than that. I'm thinking that it's no coincidence you show up and my place gets shot up."

Jaxon felt his anger begin to build, and it was getting harder for him to contain it. He kept his eyes on the old man and calmly walked toward the side of the window. He could see out, but hopefully no one would be able to see him.

He clenched his teeth as he observed a tall man, deep in shadow. The newcomer was nondescript, and was leaning against a van parked not far from the cordoned-off area in front of the diner. He could have been a curious citizen, but it was his very normalcy that shouted "Operative" to Jaxon.

He turned back to Pete and spoke with deadly calm. "Look, I know this is difficult for you to understand, and I don't have time for a lengthy explanation." He nodded toward the window. "There's another operative out there waiting for a chance to take Libby out. I need to get her to safety."

Pete hesitated, and Jaxon could see he was wavering. "Who are these people and what do they want with Libby?"

Jaxon's voice was clipped as he answered, "That, I can't say, but you can bet your ass my team will find out."

His patience was running out and he didn't want

to hurt the older gentleman, but the stakes were getting higher by the second. He knew that if he didn't get his ass out of Winterhaven soon, things were going to get ugly.

Jaxon crossed to the bed and ignored the cocked gun that was still pointed at his head.

"I said don't touch her." Pete's voice was wavering, and Jaxon's temper began to boil.

"I am her only chance to survive this night," he said, his voice hard and his deadly intent clear. "So I suggest you put the fucking gun down."

Bending over the mattress, he carefully gathered Libby into his arms. Her form seemed to melt into his hard frame, and he felt his body quiver, flush with emotion and need.

Even though she was all angles, instead of softness and the curves he remembered, she still bit into that part of him that wanted to pound the pulp out of whoever had done this to her. It struck Jaxon as ironic, considering he'd come to Winterhaven with the sole purpose of ending her life.

His arms held her close, but a moan alerted him to the fact that he was hurting her, and he loosened his grip, remembering how she'd been favoring her left side.

He shook the thoughts from his mind almost as soon as they'd come. He didn't have time to take a walk down memory lane. He didn't have time to care.

He looked at the old man again and his eyes bored into him. "I need another exit. Is there a way to leave the diner that doesn't involve the roof or the front?"

Still ignoring the gun, he plunged forward. "I need to get up to the ridge. My gear is stowed there."

He waited, restraining himself as Pete weighed his options. He watched the old man walk to the window and peer out into the darkness. He must have seen the agent down in front because he turned back abruptly and sighed heavily. "I don't like this one bit. But it seems as if I have no other choice." His eyes softened as he looked at Libby. "Promise me you'll take care of her. She's had a rough go of it."

Jaxon nodded and followed Pete out of the tiny apartment, cradling Libby in his arms. They made their way down a narrow hall until they reached another set of stairs that led down to the older man's home. Once inside, they slipped down the steep, dark stairway and into a damp, musty basement.

"The set of stairs at the end leads outside," Pete told him. "It'll put you about fifty feet from the cordoned off area in front of my diner. Give me five minutes. I'll see what I can do to get the area cleared."

He began to head back the way they'd come, then turned back. "Promise you'll let me know when she's safe?"

Jaxon didn't answer, not knowing what to say, and after a moment, Pete turned away again, slowly hiked up the stairs and disappeared.

Jaxon looked down at Libby, fighting the tenderness that threatened to overwhelm him. How could there still be feelings locked away inside of him? This woman had taken everything he'd given her and thrown it back in his face.

She'd betrayed the unit, and Diego had paid with his life. She deserved nothing from him. Angrily, he shook his head, and turned away from the angelic face that was tense even as she slumbered in his arms.

No, he would never show mercy where she was concerned.

Never.

A shout from outside brought his attention to the small basement window, and he peered through it. Some sort of disturbance had occurred. He could see Pete waving his arms wildly, and the police who were running toward the diner.

Jaxon sprang into action and leapt up the stairs, taking them two at a time. The large oak door didn't open easily, and he shoved hard, welcoming the screech as the barely used hinges gave way.

Cool night air whistled through his lungs as he cautiously poked his head out. It was close to midnight now, and the soft glow cast by the moon misted eerily along the streets. To his right he could see the commotion abating, and that Pete had been successful, with less onlookers around than before.

Jaxon quickly scanned the area while scenting the air. There was no sign of the operative he'd spotted earlier, and the smell of danger didn't grab at him. It was now or never.

He crept up the last steps and flattened his body to the side of the building, then slowly made his way around the corner, where he was out of sight. Pausing there, his eyes searched the grassy area directly in front of him, all the way up to the embankment several hundred yards away.

He still needed to gather his gear and head to his truck, which was parked a mile down the road.

He was just about to head out when Libby jerked

in his arms. And then she was struggling against him, her eyes still closed, as if caught in a nightmare. He tried to control her shaking body as he watched her eyes begin to flutter madly. The moans that had started low in her throat were now louder.

At the same time, the slithering feeling of danger slipped through his mind and he whipped his head around, listening intently.

Someone was there, around the corner and in the alley that ran behind the diner.

Libby was bucking wildly in his arms now, and he pulled her closer and did the only thing he could think of to keep her silent.

He brought his lips to hers, claiming her mouth, silencing the screams that erupted from deep within her body.

She stilled as his warmth enveloped her, and Jaxon felt her body tense even more. Her lips were soft against his, and as her scent lingered along the lines of his nasal cavity, he felt an incredible rush of emotion. The beast inside clawed at him, wanting out.

Wanting to claim what he still considered to be his.

He pulled her in even closer. He opened his mouth fully, assaulting the softness of hers with his hard, lashing tongue.

He was angry.

Mad as hell that she could still make him want, could still make him feel.

As desire raged through his body, it settled heavily between his legs, and his cock sprang to life, straining against the confines of the khaki pants he wore.

He deepened the kiss, tugging on her lip. The

taste and the feel of her cut him to the bone. He felt his insides liquefy as her intoxicating scent washed over him. It was enough to drive him crazy.

Enough to drive him over the edge.

His arms had become hard, unyielding bands of steel, and he suddenly became aware of her whimpering against his mouth. The taste of salt mingled with the headiness that was her mouth, and he realized she was crying.

Jaxon inhaled deeply before pulling away, shocked to see the eyes that had haunted him, night after night, were open now, and staring, full of terror.

"Please." She could barely speak, but managed to whisper, "Please, don't hurt me."

His eyes held hers, and for the second time in this crazy night, everything faded away. He could see the pain and confusion so clearly it was like a fucking billboard. It was a face that would melt almost any man's heart. But he wasn't just any man. He was a jaguar, and she was still his enemy. He leaned in close to her, ignoring the way she shrank from him, and whispered, "Move or make a noise, and I promise you will regret it."

She began to shake uncontrollably, and he put her down, leaning her body against the building. He put one finger to his mouth and with his right hand reached down into a concealed pocket of his pants, retrieving a large, deadly knife. Her eyes widened at the sight of it, but she remained quiet, even as her body shivered in jittery spasms.

With one last look to Libby, Jaxon turned and moved away, his body seemingly melting into the brick and mortar of the building. Silently, he made his way toward his prey, his thoughts clear and focused. He could sense the presence of a man, a human, just beyond his position, and he held the knife lightly in his hand as he slipped into the dark alley.

As he moved deeper into the darkness, his nose analyzed the myriad scents that lived there. Quickly, his eyes adjusted to the gloom. The moonlight did not penetrate here, but his enhanced vision provided him with plenty of illumination.

Jaxon stilled as the threat of danger became more pronounced and his senses went into overdrive. He located his enemy, near the back of the enclosure, slowly making his way toward him. The bastard had night vision goggles on, and even though Jaxon was sufficiently hidden in shadow, he knew his body heat would be a dead giveaway.

There was no time. He would have to be the aggressor. His emotions melted away, leaving only the deadly cunning that was so much a part of the jaguar.

Jaxon gripped the knife and shot down the alley in a burst of speed faster than any human could ever achieve. He felt his enemy pause, confusion rippling off him in waves. But it was already too late.

Jaxon could see the deadly weapon pointed at him, even as the laser beam began to look for its target. He charged forward, his speed and bulk effectively crashing him into the man with the force of a train.

The two men rolled over, and the momentum of the collision propelled them both into the hard, unyielding wall behind them. Jaxon grunted as his shoulder slammed into the solid length of brick, but his right hand was already gunning for the jugular, the blade sure and true.

He felt it slice through Kevlar, flesh, and bone. But it was already too late. *For both of them.*

A gunshot rang out and ricocheted along the brick, its loud discharge echoing into the night. Fuck. It would be a clear invitation for the other operative.

Jaxon pushed the dead man to the side and was down the alley in an instant. His only thought was to get Libby and get the hell out of Winterhaven.

She was where he'd left her. Shivering and seemingly out of it. He scooped her into his arms once more, without resistance, and took off at breakneck speed toward the knoll where he'd stashed his gear earlier.

The moon lit his path, and he hurriedly grabbed his satchel without breaking stride, and ran into the night that beckoned him, holding his cargo fast to his chest. She began to struggle weakly, but he had no problem holding her tight as she mumbled hoarsely against his chest.

Her mantra echoed into the silence that followed along behind him, a phrase she whispered over and over again, as if she were a robot.

"Please don't hurt me, please don't hurt me."

It was painful to hear, and Jaxon did his best to ignore it as he ran into the blackness that swallowed them both whole.

Chapter 4

Jaxon reached his vehicle less than half an hour later, despite carrying Libby in his arms. The run was strenuous but he'd barely broken a sweat. He crept up a steep ditch and headed for his large Tahoe. It was well-hidden, deep in a thatch of trees several yards from the paved road.

He paused, his dark head turning as he scented the wind once more. The night was full of all sorts of smells, and he inhaled them all, but none carried the scent of danger. He turned back, satisfied that he had not been followed.

Libby was shivering uncontrollably and seemed to be in a trance. Her voice had splintered into a hoarse whisper, and he winced as the words she kept repeating became harder to understand.

He didn't need to hear them to know what they were; they'd be echoing in his head for hours to come.

Please don't hurt me. Please don't hurt me. Please don't hurt me.

He opened the passenger door and gently placed her on the seat. She immediately curled into herself as if trying to disappear into the leather. She was still shivering, and he grabbed a spare blanket from the back, throwing it over her slight shoulders in an effort to give her some sort of comfort and warmth. It was a pathetic sight, and his lips tightened as he looked away.

The woman deserved nothing from him, not a goddamn thing. But she had somehow managed in less than two hours to find the one sliver of humanity that still existed inside of him.

He threw his gear into the back and grabbed his cell phone.

Hitting Redial, he climbed into the cab and turned the key. The powerful rumble of the engine broke the silence and echoed into the quiet evening as Jaxon looked to his police scanner. Turning the knob up, he hit the gas and the truck pulled away from its bed of trees as static from the scanner lessened and he was able to listen in.

The chatter that could be heard alerted him to the fact that local law enforcement had not set up roadblocks. The crime scene was contained to the diner, and so far the perimeter had not expanded beyond that. Second rate work.

Jaxon smiled harshly. He had caught one hell of a break.

Meanwhile, he held the cell phone to his ear as Declan's recorded voice droned on. He cursed silently, waited for the requisite bleep, and left a curt message.

"It's Jax. Make sure Ana is there tomorrow night. Libby is . . . not right. I want her checked out medically by someone we can trust."

He flipped the phone closed and tossed it into the console, glancing over to where she lay trembling. Exhaling harshly, he gripped the steering wheel tightly with his large hands, blackness riding him hard as turbulent emotions wove their way through his body.

What the hell happened to you Libby? Who did you manage to piss off more than me?

The headlights drifted out over the open road as darkness swallowed the large truck. Jaxon settled in for a long drive. The way he saw it, they'd be hitting Headquarters in about six hours. Hopefully the trip would be quiet and uneventful—the *opposite* of his night so far.

Libby wasn't sure how long she'd been out, but judging by the stiffness in her limbs, it had been awhile. Her body screamed for a chance to stretch, but she kept her legs and arms tucked in tight, hiding under the blanket even though the pain was becoming unbearable.

But then, she was used to living with a whole truckload of hurt. It had been her constant companion for as long as she could remember, and even further back than that. She shifted ever slightly, trying to ease the tightness in her side and give her ribs a bit of a breather. Her left side was throbbing, shooting out sharp spasms of pain that came in waves. She clenched her teeth and fought it.

The hum of a powerful engine mingled roughly with the sounds of music that filtered through the heavy blanket. The hard pounding rhythm beat in tandem with her heart, and black panic began to curl along the edge of her brain.

Someone had come for her.

They had found her.

Tears threatened as fog washed over. *They had found her.*

She couldn't remember who *they* were. Not one face, touch, or sound. But the feeling was there, a dark menace and sense of unparalleled power that hung in the air.

And the smell, there was something incredibly familiar to his smell.

It definitely was a male driving the vehicle. She knew that with every fiber of her being. Eyes as black as tar flashed through her mind. The memory of the man from the diner had her heart leaping erratically . . . and *his* very essence scared the crap out of her.

He was one of them. He had to be.

She bit her tongue as a fresh wave of terror spliced through her body, and immediately broke out into a sweat. She needed to get the hell out of the truck.

She would die before she let them get her. Images from nightmares blinked behind her eyes, and she used every bit of mental strength she possessed to push them away. If she let those pictures and feelings in, she would be done for. She just couldn't go back there.

Her survival instinct kicked in and she frantically began to plot.

When the harsh ring of a cell phone broke through the muffled music, it was everything she could do to be still and silent.

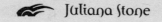

A deep voice answered the phone, and her hair stood on end as the richness of it washed over her. Whoever he was sounded powerful and pissed off. Not a good combination. She strained her ears, trying to learn what she could.

"Yeah, Jax here. You better have good news. Is Ana on board?"

Libby realized that with her captor occupied, she could depress the auto lock on her door and he might not hear it click.

Slowly, her fingers crept upward and she felt along the top of the armrest until they came across the indent of a button. She held her breath and pressed it softly. Her head lay against the door and she felt a rush of adrenaline pump through her when she heard the click as the door unlocked.

She paused, hearing bits of his conversation continue, and her heart sped up as she sensed the vehicle slowing down.

It was now or never, and she bunched her muscles tightly, waiting for the perfect opportunity, willing the truck to slow down even more. At least then, when her battered body hit the ground, it wouldn't hurt as much.

"Goddamn it, Declan! I don't give a shit what Ana feels! This isn't a request, it's a fucking order. We will deal with Libby when the time is right, and that's when *I* say so, not before."

The words exploded from her captor, shooting straight into her, and Libby wasted no more time waiting for the truck to slow down. She needed out, and it had to happen right now.

She inhaled sharply and her hand shot toward the handle. Without hesitation she yanked as hard as she could, and was out the door in a second, her body hurtling forward, taking the blanket with her.

When she hit, she hit hard. Every bone in her body reacted to the impact, and she grunted in pain. She was lucky to have landed on the soft shoulder, because it sure as hell could have been much worse. Momentum propelled her forward and she rolled down into a steep ditch, splashing into nearly a foot of water. She heard the squeal of tires as the vehicle braked and skidded into a halt. She didn't wait, pushing her discomfort to the back of her mind, and she was up and running in an instant.

For her life.

Again.

She didn't look back, only forward, and her eyes quickly adjusted to the darkened landscape.

They were out in the country. A large field ran adjacent to the paved road, and she plunged into its dark recesses. It was an orchard, filled with row after row of trees. She felt a small ray of hope as she disappeared into the darkness, her feet flying through the rows as she delved deeper into cover.

She followed the muddy path, not looking back, her entire being focused on escaping. There was no room for anything else.

She wouldn't go back.

She'd rather die first.

It seemed as if she had been running for hours, but Libby knew it was only several minutes. As her feet propelled her forward, she expected to feel the heat of his hands on her back at any moment, pulling her away from safety.

That thought alone spurred her feet even faster, but it was becoming harder to ignore the sharp fingers of pain spreading out from her rib cage. She grabbed her side, holding on tight, using sheer mental strength to keep her body moving.

Reaching the end of the field, she nearly cried aloud as the welcoming sight of a forest rose up before her. No sound came from within its dark depths, as if all the night creatures that inhabited its domain were sitting back, watching the life and death struggle being enacted for them.

Libby hopped a low-lying fence, a small grunt escaping as the jolt thudded through her aching legs and went straight to her heaving side.

But she didn't stop.

As the dark interior enveloped her, she took one second to look behind her before veering sharply to the left. The foliage looked thicker there, and she jumped over a large log, but fell as the feathery tendrils of moss caught at her feet.

She landed with a thud, hard on her left side, and screamed both in pain and frustration as it became too much for her to bear. She clutched her ribs, cursing the helplessness that slithered through her body.

If she let it, it would become all consuming. *That* couldn't happen . . . it's what *they* enjoyed, and as long as there was blood pumping through her veins, she would not give them that kind of satisfaction, not ever again. They would have to kill her first.

She took a second to focus her energy. Drawing air deep into her lungs, she pushed forward once more. Her hands grasped the slimy bark of the tree and she used it to propel her tired limbs into action, aware that he was stalking her somewhere in the distance.

Her eyes followed the tree line up past a small hill, and she quickly headed toward it, breathing heavily by the time she reached the top. She was now overlooking what appeared to be a small lake, or a pond, and on the other side a well-worn path led away from it.

She could hear vehicles somewhere in the distance, the acceleration of their motors echoing softly through the dense forest where she stood.

That was the direction she needed to go. Help was out there, somewhere.

She sprang into action as a warning screeched through the trees. Several birds began to chatter madly, and she felt fear beat at her. He was not far behind, of that she could be sure. Awkwardly, she ran down a small incline toward the water that stood silent, still and dark.

She clutched her aching side and without thought found herself standing at the edge. She heard a snap echo out behind her and bit her tongue in an effort to keep silent.

She was done showing weakness.

It was time for her to end this.

Libby slowly turned around, and her breath caught in her throat as her eyes fell upon the tall, powerful man who was just clearing the top of the hill. He came to an abrupt halt, and even though she couldn't see his face clearly, she felt the heat of his stare as he watched her in silence.

They stood like that for several long seconds, and then without warning she turned and walked into the water. The bottom was slippery so it was hard for her to keep her balance, but she managed somehow. Her body was coming down from its rush of adrenaline, and her teeth began to chatter loudly as the cold from the water took away any warmth she had possessed. She steeled herself against the frigid temperature as she slowly moved toward the center.

Her feet suddenly gave way and she was drifting in much deeper water. It was hard to stay afloat, as her side still ached incredibly, and she was treading water with only one arm to keep her head above the surface. Her body was so cold and tired.

It was then that an epiphany of sorts washed through her. What if she let go? What if, in this moment, she surrendered to fate?

Her pursuer was now halfway to the water, his voice hoarse as he shouted down to her. "What the fuck are you doing, Libby? Get your ass out of the water, you'll freeze to death."

She ignored him and closed her eyes. Without taking a last breath, Libby let her body sink below the surface. She felt darkness close over her head, as the bone chilling cold of the water seeped into her very core. But a kind of peace began to infiltrate her soul.

This is how it would end.

In a quiet body of water.

On her terms.

A sliver of sadness nicked the edge of her mind. With no memory, she had no clue who she was leaving behind. But truthfully, if there was anyone, wouldn't they have found her already? Wouldn't they have saved her from the terrible dreams that haunted her each night?

Her body drifted deeper, and she felt a burning sensation in her lungs. She just hoped it would end quickly. And if there were someone out there, waiting for her to come home, they wouldn't feel too much sadness at her passing.

Jaxon's heart nearly leapt from his chest when he saw Libby's head go under. What the hell was she doing? Was she fucking nuts? He moved faster, his eyes never leaving the surface of the water. Small bubbles slowly erupted onto the surface, but Libby remained under.

Fuck!

He dove headlong into the water, not feeling the coldness of the near icy liquid. He went deep and began to panic when the murky depths showed him nothing. He swam in circles and came up for air once more before diving under again. A flash of white caught the corner of his eye, and he was off like a shot, feeling a huge rush of relief course through him as the milky contour of her arm came into view. He kicked harder and grabbed her arm, pulling her in close to his body as he rose quickly to the surface.

They broke above the water and he inhaled air deep into his lungs. The panic he'd felt earlier was replaced by gut wrenching dread as her head lolled to the side, resting against his heaving chest. He held her firmly with one arm and reached the edge of the pond in three powerful strokes.

He pulled himself and Libby from the water and gently laid her on the muddy banks. His fingers flew to her neck, and her faint pulse gave him hope. But she wasn't breathing, and that scared the crap out of him. Libby could die. Right here and now.

His Libby.

Anger gripped him then, and he cursed as he

began to work on her feverishly. Like hell she'd die on him. Not like this. Not when he still needed answers.

His mouth gripped hers ferociously and he began to breathe life-giving air deep into her lungs. He would force her to live. There was no other option.

He continued to push his will through her lips and into her body. The anger he felt soon gave way to frustration and fear. His heart pounded so loudly he was certain it could be heard echoing across the still water.

Just when he thought her weakened body could take no more, she jerked forward and her mouth regurgitated a handful of dark water from inside her lungs. The force of it assaulted her injury, and she cried out as her arms went to her sides.

Jaxon brought her shivering form deep into the curve of his body. The night was chilled, but his jaguar blood was so heated with anger, his body was misting through his clothes as the warmth of his skin evaporated into the air.

He stared down at the pale features, taking the time to study her closely. His finger traced the small nose, continuing along high cheekbones to finally rest on the fullness of her lips. She was achingly beautiful, and the fragility of her body only enhanced the delicate features even more.

Her eyes flew open, and fear colored the violet ovals a deeper shade until they appeared black. They were huge, and she inhaled deeply, her eyes widening even more as she tried to speak.

"You! You're one of them."

Tears began to fill her eyes, and Jaxon fought the urge to wipe the dampness from her face. How in the hell had she become the victim? There was no doubt she'd been abused, but in light of her betrayal and the life it had cost, she fucking deserved it.

Didn't she?

"What do you want from me?"

His face hardened as he tried to keep his tough facade in place. Libby was crying, almost hysterical as her words lashed into him.

"Why won't you just leave me alone?"

He watched as anger began to burn in her cheeks and a fire erupted deep inside her eyes. She began to struggle, and literally spat at him, "You are going to have to kill me before I let you take me back to them." She was so agitated, he was afraid she'd hurt her injured ribs even more.

His arms pinned her tightly, their noses inches apart. He could feel her heart beating inside her chest, and took a moment to control himself.

"Who the fuck are they? What the hell happened to you, Libby?"

At the sound of his words she stilled, her eyes closing as a fresh batch of tears coursed down her face.

"They are pain, anger, and madness." She whimpered. "They are evil."

Her eyes flew open but her voice quieted as her shoulders sagged in defeat.

"You are just like them."

 Chapter 5

Libby's words hung in the air, and Jaxon felt the fight leave her body. Physically she was done. She just didn't have anything more left in her.

Her words made no sense to him. *You are just like them.* She was comparing *him* to the bastards that had literally beaten the life out of her?

He didn't say a word, but picked her up carefully and began the trek up the hill and through the forest. The birds that had heralded his approach remained quiet as he slowly made his way back. He could feel their eyes on him, not trusting the shifter that had invaded their sanctuary.

When he cleared the apple trees, he quickly ran to the truck, balancing Libby against his chest, feeling the steady rhythm of her breathing. Even though he would deny it until hell froze over, there was that small sliver of comfort in knowing she was finally calm.

And free of her nightmares for the moment.

He reached the truck and loaded her into the passenger side for the second time, looking around for the blanket that had flown out with her. He noticed it a few yards back and quickly retrieved it, tucking her in with the added warmth of the wool.

He jumped into the cab, started the truck, and looked to his passenger before accelerating slowly. Libby was fast asleep, but he didn't trust her. He flicked on the child safety locks and ran his hand through his hair in agitation.

He needed to find out whoever the hell *them* was.

Somehow this whole mess was connected. Everything, starting back three years ago, when his unit had been ambushed and Diego murdered.

He just had to connect the dots. He needed to link them all together. His face hardened as Libby's image floated through his mind.

He had the first dot.

Now he had to find the rest.

With Declan's help they should be able to hurry her memory from its hiding place, and then the answers would come. Jaxon felt the coldness that lived inside of him spread out and caress his fast beating heart. His small shred of humanity disappeared and his handsome features settled into a tense frown.

The woman in his thoughts moaned as she turned toward him. Her arm was flung over her head, as if warding off . . . *something*.

Libby Jamieson had all of the answers locked deep inside of her. He snarled softly as he looked away from her and back to the road. He had a shit-load of questions and wouldn't let her rest until she was able to answer them. He'd rip them from her if he had to.

The glowing clock on the dashboard told him it was three. He had been making great time until Libby's mad dash for freedom. Without any more problems, he'd reach the loft by four.

Jaxon cranked up the volume and carried on down the road as the hypnotic melody of a Doors classic filled the cab.

This is the end, my only friend the end.

He snorted as the lyrics floated through his brain. Hell no, this is the *beginning of the end*.

Hardly anyone was on the road and it was just before 4:00 A.M. that the beams of light from the Tahoe flickered across the empty parking lot of an old abandoned warehouse, deep in the heart of the waterfront near Manhattan.

Old, indeed it was.

Abandoned, it most certainly was not.

He slowed down as the truck maneuvered through a narrow entrance, stopping near the booth that housed Cracker, the night security guard. It had been almost a year since Jaxon had visited the prem-ises, but Cracker was used to the secretive comings and goings of the certain select few who were al-lowed access.

The truck ground to a halt as Cracker stepped from his safe haven, a large semiautomatic perched lazily against his leg. The man was about forty-five, tall, broad-shouldered, and mean as all hell. He was ex-military, having resigned his commission after being in Iraq for several years.

He wasn't one hundred percent human either.

His scent had always thrown Jaxon for a loop; it was something he'd never come across before. The man had never volunteered his lineage, but as long as he did his job, and did it well, Jaxon didn't give a shit if oil ran through his veins.

As the truck slowly pulled up alongside him, Cracker's eyes—so pale they were almost white—drifted toward the passenger that lay huddled against the door. They narrowed. It was the only noticeable sign of surprise, and his face quickly resumed the blank facade that was the norm, before acknowledging his boss.

"Evening, Castille. Declan's already inside."

"Thanks."

With those few words, Jaxon proceeded through the gates until he was inside the center of a large courtyard type area. The entire perimeter was fenced in, with full coverage from security cameras and two roving dogs that were trained to kill on command.

In front of him was a series of eight large doors that led to a large underground parking facility. He drove the truck to the very end, depressing the remote inside his cab. The heavy steel door began to slowly recede, and he was able to drive through.

Once inside, he pulled into his spot and cut the motor. Jaxon sighed softly, his lips pursed into a hard thin line as he glanced at the still slumbering woman.

Libby had slept fitfully on and off the last forty-five minutes of the drive, occasionally moaning loudly and jerking her body wildly. Nightmares.

That was something they both shared.

He glanced to the left, smiling for the first time at the sight of the vehicle parked there. The long, sleek lines of the low riding viper were so Declan. It had been much too long since he'd been with his fellow operatives.

They'd been family once.

Until a little slip of ass had decided it would be a great idea to betray them. Once again anger flared. His eyes raked sparks of fire over Libby as the intensity of his emotions flushed his skin a deep red.

She'd stolen a lot more than Diego from him that day.

And she would pay dearly.

Jaxon swung the door open, sliding from the cab with the sinuous grace that came so naturally to his kind. His eyes were always moving, and he noticed there was only the one other vehicle parked inside the cavernous garage.

Guess Ana had decided not to join the party early. He slowly rubbed the kinks from the tense cords in his neck. She'd show. Although with the coming dawn, it wouldn't be until later in the afternoon or early evening.

Yeah, he'd been away far too long. It felt good to be back, with a mission in hand, and a host of butts out there just waiting to be kicked.

He turned back to the vehicle and lugged the large bag from the back of the truck. After securing it around his shoulders, he opened the passenger door and grabbed Libby as if she weighed nothing. Which, given her state, wasn't an exaggeration. The woman had lost some serious weight and probably tipped the scales at a buck ten, if that, soaking wet.

He quickly crossed to an elevator that opened only after a successful retinal scan and palm print. Once he'd initiated the procedure, it took less than a minute for him to exit the lift and step into the main area of the loft.

His loft.

And headquarters to the best damn paranormal antiterrorist team on the planet.

Magicks, lycans, vampires, and shifters had always existed alongside humans, invisible and silent, governed by their own. But over the last century things had shifted. Lines that were drawn straight and true had become blurred. New alliances had been formed as old ones were broken.

The general human populace was still unaware of the various creatures that walked the earth alongside them. And while most of the paranormals were content to exist in silence, there was a faction that needed to be watched closely. The ones that had no mind to heed their own laws, let alone the human ones.

It was up to organizations like PATU to police them. They were government sanctioned, and his unit had been the best. But after Diego's death the team had disbanded and Declan turned to freelance work, while Ana was reassigned.

As for himself, Jaxon had always worked when he chose to, and had just recently returned from a particular nasty mission in the wilds of South America. It had taken well over a year out of his life, and he'd truly been at a crossroads when the information on Libby just fell into his lap.

Nice and easy. And like a fool he'd run with it and almost gotten killed.

He continued into the large atrium that was the focal point of the loft, his long legs quickly eating up the ground as he passed the greenery to continue down the hall to his right. There was a series of rooms down here. They were in fact interrogation rooms, but one had a bed, so she'd be comfortable.

He could leave Libby there and not worry about her trying to escape, as the heavy steel doors came equipped with locks that couldn't be breached by a human, or otherwise. They were supposedly both charm safe and bomb safe. The only way to open them, once locked, was with a series of codes.

Declan O'Hara had managed to open them several times, *from the inside*, just to annoy the hell out of Jaxon, and he'd not given up his secrets.

Jaxon stepped into the cold room, wincing as the harsh lights flickered on, enhancing the dull, muted space. He shrugged; beggars couldn't be choosers, and right now Libby Jamieson was at his mercy.

He lowered her to the bed, keeping her body tucked into the blanket. She immediately rolled to her side, and he had the distinct impression that she was no longer asleep. Her long blond hair was a mess about her head, the once lustrous tendrils devoid of shine and health. They hid her face from view, and he stepped away, turning his back to the woman who'd once been his lover.

He left her there, without a word, and smiled in satisfaction as the heavy clang locked her in. He'd left only the day before to put a bullet in her head, but it was somehow much more fitting that she was here, in New York City, and she would know the wrath of a Castille.

She would learn what it was to cross a jaguar. For an animal like Jaxon, the hunt wasn't over until his enemy was dead.

Despite the fact that she had momentarily aroused his dormant softer side, Libby Jamieson was still his enemy. That someone had used her to get to him only bought her a bit of breathing room. Her reckoning would come. Once he flushed out the bastard that had taken a hit out on him, he would turn all of his energies toward Libby.

And she would suffer as he had. Whatever she'd been through in the last three years would be nothing compared to the wrath he would bring down on her head.

No one crossed a Castille and lived to tell the tale. No one.

He left her and ignored the soft whispers that clung to the edge of reason that still lived in his head. The ones that told him he was no better than *them*.

The familiar scent of Declan O'Hara wafted toward him as he made his way around the center of the atrium and headed to the hub of operations. It was a huge room, full of state-of-the-art computers and surveillance equipment, with another chamber deeper in, filled to the brink with an eclectic collection of weaponry.

Weapons that could kill humans but for the most part were specialized for use against vamps, wolves, shifters of all sorts, and magicks.

Jaxon could command a small army from here,

and he'd indeed done just that many times in the past.

As his eyes alighted on the tall man leaning over a computer screen, a genuine smile transformed his harsh features into the handsome man that he was.

Declan O'Hara had been part of this unit long before Diego even recruited Jaxon. He was a man of mystery, and one with a dangerous edge. He was a formidable opponent who not only was a great soldier, but had a powerful command of magick. He'd been known to dabble in the dark arts when the occasion called for it.

Jaxon didn't know much about his personal life, only that his father had been a warlock cast out of his coven for using the dark arts. He'd always believed there was more to the story, but Declan had never volunteered and he'd never asked.

A man should be allowed to keep his personal shit to himself.

"Where is she?"

Declan turned from the task he was performing, his face dark and unreadable. Jaxon could well understand his hatred toward Libby. They all felt it.

The day Diego had died, Declan attempted to use dark magick to bring him back, but the sacrifice would have been too much, and Jaxon stopped him. He had seen the struggle, the darkness growing inside, and knew if Declan was successful, he would be doomed.

The dark magick would have claimed him. Such was the delicate line between good and evil. Between love and hate.

Jaxon's smile faded and he wondered, for the first time, if he would have been able to carry through with his intent to take Libby out. What if she'd not looked out into the darkness at him? Would he have pulled the trigger and left her there to die?

"Christ, Jax, don't tell me she's gotten to you already? What did she do? Bat those baby blues and open her legs for you?"

"Her eyes are violet."

Jaxon's voice was deadly in its softness, and it was obvious that Declan knew he'd crossed the line. Tense silence filled the space between them until Declan turned back to the computer screen. "Is she in one of the interrogation rooms?"

"Yeah, and you're not to go anywhere near her until I say so."

Declan ignored the last comment as he rubbed his eyes wearily. He pushed his fingers through the thick wavy hair he left long, curling around his neck. He certainly did not look military, but the lean and muscled frame beneath the faded jeans and T-shirt became one hell of a fighting machine when in combat. He could kick most anyone's ass.

"I tried to make sense of the transmission you received but I have no freaking clue where it originated. You'll have to get Ana to look at it," Declan said.

The dark green eyes turned into hard emeralds as his face narrowed in anger. "I'll tell you one thing, Jax. Your intel came from someone with the highest level security clearance. Maybe whoever it was just covered all the bases and had a second player in motion, in case you couldn't complete the mission. Which, I hate to point out, you didn't." Declan ignored the black eyes throwing flames of anger his way. "Maybe the shot was just a coincidence."

"No, it was no coincidence. It was a setup. I took out the sniper. He was a paid assassin. The poor bastard was human. Someone was stupid enough to send a human soldier out to kill a jaguar. He knew nothing, but I heard his phone conversation and he was definitely taking orders."

Jaxon's face darkened even more as he felt the animal inside of him begin to stir in reaction to his intense, warring emotions. He took a deep breath, noticing the way Declan retreated.

"Someone was using Libby as bait to get me out in the open, and whoever the hell it is, knew where she was. I've been hunting her for the last three years and had no clue she was working in some dead end diner in northern Michigan."

His skin began to burn and he growled deeply from his chest. "I'm going to find the bastard that ordered the hit and rip him to pieces with my bare claws." Jaxon flexed his powerful forearms and his skin itched to let the beast free.

"Someone wants me dead. The only reason I'm standing here right now is the fact that Libby fainted and I reacted on instinct and broke her fall."

"Well, looks like the bitch was good for something after all."

Both men turned in surprise as a small compact woman walked into the room. She was petite, yes, but hard as nails. Dressed from head to toe in tight black leather, she moved as if walking on air. Her long auburn hair hung in waves to her waist, flowing softly as if a breeze lived amidst the luxurious length. Freckles sprinkled across a small upturned nose, and her expressive sapphire eyes were almost overpowering on such a delicate childlike face.

But the woman who stood before them was anything but a child. She was a lethal killing machine who needed blood to survive. Lots and lots of blood.

Her name was Ana and she was the missing member of his team.

She was also a three-hundred-year-old vampire who loved to kick ass, and at the moment there was no mistake as to whose ass was next in line.

Chapter 6

"What, no hug? No kisses?" Ana's soft voice purred as she smiled at the two of them, but Jaxon knew better. She was pissed.

He was quiet for a few seconds. His face darkened and the air seemed to swirl around him as he spoke. "You will not go near her unless I'm present, Ana. Are we clear?"

Her eyes narrowed and she hissed in anger. Her fangs began to elongate and she growled loudly as she took a step closer.

Declan stepped between the two of them, his voice harsh and commanding.

"Back off, both of you! This is bullshit!" He turned to Jaxon. Both men were of equal height, and formidable opponents when the need arose. "Ana and I came because *you* asked us for help. We both dropped everything and we're here, aren't we?"

Declan shook his head in disgust, his voice barely

controlled. "You will not deny us the satisfaction of making that bitch pay for what she did to Diego. Hell, what she did to all of us."

His eyes sought out the intense blue ones of the vampire, softening at the pain so ill concealed behind the bejeweled depths.

"And we will. *We all will*, when the time is right. Libby is the key here. Everything comes back to her. Right now we need her alive, but once we have the answers—"

"All bets are off," Ana's voice bit through. Bitterness and anger hardened the soft features of her face.

"I won't tell you again, Ana. Leave her alone. She has no memory of her life, she has no answers for you, and I don't trust you around her. You can't be objective where she's concerned."

Jaxon clenched his teeth together as his anger got the better of him.

"The sun is waking up. I need to rest."

Ana abruptly turned on her heel and headed toward the private quarters, where they each had their own space. "Thanks for the warm welcome, Castille . . . so glad to be back."

Her voice gently drifted back toward them and Jaxon swore in frustration. She was the one person he had no desire to alienate. He had lost his cousin the day Diego died, but Ana . . . she had lost so much more.

Roughly, he ran his hands through the black hair on top of his head. Weariness was starting to settle into his bones, and he knew he needed sleep in order to function properly.

"You should get some rest too, Dec. We'll start fresh in a few hours."

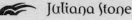

Jaxon turned and headed toward his own room, pausing as the urge to check on Libby tore through his body. He had to physically force himself to follow in Ana's footsteps.

He reached his quarters and tiredly flopped onto the bed, dirty clothes and all. His eyes closed and he was immediately assaulted with images of Libby.

The sight of her blond hair floating lazily along the top of the water as she sank beneath its cold dark surface was one he'd like to forget he'd ever witnessed.

He had tried to convince himself over the last few years that she never meant anything to him. That Libby Jamieson was nothing more then a woman he'd had sex with. Great sex, actually, but nothing more. He was a jaguar, and like most of his kind, had somewhat insatiable needs. Women were like candy. They were gobbled up and spat out when the flavor began to get stale.

He had first met Libby when she was called in to work with his team on an assignment in China. She'd been trained in the paranormal sector at Quantico, even though she was wholly human.

She'd been a kick-ass trainee, and came to his unit highly recommended. She thought quickly on her feet, was amazing in hand-to-hand combat, and her pale beauty was an added bonus.

Most men, whether human or other, were easily led astray and thought with their dicks when a beautiful woman was about. She'd been used many times to trap a target, and after a few months of working together, Jaxon had been unable to resist her charms.

They'd fallen into a passionate, sometimes volatile

relationship that lasted two years. They fought and then had the most amazing makeup sex ever. She even embraced the jaguar that lived inside of him.

Jaxon groaned, feeling his groin tighten as memories of pounding his cock deep into her body flooded his mind. She had been wildly passionate, funny, annoying, and tender. She lived life to the fullest, and with her, he had felt complete in a way he'd never experienced before.

But then, like all females, she had wanted more than he could give, and the last few months had not been great. They fought a lot. She wanted the white picket fence, and he didn't.

Up to that point he had never envisioned a life shared with anyone. He knew that when he took a mate, it would be forever, and he just wasn't ready for that. His life *was* and always *had been* the hunt.

The last night they spent together had been more volatile than most. He grunted, trying to force the memories away. But it was impossible.

She'd been so emotional in the preceding weeks. Either up or down. There was no pleasing Libby, but even he was shocked to find out that she'd applied for a transfer to a different unit.

At the time, he was getting ready to take off with Declan and Diego. The mission was routine. Ana hadn't been involved, and Libby's part in the initial legwork was over. He had been livid when he found out about the transfer, and that led to one of their most heated blowouts.

As always, their argument turned into passionate sex.

Jaxon groaned and his eyes closed as memories of her smell washed over him. Images of her long blond hair cascading down, caressing the dark skin of his body, pulled at him, and his shaft became painfully engorged as he tried to wipe the pictures from his mind.

But it was as fresh as if they'd just made love.

Her eyes had been sad; he remembered the tears that gathered in the corners. He remembered reaching for them and kissing them away as she rode him hard. When they had both come to orgasm, she cried against his chest, and he felt like the biggest loser on the planet.

He'd left her there, lying in his bed alone, huddled in the mess of blankets. He remembered telling her they'd sort things out when he returned.

That was the last time he had laid eyes on Libby.

Until tonight.

Jaxon threw his head back, willing his hard body to succumb to the bone deep weariness that lay heavy in his heart and soul. He needed to sleep. He needed to forget. For surely, on that last night, the betrayal had already been in place. As surely as he'd pumped furiously into her, trying to forget their problems in the softness of her body, she had already signed Diego's death warrant.

And perhaps her own.

Libby came awake with a start. It was dark, cold, and hard where she lay. Slowly, her hand cupped the side of her body, and she groaned in protest as tight muscles competed with the pain that rifled like fire through her rib cage.

The burn was intense, and she sat up carefully, hissing loudly as every single cell in her body shrieked against the movement.

She began to focus and breathe through the discomfort, trying to force a calm that she was nowhere near feeling. But it was no use and blood began to pump through her veins rapidly as her heart rate increased. A slow burn unfurled, deep in the pit of her stomach. It wove its way rapidly through her body, until her chest was heaving with a mixture of emotions that were making her light-headed.

She welcomed it.

For the first time in a long time, she felt alive. She laughed then, the sound strained and bordering on hysterical.

How crazy was that?

Her body was a mess of injuries, old and new; she had no idea who the hell she was, or why people were shooting at her. And the tall dark man? Who the hell was he?

Her brain protested all the questions and feelings swirling about, and as she recalled his face, Libby was startled at the intensity of emotion that washed over her. She realized then that the tall dark stranger who brought her here was the reason she felt alive. As if she'd lived the last two months—which in fact were the only two months she could remember—in slow motion.

And truthfully, they had been. It was all a blur, and she was suddenly so tired of being the helpless victim. It somehow didn't seem the right fit to her. As if in her former life—whatever that meant—she would not have taken any of this shit lying down.

She felt newfound strength begin to pour through her as she sat there in the dark, methodically looking around, trying to find an escape. Her eyes had adjusted to the dim interior, and she slowly lowered her feet to the cold tiles, feeling the shock of them against her bare toes.

Her arms still cradled her side, and her body odor hit her smack in the face. God, she was a mess. She needed out of this place, if not for any reason other than to wash the grime and smell from her body.

Her prison was small but had enough room for a bed, and as her eyes skimmed the far recesses, she smiled at the sight of a toilet and sink. Each step that drew her closer to the sink seemed lighter, more assured, and then she quickly set about washing her face and hands.

Her tummy growled, and Libby tried to remember the last time she'd eaten, but shrugged it off. She would have to worry about that later. After she escaped.

There was no window other than a small insert in the heavy door. And she knew how heavy it was. When the stranger lowered her to the bed, she'd rolled over, pretending sleep, but cringed at the sound of the door locking behind him as he left.

She ran her fingers over the door's surface and swore when it became evident there was no way she'd be able to budge it an inch. Quickly her mind moved on, and she knew her only chance to escape would be when they came for her.

But she'd have to be smart about it. Take a chance. *The right chance.*

Libby's heart leapt to her throat as the handle began to turn.

Someone was there!

She jumped back to the bed, grabbing the blankets around her, her heart thumping rapidly. She inhaled one deep cleansing breath and prayed that whoever it was would believe she was still fast asleep. She turned her back to the door and closed her eyes tightly.

The door swung open, its hinges creaking ever so softly, the sound hanging dully in the air. Libby felt the hairs rise on the back of her neck, and held her breath, forcing it out slowly, mimicking the sounds of sleep. It felt as if a million tiny fingers were running up and down her back, and her body screamed at her to move, to flee. But she held fast.

No footfalls or any other sound heralded the approach of her captor, but she knew someone was there, just inches from her.

Were they going to kill her now?

Panic began to creep through her. She felt helpless and exposed to her enemy. She felt the familiar choking sensation weave its way up from her chest, as blackness once more curled around the edges of her brain. But she held on, gritted her teeth and pushed it away.

"Is this a new game, Libby? Did you think you could escape me so easily?"

The low voice fell upon her—a woman's voice—and she exhaled slowly, not recognizing it. But she could sense that the woman who stood behind her was furious. She could feel it in the quiet words; it colored them with a ferocity that needed no amplification.

Libby's eyes opened slowly, and she was grateful that she'd successfully fought off the panic attack that would have rendered her helpless.

It was time to face the enemy.

Slowly, she pushed her body from the bed, turning toward the woman, who stood a foot away. The splice of pain that crossed her face did not go unnoticed, but Libby held her own and met the black eyes with a direct stare.

The woman who stood before her was incredibly beautiful, in a way that seemed almost surreal. She had long wavy dark chestnut hair that surrounded delicate features and pale skin. She was clothed from head to toe in black, and though petite, projected a menacing aura.

Her eyes were dark, like round pebbles of onyx dipped in sapphire. And they were staring at her hard, full of malice, dislike, and something else.

When the woman spoke again, Libby jumped, surprised at her harsh words.

"So it's true, then? You claim to have no memory of who you are and what you've done to us?"

The stranger took one step forward until her body was almost touching Libby's. Her voice dropped an octave and the warmth from her breath caressed Libby's cheeks. "Did you forget how to talk as well? I see you've forgotten how to bathe. I used to be envious of the long blond hair that fell from your head, and now . . ." Her fingers reached out for a strand that fell down to Libby's breast. Libby flinched as the fingers drew near, and closed her eyes as the woman tugged softly on the strand. "I see that personal hygiene has fallen by the wayside."

The woman stepped back, her eyes critical. "As has your fashion sense."

Libby flushed in embarrassment. The words rang too close to the truth.

"I don't know you."

The words slipped from Libby's mouth, and she

immediately wished she could take them back. The woman's eyes widened and she laughed. The sound was fake and tinny as it echoed against the sterile walls.

"Let me introduce myself. I'm Ana, and I can assure you we will be doing everything in our power to enable you to remember *exactly* who you are. I have a personal interest invested in your memory returning. We all do."

Cold fear began to knot Libby's belly at the woman's words. Blank pictures flashed behind her eyes, empty scenes that held no form but the feelings they aroused were devastating. It was bone chilling terror and she began to tremble, her eyes looking to the floor and away from the probing black ones that had narrowed suddenly.

"Are you scared, Libby?"

Ana knelt down in front of her, forcing Libby's head up until her violet eyes were captured by the blackness of her own. "You should be," she whispered, and Libby's eyes widened. She felt the scream that was trapped at the back of her throat rush to the surface and burst from her in a loud wail.

Ana's eyes had darkened even further, until there were no whites to them, and she growled loudly as her mouth flashed a set of very long, very sharp fangs at Libby.

"Enough! Ana, leave at once."

Libby's eyes flew up and she felt immediate relief at the sight of the tall dark stranger who stood in the doorway. She jumped past Ana and flew into his arms, ignoring all the aches of her protesting limbs and the need for escape.

Her one and only thought was to get to him. For some reason, she knew he would not let harm come to her.

She buried her face into the hardness of his chest, and her limbs were shaking uncontrollably as she closed her eyes, trying to blot out the image of Ana's fangs. What the hell was she? And who were these people?

"Please, I don't know anything. I can't remember anything. Can't you let me go?"

Strength and warmth seeped from his pores into her body, and he hesitated before loosely encompassing her into the circle of his arms. He spoke then, and the rumble of his voice vibrated his chest against her cheeks. He smelled of the earth and of comfort. He held an undeniable male scent that even amidst all the turmoil awakened something inside her.

Libby felt heat begin to finger outward, caressing her breasts and winding down to her tummy. She was aware of every hard plane of his chest and abs, and in that moment, she wanted nothing more than to lose herself in the sensations. To just close her eyes and to pretend she was somewhere else.

With him.

"You need to leave now, Ana."

Libby expected the woman to argue, but she walked past them, her voice insolent. "I was just welcoming your little pet back to the fold, Jaxon. I told her we were going to help her get her memory back." Ana paused, her voice turning harsh as she left the room. "I've been waiting three long years to hear why she betrayed us all and murdered my lover."

Libby's eyes widened in disbelief at the absurd

accusations the woman had spat at her. She felt her blood begin to burn and she whispered hoarsely, "Liar."

Ana's eyebrows arched in perfect sync but she remained silent.

A third voice joined the discussion, and Libby's eyes opened up to a tall, handsome man wiping sleep from features that seemed as if carved from stone.

"So nice to see the whole gang back together again."

Libby felt the stranger—*Jaxon's*—arms tense as they tightened around her.

"Declan, she's had enough this morning."

"Christ, Jax, I know that. I was going to make some breakfast and thought we could all sit down together and eat our eggs and bacon like normal people. Well, as normal as a human, which would be you," the man called Declan said as he winked at her, smiling widely, though the warmth never quite reached his eyes, "a vampire, shapeshifter, and a practitioner of magick can have."

Chapter 7

ampire!"

Libby's eyes opened in horror and she looked up at Jaxon. His face was blank but she noted the tick that throbbed at his temple, and the tense set of his mouth. He looked pissed, and the resignation that flickered in his eyes scared the crap out of her.

"Did you think these were fake?" Ana hissed at her from behind, and Libby's body started to tremble. Her tummy roiled in protest and she tried to push away, but the arms that held her tightened to the point of pain.

"Who are you people?" The words were barely louder than a whisper and fell from her white lips as her brain tried to wrap around everything.

"We used to be your family Libby, but that was a long time ago." Declan moved away, his posture a testament to the turmoil that lived inside him.

"I don't remember any of you."

Declan paused, his eyes sweeping over her dismissively, his voice dry when he finally spoke. "Oh, don't worry, darlin', it will all come back in time . . . one way or another."

She watched from the corner of her eye as Declan put his arm around Ana, his fingers caressing her shoulders in a show of comfort. The two of them left quietly, disappearing around the corner.

Jaxon immediately pushed her away from him, as if the touch of her skin burned like acid. Her stomach grumbled loudly and she cradled her midsection, feeling both nauseous and hungry. She couldn't remember the last time she'd eaten, and her strength was waning fast. She knew she needed nourishment in order to regain some strength, and *maybe* have a slim chance at escape.

"I'll bring you a plate of food," Jaxon said, "and once you've eaten, a shower will be made available."

Libby's cheeks burned hot as she watched him turn to leave. He was so tall, yet moved with silence and deadly grace.

Like an animal.

"Wait!"

He angled his head back at her, his eyebrows arched questioningly.

Libby found herself frozen in place, her eyes lost in the dark depths of his own. They were incredibly expressive. With lashes so long she just knew they would whisper against her skin, if she were ever to get that close to him.

She watched his sensual lips compress into a tight line, and his eyes once more became aloof.

"Please, I . . . I'm really confused, and if you all know me, or know where I come from, why the hell can't you just tell me?"

She became unnerved at his continued silence. His dark features studied her and she could see his brain at work, weighing his options.

"I won't let you take me back to them." Libby jutted her chin out in defiance, shuddering as his eyes narrowed. His voice was soft when he spoke, and it slid over her like hot liquid.

"You don't have to worry about that, Libby."

She swallowed thickly as he shook his head, and she waited for him to continue, not sure if his words were meant to intimidate or comfort.

He opened his mouth once more, his eyes boring into hers, but then turned abruptly and silently left the room.

Slowly, her fingers wound their way up to her face, and she pushed back the straggly tendrils of hair that had fallen forward.

Her fingers trembled as they traced the lines of her cheek, following the sharp curve until they came to rest on her lips. Her eyes were drawn to her reflection in the window of the door, and she stared at herself in shame. As if she *knew* that at one time there had been so much more than the gaunt, filthy, weak person who stared back at her.

"Who are you?"

She watched as her mouth moved, letting the words slip from between pale lips. The woman, *vampire*, Ana, had said she was a murderer.

That just couldn't be possible. Could it?

Everything seemed so overwhelming all of a sudden. She collapsed back onto the bed as her strength fled in a rush. Her head began to ache, dull throbs that splintered through her skull, and she groaned as she tried to make sense of everything that had happened to her in the past twenty-four hours.

Jaxon had been ruthless in his pursuit of her, but if he had wanted her dead, then surely he would have left her to slip below the water to die. Wouldn't he?

His dark eyes burned behind her own as she closed them tightly. He was so large, intimidating and angry, but she somehow knew he wouldn't harm her. When he had first pulled her from the water, she was terrified—terrified of going back to the nameless monsters that chased her dreams every night.

She'd truly believed that he was one of them, and if she'd had the chance, she would have jumped back into the water and let its gentle caress take her into oblivion.

But she hadn't jumped back in, and for that she could be grateful.

A spark had been stoked and was slowly growing into a heated desire to live. For the first time in many weeks, Libby had the urge to look at herself. *Really look at herself.*

She no longer wanted to be the victim.

Her first memories were so very new, only months old.

She had heard all the whispers from the townspeople of Winterhaven. Some were incredibly hurtful, while others had just been truthful. She'd been the poor little Raggedy Ann who showed up at the diner in Winterhaven two months earlier; a socially inept female with sad eyes and a broken mind. Pete took her under his wing, and for that she would always be thankful, but each day had been torture, and truthfully, most of the time she had no concern or thought for the future.

But now, suddenly, it became vital that she survive. *That she remember.* Not only to lay to rest the demons that stalked her, but to answer the haunted look she'd glimpsed in Jaxon's eyes when he brought her here only a few hours ago.

Declan had said they were family once.

Ana had said she was a murderer.

Jaxon had said nothing.

It was up to her to find the answers.

Libby's eyes flew open as the door creaked and slowly inched forward. She held her breath, feeling a small tug of disappointment when Declan returned with a tray of food. She sat up, wincing at the pain in her side and the shards of glass that seemed to be breaking inside her head. It felt as if tiny pieces of her brain were slipping away and hitting the side of her skull.

The smell of food had her mouth watering, and spittle began to pool inside her cheeks as a tray of eggs, bacon, hash browns, and toast was set on the table beside her bed.

Libby kept her eyes averted, not wanting to see the dislike Declan made no attempt to hide. She willed him to walk away, but as her luck would have it, the tall man had other things on his mind.

"So, Libby, I'm curious. How much do you remember exactly? Can you at least share that with us? Can you tell me how far back your addled brain lets you wander?"

The insult stung, and she swallowed thickly, wanting only to eat in peace.

She paused for a moment and hoped if she answered his questions truthfully, Declan would leave her alone. Her eyes wandered toward the plate of food, set just out of reach, and she realized he was trying his own form of torture.

She sighed, having no desire to play this game.

"I remember riding on a bus. It was dark, and had rained recently. I could smell it in the air when I got off . . . the rain and the grass." She closed her eyes, picturing the stormy night she'd arrived in Winterhaven.

"Someone had just cut their lawn and it lingered. It smelled nice . . . the grass."

She paused, drinking in details that only now her mind was allowing her to see. The pain began to sharpen inside her skull, but she ignored it, clenching her teeth and willing the pictures to come.

"I had to get off in Winterhaven because I had no more money left. It was as far as I could go."

"Where did you get money? Who gave it to you?" Declan's hard words rained down on her, and she flinched at the heaviness of his anger. It was obvious he didn't believe a word she was saying.

"I don't know. I mean, I had none with me. I just woke up on the bus and the driver told me to get off."

"Did anyone else get off with you?"

"No. At least I don't think so." Her mind whirled into a vortex of images, and she pressed her hands against her head as the ripples of pain became much more intense. A blurred image ran across her memory. A man? Had someone gotten off with her?

"There might have been someone, I just . . . I'm

sorry. I remember the rain and being soaked, and the feeling of panic that came over me because I had no clue where I was, or why I was out in a storm in the dark." She paused, whispering. "And the noise was so terrifying."

"What noise?"

Libby blinked up at Declan and felt a small moment of triumph wash through her. She smiled. Her lips were tremulous and eyes shadowed. "There were heavy footsteps. They were following me. I remember running and the only warm place to go to was the diner."

She paused, trying not to let the emotions overwhelm her.

"I was so scared it was them. All I wanted to do was disappear, and I wanted the pain to stop."

A single, solitary tear escaped, slowly sliding down her cheek until it disappeared. "I must have fainted, I guess, because the next thing I remember is Pete. It was two full days later." Her voice became hoarse with emotion as she continued. "I got away from the footsteps but the pain was still there." Her voice dropped, "I don't think it will ever go away. It's inside of me to stay."

Declan moved back, allowing her access to the food. Her violet eyes were shadowed, heavy with tears, and something slithered across his features and was gone just as quick. He stood there, staring down at her intently, and then turned abruptly, leaving her to the quiet.

She grabbed at the food, greedily stuffing the bacon into her mouth, closing her eyes to savor the taste and aroma as it awakened a ravenous hunger.

Not more than five minutes later she was licking the last of the grease from her fingers—she'd already licked every last bit from the plate—when Jaxon appeared suddenly in her room.

The entire area seemed to shrink and fall in upon itself. The man was huge, dangerous, and incredible to look at. He was fresh from the shower, his blue black hair waving thickly atop his closely cropped head. The dark beard that had graced the sharp, chiseled features was gone, and his clothes were much more casual.

And way too sexy.

That thought wove its way through her brain, and Libby felt the heat of a blush ride her cheeks once more. What was it about this man that affected her so?

Yeah, so he was tall, muscled with a ripped six pack, and he looked amazing in a tight T-shirt and faded jeans. So what? He was also the man who'd taken her from Pete and brought her here for an undetermined reason. She didn't wholly believe it was all about regaining her memory. That seemed a little too cut-and-dried.

He had an ulterior motive, of that Libby was sure.

She just hoped that she lived through whatever the hell it was they were after.

"The shower is down the hall. I'll show you."

He waited for her, his face closed, distant. Libby arose from the bed, her movements stiff and forced. It seemed that every bone and muscle in her body ached, and the thought of a warm shower seemed too good to be true.

"After your shower, Ana will examine you."

Yup, too good to be true.

"I am not letting that . . . that *deranged woman* near me. Can't you see that she wants to kill me?"

"We all want to kill you, Libby, but that doesn't mean it will happen. I've talked to Ana and she knows not to cross me. She has given me her word that no harm will come to you."

With that he turned on his heel and walked out the door, obviously expecting her to follow in his footsteps like a little puppy dog.

"You have got to be joking."

Libby inhaled softly as Jaxon paused. He was so tense, his body hummed like an energy field. When he spoke, is voice was low, deadly, and the hairs rose on her neck at its the menace.

"I don't joke. About anything. You will have a shower and then Ana will examine you. It's the only way we can hope to gather evidence of where you've been for the past three years."

He turned then and nailed her with a look that told Libby they were done. She sighed, overwhelmed, and adopted the submissive posture she'd only recently begun to fight.

She followed him quietly, stopping only to take two large white towels that he'd procured. A cold knot of fear began to tighten deep in her gut, and the food she had all but inhaled moments before left her feeling sickly.

She opened the door that he indicated with a quick nod and disappeared inside, closing it quickly behind her.

Libby felt like she'd just come off the world's craziest roller coaster. And she hated roller coasters. She knew that as surely as she knew she was screwed. She was frazzled, sore, sick to her stomach, and wished more then anything that she was somewhere else.

That she was someone else.

Like a normal person with a family and people to love her. What did she have? Who did she have?

She pushed herself away from the door and tried to banish the thoughts that were trying to crowd her too tired brain. Stripping the dirty clothes from her back, she walked toward the welcoming hot spray and hoped it would wash her troubles down the drain.

Better yet, wash *her* down the drain. Stepping under the hot water, Libby closed her eyes and let everything out. Her tears mingled with the water that fell upon her body, the pathetic sounds she made muffled by the hard spray.

Her eyes fell to the drain at her feet and she watched the water slip away. There was no escape for her. She knew that now. With deep resignation, she reached for the soap and began to scrub the grime and exhaustion from her limbs.

Outside the shower room, Jaxon leaned his tall frame against the cold cement wall. Her scent lingered deep in his nostrils. She'd been dirty, unwashed, and it still called to the primal part of him that wanted her. The animal inside him grumbled at being denied the chance to taste its woman.

He clenched his hands tightly, trying to fight the wave of desire that rushed through him. Visions of her naked and wet form began to dance in front of his eyes. He pictured her hands flowing across the milky white of her breasts and then down her tummy, to rest at the juncture between her legs.

She was so fucking beautiful. Even now, as beaten down as she was, his senses came alive at the sight of her, at the very smell of her. If he could, he would join her in the shower and take what was his.

Savagely, he swore, and in that moment hated Libby with a ferocity that startled even him. He hated the fact that she made him feel, made him want her. After all she'd done to destroy his life.

He still wanted her.

Jaxon shifted his jeans, trying to alleviate the pressure between his legs. Unfortunately it didn't help. The sensation of the material as it caressed his shaft only intensified the need.

For her.

His skin broke out into a cold sweat, and he inhaled deeply, trying to calm the frazzled nerves that hummed along his entire body.

"Why are you doing this to yourself?"

Jaxon hissed from between his teeth as he opened his eyes to gaze into ones as conflicted as his. Concern and irritation were evident in Ana's delicate features. She looked tired, which was strange, since she was a vampire, but then again, the whole situation was fucked.

It must be damn hard for her to stand by and not take out the woman who'd signed Diego's death warrant, he thought. It should have been hard for him too, but it wasn't.

"She's showering. I told her you would perform a routine examination."

Ana studied him, her eyes narrowed to half slits,

and Jaxon felt his emotions continue to swirl into a large ball of mixed soup.

He looked away from her, resenting the fact that she knew him so well. Knew how hard all of this was.

He was a Castille, for Christ sakes. He wasn't supposed to have any weaknesses. And he hadn't, until a slip of blond ass walked into his life over five years ago. Nothing had ever been the same since.

"Well, I'm here now," Ana said. "You don't need to guard her door. I think it's safe to say Declan has no designs on your woman."

Jaxon sprang forward and the vampire stepped back quickly. "Watch where you tread, Ana." Something in his eyes became feral and his voice was low as he continued, "I need to run. I'll be in the jungle room if you want me."

He moved away from her, heading down the hall, his heart beating a staccato rhythm that was painfully loud.

"Do not harm her, or you'll have me to deal with."

Ana watched him leave and tried to push away the sadness that pressed into her. Jaxon Castille had always been a bad ass, a man apart from the rest of them. He had never needed anybody in his life, only the companionship of the people in his unit.

She shook her head in agitation. That had all changed the day Libby Jamieson was transferred to their unit at PATU.

The moment she'd first laid eyes on Libby, Ana knew she would be trouble.

It was in the way she walked. In the way her long blond hair hung down her back, just so. It was in the way Jaxon immediately focused on her with an intensity that signaled the beginning of the end for the both of them. She had known nothing but heartache could come from their joining.

Jaxon wasn't ready to take a mate, and considering the shitty relationship his parents had endured, she wasn't sure he would ever be willing to give it all up for one woman. And if he did, there was no way he'd let Libby live the life that she thrived on. The danger alone would have been enough to put a serious dent in their relationship.

When a jaguar mated, it was for life, and even though Jaxon would have liked to believe he could escape that genetic trait, it seemed that Libby was the one female who posed a serious threat to his singular status.

Ana sighed. Too bad he hadn't listened to her and had Libby transferred immediately from their unit. It wasn't like she'd ever truly belonged. She was a fucking human, for Christ sakes!

Her eyes darkened and her hands clenched into small tight balls. Libby Jamieson was the human solely responsible for the death of her lover. Memories of Diego washed through her, and she felt her body soften as the weight of them cracked her heart.

Ana pushed herself forward angrily.

Enough with the memories.

She yanked the door open, smiling at the shriek that flew from deep inside the steamy room. She wouldn't harm Libby, but no one said she couldn't have a little fun with the bitch.

"Time for your physical."

Ana grabbed a large towel and stepped closer to

the shower, her eyes smiling in malicious enjoyment as she yanked the curtain back.

The smile soon fell from her face as the towel slipped from her suddenly weak fingers. Her mind was having a hard time comprehending what she saw.

Libby had turned toward the wall in an attempt to hide, but in the process had exposed the flesh that covered her back, buttocks, and legs. She was painfully thin, compared to the healthy workout nut she'd been back in the day.

But it wasn't her thinness that was so shocking.

Her back was full of scars that started just below her shoulders and raised ridges that ran down along her rib cage. Deep grooves had been carved into her flesh, and some were burns. Angry red marks that shouted torture and abuse. Ana walked into the shower without thinking; her fingers, reaching forward on their own, gently touched the marred flesh.

Libby was trembling uncontrollably, and she flinched as contact was made.

"Please don't look."

Ana continued to trace the puckered red flesh, wincing as the sobs escaped Libby, gut wrenching and full of pain, both physical and emotional.

Her eyes continued to wander over the mutilated area, and she could see that Libby favored her left side. Her ribs there were swollen, suggesting an injury that hadn't healed.

Ana turned away, sickened by the obvious signs of torture. She grabbed the towel from the floor and gently wrapped it around Libby's shaking form. Less than twelve hours ago she had wanted nothing more than Libby's blood. Nothing more than for Libby to experience the darkness of death.

She'd been alive for over three hundred years, and in that time had seen a lot. She'd traveled to every corner of the globe, and beyond. She'd suffered losses and endured indescribable anguish, both mental and physical, as she lost everyone she'd ever loved.

Ana was cursed and she knew it.

She could feel the darkness that was slowly chipping away at her soul. Or what was left of it. Diego had been her anchor. With him, she'd been able to push it back. She'd been able to hope. She'd been able to live once more.

Even among all the death and destruction they fought against every day.

When he'd been murdered, it was almost her undoing. The only thing that kept her from walking into the sun was a thirst for revenge. It ate at her with a ferocity that made blood lust pale in comparison. It was insatiable, relentless.

Now she was confused as all hell, and feeling something a three-hundred-year-old vampire rarely felt: shocked.

She exhaled softly. It looked like Libby had found her own nightmare punishment.

She led Libby from the shower room then, trying her best to ignore the sobs that escaped Libby's clenched, chattering teeth. It was starting to look like Libby's years in limbo had been no picnic at all. But for Ana, the question still remained. Did she deserve the sympathy that was knocking hard at her door?

As they entered the medical facility, the vampire's steel resolve was once more in place. She was focused and determined to find out what the hell had happened.

And no amount of scars, burns, and broken bones would keep her from vengeance if Libby was complicit in the attack on their unit, in the death of Diego.

That was the one thing she *was* sure of.

Chapter 8

The large black jaguar swam through deep water, his powerful strokes carrying him forward until he reached the edge. Using claws as sharp as razors, he pulled his heavy body out and onto the bank. Midnight colored flanks heaved from exhaustion, the rosettes barely noticeable underneath the palette of black, as they glistened underneath the artificial light that gently illuminated the jungle room.

The cat barked a warning and jumped easily up onto a large branch that jutted out over the water. His tail flickered back and forth lazily. The animal was anything but. His mouth hung loose and he began to pant as anxiety once more drifted through his veins.

It roared once more, angered that the woman he wanted to claim, *needed to claim*, was being denied him. He was at war with the humanity that lived deep inside his soul. The part of him that held back, the part that ran on emotion.

The animal in him only wanted to mate. And no one but Libby would do.

It was a pleasure long denied.

A noise broke through the eerie silence, and the cat swung his great head toward the far corner. He growled low and deep from his chest, standing up and scenting the air. Without a sound he jumped back toward the embankment and crept slowly through the underbrush, disappearing into his surroundings.

With great stealth the cat moved forward, creeping low amidst the underbrush. He sensed a presence to his left and veered to the right, quickly circling back until a scent reached his nostrils. The cat began to tremble then, so great was his excitement, and as he stalked ever closer to his prey, it was harder for the human side to maintain control.

Up ahead a shadow passed before him, and with a mighty run and leap his great paws knocked his prey to the ground, landing on top in a rush of muscle and bone.

"For Christ sakes Jaxon, get the hell off of me."

With a powerful push Declan wrangled his way from beneath the heavy animal, his face thunderous. "You weigh a fucking ton. Do that again and I'll be forced to use dark magick on you. You wanna stay a pussy forever?"

The two of them stood for a few seconds, chests heaving, and then mist began to creep around the black cat. It lovingly caressed the powerful beast, enveloping it in its tendrils, encouraging the change until, a few seconds later, Jaxon stood in its place.

His tall frame was awash in sweat, glistening under the light that made its way through the heavy overhang of jungle fauna. His lips were pulled back into a rakish grin, and he flexed the long muscles in his arms, rotating his neck in an effort to calm the beast that still wanted to hunt.

His naked form slowly crossed to a pile of clothes left near the hidden entrance, and he pulled his jeans on, letting his chest fill with air. The clan tattoos that colored his left shoulder and curved down around his abs seemed luminescent.

Declan waited until Jaxon's breathing slowed down, then he joined him near the entrance. His face was tense, putting Jaxon on alert.

"We need to go. Ana's done her exam and she wants us both in the war room, pronto."

"How does she seem?"

"She's extremely concerned."

Jaxon paused for a moment, exhaling slowly. "I wasn't talking about Ana."

Declan avoided his eyes, mumbling under his breath, "Ana will explain everything."

He turned and exited Jaxon's sanctuary.

Jaxon followed, trying his best to push back the heavy knot of dread that hung low in his belly. Declan wasn't himself. He wasn't screaming for Libby's blood, shouting sarcastic comments at him. He was aloof.

Fuck. That couldn't be good.

He quickly walked down the hall, turning right until he came into the open atrium that led to the war room. Declan and Ana were already inside, settled in front of a bank of computer screens. As he entered, they both stopped talking, and Ana turned, indicating he take a seat at the table.

She was avoiding his eyes.

The knot deep in his gut was getting bigger. He quietly moved toward the long table, but leaned his hip against it, refusing to sit.

It was never a good idea to sit when you were about to receive bad news. And he knew, as surely as the sun would rise, that a whole lot of crap was about to be dropped in his lap.

Ana was fidgeting with her notes. Exasperated, impatience clawed at him. He wasn't someone to wait and take things as they would come. He was a jaguar warrior, and had always run head first into battle.

This was no different.

"What the hell did you find out, Ana?" he demanded. "I don't have all day to wait. Someone shot at my ass last night and I need to figure out who the hell it is before they try again."

The vampire cleared her throat and lifted her troubled eyes unit they met Jaxon's. The confusion and pain that lay there hit him hard in the gut.

"Is Libby all right? What the hell did you do to her?" He growled deeply and sprang forward, stopping when Declan's hand pushed him back.

"Jax! Let her speak."

Ana paused, before plunging forward, her voice soft, but her tone determined.

"I can give you the bad news first . . . actually there is no good news, so I'll just start at the top."

Jaxon's eyes narrowed and his face became blank, but his eyes never left the petite vampire.

"First off, I'm not sure how much time we have. I found a chip embedded on the side of her hip. I removed it, ran a few tests, and confirmed exactly what it was."

"And that would be?"

"A tracking device."

"Son of a bitch." Declan spoke up. "That's just fucking lovely."

Jaxon shot a furious look at him and turned back to Ana. "We'll deal with that after I find out what the hell happened to her."

Ana exhaled softly before she continued. "I ran a number of tests on Libby, and while I can't tell exactly where she has been these last three years, I can at least tell you what was done to her." Her dark eyes moved to Declan and back to Jaxon before falling to the notes in front of her.

"She's been tortured over a long period of time. How long, I can't really tell, but if I had to guess I would say years. She has a number of fractures, some of which are the result of old injuries. She also has a number of newer ones, including two ribs that were broken on her left side. That particular fracture hasn't healed properly and is causing her a lot of discomfort."

Ana looked to Declan. "I'm hoping you can help in regards to that. I did give her something for the pain, but that's only a short-term solution."

She sighed heavily before returning to her notes, and Jaxon felt his insides thicken into ice at the sight of a woman, usually so in control, now shaken and disturbed.

"She was tortured with knives. There are a series of wounds along her back and crossing over the top of her buttocks. They are deep and would have been extremely painful. I also found evidence of old burn marks that were inflicted in the same area."

The knot inside Jaxon exploded and his fist pounded the table. Then he grabbed a chair and flung it hard against the door. His fury was so strong and all consuming that Declan had to grab him, pinning his arms behind his back in an effort to contain the beast that was roaring for release.

Ana jumped up and went to Jaxon, her arms going around him, calming him with her softness and compassion. "Please, Jax, let me finish and then we can figure out how to get the bastards who did this."

Jaxon inhaled deeply, relaxing gradually, until Declan felt it was safe to release his arms. Nothing more was said, and Ana returned to her notes, though Jaxon had the impression it was only to keep her eyes away from his. She knew damn well what she'd written in her report.

"There were also similar signs of torture on the bottom of her feet. I did a CT scan, and other than a few smaller fractures to her skull, I thought everything was normal. At first nothing jumped out at me, but then I noticed a blemish that seems almost unnatural. I'm not convinced the amnesia is linked to the torture and abuse she experienced. I'm more inclined to think that there has been some sort of block put on her memories."

"But that would mean—" Declan stopped as his eyes flew to Jaxon's.

"Yeah, Dec," Ana said. "It would mean dark arts are at play here."

Jaxon watched her bite her lip, fighting the emotions that threatened to overwhelm her—and that, more than anything, scared the crap out of him. Ana was always cool under pressure. She could take anything thrown at her and remain calm, but this—*this* was hitting far too close to home.

Mind rape hurt, almost as much as—

He couldn't finish his thought, but he managed to say, "Was she . . . ?"

Ana shook her head, "I don't know, Jaxon. At that point during my physical examination she was getting too emotional and wouldn't let me continue. I can't tell you if she was assaulted or not. What I can say is that I noticed a long thin scar, low on her abdomen."

"Well, what the hell does that mean?"

"It could mean nothing." Ana took a deep breath. "But it looks to me like a scar indicating a birth by cesarean section."

"What!" Jaxon's voice was hoarse and his eyes full of disbelief.

"Jaxon, I'm sorry. I can't be sure unless I do a further examination, but the scar's diameter and positioning lend itself to my theory."

"Well, if she had a fucking baby, where the hell is it?"

"I wish I could answer that."

Ana was about to go on when a resounding explosion rocked the building.

Jaxon swore a long string of profanities as he moved quickly to the computers. Declan, close on his heels, looked back to Ana. "Guess that's them shouting hell-fucking-O."

Within seconds a light began to flash above the

door, illuminating them in a wash of red. A buzzer sounded and a large screen to their right came alive. Then Cracker's large mug was staring down at them, and they watched him calmly look away and spit as another blast tore through the outer perimeter.

"Jaxon," he said calmly, "as I'm sure you can tell, we're under attack."

"Yeah, I can see that. How the hell did they get near us without you knowing?"

"Not sure. But judging by the vibrations and harmonics that are ripping through the area, Declan's protection wards are not going to last much longer. It doesn't look good. There is a large and well-trained group of men on the other side of the courtyard, and I think it's time to vamoose."

"Call the dogs and get inside the building. Declan is on his way to put more wards in place. We need time to follow protocol before we leave."

"Roger that. I'll be up in a few."

The screen went blank, and Jaxon flexed his hands as hot anger began to boil deep inside him. He also felt excitement at the thought of a fight, and tried to maintain a professional manner when all he wanted to do was unleash the power that lay within him, waiting for the chance to attack.

"How the hell did they breach our perimeter and go undetected until they were able to set off charges?" His voice thundered from his chest, but no one could answer his question.

Declan crossed to a large cabinet and grabbed a satchel. He filled the bag with an assortment of weapons, going heavy on anything antimagick. His stash included a charmed serrated knife, a Glock,

and several charges. When he was done, he shoul-
dered the bag and turned toward Jaxon. His body
hummed with energy but his face was tense and
when he spoke, his voice was low. They both knew
this was about as serious as it got. No one had ever
been able to breach their defenses.

"Someone with knowledge of the dark arts is
here. It's all connected. Libby, you, and what happened to Diego three years ago as well."

Declan gave a quick nod and then headed for the
door, "I'll set up some stronger protection wards,
but I can only buy us maybe ten minutes, if that. We
need to start destruction protocol and get the hell
out of here."

As he disappeared, Ana's fingers began flying
over the keyboard. Jaxon watched as she dumped
any sensitive material still on the hard drives, before
destroying all that remained.

He grabbed a phone and waited impatiently to
be connected with the head of PATU in Washington, D.C. It was a direct line and only to be used in
case of emergency. He felt the building shake, and
snorted. If ever there was a time . . .

After three rings it was answered.

"Identification?"

"Alpha nine two nine zero three."

"Code?"

"Blood fucking red! Get Drake on the phone
now." His growl was loud, savage, and he was immediately patched through to Commander Joshua
Drake, who answered on the first ring.

"Castille, what's the situation?"

"We're under attack, sir. Not sure who the enemy

is, but there are definite dark arts involved, and the players are well-organized and well-trained."

"You've begun destructive protocol?"

"Yes sir. Ana is dumping everything right now."

There was a slight pause before Commander Drake continued. "Ana? I thought she was on a job in Alaska."

"She was, but I called her in. I can't go into specifics but Declan is here as well. We'll be in touch at some point tomorrow, but you'd better send a cleanup crew here ASAP."

"Now, Jaxon, hold on. I need to know what you're up to and where the hell you're going—"

But Jaxon had already hung up and turned to Ana. "We have everything we need?"

"Yes, I'm dumping the last of the files now and then I'll run the destruct program. That should only take a couple of minutes."

"Good, I'm going to grab some extra weapons and then get Libby. We'll head out through the tunnels." His eyes pierced the dark eyes of the vampire. "If we get separated, we'll regroup at Jagger's cabin up north."

Ana shook her head. "No problem. Just make sure you get your ass out to the boat before this building goes up in smoke. My skin doesn't mix well with fire, and I really don't want to have to brave a wall of flames looking for an overgrown kitty."

Jaxon ignored her comment, his mind already running ahead, making plans, fighting the urge to grab Libby and run.

Cracker and Declan arrived just as he was leaving, their faces red with exertion. The two large patrol dogs panted alongside their master, and Jaxon waved him through.

"Take the tunnels. We rendezvous in Jersey and then head north to Jagger's cabin. He's been off the grid for a while, don't think he'll mind."

Cracker nodded coolly, grabbed a few more guns from the rack, and called the dogs to follow him out. Declan's eyes were troubled as they settled on Jaxon.

"We don't have long before they breach the wards. That was some heavy shit surrounding the perimeter. Real dark stuff; I don't recognize the signature." His eyes narrowed and his voice became deadly. "Looks like we have a new player in town."

Jaxon snarled then, the beast clawing hard at him, wanting out. "I say bring it on."

He turned as Ana piped in, "Okay, I have all we need. The destruct program is almost finished and the timer has been set. We have exactly ten minutes before this whole place goes to shit. So I suggest we make haste and get the hell out of here."

Declan flashed a wicked smile at them both, "I know the shit is literally hitting the fan, but man, I haven't had this much fun in a long time. Feels good. Can't wait to kick me some fucking ass."

"Good," Jaxon said. "You accompany Ana through the tunnels." He looked at his watch. "The sun is already setting so you're good to go. I'm going to grab Libby and I'll meet you at the docks."

Ana tucked a large laptop under her arm and retrieved the bag full of disks, while Declan waited for her. Then she pulled up short and whirled around. "Christ! Jaxon, about Libby."

"What now?" Exasperation exploded from him as

the need to get Libby to safety weighed down on him.

"I had to give her a sedative to calm her. Sorry, she'll slow you down."

Jaxon nodded, his lips tight, and then he sprinted down the hall to Libby's room.

She was sitting on the bed, her body covered by a thin gown, shaking her head slowly, with jerky uncoordinated movements. He crossed to her quickly, flinching at her violent reaction when another blast shook the foundation of the building.

To her right a fresh pile of clothes had been laid out, and he grabbed for them, snatching up a shirt and a pair of jeans. His hands stilled as her scent wafted up into his nose. Ana had managed to find some of Libby's old clothes, and for that he was grateful.

His eyes moved over her slight form and he knew they would no longer fit, but it was all they had.

Her head slowly lolled to the side and her eyes shifted up toward his. There was no reaction; no fear, anxiety . . . nothing but shadowed violet. Damn, what the hell had Ana given her? A goddamn horse tranquilizer?

He reached for her and met no resistance, and even though her body was trembling in wild rapid movements, he managed to lift her up until she was leaning against him.

The feel of her soft curves against his hardness was so familiar, an ache formed immediately, deep in his gut. The intensity of it stunned him, and Jaxon shook his head angrily.

His fingers fell to the tie at the top of her gown and he yanked it undone, but he was gentle while pulling the fabric from her body. She whimpered then, and he froze, not wanting to alarm her, but the need for speed propelled his hands and he turned her to the side, his eyes avoiding her nakedness as he grabbed the jeans and bent to help her legs into them.

He pulled them up, the worn denim slipping over her soft skin and hips. He looked away from the soft center between her legs, but his hands stilled as they reached the scar now visible to him, low on her abdomen. His fingers reached for it, and he softly caressed the thin, faded line, feeling her muscles clench against his touch.

His eyes slowly traveled up, past the flat stomach, before settling on the gentle swell of her breasts. The rosy nipples were puckered from the cold, but the soft globes were firm and well rounded.

At the moment, they were slowly rocking as she inhaled deeply. His eyes moved from them until they locked onto the deep violet orbs that stared down at him intently.

He sucked in deeply at the look that lay there.

Jaxon's groin tightened sharply and intense desire shot through him, slamming through every cell in his body like a bolt of electricity. He slowly rose to stand in front of her. The softness of Libby's breasts called to him, and he inhaled the subtle scent that belonged only to her, groaning inside as the turgid tips caressed the hard flesh of his body.

"You're so fucking beautiful."

His voice was harsh, thick with emotion, and he clenched his fists tightly to his sides, forcing them away when all they wanted to do was grab her breasts and lift them to his watering mouth.

"So are you."

Her simple words inflamed the heat that was slowly turning his blood to molten lava.

Her eyes were fastened onto his flesh, and they wandered from his shoulders and then down, lower, her fingers following suit, tracing the intricate lines of his clan tattoos. When she touched him, the intense fire inside begged to be let out, but Jaxon grabbed her hand and turned her tempting breasts away from him.

What the hell was wrong with him? He needed to get them the hell out before the enemy broke through Declan's wards. And he probably had about seven minutes until the entire building went the way of Armageddon.

"Libby, I need you to put this shirt on. We have to leave right now."

His voice bellowed louder then he'd intended, and she winced, but then wariness crept into her eyes as she grabbed the shirt and held it close to her exposed flesh. She turned, and what he saw sent him for a loop.

He hissed at the scars on her back, raw and angry. They stood out in stark relief against her white skin, as if she'd been branded.

Something clicked, deep inside, and he felt his anger recede. It buried itself deep in the dark corner of his soul, the place where the jaguar roared in despair.

There it would wait, festering into something mammoth before he unleashed it upon the animals that had done this to her.

Libby's movements were still slow, jerky from the effects of the sedative, and he gently pulled the top down over her head. He nodded toward the shoes, and she slipped her feet into them, leaning against his hard frame for support.

He grabbed her elbow then and they both turned toward the exit.

But there was a huge problem between them and freedom.

A rather large, menacing gun aimed straight at his head.

Chapter 9

Jaxon swore and pushed Libby behind him.

Good thing a cat had nine lives, and the way he figured it, he still had about five to go.

He glanced quickly at his watch. Five minutes and counting before the big kaboom.

His eyes met the helmet-encased head of his enemy full on as he let the power inside him out.

Yeah. This should be a piece of cake.

"Shit! Never thought I'd snag me a Castille jaguar. Damn, must be my lucky day."

The arrogance of his enemy was astounding. Normally, he would have enjoyed a little game of cat and mouse, but he didn't fancy frying his ass over such a pitiful excuse of a soldier. His nostrils flared and he sneered as a low growl erupted. The scent told him the asshole was human.

As if a human with a gun could stop him.

Even in human form Jaxon was a formidable

opponent. He still retained many of his enhanced jaguar traits, including speed and strength. With a roar, he moved so fast that the soldier barely had time to react. The rifle was smacked from his hands as if it were a play toy, and Jaxon had him pinned to the wall in two seconds flat.

His teeth were bared and his eyes feral, the violence running through his veins almost bringing the cat to the fore. He felt the familiar burn as his skin began to shift.

"Who the fuck do you work for?"

Silence greeted his question, and with a mighty roar, he shook the man until his head hit the wall behind him with a resounding thud. "One more chance."

The soldier began to tremble as the finality of his situation became apparent. "You're just going to kill me anyway, so fuck you."

He sprayed the air with spittle, and Jaxon savagely pressed his thumb deep into his enemy's carotid artery, rendering him unconscious within seconds.

The shock on Libby's face quickly changed to fear and she shrank from him, shaking her head, trying to move away.

Jaxon grabbed her roughly, ignoring the huge eyes, and yanked her along behind him. He had no time to pamper her. The clock was ticking away, and he knew if he didn't get them the hell out of there, his remaining five lives would definitely be toast.

Libby's movements were sluggish, her arm still favoring her ribs, and with a curse he grabbed her up into the hard embrace of his arms, balancing his bag of weapons on his hip, before running with the speed only a jaguar possessed toward his sanctuary. There, hidden in his precious jungle, was a trapdoor that led directly to the escape tunnels below.

Shouts rang out behind him, and his eyes glanced off a red laser beam that hit the wall to his right. He ducked just as a shot decimated the wall, building up speed as he flew down the darkened halls.

Libby clung to his neck as if her life depended on it, and he yanked the door to the jungle room open, slipped inside, and locked it. Within seconds loud banging and gunfire was heard on the other side, but Jaxon disappeared into the thick foliage, making his way quickly through the hot, damp interior until he reached the hatch.

Carefully, he placed Libby on the ground and moved a massive tree trunk that to anyone else would have appeared part of the rotting vegetation that littered the earthen floor. His muscles contracted as the heavy piece of wood was moved back, and he gestured toward Libby to climb down the stairs he had exposed.

She hesitated, and he swore under his breath.

"Libby, I know you're scared, but you need to trust me and do as I say."

A blast ripped through the room, and he wasn't sure if it was his words or the shouts that now resounded in the sanctuary, but she hurried as best she could to do his bidding.

Thick, black anger pulsed through his body with every beat of his heart at the thought of his private area being invaded by an enemy. The jaguar inside wanted nothing more than to attack, kill, and destroy.

But there was no time.

Jaxon jumped down, grabbing his bag before the tree fell back into place.

He found a shivering, confused Libby waiting for him at the bottom of the stairs. Without words, he once more lifted her up to his chest and ran like hell toward freedom.

Underneath the mammoth building that housed his branch of operations for PATU, there were a series of tunnels that had been put in place for such a situation as this. He'd never had to use them before, and as he ran, his body dripping with sweat from exertion, his memories of the layout were not as sharp as he would have liked.

If he took the wrong exit, well, he'd be screwed.

Familiar scents called to him, and with a grin, his nose led him down the same path Ana, Declan, and Cracker had taken minutes earlier.

He knew it was going to be close, and the adrenaline his body was producing went into overdrive as he spotted the clear night sky up ahead. The concrete ground was slowly elevating, and Jaxon burst through, hearing the motor of a boat as it pulled away from the dock.

Without stopping, still holding Libby firmly in his arms, his long powerful legs carried him forward and he ran to the end of the pier and leapt high into the air. He landed with a jarring force that brought him to his knees, but relief washed over him as Ana revved the throttle and the powerful boat took off like a rocket.

They were speeding up the Hudson River when a massive blast rocked the entire dock area. Fire, debris, and heat rent the air as Jaxon covered Libby, pulling her into his chest. A shriek tore from her throat as several smaller explosions continued to combust.

"Damn," Declan said. "If we'd have put music to that, it could have been entered in the Fourth of July fireworks contest."

Jaxon shook his head, marveling at the way Declan was able to make light of any situation.

"No, I'm serious. We could have called it, 'Reign of Fire' or something like that. It would have won, hands down."

Ignoring the attempt at humor, Jaxon's eyes swept the waterfront where his headquarters had lived in secrecy for well over ten years. The beautiful sanctuary he'd built with painstaking care was no more, reduced to a pile of rubble and ash.

His eyes hardened at the glow that swept through the air, and he hoped that each and every bastard who dared to enter his domain had died horribly. He grabbed some blankets and wrapped them around Libby before settling in for the short boat ride.

They were rounding Ellis Island and would reach their safe house located on the Jersey shore in no time. He closed his eyes, shaking his head at the deadly situation he'd been thrust into.

The woman in his arms held the key. Of that he was certain. Somewhere, locked away deep inside her damaged mind, were the answers he was looking for.

He sighed, letting the tension fall from his body and feeling the warmth from hers help alleviate the stress he was under.

Tomorrow they'd be up north and far away from here. He growled softly, as a wicked smile slashed over his features.

Once he found out who the hell *them* was, he'd be gunning for their asses. Anticipation licked at his insides as the cat relished the thought of a hunt. Bring it on, he thought. Bring it on.

Libby slowly crawled back from the edge of unconsciousness. Her brain was feeling fuzzy, but that was pretty much par for the course. She licked her lips, grimacing at the feel of her thick tongue. Her muscles ached and she became aware of voices, low and stilted, just beyond the fringe of black her closed eyelids afforded her.

Every muscle in her body was screaming at her to stretch, but she resisted, staying as still as she could. She strained her ears, hoping to hear a clue as to her whereabouts. For one brief moment pure, raw terror swept through her body like a flash flood. Was she back with *them*? Had they come for her?

Images, bits and pieces of emotions, flew at her.

She remembered the tall one, Jaxon, running with her toward a black wall of nothingness, and then there'd been an explosion, great balls of fire erupting into the blackness.

But the images were blurry, incoherent.

A dull ache was beginning to throb at the base of her skull, and the ever near presence of tears threatened to spill from her tightly closed lids.

When would this all end? Wearily, she tried to make sense of the last few days, but it only confused her even more.

A woman's voice drifted lazily over to her, and

Libby's body stilled as she concentrated to gather as much information as she could.

"Not sure if we should tell her. It could do more harm than good."

"I'm sorry, Jaxon. I have to side with Ana on this one. She doesn't know us from shit. So if we sit her down, tell her who she is and what she's done, it could scramble what little bit of usable gray matter is in there all to hell."

Libby winced at the analogy Declan used with such obvious contempt, his deep voice clearer than Ana's soft one. She could picture their faces clearly as memories tugged at her mind. They were fresh, new ones, only hours old.

Her heart began to flutter, and she fought the panic that seemed to forever live in hiding, waiting for the chance to explode. She'd escaped the faceless monsters from her past, but for how long? She wasn't sure.

This trio confused and frightened her on a different level all together. Jaxon confused her most. He was haunted as much by his past as she was. When he looked at her, his eyes were filled with a whole host of emotions, all of them dark, and they made *her* ache inside. But it was the other emotions that she had caught glimpses of, the ones he tried to hide from her, that scared the crap out of her. They were incredibly raw and almost animalistic.

"Best bet would be to get her to trust you. Once she relaxes some, she might start to remember and we can finally begin to put the pieces to this puzzle together."

"I can barely stand to touch her, Dec. How the hell am I going to get her to trust me?"

That last was Jaxon, and Libby cringed at the words he'd uttered so harshly, her stomach clenching at the bitter tone. Yeah, it was obvious his dislike for her bordered on hatred, but he was a liar. She blushed at the vague memory of him helping her get dressed. He'd told her that she was beautiful. She sighed again, not understanding any of it.

"Declan is right, Jax. You are the only one she might open up to."

"Why the hell can't Declan perform his freaking voodoo on her and crack her brain wide open?"

"Because, Jax, if I go in and fool around with a mind block that wasn't put there by me, I could kill her. And last time I looked, we need her alive to find out who's after you. Hell, considering my ass was involved in the latest attempt, and my restored viper has just been blown to bits, it's become slightly more personal."

Libby felt sick at Declan's words, wishing she knew the answers as he continued speaking.

"Once we've figured this all out, I really don't care what the hell you do with her."

"Declan," Ana said, "if you could have seen what they did to her—"

"Ana, what she did, three years ago—"

"Enough. I'll see what I can do. In the meantime, Ana, you need to work on tracing the origin of my intel . . . and Declan, I need you to contact anyone who's running under the wire. See what kind of chatter you can dig up, but don't go through our regular channels. Right now, I don't trust anyone."

Jaxon's words effectively ended the powwow, and Libby tensed, feeling a huge sense of relief wash through her as their voices faded and silence filled the space around her. She was safe, for now.

She inched her eyes open one at a time, squinting for a few seconds until she adjusted to the light.

She was lying on a bed in a small room. Soft cotton sheets tickled her nose; they smelled fresh. She kept still, but her eyes wandered the perimeter. Though the room was sparse, it was clean and tidy. There was a small dresser next to the door, with gingham curtains at the window that blocked most of the sunlight from streaming in from outside.

If she had to guess, she'd say it was some sort of rustic getaway, just like the ones her father used to take her to when she was a little girl.

She bolted upright then, ignoring the rush of blood that flooded her head and left her feeling nauseous. There was more there . . . just on the edge, but she couldn't grasp it. Frustrated, she sank back and closed her eyes again, willing herself to see a face, to see anything that was from her past.

But the canvas was empty and there was nothing more there. Just that one echo from the past.

Gritting her teeth, she sat up once more, squaring her shoulders. That echo was more then she'd had yesterday. That was something, wasn't it?

She threw her legs over the side of the bed. Her tummy was grumbling and she needed to find a washroom. Her fingers caressed the soft denim that covered her long legs, and the memory of Jaxon watching her flitted into her brain.

Jaxon staring at her bare breasts with an intense hunger that now made her cheeks heat up to a bright, rosy red.

Shakily, Libby pressed her cool palms to her face and stood up on wobbly feet. She took a few moments, listening intently at the door, and when she was sure there was no one outside, she gently pulled it open, grimacing as a soft creak echoed into the empty hall beyond.

Cautiously, she poked her head out, then followed with her body as she turned right and headed in the direction she thought might house both a bathroom and a kitchen. She found the washroom, and after she was done, came back out and continued her exploration.

The hall opened up to a great room.

Libby felt the first splash of pleasure sift through her body as she faced a wall of floor-to-ceiling windows that opened up to a vast, rugged wilderness. It was magnificent, and she found herself drawn to the beauty of it, almost like a child pressing its nose up against the window in a toy shop at Christmas.

A large, silent forest surrounded the cabin. Tall, thick stands of trees guarded this little slice of paradise and sloped gently down to the right, where the shimmering blue of water beckoned. It was spring, yet patches of snow could still be seen lingering near the darkened areas the sun was unable to reach.

They must be either at a much higher elevation, or farther north than Winterhaven had been.

Her tummy grumbled loudly, the pangs of hunger fueling her desire to find food. The main living area was open, without walls, and she saw the kitchen to her left. A basket of fruit lay on the counter, and she grabbed an apple before opening the large and well-stocked refrigerator, her eyes alighting on the interior.

Well-stocked, yes, but with an eclectic assortment of foods. There were several plastic bags filled with a thick red substance that took up the entire top shelf. She didn't even *want* to know what that was, and snorted at the idea of Ana being a vampire. Surely Declan had been playing some kind of mind game with her. There were no such things as vampires.

The shelf below was full of brown paper packages, presumably some sort of meat. There were a few cartons of milk, more fruit, and a large block of cheese.

Libby grabbed the cheese and quickly cut herself a large piece, happy to find a box of crackers in the cupboard to keep it company. She poured a glass of milk and silently made her way toward the front door.

She hesitated for a second, looking back over her shoulder before exhaling softly and pushing the large, heavy oak door open.

Stepping out onto a deep, wide porch, her face broke into a spontaneous smile at the sight of a comfy-looking swing to her right. It overlooked the water she'd spied from inside, and she quickly settled her butt into its cozy confines. She took a long swig of milk and attacked her cheese and crackers with gusto.

It had been a while since she could remember having any kind of appetite. It felt good. To eat, breathe the air, and enjoy nature.

She finished her cheese and was half done with the box of crackers when a thought occurred to her that stopped her cold. She had made it through the previous evening, as chaotic as it had been, without one nightmare.

No faceless monsters had terrified her last night. She munched on a corner of a salted cracker, welcoming the ray of hope that sprang up inside her.

Maybe there was a chance for her after all.

If she could stay alive, that is.

It didn't take long before her stomach protested at the amount of food she'd shoved down her throat. Feeling like a small pig, she set the box of crackers aside, then gulped down the last bit of milk in her cup.

Settling back into the swing, she closed her eyes. A feeling of contentment slipped through her veins, and she grabbed hold of it fiercely. The sun was warm on her face, her belly was full, and for once she let all the dark thoughts drift away.

Slowly, Libby became aware of the abundance of nature that inhabited this little corner of the world. Trees stood guard over a vast number of birds, and she caught glimpses of a couple of morning doves, as well as several robins. Their fat bellies flashed red as they zipped through the trees, wildly screeching to all the arrival of spring.

The antics of a little brown squirrel brought a smile to her face, its body darting madly about in search of something just out of reach. Kind of like her, she thought.

She stood then, answering the restless call of the little animal. Looking back toward the door, she slipped down the steps and began to make her way into the silent realm of the forest. It was quite a bit colder there, and she wrapped her arms around her body, trying to hold in some of the warmth that the light cotton shirt afforded her.

Sapphire blue water glistened to the right, and

she headed toward it, as if following a path she'd trodden before. Strange, that thought.

The hair on the back of her neck quaked, and Libby stopped abruptly. She remained still, feeling the soft breeze that caressed her cheeks and blew her loose blond hair about her face. Her heart began to beat faster as a feeling of unease rifled through her veins in a fierce rush.

She knew this feeling well.

Someone was watching her.

She let out a slow breath as her eyes frantically scoped out the terrain in the immediate area. She was surrounded by trees that continued down to the water. It appeared they couldn't be climbed, and certainly not by someone with damaged ribs and no strength.

She put one foot in front of the other, trying to appear as nonchalant as possible, which was hard; her entire body was yelling at her to run from the danger.

And there was definitely something there. She could feel it with every fiber of her being. Someone was stalking her with deadly precision.

A flash to her right was enough to kick-start her legs, and she took off toward the water, eyes searching in vain for a weapon or means of escape. The stitch in her side became sharper, but she kept on, and less than a minute later stumbled to the edge of the small, pristine lake.

A large piece of driftwood stuck out of the mucky earth close to water, and she grabbed it, yanking to get it out. Slivers punctured the skin of her fingers, but she didn't care. A sound behind her sent shivers up her spine and she renewed her effort, feeling desperation begin to tear at her insides as fear plopped itself deep into her belly.

Something burst inside of Libby then. She felt the crack, as if a well of emotion that had been bottled deep inside her had been shaken and exploded into a storm.

She was pissed off.

Actually, she was more than pissed off. She was fucking furious.

Enough!

She wasn't going to cower any longer.

With a mighty heave, she yelled loudly as she freed the large piece of wood, but the momentum knocked her off her feet and she landed on her back.

Hard.

Her head smacked the soft ground behind her, and the breath was knocked from her body.

Libby lay there, chest heaving, willing her body to get up and fight.

But then things changed in a way she'd never expected.

Feet came into view. Not feet exactly, but large paws.

Slowly, she lifted her head and pushed her body up until she was kneeling in the muck, brandishing a piece of driftwood and inches away from the most magnificent animal she'd ever seen.

Time stilled for a few seconds. She was aware of her lungs deeply inhaling air as her heart furiously pumped blood through her body, screaming at her to defend herself.

Warm air blew from the creature's nose and caressed her face. Libby shivered at the sensation as she stared, mesmerized, at the dark intelligent eyes that peered at her from the exotic face of the powerful black cat.

She gulped thickly as a low keening growl vibrated deep from its chest.

The animal moved away and began to pace back and forth, its movements agitated but not aggressive. She found herself relaxing, and when the animal stopped so close that she could touch it, her hands moved toward it on their own accord.

Trembling fingers hesitated, then softly skimmed over the thick fur that surrounded its head. The pelt was deep black, but as the sun caressed it, outlines of its rosettes were plainly visible. In fact they shimmered under her touch.

The cat was beautiful, and as she studied the animal, her fear left her completely. She had no clue what it was. A panther, maybe? Weren't they black?

"What are you?" she whispered, and fought the urge to wrap her arms around the beast. That would be crazy, wouldn't it?

The magical moment was broken as the animal jumped back, barking roughly from its chest. It resumed pacing once more, and Libby started to feel nervous. Then waves of anxiety pummeled her and she looked to the wimpy piece of driftwood she'd managed to dislodge.

There was no way in hell *that* was going to save her if kitty cat decided she looked like a tasty treat.

The animal howled, and fear crept up her spine again. Her mouth went dry and she shivered as fog began to encircle the cat. Long tendrils crept up and over the powerful muscles of its hind legs, until the entire body was shrouded in mist.

Libby fell back as the animal began to move and

shift, fear clogging her mouth, blocking her scream. Her eyes widened in horror as the dark shape mutated. Grunts and popping noises reverberated through the small clearing. She began to back away, trying to ignore the terror that clawed at her insides.

As long as the animal wasn't hungry, she should be all right. Now was not the time to panic. She needed to keep a cool head.

But that was going to be freaking hard.

Her mouth fell open and she shook her head in denial as a man walked toward her from the mist; slowly, with predatory grace.

A powerfully tall and naked man.

Intricate tattoos glistened in the sun as a fine sheen of mist clung to his skin. They shimmered as he walked toward her.

It was Jaxon, and his eyes were alive with a fever that hit her hard in the gut.

As Libby's eyes slowly wandered over the magnificent specimen, they widened even more. His straining erection pointed toward her like a weapon, and she licked her lips.

Jaxon was hungry all right. And it wasn't for food.

Chapter 10

If anyone had told Libby such a ridiculous story, she would have said they were full of shit. An animal changing into a man was unbelievable. It had to be an illusion, an elaborate hoax meant to intimidate and frighten.

Declan's words rumbled through her brain, their import penetrating her disbelief.

Vampire, shifter, and practitioner of magick.

That's what he had said to her the day before. At the time, she'd dismissed them as outrageous, intended to scare the crap out of her. And they'd worked. She shuddered at the image of Ana and her ferocious fangs. But now? Now she didn't know what to think.

Was this some elaborate trick? Or was it all true?

Libby's eyes flew to Jaxon's, and sharp jolts of awareness plummeted through her body. They sent shock waves of energy sliding outward, until her entire frame literally hummed.

Her heart sped up, pounding a pagan beat as adrenaline poured through her veins. His lips parted as he watched her. His eyes darkened even more, and he growled lightly as he stopped only a few inches from her.

His hands were clenched at his sides, and she tried to avert her gaze but was drawn once more to the large male appendage that bobbed as his chest heaved. He was so incredibly beautiful, as if carved from stone: tall, muscular, and loaded to the brim with testosterone.

His face was dark, unreadable, but something fierce smoldered deep within his eyes that called to her soul. It told her things, secrets that he'd left hidden. And then there was the part of his body that stood at attention, screaming at her to listen.

He wanted her.

And God help her, she felt more alive right now, in this moment, than she could ever recall being. She wanted nothing more than to bask in the feeling and never let go.

Without thought, purely on instinct, her fingers crept forward, hesitating only a second before making contact with the firm flesh of his chest. Heat licked at her, scorching a path up her forearms, and she gasped at the intensity, as flames of need erupted deep inside her. Her hands flattened and the palms lingered there, slowly tracing the colorful tattoos that caressed his chest and rose up toward his left shoulder.

Their design was bold. A series of symbols that looked to be ancient Aztec markings. She shook her head sharply at that thought. Aztec markings? Yes. She *knew* this, and that excited her. Her eyes flew to his dark ones again, and they claimed her hotly. All her thoughts of tattoos and Aztec markings fled.

Her body shifted as hot liquid slithered through her veins. She felt light-headed and swayed weakly until her body was crushed to him in a hard embrace.

Jaxon pulled Libby into him, his body aflame. The animal roared inside, impatient for what belonged to him, and he gritted his teeth in an effort to tame the beast. But it was so difficult to ignore the animal when his body was hot, heavy with need, and he closed his eyes as he took her scent deep into his lungs.

It was sweet and incredibly feminine. The familiar muskiness that was unique to her, blended magically with vanilla, pulled at him.

Hard.

He groaned loudly as his cock filled, and he was painfully aware of the softness it was pressed up against. It had been so long. So incredibly long since his body had felt like this.

There had been other women. Needs had to be met, but none had touched him as deeply and as profoundly as Libby.

No one had been able to match the passion he had shared with her. He groaned once more, running his lips over the hair that lay at her neck. Yeah, it had been too long.

Three years to be exact, and Jaxon found his emotions warring with each other as he fought the urge to punish and dominate. He couldn't hurt her. Not now. Not when he needed answers to the questions that had been rolling around his head.

His hands began to wander over her body, enjoying the feel of softness in such direct contrast to the hardness of his own. She'd lost weight, yes, but she was still wholly female.

His female.

His mouth sought hers, with a ferocity that only fueled the fire more. His only thought was to claim her body as his.

He groaned deeply into her mouth and nudged the soft lips open, allowing his tongue to venture into the heated warmth that lived there. She tasted exactly like he remembered, and the flames that licked at him erupted into an inferno as she surrendered to him, a soft whimper escaping as she melted into his hardness.

His left hand moved up, under her shirt, and he felt the shiver as he traced the curve of her spine, carefully caressing the damaged skin. He then moved with purpose around her rib cage, until he was able to cup the heavy underside of her breasts.

She arched against him, her hands slowly sliding up behind his neck, and kissed him back, her tongue dancing with his in a feverish tango that left them both breathless. His free hand held her head tightly as he continued to ravage her soft lips.

After what seemed like forever, Jaxon broke away and, chest heaving, his eyes captured her violet ones. He wanted her to see exactly what it was that he was going to do to her. He watched as the deep recesses of her eyes darkened, her swollen lips parted as her breathing quickened.

His hand reached out slowly, his fingers traveling over her delicate features, following the gentle curve of cheek, past the generous mouth and petite chin. Her neck was long and graceful, the pulse at the base beating fast and hard against his touch. It felt intoxicating.

His eyes fell to the heaving chest that was covered by only a thin layer of cotton. He could see the outline of his other hand as it cupped her left breast, his thumb aching to stroke the turgid nipple that stood in relief against the soft material.

She whimpered, grinding her hips against his hardness as he lowered his mouth. He blew hot air over the puckered bit of flesh, and without warning latched onto it, his mouth hot, wet, and demanding. Even through thin fabric she tasted like heaven.

He felt her breast swell against him, and strengthened his hold on her as her knees buckled. She would have fallen otherwise. It was too much for him, and he gently lowered her to the ground, laying her out as if she were a banquet he was about to feast from.

And feast he would.

His eyes caught hers, and he held them captive as he growled, "It's been so long, Libby. God help me, but I can't deny myself any longer."

He was burning with desire, his lips hot with need. He ripped the shirt in two in an effort to get to the flesh that called to him. He ignored the heavy ache between his legs and focused on the heaving globes mere inches from his lips.

He smiled wickedly as he lowered his head. His mouth was watering in anticipation, and as he slowly flicked his tongue across the dusky pink of her nipples, her hands found their way into the thickness of the hair on his head and she pulled him into her.

"Oh my God, that feels so good," she gasped.

He smiled against the soft flesh and then opened wide, bringing his heated tongue to swirl around the buds that begged to be kissed. Slowly, he teased and caressed, and when her whimpers became hoarse and the pressure from her hands was hard, he took one of the tips deep into his mouth and suckled hard.

She tasted like candy, and he felt her stiffen as he savored the sweetness and gently caressed her other breast. They had always been beautiful, perfect and feminine, but today they were like gifts from the gods, and he suckled hungrily.

Her hands began to make their way down past his shoulders, and Jaxon shuddered at her tentative caresses. They felt unsure, virginal, and that nearly drove him to the brink.

His skin was burning up and he felt the beast scratching at him. Begging him to take what was his. Mark her with his brand.

He tore his mouth from her breasts, trailing a path of fire down, his hands grabbing the waistband of her jeans. He would have ripped them, but her hips were so slim they slid down with no effort at all.

The scent of her arousal was heavy in the air, and Jaxon felt close to losing control. He leaned back onto his haunches, breathing in deeply, trying to maintain a bit of calm, his eyes taking in every inch of her beautiful body.

Her long hair was wild about her face, half covering her eyes as they trailed in long tendrils over her panting mouth and down toward her heaving breasts. His eyes wandered past the ribs, which were too noticeable for his liking, to the flat belly and the neat patch of blond that harbored her greatest treasure. His heart ached at the beauty before him, and it took a few moments until he realized there was a flaw to her, one that hadn't been there before.

The long, thin white scar seemed to mock him as it sat low on her abdomen. The anger that rushed through him upon seeing it was instant and cold. It felt as if he'd been punched in the gut. The scar represented a whole host of things he wasn't ready to deal with. And as his desire fled, the questions that had been burning in his mind since the night before could no longer be denied. Had she had a baby? And if so, who the hell was the father? Had she loved another the way she'd loved him?

Images and memories clouded his mind, and his hot flesh cooled as a rush of emptiness threatened to overwhelm him. It sat heavy and unwanted deep in his chest. He felt betrayed, and as his eyes skimmed the scar, he couldn't help but wonder if she'd screwed the bastards who had ultimately screwed *him* over.

He pushed away violently, and was ten yards away before he could speak. He'd been so close to losing himself in her. *Again.* Something he had promised he would never do.

"You need to go back to the cabin."

Libby sat up, trying to hide her nakedness, and when she spoke, she sounded confused. "Jaxon, I don't understand."

Her voice broke on a sob, and he fought the savage need to take her. To punish her. To pound his body into hers and hope for some sense of relief from the darkness that had stalked him for the last three years.

"Jaxon, help me understand all of this. *Please, I need to know.*"

"Libby, what you need to do is get away from me." His voice, thick with anger and need, was almost incoherent.

"I just—"

Jaxon exploded into action and was at her side in a second. He leaned down, enjoying the fear that clouded her eyes as she stared back at him. Her body trembled and she shrank from him.

"If you don't get out of my sight I will do one of two things to you. I will either fuck you until you can't see anymore, or I will wrap my hands around that lovely, long neck of yours and wring the very last breath you'll ever breathe from your body."

Then Jaxon pulled back from her again, his body flushed with fury as he spat, "My problem is that I don't know which one I want to do more."

The hurt that flashed across her face slammed into him, but he angrily pushed it aside. What the hell did it matter if she was upset? He could give a rat's ass.

He watched her through hooded eyes as she rolled over and pulled her jeans back up over her hips. Her movements were stiff, but she held her head high as she clasped the two ends of her shredded shirt together, trying to cover her exposed breasts.

Without much success.

She gained her footing and faced him with a bravado he knew she didn't feel. He had to give her credit. She was finally regaining some of the spunk that had attracted him to her in the first place.

"I'm leaving now."

Her voice was small, and the anguish she felt was

laced throughout her words. "I don't know what I did
to you and the others . . ." She paused again, struggling to maintain her composure. "I can't say I'm
sorry for something I don't remember, but if I hurt
you in the past, there must have been a reason."

He turned on his heel and walked toward the
forest, flinching at the hoarsely whispered words
that followed.

"There *has* to be a reason."

He stalked through the trees, ignoring the shrieks
and alarm that rent the air as two blue jays and a host
of sparrows heralded his approach. For an animal
known for its ability to hunt and stalk its prey with
silence and stealth, he was doing a poor job melting
into the local habitat, but he didn't give a shit.

His body trembled with anger. He was furious,
and as he glanced down at himself, the lines around
his mouth whitened even more. He snarled savagely; his dick was still hard as hell. It ached painfully, begging for release and the warm softness it
had been denied.

Onward he marched, each large step taking him
farther into the wilderness that surrounded his
brother's cabin. It was quiet here, peaceful. A place
that in the past had been able to soothe his spirit
and free his mind of all the crap his world was constantly throwing at him.

But no more.

Would he ever be free from her betrayal? *Would he
ever be free from the want and need that ate at him?* That
was the question that confused him most and, if he
were truthful, scared the crap out of him.

He was a jaguar. He lived for the hunt and loved
the work he did at PATU. He'd decided long ago that

he would not take a mate. Most jaguar shifters didn't settle on one woman.

Bitterly, Jaxon thought of his father. He certainly hadn't.

But he was a true jaguar warrior, which set him aside from the common shifters, like his older brother and his father.

Jaguar warriors mated for life. It was part of their genetic code.

It was the reason his mother, who was a rare female warrior, had stayed with his father even though he'd betrayed their bond over and over again.

The now elderly Castille had married his mother and fathered three sons. He'd spent the bulk of his younger years expanding an empire that even by today's standards was considered impressive. Blue Heaven Industries was a multifaceted company that dabbled in both military and communications, and it was a major bone of contention that he was not at his father's side along with his brother Julian.

But then again, Julian hadn't been born with the warrior tattoos that both he and his younger brother had. Tattoos that at times seemed almost a curse. To be a jaguar shifter was one thing, but to be born a warrior was something else entirely.

The need to fight and to hunt was a constant that burned beneath his skin. Regular jaguar shifters had always existed, but the warriors came into existence because of dark magick used by the ancient Aztecs. They succeeded in creating the ultimate predator, and the genetic code had been passed down through centuries.

Jaxon continued on, mindless of direction, only wanting the painful need that clawed at him to go away. He wasn't sure when his senses started screaming at him, but he noticed it as he stepped into a small clearing, deep into the brush, and discovered the remnants of a fire.

Quickly, he scanned the perimeter as his body remained still. He scented the air, pulling in many different smells that his olfactory senses were able to pick apart in seconds.

He knew there was a carcass, half decomposed to his left, just under the brush—animal, not human. He also knew that a shifter had lingered here, but vacated, probably within the last day or so. The signature was jumbled, and he was certain some sort of agent was used to cover its exact origin. Whether that agent was human or a result of magick, he couldn't be sure. But he did know one thing: the act of hiding one's origins was something an enemy would use.

He growled low in his belly, senses high at the thought of a hunt.

"Damn, Jax! By the looks of things, I'd say you were happy to see me, but since I'm your brother, I'm really hoping that's not the case."

Jaxon's tense muscles deflated in an instant, and luckily for him, that included the large one that had been standing at attention between his legs. He kept absolutely still, his enhanced senses quivering, and at just the right moment jabbed his left hand out to the side, feeling a keen sense of satisfaction when he connected hard with the flesh of his younger brother's chest.

He heard a soft thump as his brother hit the ground, and he whirled around, crouching low, a wicked smile playing across his features.

He hadn't seen Jagger in almost six months.

They'd hooked up when Jaxon had returned to the States briefly, but since then he'd remained incognito. Jaxon was hoping to run into him at some point, considering the cabin belonged to him, but when he arrived last night, it was obvious the place had been deserted for quite a while.

His brother rubbed the back of his head gingerly as he slowly gained his feet. "I should have downed you ten minutes ago. I would have too, but seeing as certain parts of your body were a little vulnerable, I thought it best to give you a chance to wind down. I mean, that thing looked so rigid I was afraid it would snap in two." He cracked a grin of his own. "My mistake, but it won't happen again."

Jaxon stared at his brother, noticing a hardness that gripped the features so like his own. Jagger was taller then he was, by a couple of inches, putting him at six-foot-six, his frame powerful and deadly. He had followed in his older brother's footsteps and gone into the military, much to their father's dismay, and done several tours of duty in Iraq.

All black ops, all deadly; the kind of missions a jaguar craved.

Something had happened over there. Jaxon wasn't sure exactly what, but his brother returned from Iraq a changed man. Jagger resigned his commission when his last tour was over and had then spent the majority of his time on the road. Where he'd been and what he had been up to wasn't something he'd shared.

Jaxon knew his brother was finding his way. And a hard one, that was. Being a jaguar, especially one born with the warrior tattoo, was not an easy path to follow. The animal fought with the human side constantly. It was a never-ending struggle, and one that could lead to destruction if not handled with maturity and balance. Something both his father and older brother had never had to deal with.

But he knew that his brother would be fine. Jagger was a Castille, after all.

"I see you finally found Libby."

Jaxon's head whipped up at his brother's comment, his eyes narrowing at the mention of her name. "When did you see Libby?"

Jagger paused, a wicked glint lighting his eyes a deeper shade of green. "Well, hell Jaxon, I've already had tea and cookies with her."

Jaxon hissed his displeasure at the thought of Jagger anywhere near Libby, and took an aggressive step toward him, stopping just short of physical action when his brother laughingly slapped him in the chest.

"Down boy! I'm just playing ya. Christ, I haven't been close enough to even lay eyes on her. I had just caught her scent and begun to follow it when I saw you crashing through my trees all bent out of shape and, well . . ." His voice trailed off, and the two brothers laughed, their voices echoing through the thick stand of trees that surrounded them.

"So, what's her story? When did you track her down?" Jagger asked.

Jaxon sighed tiredly, easing his way back from the edge that had been riding him for the last couple of days.

"I was sent intel, pointing me in her direction. She's been in Michigan for about two months, as far as I can gather. Before that, who knows where the hell she was." His voice thickened as the still lingering anger began to brew once more.

"It was a setup. I went to Michigan, meant to put a bullet in her head, but something held me back. Instead, I deviated from protocol, went to the diner where she was working and gave some fucking bastard a nice clear shot at my ass. I took Libby, and we've been running ever since. They used her to follow my movements, and attacked the loft in Manhattan." Jaxon shook his head, remembering the carnage and chaos. "We had to bail and destroy the base. We arrived here several hours ago."

"Who's we?"

"I called in Declan and Ana."

"I'm sure that was one hell of a reunion. It's a wonder Libby is still alive and breathing."

Jaxon snarled, "She's alive for now only because we need her."

Jagger moved away, his voice soft as he contemplated his brother. "You sure that's the only reason?"

"What are you getting at?" Jaxon was breathing hard as he rounded on his brother, his body humming with an energy that was shouting for release. He was itching for a fight, and Jagger knew it.

"All I'm saying is you went to Michigan to take out the bitch who basically put a bullet in Diego's brain." He shrugged, and met his brother's eyes dead on. "She's still alive, and you're walking around with a raging hard-on," Jagger continued, even as Jaxon snarled savagely and lunged for his brother. "You do the math."

The two of them tumbled to the ground hard, Jagger grunting at the force of Jaxon's hit. They both rolled toward the center of the clearing, chests heaving and curses flying. When Jaxon's bare back slammed into the sharpened wood remains that littered the ground, he swore loudly and threw his brother off.

They were up and facing each other in seconds, both aggressive and smiling wickedly at the joy they got out of physical sparring. Jaxon's eyes briefly flickered over the remains of the fire, and the joy he felt left him quickly.

He relaxed his stance and pointed out the area to his brother. Jagger knelt down and sniffed the ground. "Seems a shifter has been trespassing on my land. You recognize the scent? Because I sure as hell don't."

"It's not something I've come across before." Jaxon continued to peer deep into the forest, but he knew there would be no more clues. "Whoever it was is long gone. I'd say about a day or so. I don't think it's connected to Libby. We only just got here."

Jagger was quiet, his lips tense, and Jaxon was beginning to think his brother wasn't so surprised to see evidence of someone on his land.

"You have any ideas?"

His brother turned toward him, face blank and unreadable. "A few."

Jaxon eyed him closely. "You sure everything's all right?"

Jagger laughed at that. "Last time I looked, I wasn't the one running around in the woods with a hardon." His grin didn't let up even as Jaxon scowled. "Yeah, I'm good."

Jaxon turned and began to head back toward the cabin. "I need to get back to the house. Ana and

Declan should hopefully have some answers for me. You care to come along?"

Jagger laughed as he smacked Jaxon on the back. "So now I need an invitation to enter my own home?" He snorted as a new round of laughter bubbled up from deep in his chest. "Is everybody naked? Or are you the only one feeling the need to air out your junk?"

Chapter 11

Libby ran as hard and as fast as she could, not stopping until she reached the cabin. The stitch in her side ached beyond belief, and her fingers itched to massage the throbbing area, but they were busy holding the shredded remains of her top together.

The top *he* had ripped apart.

Her face flushed a deep crimson. She could still feel the imprint of his hands on her body, the roughness of them as they'd touched her flesh. She couldn't lie to herself. She had wanted him as much as he'd wanted him, if not more. She groaned softly as she thought of his hot, wet mouth against her breast.

When he took her aching nipple deep into his mouth, even through the material of her top she'd felt the heat began to burn bright, hard, and demanding deep within. The ache she felt at her core still throbbed, painfully unfulfilled.

Their bodies had connected and it felt . . . so natural.

As if they'd done it before.

That thought brought her to a jarring halt just as her hand was reaching for the door. Had they been lovers? Was that the answer to the bitterness that haunted his eyes when he looked at her?

She hesitated, her teeth nibbling at her lips as she contemplated that thought. Images of the two of them, naked, limbs entwined, flew behind her eyes, and she blinked rapidly, wondering if they were imagined or memories from her past.

Why can't I remember?

"Guess we'll have to see if Ana has any clothes she can lend you. Don't think they'll fit, though. She's a little less endowed up top."

Libby turned toward the swing, noticing, for the first time, Declan sitting there, drinking in her state of undress.

"What happened? Didn't like the fashion choice Ana picked for you?"

Tears began to prick the backs of her eyes, and Libby struggled to maintain control of her emotions, her fingers desperately trying to keep the ends of the shirt held tight over her heaving breasts.

His eyes followed her movements, and humiliation was added to the host of emotions that ripped through her.

"You must love seeing me like this." Her voice was tremulous, but she held on, fighting to remain steady. "Confused and pathetic."

She shuffled over until she was a few feet from him, feeling as if the weight of a thousand lifetimes sat on her slight shoulders. The tears she'd tried to hold back burst through, coursing down her cheeks.

"Why can't you people just tell me who I am and what I've done? Why these games? Why can't I remember anything past the last two months of my life? And why is this ache inside of me getting bigger?"

Declan continued to study her in silence, his face unreadable.

"Why am I not totally freaked out by the fact that Ana appears to be a vampire? I mean, that can't be possible, and Jaxon just . . . just . . ." She couldn't finish the thought. She was so tired of being confused.

"We think someone has used a memory charm on you, a powerful one at that. It's preventing you from remembering all the delicious little details that I would love nothing more than to pull from your brain." He smiled coldly at her, his loathing barely contained. "And I would try, but you would most likely not live through it."

He looked away, as if the sight of her made him sick. "It will eventually fade, as the originator of the spell is no longer with you. Once that happens, you will remember everything, whether you want to or not."

Declan's words were matter of fact, nonchalant even, but his body language told a different story. There was so much more to all of this, but one thing was clear: if she jumped in the lake and never resurfaced, he would not jump in to save her.

His dislike was thick and meaty.

"Why won't you just tell me who the fuck I am?" Her voice came from deep inside her chest, shooting upward with an anger that hung in the air between them.

"Your name is Libby Jamieson, and once you were part of a military unit." Ana's voice was soft and floated on the wind, winding its way toward Libby, encircling her with its silky texture. "Our unit, actually." Ana paused briefly, her eyes sweeping over Libby to land on Declan.

"We were antiterror and specialized in operations that our counterparts were ill-equipped to handle. It was a unique unit and one that you really didn't belong in."

Libby stared at her, not comprehending the meaning of her words.

Ana sighed impatiently. "You were human, and the rest of us . . . well, we're not."

Libby opened her mouth to speak and shook her head, not believing what she was hearing. But then, recalling Jaxon morphing from a wild animal into man, she stared at the other woman and remained silent.

"I know it's a lot to comprehend," Ana said. "Most humans don't know any of us exist. It seems these days the only ones that do are looking to use our strengths and differences in order to do something illegal."

Ana smiled hesitantly. "Yes, I'm a vampire. I've lived for over three hundred years, and no, I wasn't *made*. It is forbidden for my kind to do so. I was born what I am." She motioned toward Declan. "As was Dec, and Jaxon our resident jaguar."

Ana motioned for her to follow her back inside the cabin, and Libby looked to Declan, but he had already turned away from her. She inhaled a deep, cleansing breath and squared her shoulders. She wasn't sure what to believe anymore, and the pounding behind her eyes was slowly wearing her down.

She rubbed her temple wearily and joined Ana inside the cabin. The other woman gently grabbed her arm. The touch of Ana's hand was bittersweet. It had been so long since anyone had touched her with compassion, but still, she could sense that the woman was holding back. As if it was a struggle for her to touch and to comfort.

Wild thoughts began to race through her mind. As she shook her head, they became louder, the pain building into a pounding migraine that set her teeth on edge as wave after wave crashed through her. So many thoughts and pictures.

What had she done to them? *What had she done to herself?*

Her mind was reeling, but the cool touch of Ana's fingers at her back, stiff as they were, felt somehow reassuring. It was sad, really, how starved for a connection she'd become.

Any kind of connection.

"I am so tired."

She felt beat, and let Ana lead her back to the bedroom that she'd woken up in a few hours earlier. She still clutched the two ends of her shirt together, and cringed when Ana turned abruptly and spoke softly. "I have another shirt that should fit you. Hold on and I'll grab it."

Shame darkened her cheeks a deep red, and she could only nod in acceptance of the other woman's kind gesture.

Libby sat down on the bed and turned onto her side, welcoming the soft feel of cotton against her cheek.

She closed her eyes, and exhaustion hung on her slight frame, weighing her down until she succumbed to its demanding pull.

When Ana returned a few minutes later, she found Libby fast asleep. She placed a clean T-shirt on the table next to the bed and left as silently as she'd come.

The smell of food eventually brought her around.

Libby's eyes flew open and nightfall was evident from the shadows lurking about the corners. She was still in the room she'd woken up in, and someone had been kind enough to leave a small nightlight glowing. Its arc was small but it lit the room enough for her to see, and for that she was grateful. She hated the dark and all the monsters that accompanied it.

Voices could be heard outside her room and down the hall, several in fact, and she strained her ears trying to discern their identities. After a few moments she knew that Jaxon, Declan, and Ana were all present, and two other men.

She would have preferred to stay in her room, safely hidden. But her stomach was painfully protesting its empty state, and if she wasn't mistaken, the scent of barbecue was wafting deliciously in the air.

She swung her legs over, and was up before she convinced herself to stay behind, which was something she might have done a few days earlier. Hell, a week ago she'd have stayed holed up in the bedroom until she passed out from hunger.

The thought of confronting the man she'd almost made love to would have been unimaginable. Especially considering he could change from a deadly predator into just about the sexiest male she had ever laid eyes on.

Cool air caressed her breasts, and she swore. *Shit!* She'd forgotten about the torn shirt.

Her fingers closed the gaping fabric as her eyes frantically searched the room. She breathed a sigh of relief when she spotted a neatly folded shirt left on the side table, and immediately made the switch.

The T-shirt was a little on the small side, way too tight across the chest for comfort, and she hesitated for a moment, hating the way it drew attention to her body.

Well, it's not like he hasn't seen them.

Libby snorted at that thought, not liking the heat that flushed her cheeks, and in the end it was the sharp emptiness in her gut that urged her forward. She quickly left the room and walked with calm steps, head held high, until she entered the large open area where everyone was congregated.

All conversation stopped, and she felt the heat of five separate pairs of eyes. Jaxon was to her extreme right, so she ignored that direction completely, focusing on the one friendly face she could see.

It belonged to an older gentleman, his weathered eyes crinkled in greeting, but the warmth disappeared entirely as Jaxon growled like an animal from the end of the table.

She faltered for a second, smiled tentatively at the older man, and walked toward the kitchen counter where the remnants of a meal lay scattered on several plates.

All that was left was the discards. Well, that and a glass that held about an inch of a dark red substance. Thinking of Ana, her stomach flipped over, and she looked away from what was obviously blood.

Libby stood there like an idiot, trying to ignore the silence that weighed on her like a slab of concrete. She knew everyone at the table was watching her, and she had the insane urge to make an obscene gesture behind her back. She actually raised her hand, but thought better of it, and walked around the counter, hoping there might be some leftovers.

There was nothing.

To her right, past the wall of windows, she spied two large dogs sprawled on the porch. They were happily gnawing away at several large bones. Pain sliced through her at the sight.

Jaxon had thought to feed his dogs. Nice.

The dogs got steak and bones, and she . . . well, she got dick all.

Once again she was at the low end of the pecking order. She inhaled softly, wanting to cry but fighting it.

She would no longer show weakness.

If she was to survive these next few days, she would have to toughen up and look after herself.

Screw Jaxon and his crew.

She turned toward the cupboards then and opened the nearest ones. They were empty, save for a few pots and pans and several boxes of cereal. She grabbed the first box, but as she lifted it, realized it was empty.

Figures.

The cheese!

She slammed the cupboard closed, maybe too loudly, but by now she didn't give a shit. She was starving, and if there was nothing left but cheese again, well, that sure as hell beat sucking back a cup of blood.

Her hopes were once more dashed by the pitiful lump of cheese that had been left in place of the large block she had seen earlier. She grabbed the measly leftover and turned back toward the far cupboard, wanting to grab the box of crackers she'd spotted before.

As luck would have it, the box had been stowed away on a shelf just out of her reach. Blind anger shot through her, and she hissed as she tried to grab it with the tips of her fingers. Her side ached as the muscles pulled, but she ignored the twinge and focused on getting the box down.

The room was still silent, and knowing that all five of them were watching her struggle, her body was flushed with heat. She pictured the smirks that were likely on their faces and gritted her teeth.

She couldn't get to the box and hung her head in defeat. Her stomach growled loudly, echoing into the silence that surrounded her, and she turned abruptly, ignoring the faces to her left, and walked toward a large chair that overlooked the magnificent view.

Libby fell into its softness with a thump, a small gasp escaping her as the impact jarred her already aching ribs. She held her head proudly as she began to gnaw on the cheese.

A chair was scraped back loudly, and then she heard footsteps banging across the tiles. It was followed by grumbling, cursing, and cupboards slamming, and she paused, chewing her food softly while trying to appear uninterested.

She heard the spray of water and cringed, turning her head to avoid whoever was making a beeline for her.

A hand at her shoulder startled her. It was the old man, and he offered her a plate of crackers that also held a bunch of freshly washed grapes.

Libby was touched. She took the plate from him, nodding in thanks, not trusting her voice.

"We're not all animals here. I'm ashamed to say I didn't think to leave you a plate myself."

The man turned around and headed toward the front door. "I'm going for a smoke, and don't want no company."

The door slammed behind him, and Libby smiled at his grumbling words. Yep, screw Jaxon and his crew.

She hungrily attacked the cheese and crackers, thinking they tasted even better than earlier in the day. The grapes were large, green, and incredibly sweet. She enjoyed every single one immensely, and when she was done, licked her fingers slowly, savoring the last sweet taste.

Movement in the window drew her eyes, and she was startled at the clear picture reflected in the large panes. She could observe the table behind her unnoticed, and she sank farther into the comfort of the chair as she settled back to look.

Conversation had resumed, but the words were soft, muted, and even though she strained her ears, she couldn't catch anything.

She could see them all clearly, and found herself

searching for Jaxon. He was sitting at the end of the table, deep in serious conversation with Declan. To his right sat a man who leaned back carelessly in his chair, long legs sprawled out in front of him. He was massive, and as her eyes met his in the window, she gasped loudly.

He was Jaxon's double, and a slow grin fell across the handsome face, illuminating the similarities but also highlighting the differences.

His eyes were incredible, not the dark black of his brother's, but even through the glass she could see the electric green. It was a devastating combination when paired with his dark hair and deeply tanned skin. She could also see the beginnings of a similar tattoo that graced the left side of his neck, but it disappeared beneath his tight black T-shirt.

A low growl grabbed her attention, and her eyes slammed into the furious gaze that Jaxon directed at her. He said something to the man with the green eyes, and Green Eyes laughed outright. This seemed to piss Jaxon off even more and he jumped to his feet.

The table erupted into chaos, with everyone standing and shouting, but not the green-eyed devil. His eyes pulled at hers and she found herself smiling back at him.

"Enough!"

Jaxon's deep voice rang out, and silence once more reigned supreme.

Tension emanated from within the group at the table. At some point the rhythm and tone had changed. All the men were now scowling, and Ana retreated to the kitchen, gathering up the mess on the counter.

Jaxon's face was as black as she'd ever seen it, and she looked away, suddenly frightened by the ferocious set to his features.

A phone rang then, its shrill tone grating as it loudly pierced the air. The tall stranger, so like Jaxon, moved quickly, bearing the same grace and stealth. Her eyes followed his movements until her view was blocked by the long muscular legs of the man she'd been trying to avoid.

She refused to meet his eyes, and pointedly tried to look around him. He had other plans, and knelt down in front of her. Still, she kept her eyes lowered and tried not to notice how his large frame enveloped the chair, effectively locking her between his two legs.

Tried, being the key word, and one that wasn't successful.

Her eyes skimmed the powerful muscles that flexed underneath his faded jeans, and his scent crowded her, awakening an ache that struck hard and fast.

"My brother is off limits. Don't even think of using your assets to sway him." His breath was hot on her cheeks as he moved in closer, his words meant to insult. "He knows you're damaged goods."

Heat flushed through her body and she inhaled sharply at the hurtful slam. Her chest began to pound as her heart sped up.

"Go fuck yourself." The words slipped from between her lips of their own accord. Even she was shocked at them, but tried not to let it show.

Jaxon felt his temper knocking hard and he wanted nothing more than to let it fly. Instead he took a few seconds and calmed himself. He grabbed her chin, forcing her eyes up until his dark ones held hers prisoner. "You've done that to me, Libby, many times over. You'll not hurt another Castille as long as there is breath in my body."

He shoved her away from him and stood quickly.

Her wounded eyes affected him more than he would like to admit, but the fury that clawed at him incited the jaguar to a point of violence that was almost overwhelming. He snarled at the thought of Jagger anywhere near Libby.

He stalked back to the table, head swiveling toward his brother as he came back into the room. Jagger was tense, his features closed.

"I have to hit the road, Jax," he said. "I was wondering if it would be all right for Cracker to ride along with me. Something's come up and I could use his expertise. I know you have your hands full with this situation and all."

Jaxon studied his younger brother, not liking the light tone he'd adopted. It was in direct contrast to the black energy that haloed him like a blanket. Some deep shit was about to hit the fan.

For both Castille brothers.

"Anything you want to discuss before you leave?"

Jagger smiled wickedly, already heading toward the door. "Nah, I'm good. Just make sure to lock up before you leave."

As he passed Libby, he ignored the warning growl from behind and leaned over, his impressive bulk responsible for the look of panic that flashed across her face. He grinned wickedly, winked and whispered, loud enough for all to hear, "It's good to see you, Libs. About time you popped up from off the grid." He chuckled softly. "A lot of things have changed, but Jaxon's still an ass of epic proportions. Don't take any crap from him."

He turned then and shot a sly grin at his brother before heading out into the night.

Cracker returned briefly and grabbed a bag before nodding in his general direction. The ex-soldier was pissed at him. That was plain for all to see.

Jaxon shrugged it off. Cracker would get over it.

He watched him closely, his shoulders tensing as the older man leaned down and whispered into Libby's ear. Christ, he had to get over the whole territorial thing. Libby wasn't his. Hadn't been for a long time. Even back in the day, they'd been lovers, sure, but nothing more.

Yeah right.

Jaxon ignored the silent taunt that rippled through his brain, choosing to focus on other things. He didn't want to think about Libby anymore. At least, not right now.

The door slammed shut behind Cracker, and suddenly the room seemed too quiet. Declan had gone down to the office, waiting to hear back from his contacts, and Ana was banging around in the kitchen, muttering things he didn't care to listen to.

Great. Just fucking great. The tension was so thick he could hardly breathe. Darkly, he pinned Libby with furious, bitter eyes.

Ever since that intel landed in his lap, his life had spiraled out of control, and the direction hadn't been up. He was the kind of man used to being in control of all areas of his life, and damned if this little slip of a blonde was gonna screw him over.

Again.

Her violet eyes shadowed and he felt a splinter of pleasure as she looked away. His eyes held fast, knowing the direct stare was making Libby uncomfortable, and he kept them pasted to her as she walked stiffly past him.

He followed her progress until she disappeared, and then caught the surprised look Ana sent him.

"What?" he barked.

She opened her mouth to speak, but closed it without uttering a word. Moving past him, Ana headed toward the office at the other end of the house. "I hope she doesn't wander away again, considering the dangerous creatures that lurk about these woods," she said, her voice softening as she added, "I'm fresh out of extra shirts."

Jaxon scowled darkly but by then he was alone. His body hummed with tension and he wanted nothing more then to become a jaguar and run it off. He swung around, gazing out at the vast stretch of darkness longingly.

Sighing tiredly, he turned and followed Ana's footsteps. He was hoping they'd each have the answers they were looking for.

He reached the office to find Ana and Declan crouched together in front of the lone computer they'd been left to work with. Everything else had been destroyed in the blast.

Ana looked upset when her eyes finally turned to him.

"This is bad, Jaxon. I don't know what to make of it. The intel you received can be traced directly back to Drake's office. A secure channel was used, one that would need the highest security clearance to even gain access."

Her long hair fell over her eyes, and she pushed it back impatiently. "There are probably only a handful of people with that kind of clearance."

"Hey, you're sharing space with one of them."

Ana looked at Declan in disbelief, "You have level five security clearance? Since when?"

"Since Borneo."

"Borneo, that was over a year ago. You didn't tell me your situation with Drake had changed."

"I didn't know we reported back to each other, Ana. But now that you know, got something to share in return?"

"Enough, guys. You two are not helping me right now. And since I'm the one who was shot at, I need you both to chill. Any ideas on who sent the intel? Do you think Drake's involved?"

Ana sighed, shaking her head, "I've checked, and from what I can tell, he wasn't in the building when the intel was sent. But we all know that means nothing."

Declan cut in, "Either way, we need to go to Washington to investigate."

Ana piped in as well, "I agree, the sooner the better. I'll leave tonight."

Jaxon balked at the thought that his boss was somehow linked to an attempt on his life, but in this business, stranger things had happened.

"Good, then. The both of you will leave tonight, but this has to run under the radar. Right now we don't know who to trust, and Drake knows the two of you are working with me. You could be walking right into a trap."

Declan and Ana headed up the stairs, while

Jaxon's thoughts swirled in several different directions.

Who the hell wanted him dead?

But the bigger question remained: what part did Libby have in all of this? Was she being used by a higher power, or was she actively, willingly, involved in a plot to take him out?

He growled at the thought.

He would give her exactly twenty-four hours to regain her memory.

If it didn't come back by the time Ana and Declan returned, he'd let the sorcerer have at her.

And God help her if she was complicit.

Chapter 12

Screams woke him from a dead sleep. They tore at him, animalistic squeals and sharp moans of terror.

Jaxon had dozed off on the couch and was up in a flash. He flew down the hall, hesitating outside Libby's room, confused and disturbed at the raw agony that he heard beyond her door. He sensed no other presence, and after a few moments the screams lessened and then quieted altogether.

He exhaled slowly, on edge and fighting the urge to go to her. He growled in frustration, hating the way she'd managed to crawl underneath his thick skin.

He pictured the scars that laced her back, knowing the suffering that she'd endured, yet still took a step back.

Hands clenched at his sides, he turned away, intending to leave her wallowing in her own misery and took a few steps way. But he stopped when he heard a thud inside, and then sobbing, which was heart wrenching. He cursed his weakness—he'd always been softer around Libby—as he whirled back around and pushed the door open.

He found Libby curled up tight in the fetal position, on the floor beside her bed. She'd obviously fallen out, but was still deep in the throes of a nightmare. She was clad only in the thin T-shirt Ana had given her and a pair of underwear.

The shirt was soaked with sweat, and long strands of blond hair clung to the moisture at her face and neck. Her body was shaking. Jerks and spasms rocked her limbs, punctuated by a series of deep, guttural moans that sounded as if they were forced from her throat.

He stood still, unsure how to proceed.

She rolled onto her back, eyes open but not seeing him.

She was definitely under the spell of something dark. Her long graceful arms held herself protectively around the midsection and she began to mumble words that erupted into harsh whispers.

"Castille's whore. Castille's whore. Castille's whore."

Jaxon's blood turned to ice at the words and he fell to his knees, feeling the heat from her body even though he was careful not to touch her.

She stilled as if sensing a presence beside her, and then her spasms, which had abated, returned, her body quaking with a ferocity that surprised him. His eyes raked her near naked form, and he was disgusted at the sharp spike of desire that flooded his body.

He clenched his teeth, trying to ignore the pull

that she wrenched from him. But it was no use. He cupped Libby around the shoulders with one arm, the other arm under her knees, and pulled her to him. As he lifted her up, she grabbed hold of his neck and clung to him, her thin arms digging into the hardness of his flesh as if the very devil were after her.

Her head lolled back, falling against his chest, and the dark eyes that had never faded from his memory implored him with such anguish, he felt the cracks around his heart widening even more.

"Please help me."

Gently, Jaxon cradled her there, tight against his heaving chest, feeling every heartbeat her body took, fighting the overwhelming urge to protect and soothe.

It was a losing battle, and he knew it.

This woman that he held, shivering, damaged, weak and traitorous, belonged to him on a level he couldn't even begin to comprehend. He stumbled, the realization nearly bringing him to his knees.

Jaxon Castille, jaguar warrior, felled by someone like Libby Jamieson.

He cursed the irony.

The last three years of his life had been hell. The only thing that had kept him sane and functioning was the intense desire for revenge. The hunt for Libby had remained his number one priority, even as he took the odd mission for Drake. His team had broken up, life pretty much fell apart, but one constant was threaded throughout.

Libby.

He had dreamed of numerous ways to make her

pay for the death of his cousin Diego, all of them painful. He had lain awake so many nights, fighting the desire that ravaged his body at just the thought of her. It mingled equally and freely with a deadly rage that simmered below the surface.

A rage that fed the cat, enticing it into a frenzy of need that drove him, day after day, fueling the hunt.

And look where that got him.

Here he stood, quivering with need, holding onto the woman who'd effectively shredded his life into slices of want, need, and emptiness.

She whimpered softly in his arms, relaxing into the crook between his shoulder and elbow. The frailty of her body inflamed his senses, and he found her hair—so blond and pale against the dark of his skin—incredibly erotic. He groaned as his body reacted, instantly becoming hard.

Her feminine scent colored the air around him, and he inhaled deeply, letting her essence filter through his lungs until it seemed every cell in his body was alive with a craving that bordered on obsession. Savagely, he shook his head, trying to clear the images of their bodies naked, writhing together in passion.

Her arms around his neck tightened even more as she melted into him. Christ, he needed a cold swim in the lake to put out the fire she'd inadvertently started. He looked down at her face, relaxed and deeply ensconced in slumber. The nightmares were gone, for now.

Jaxon glanced behind him, at the door standing open, mocking his stupidity. Then he knelt down on the mattress. which still held the warmth from her skin, and slid his hard body down until he was on his side, with Libby safely tucked in his embrace.

His dick, inflamed and hard, rested against her back, and he cursed loudly as she sighed and moved her ass against him seductively.

As if she was home.

Fuck, it was gonna be a long night.

Soft rays of sunlight fell across her face, caressing cheeks and awakening her psyche.

Libby couldn't remember ever feeling so warm, settled . . . almost happy. Deliciously content. She and happy didn't usually go hand and hand, but there was no denying the way her body felt.

She snuggled closer to the warmth that wrapped itself around her limbs, then froze.

She wasn't alone.

Her eyes flew open and to a broad expanse of bronzed, hard flesh. The tattoos she found herself staring at were Jaxon's. They mesmerized her, seeming to be alive. As he inhaled deeply, the images and symbols on his hard chest contracted, giving the illusion of movement.

But why the hell was he in bed beside her?

Her memories from the previous evening were fuzzy, her mind still heavy with sleep. The last thing she remembered clearly was his black eyes looking at her with such contempt that he'd scared her back into the safe confines of the bedroom she was given when she arrived here.

Wherever the hell *here* was.

She tried to push away, but his right arm was at her back, while the left lay at her hip, his large hand cupped there, almost possessively. With the wall behind her, his large form in front, she was definitely good and trapped. Sighing softly, she basked in the moment, thinking that it all felt, somehow, so right.

She relaxed her limbs, her eyes drinking in the sheer male beauty that lay in every perfect feature before her: from the deeply expressive eyes with the sinfully thick long lashes to the wide jaw that encased the most amazingly kissable lips she'd ever seen on a man.

Not that she remembered many, but she knew that if she had the ability to remember a thousand different faces, Jaxon Castille's would end up on top. Even though he scared the crap out of her most of the time, there was no denying the fact that the man was incredibly hot.

Volcanic hot, to be exact.

The eyes she'd been fantasizing about opened without warning, pinning hers with a hard, direct glare that set her insides on fire. Suddenly, nerve endings that she hadn't known existed roared to life and her entire body was suffused with heat. She felt her nipples harden, even as liquid fire melted into the very center of her, erupting into a wall of need.

A throb began in earnest, pulsing low, deep within her body. Her breath quickened and she fought the urge to rub her hips against his hardness. The ache between her legs magnified at the very thought, and Libby blushed, embarrassed at her body's reaction to someone who made no attempt to hide the dislike he felt for her.

His eyes remained focused, hard and unreadable. She had no clue what he was thinking, but from the feel of his pulsating length burning against her thigh, she knew he was equally aroused. She groaned softly, and unable to stop herself, rubbed her hips gently against him, loving the feel of his heated flesh against the softness of her own.

He hissed in reaction, and his hands pulled her up along his body until her lips were but inches from his. She could see the white teeth, his tongue languishing between parted lips as he continued to breathe heavily.

"Careful to fan the flames of desire, Libs . . . I'm not feeling in a gentlemanly frame of mind this morning."

"I'm sorry, I can't help myself." Her soft honest words slipped from between her lips without thought. "I want you. I don't even know why. It's like my body craves your touch, and the need inside of me is almost painful."

She heard his rough groan and it only excited her more.

"I feel like I'm finally home." She felt him still at her words, and she whispered quietly, "Like I'm where I belong."

Jaxon's natural scent was like a beacon to the wildly fluttering heart that pumped blood through her veins furiously. She wanted to bury her nose against his throat, inhale the heady musk, and acting purely on the animalistic needs that clawed at her, that's exactly what she did.

Libby closed her eyes and nuzzled against the pulse that pounded at the base of his neck. Her tongue slipped from her mouth and she licked the delicious pressure point, delighting in the feel of power as his life force rushed through his veins with each powerful beat of his heart. He threw his head back, his arms holding her to him tightly, and she nipped playfully before slowly trailing a path of butterfly kisses up along his jaw until she reached the lips that were awakening incredibly erotic images in her mind.

She paused, her eyes seeking the deep brown of his, and as they met, the fire that raged inside her intensified, and he grabbed her to him, his mouth plundering the softness of her own, his tongue invading, commanding.

Libby opened up to him fully, not caring about anything other than the man who'd awakened such a need, such a desire, that she didn't think the fire would ever be extinguished. Her nipples were fully engorged, the sensitive peaks aching from the friction of the cloth of the T-shirt and the hardness of his chest.

She groaned loudly as his mouth left hers, to trail a path of molten lava down her neck. He sniffed along the side, sending scattered shards of desire to flicker over the supersensitive area, and when he began to suckle the flesh directly under her ear, Libby felt a rush of warm wet honey spill from between her legs.

Anxiously, she began to move against him, her body finding a rhythm long denied, and one that it recognized even if she didn't.

She felt his arms wrap themselves around her tightly, and the growl that erupted from deep within his chest vibrated through her, electrifying already taut nerves to an unheard of level of desire. He pulled her into his embrace, twisting until he was flat on his back and she lay panting, sprawled on top. Libby stilled then, and slowly brought her legs up until she was straddling his hardness.

Her hands held fast to his chest, pushing her body up and away from the lips that so tantalized her. She watched him through half-lidded eyes, as his own eyes scanned her body, settling hotly on her generous breasts. The T-shirt Ana had given her wrapped itself tightly against the gently rounded globes, accentuating the boldly erect nipples that stood out in sharp relief, begging for his touch.

When his hands reached underneath her T-shirt to caress her belly, Libby hissed in a torturous sigh, ignoring the ache in her side as she lifted her arms straight up, willing him to pull the shirt from her.

His hands were rough, the fingertips callused as he trailed them over her ribs, pausing a moment at the wince of pain as he crossed over her injured bones. Up, his hands traveled. Gently tugging the ends of her T-shirt, he used a bit of extra effort to drag the material over her breasts, and she groaned as he licked his lips in anticipation.

When the soft mounds popped free from their constraints, Jaxon immediately claimed one turgid nipple deep into his hot, wet mouth, while his other hand ripped the T-shirt up and over her head, sending it sailing to the floor in a heap.

Libby's arms wrapped around Jaxon, encouraging his exploration, needing to feel him in the most basic way a woman could want a man. His mouth blazed a wicked path of heat along her flesh. Deep spirals of desire formed inside her belly as his tongue continued to assault her flesh. The need became intense, and it seemed every cell in her body was starved for his touch.

She was on fire and a rush of blood roared in her ears as he continued to feed upon her flesh.

Each gentle and not so gentle tug to her nipple elicited a wild response that pounded through her body, sending spasms of pleasure that settled into the deep, pulsating core between her legs. The ache was becoming unbearable, and her body began to cream in anticipation.

Wanting what was next. *Needing* to feel Jaxon's hardness, deep inside, assuaging the ache that only increased as his mouth washed over her body.

She felt his muscles bunch beneath her hands as she ran them over his powerful shoulders and down his back. His mouth began to trail its wicked path away from her breasts, and she arched back, giving him ample room as he explored the valley between them, his tongue lapping at the underside of each heavy breast.

She felt his hard cock between her legs and ground her soft center against it, smiling as he growled and tensed, enjoying the power her body had over his.

"It's been so long." The words fell unbidden from her lips, but Libby paid no mind, moaning loudly as her needs became overwhelming.

Jaxon's hands fell to her hips and held her still even as she tried to move against him. Her eyes flew open and she looked down at him, feeling a sense of abandonment as his own eyes blackened, the whites disappearing, the growl that fell from his lips not wholly human.

Something burned there, something dangerous, and it licked at the flames of her desire until she was nothing but a whimpering mess of flesh and bone.

"I need you."

Her soft words echoed in the still and quiet. They lay heavy between them, and inside Libby felt a wash of sadness run through her.

"I need you to help me remember."

Jaxon trembled at Libby's words and closed his eyes against her beauty, needing to regain some semblance of control. He was letting go too fast, and the beast was raging, wanting out with a brutal intensity that made coherent thought impossible.

Her scent was everywhere, scattered over his flesh and invading the cells of his body. Savagely he pulled her to him, knowing that he had crossed the line. Hell, he had jumped over it the night before. He didn't care.

The jaguar would be denied no longer.

Once more he claimed the lips that had driven him mad with revenge for three long years. He parted their softness with his tongue, loving the taste of her, the smell of her, the feel of her. Her body moved frantically against his, and he roared inside, welcoming the aggressive passion that wracked her limbs.

He continued to delve deeper into her mouth, sucking, licking, tugging until Libby's moans became a continuous chorus of need. His hands found her breasts and they filled his palms. He reveled in the feminine flesh, once again rewarded with a loud groan as his thumbs worked the hard peaks, the callused pads rubbing the sensitive nipples roughly and eliciting trembles each time he claimed them.

The fire that licked at his body began to pulse, and Jaxon tensed, fighting the urge to dominate, wanting the exquisite sensations to last as long as possible.

Libby was right. It had been way too fucking long.

Abruptly, he pushed her back, pulling himself up, needing to see every delicious inch of her body. Libby's eyes darkened as his intent became clear, and soft mewing sounds fell from her parted lips as she spread her legs in anticipation.

Her fragrant arousal flooded the air, the heady musk thick and tangible, so incredibly sweet that he could almost taste it.

His eyes drank in her beauty, from the delicate features of her face, to the heaving breasts, down the creamy expanse of skin, until they settled onto the small scrap of fabric that clung to the prize he sought above all others.

He grinned wickedly up at her and his tongue once more lapped hungrily at the dusky pink nipples that lay before him. They begged and taunted him with their ripeness, an appetizer before the main course.

One that was meant to be enjoyed and savored. He suckled, nipped, and teased each hard bud as his hands moved possessively down her body. He felt a hard tug in his groin at Libby's hiss of pleasure as he spread liquid heat along her breasts. He continued down past her heaving chest, worshiping her rib cage and soft belly as he headed straight toward the honey spot.

His fingers hooked into the top of her panties and he ripped them from her flesh, his hands and mouth seeking the warmth that was no longer hidden. He felt her body contort, arching away and into him at the same time, and he growled loudly as her fingers found his head, the nails digging into his scalp, urging him on as she opened herself even more for him.

He flicked his tongue teasingly, finding the engorged bud that glistened with the cream of her sex. Her body jerked and he growled deeply against her warmth, and without hesitation his hot mouth opened wide and he took all of her deep into him, his tongue working her into a frenzy that erupted within seconds, filling his mouth with the sweet taste of her orgasm.

His large hands cupped her butt tightly and he held her there, enjoying the taste and smell. Only when the last shudder quietly slipped from her did he let go, to continue his journey down her body, on which he feasted at her thighs, knees, and toes.

His own arousal pulsed with life, the heavy ache between his legs becoming almost unbearable. Then, with restrained grace, he flipped her body over, and abruptly stilled at the sight that greeted him.

He felt Libby's immediate withdrawal, her hands going to her face, which she buried deep into the pillows and covers.

He let his eyes wander over the damaged and torn flesh of her back, then reached down to touch the puckered, ruined skin. With a groan, his mouth rained kisses along each blemish.

"Please don't look."

Libby's muffled cry tore at him, and Jaxon slowly brought his lips to the sensitive area underneath her ear, feeling her shudder against his words. "You taste of heaven, feel like sin, but you always have and always will look like an angel to me. There is not one inch of flesh on your body that I don't want to taste."

His hands and mouth proceeded to demonstrate the passion in his words, and when her cries turned from anguish to wails of pleasure again, he hoisted her hips into the air and plunged his shaft hard and deep into her waiting wetness.

Jaxon literally saw stars as her hot velvet channel welcomed his hardness, gripping him tightly as he began to move to a rhythm older than time. Their bodies strained against each other, the wet, sweaty flesh of his slapping against the rounded softness of her buttocks, creating a symphony of sound.

She was incredibly tight, and his body—though large—went deep, and she took every long hard inch of him. He could feel her quivering, pulsing against him, and he clenched his teeth in an effort to pro-long the exquisite sensations that were so incredible they were almost painful. He could feel the pressure building; his balls clenched and he increased his tempo, pounding into her ferociously, as the beast began to howl in triumph.

Her slick channel contracted hard, and Jaxon roared as his release washed over and through him, to bury itself deep inside her sweetness. And then he held her to him hard, biting her shoulder as he continued to empty himself.

After a few moments their hearts calmed, the beats slowing down in time with their breathing. Jaxon slipped from her body and pulled her close to him as he collapsed back onto the bed. His mind was jumbled and he felt a sliver of madness run through him as the reality of his losing control over-came him.

What the hell had he just done?

What power had he once more given Libby Jamieson over him?

Libby felt it.

Something had changed. Shifted. Something else irrevocably lost.

She felt the cool morning air as it wafted in from the window at her back, caressing her heated skin and leaving a hoard of goose bumps in its wake. Her arms slowly crept back from his body as the black of his eyes began to pulsate with color; amber, gold, and red ran through the darkness like bolts of lightning. The effect was startling, unsettling.

His face became a blank mask, the one that faced the world most of the time. It was impenetrable and harsh.

She shivered as his hands fell away from her body, and felt even more bereft as his body heat left hers. It was as if he had only just woken up and realized that the woman he'd held so passionately was not the one he'd imagined. That she was damaged.

Sorrow laced through Libby then. Sorrow for what she'd just shared, because it was already lost to her. It was sharp, and struck her deeply. She could feel the heat of unshed tears gathering behind her lids, and she fought to keep them at bay.

She would not cry in front of Jaxon Castille again.

No matter what.

Scorching shame spilled over her, and she covered her exposed nakedness with trembling hands, wishing she could just close her eyes and make everything go away.

His hands pushed her away, and she kept her

eyes downcast as he leapt from her bed. The imprint of his body still lay next to her, his scent was everywhere, but already his heat was replaced with a cool whisper. Inside, she cried out for the warmth lost, for the heated feel of his body next to hers. She heard him move toward the door, felt the tension emanating from him like long fingers.

"Jaxon, don't leave." She cringed at the pathetic sound of her voice and felt the sting of heat as her cheeks reddened in shame.

He paused at the door but did not turn toward her as he spoke. "Libby, you and I . . . we can't do this. There's too much shit going on, and I don't think we can just go back to the way it was." He took another step, and she was left with only the sound of his voice, "I can't do this with you. I'm sorry, it won't happen again."

His words startled her, but on some level they only confirmed what her body already knew. She and Jaxon had been involved at one point in her life. And whatever she had done—that thing her addled brain couldn't remember—it destroyed whatever it was they had shared.

As Libby stared at the empty doorway, her heart plummeted.

She didn't know what *it* was exactly, only that she wanted it back.

She drew the covers up around her shaking form and closed her eyes, trying to block out the sunlight that seemed determined to find her.

Yeah, she should have known better.

Happy and Libby just didn't go hand in hand.

Chapter 13

Libby woke to a room shrouded in shadows and a house that was eerily silent. She yawned and stretched tight limbs, groaning softly as aching muscles protested. She was sore, no doubt about it, certain parts of her anatomy more so than others. And once more she felt the stain of heat on her cheeks as images of the reason for it danced before her eyes.

There was a heaviness blanketing her limbs, and it seeped deep into her soul as memories of her lovemaking with Jaxon filtered through the fog. He had been amazing. Her body began to tingle at just the thought of his hands on her flesh, and she sighed softly, wanting to go back six hours, needing him there with her.

But Jaxon had made it very clear she was a mistake he didn't plan on repeating. The ache that sat near her heart blossomed sharply, and she wanted nothing more then to bury herself deep in the covers and wallow in self-pity.

And that's exactly what she did. For about two minutes.

But as she lay there, Libby began to realize that she wasn't a weak, broken person anymore. Sure, she'd been through more than most people would ever face in a lifetime, but she was alive. And she felt there was a purpose for her, yet unfulfilled. Even if it was only to find her way back to what she had been before.

Before she could do that, she needed to pull up her big girl pants and deal with the mess her life had become. A tremulous smile played along the edges of her mouth. Yeah, it was time to say a big *fuck you* to the demons from her past and move on. She flung her body from the bed, pausing for a moment as she caught sight of her nakedness in the mirror above the dresser to her left.

She flinched at the sight of the scars on her back and was pummeled with a deluge of disgust and anxiety. That someone could do this to her and she had no clue who or why was something she'd struggled with since she first discovered the marred flesh back in Winterhaven.

Her cheeks burned and her hands went to them, the coolness of her fingers against the heated flesh bringing a modicum of relief. She winced, wanting to turn away from the hideous sight, but not before the violet eyes that stared back at her grabbed her attention fully.

Slowly, Libby walked toward the mirror. Huge dark eyes widened as she wondered at the changes that had transpired in her appearance in only a few days.

Her cheeks were flushed, lips bruised and full. Her hair was a chaotic mess about her shoulders. The long blond strands seemed to glisten with a new energy that shimmered in the waning sunlight, haloing her head in a wash of gold.

Her eyes were arresting, no longer dull and beaten down. They held a sparkle. Somewhere deep, a tiny sprinkling of stardust glittered from within, and left them shiny with a new vibrant energy that brought a tremulous smile to her generous lips.

She smiled broadly, her reflection showing a face from the past, and it was one she wanted to grab hold of and never let go.

Surely it was the face that Jaxon knew. But was it one he had loved?

Her hands fell from her face and she scooped up the T-shirt from the floor and padded over to where the rest of her clothes lay. Shaking her head, she sighed as a whisper floated through her mind.

Careful what you wish for.

And she knew that was the crux of the matter. She needed to remember before she could move on. But if the memories were as bad as she suspected, maybe they were better left buried, deep in her past.

She opened the door, peered out into the empty hall, and when she was satisfied that Jaxon wasn't in the immediate area, scooted through and down to the bathroom, where she got dressed.

Her belly led the way toward the kitchen, and she was relieved to discover she was alone. She would have to face Jaxon sooner or later, but right now later sounded so much better.

She raided the cupboards, even though the thought of dining on crackers again held little appeal. But it was nice to feel hungry. Days ago her appetite had been nearly nonexistent. Pete had tried every way imaginable to tempt her to eat, and it was a daily struggle on his part. But truthfully, why eat when you had no desire to live?

He would be happy to see her raking through cupboards in search of sustenance, she thought. Opening the fridge, her face contorted at the sight of two large plastic bags, which she now knew contained blood. Her eyes latched onto a small piece of steak that had been carefully wrapped, along with a baked potato and veggies. Her name was printed neatly on a piece of paper and taped to the items.

It brought a smile to her face, and she found herself humming a tune as she grabbed the food and threw it in the microwave. While her meal circled inside for a couple minutes, Libby twirled the paper around, looking at the writing, wondering who had been nice enough to think of her needs.

Jaxon? She shook her head.

It's much too neat to be Jaxon's.

The thought came from nowhere, and she froze, her mind clicking as it leapt forward in a blur. She could see something just beyond the veil of her past.

She clearly envisioned papers, typed memos with scrawls highlighting segments, scrawls that belonged to Jaxon. She *knew* this!

Desperately, she closed her eyes, trying to remember. Bits and pieces flew by, and she knew the price for this window into her past would not be pleasant. Even now, as she struggled to regain a sense of time, her head felt as if it were cracking apart. Flashes, spikes of lightning, flew around inside her skull, and as her stomach heaved, she grabbed the counter for support.

Blinding pain shot through her brain, and the piece of paper floated to the floor as her hands went to her head, pushing against her skull in an effort to stop the pain. She screamed at the brutality of the attack, and fell to her knees as images burst through the darkness, coming at her fast and sharp. Too many to focus on just one, but the predominant face that stalked these patches of memory was one she knew well.

Jaxon's dark visage flew past like a ribbon blowing in the wind. His image twisted and turned, his face laughing at her, his eyes full of passion, his brightly colored tattoo vibrant and moving against her skin.

Emotions pounded her, both dark and light, and she groaned at the amount of information her mind was struggling with. It was all jumbled, confused, and as she held her head, she rocked back and forth in an effort to stop it.

Her soft whimpers echoed in the room, and what seemed like hours later, the images began to fade along with the pain.

She was wrecked. In that short period of time, she was done for.

Everything around her seemed thick, as if crawling with a layer of reality that wasn't truly real. Dull though her mind had become, she tried to get to her feet. But her body was drained of energy and she fell back onto her butt.

The microwave emitted a loud, high-pitched

bleep that just about shattered the last few nerve endings that still remained untouched, and she winced from the agony of it.

Outside, it was dusk now, and her eyes skimmed the large expanse of wilderness through the windows, feeling a twinge of unease as a shadow drifted across the porch.

Was it just the wind playing tricks on her mind? She tried to focus her eyes but there was nothing there, and for a moment she wondered if she had imagined it.

A soft click at the door convinced her otherwise, and her heart leapt deep into her throat, pounding out a rhythm of fear that rushed through her veins.

She inhaled sharply and felt her mouth go dry as fear began to invade and conquer, turning muscle to jelly in seconds. The sound of silence echoed louder than anything she'd heard before, and white hot jolts of pressure jump-started her heart, making it harder to breathe. Along with the nausea that lay at the pit of her tummy, she felt light-headed.

It was not Jaxon who had entered the cabin. Of that she was sure.

She held her breath as hesitant footfalls crept closer, and then she felt a small moment of relief as they moved farther away, and closer to the stairs that led to the basement.

Libby slumped down, hidden behind the large granite countertop. Her eyes quickly moved about looking for a weapon. She felt a sliver of adrenaline shoot through her body as she spied the large drawers directly in front of her. Surely something of use could be found there.

She glanced toward the massive window that ran along the front of the cabin, but from where she hid, there was no reflection that she could see.

Closing her eyes tightly, she tried to blot out the fear that was burgeoning within her.

Whoever had just entered was no friend of hers. The scent that filtered down to where she hid was not Jaxon's. It was full of darkness, depravity, and malice.

And it was a scent she recognized all too well.

It was one of the monsters! *They had found her.*

She swallowed the lump of tension that rode the back of her throat, wondering where the hell Jaxon was. With that thought a new one struck, spreading agony to her heart. It hit fast and hard, heightening the emotions that were already jumbled deep inside her.

What if they had harmed Jaxon? What if at this very moment he was out there in the woods, dying and in need of her help?

Her eyes fell to her hands, watching them shake as she slipped them between her thighs in an effort to control her weakness. The ever present ache at her side began to burn, and she hissed softly as her ribs contracted and the pain worsened.

They had done this to her. They had weakened and broken her spirit.

In that moment of contemplation a spark ignited. It fed on the remnants of adrenaline that moved through her body, feasted on the tattered bits of memories that had both teased and tormented her only moments before.

And it grew, with a heat and ferocity that should

have surprised her but somehow didn't. This was her time, her window of opportunity to do the right thing. It was time for her to reclaim her life, even if it was about to end.

Libby calmed her mind and felt a sense of peace wash over her. No longer would she let them pull her strings as if she were a puppet. They had taken many things from her, but if this was to be her final battle, then so be it. She would make it a battle they sure as hell wouldn't forget.

She eyed the deep drawer that was at her level and quietly eased it open, but found only lids and containers inside. One after the other she slowly opened the drawers, until only the top one remained. She couldn't see into it, unless she exposed herself, so her fingers flew over the utensils before settling across the cold, solid length of a large knife.

A scuff slid across the tiles behind her, followed by another . . . and then another.

She grabbed the knife and held it to her chest, willing the pounding beats to slow so that she could think. He wasn't even trying to hide his presence.

Her enemy thought her weak, pathetic, and up until a few days ago that's exactly what she had been. Good. That should work to her advantage. Right now it was the only one she had.

She stilled and listened with all her senses, once more glancing toward the window to her right. It was now almost completely dark outside, with a hint of light falling from a mostly hidden moon. Mist was gathering, slithering across the edge of the forest, and she shivered as a feeling of dread punched her low in the gut.

There were no lights on inside the cabin, and she could barely make out the reflection of the large male who stood not more then ten feet from her. He was tall and heavily muscled, judging by the bulk of him.

Even though she could not see clearly, aggression poured from every inch of his lethal frame, which was confirmed when he spoke, his voice harsh with barely contained anger.

"I can smell your fear, Libby. I know you're here. Why don't we skip the games and you can tell me what I need to know, and maybe, just maybe, I might let you die . . . easily."

His words shot through the air, hitting her in the chest with a force she recognized.

She knew that timbre well. One of the monsters from her past finally had a face, and a living, breathing body to go with it.

"Where is the shifter? I can smell his stink all over this place." He paused then, and Libby shuddered as he inhaled deep and long, growling wickedly as his anger built. "His brother has been here recently as well. Too bad we didn't find this place sooner. Two dead Castilles would have been quite a coup."

He laughed, each deep guffaw slicing through Libby's resolve with clean precision. Her fingers began to shake. She closed her eyes and willed herself to stay calm and focused. She needed to be strong. There was no alternative.

She gripped the knife tight in her hands, her head pounding as long buried memories began to crack open. She welcomed the flood of emotion, grabbing hold of it greedily, using it to fuel the anger growing from deep within.

His laughter stopped abruptly and she held her breath, trying to stave off the fear that was along for the ride.

"Still a Castille whore, I see. I can smell your sex from here." His voice was getting closer, and she gripped the handle, moving toward the end of the counter. "Was it worth it Libby? Was all of it worth one more night with Castille?"

With a roar, the large man jumped up and over the counter, landing not more then a few feet from Libby. She screamed at the sudden movement, unable to help herself.

He laughed outright, and she cringed beneath the fury that laced his features. Eyes as black as onyx burned down at her, and he smiled wickedly, enjoying the fear that draped her shoulders like a shroud.

"Been a long time, bitch. Miss me much?"

He knelt down in front of her then, and his powerful arm knocked the knife from her hands. Libby heard it skitter across the tiles, the metallic clanging echoing eerily in the empty cabin.

She felt in her heart that this was it. The proverbial climax to the story of her life. Her eyes slowly moved to the man in front of her and she felt the hatred, anger, and pain inside her seeping into her veins. It sped along inside her body, giving her strength even in the face of certain death.

She would not go quietly.

"That the best you can do, asshole?" she said hoarsely.

He leaned in so close she could see the whites of his eyes. He snarled savagely. "Nice to see you've got a bit of your spunk back." Then he laughed loudly. "I was afraid you'd be a bit of a dead fuck."

Libby hissed at his words and tried to slap his face, but his hands grabbed hers and held them steady.

"You know how hard it was for me to keep my hands off of you?" His tongue flicked out wickedly, and she shrank away from him. "Every night I ached to claim you as my own, but my cousins forbade it. Said you were a Castille whore and no DaCosta would dare dip his cock into something as tainted as you."

His voice quieted into a deadly whisper, and his long fingers reached for the golden strands of hair that fell about her face. He grabbed hold of them and pulled her closer, inhaling her scent deeply as a growl rumbled from deep within his chest.

"I don't care if you tell me where the shifter is or not. I didn't come alone. Right now several of my men are out there," he nodded toward the forest, "and they will hunt him down and bring him to me. I will kill him, as is my right."

Libby gritted her teeth as his tongue licked along the edge of her jaw, her mind frantically looking for a way out.

"I can smell him all over you . . . *inside* of you. Even now his seed rests where mine should be."

He lifted her up and threw her onto the counter. Libby yelped as her skull whacked the granite with such force that stars flashed before her eyes. Savagely, he yanked her head back, his eyes resting on her shaking lips, his voice deadly and full of intent.

"I will taste you. Have my fill of you. You will know what it feels like to mate with a DaCosta." Black laughter trickled from even white teeth. "And then you will die."

She tried to struggle, but he was just too strong, and she watched helplessly as his hands fell to his pants. Now, for the first time, she noticed tattoos and markings on his left arm, peeking up from beneath the neckline of the shirt he wore. They were so like Jaxon's, yet different somehow. A small trickle of awareness slipped through her brain, and an image flashed in front of her.

And then another.

Realization hit her hard, and her lungs contracted painfully as she struggled to breathe. Agony coursed through her veins.

He had held her tightly while fat Frank had burned her flesh. *He* had carved his knife deep into her flesh. *He* had beaten her with his hands.

He had a name . . . Alexio. She remembered it with perfect clarity. He was a member of the Da-Costa crime family.

He had tried to beat information from her, all in an effort to . . .

The canvas remained blank, and she cried out as she tried to remember.

His hands stilled and he grinned down at her. "You remember me now? He said the mind block would crumble once you started gaining memories." He leaned closer to her, and Libby pushed back against him, but it only fed his enjoyment. "I'll make sure Castille knows I was able to pleasure his woman before she died."

Alexio moved back briefly, intent on loosening

his pants, and Libby saw her chance. She kicked out as hard as she could, her aim strong and true as she connected with his groin area.

He roared as she rolled to the side, falling to the floor. She hissed as her side throbbed from the impact, but her eyes had already latched onto the knife that lay inches from her hands and she scrambled to grab it.

A loud crash echoed through the dark cabin, but Libby pushed aside the fear clawing at her as the furious roar rent the air. Her mind was moving in a chaotic mess, but the need to survive held strong, and she clenched her teeth together tightly, as her fingers closed around the handle of the knife.

Strong hands grabbed her legs and began to pull her back, but she bucked and kicked, twisting her body around until she was able to aim for his face. Alexio was furious beyond reason, and his eyes bulged with a fanatical madness as spittle gathered at the corners of his mouth.

Someone, or something, was there, just beyond her vision, but Alexio was so enraged his focus had not shifted from her. Resignation fell over Libby, but it was accompanied with determination and grit.

If this was to be her final moment, she would not die in vain.

She would take the fucking bastard with her.

Time slowed then, like in the movies.

She heard the roar once more, but the sound was muffled and seemed so far away. Everything, in fact, seemed hazy, condensed but amplified.

She saw Alexio lunge for her at the same time she brought the knife up, its steel shaft glinting in the moonlight as the arc carried it straight toward his chest. Sweat dripped from his forehead and she could feel the heat from his body as he fell upon her, his breath hot at her neck and his hands reaching out.

They grasped her, and she felt the long fingers dig deep into her flesh, but it was surreal, and for a moment Libby thought it was a dream. Pressure began to build, and she winced at the blackness that edged the broken remains of her mind.

Blackness that parted as the gates opened and a flood of memories washed over her. Jaxon, Ana, Declan . . . and Diego.

They were all there, jumbled into a mass of incoherent thoughts and feelings. All mixed up with the pain and anguish she'd endured over the last three years.

Her mind wandered back, further than she'd gone in ages, and the scream that flew from her lungs was like a cry to heaven. It was full of anger, hatred, and betrayal.

It was a cry for all things lost.

She felt her body liquefy and she let go, slumped beneath the heavy weight of Alexio atop of her.

When he was wrenched away and thrown to the side, she didn't care.

When strong arms lifted her and gathered her close, she didn't care.

When Jaxon grabbed her chin and forced her eyes to his, she felt a spark of something rush through her. It was hot, heavy, and full with the need for vengeance.

She drew her arm back and slapped his face as hard as she could, struggling to leave his embrace, feeling her flesh rail against his touch.

She had spent the last three years hating this man with every fiber of her being. Oh, how she had plotted and designed his demise. He might not have had a physical hand in her torture and subsequent captivity, but he was the only reason she'd been taken.

The reason she had lost so much.

Wicked pain shot through her breast and an ache settled around her heart as he lifted her. It was one she knew well, and she screamed again as anguish rolled over her, coming in waves and getting stronger as the seconds ticked by.

Her sorrow was heartbreaking.

Her mind stilled as the images and memories finally stopped. But the emotions continued unabated, and she continued to struggle until he gently put her down.

Libby stumbled away from him, her legs wobbly and barely holding her upright.

She was covered in blood. Dully, she glanced down at the body of Alexio DaCosta, before returning to the dark eyes of her former lover. He too had sustained injuries, no doubt fighting the fellow shifters that DaCosta would have brought with him.

Pity they'd not done more damage.

Oh, yeah, Alexio was right. Her memories were fully intact.

Ana and Declan rushed into the cabin, both shouting in surprise at the carnage and stopping in their tracks at the sight of so much blood.

Libby ignored all three of them and limped toward the bathroom. She would clean herself up and then plan a course of action.

Jaxon reached for her as she passed him, and she

hissed sharply, the deadly venom in her voice cutting through the air.

"Don't touch me." She couldn't look at him as she continued on toward the hall.

No one would stop her this time.

She would make Jaxon Castille pay dearly for the wrongs he'd committed against her.

But first she needed to find her son.

Chapter 14

Jaxon's heart felt about to burst, so great was the adrenaline rush that had fueled his run to the cabin. His chest heaved with the effort it took to control the fury that emanated off him in waves. His hands were coiled into tight balls of flesh, and he paced back and forth, so full of the need to act, to kill, that it was painful.

To think that someone had the balls to come after Libby, here, in a Castille home, for Christ sakes, made his blood boil. He roared once more, his anger reverberating through the cabin.

His eyes swept the floor, alighting on the still, bloody form that lay quiet in death's repose on the cold tiles. He was upon the body in seconds, inhaling its scent, taking the trace odor deep into his lungs so he could confirm what his mind already knew.

He had killed three jaguars out in the forest.

None were warriors, but they'd been deadly just the same. This one bore the tattoos of a jaguar warrior. Jaxon's anger intensified as he recognized the markings on the skin, even before the scent signatures had cleared his olfactory glands.

DaCosta!

He trembled as impotent fury rode him hard, and snarling savagely, he threw the body away from him. He closed his eyes, trying to blot out the red haze that threatened to engulf him. He could not lose control now. He needed his wits about him.

With cold precision, Jaxon calmed his mind and body. He needed to be smart, calculating. Only then would he be able to sort out the puzzle.

Only then would he be able to begin the hunt.

As his body began to quiet and the last remnants of jaguar faded from his skin, Jaxon became aware of Ana and Declan. Covered in blood, he stood up quickly, unashamed of his nakedness. He glanced toward the hall that led to Libby, and turned quickly in the opposite direction.

"Go, Jax, we'll take care of this piece of garbage. We've a lot to discuss." Declan's voice filtered through, and Jaxon acknowledged his words.

He didn't trust his vocal cords just yet; his mind was a mess of thoughts and images. He stopped and looked back once more toward the bedrooms.

"Don't worry about Libby. I'll look in on her. You go and look after yourself." Ana's soft voice caressed his wounded soul, and without another thought, Jaxon headed out into the night.

The water from the lake called to him, and when its coolness rippled over his head, the hard shell around his heart cracked wide open. The pain he felt was immense. It ripped through every cell in his body, tearing deep through tissue and bone.

Had the DaCosta clan been responsible for Libby's disappearance?

His mind moved at a savage pace as thoughts of Libby at their mercy bombarded his brain. It left him feeling helpless, which was something he was not used to feeling. He dove deep, the cold water somewhat alleviating the heat of his emotions, before finally coming up for air.

His long length moved forward quickly, the powerful arms slicing through water, carrying him to the other side of the lake and back. Jaxon repeated the process, again and again, and when he finally heaved his tired limbs from the lake, two hours had passed.

Physically, his body was spent, but his mind was still tortured, filled to the brim with questions that begged for answers he wasn't sure he wanted to hear.

The DaCosta jaguar clan had been under PATU's radar for years, but he knew personally how corrupt and evil the clan had become. Always on the fringes of jaguar society, they'd built an impressive empire that worked black market weapons and intel, all of it run by the patriarch, Jakobi.

The youngest DaCosta, a man by the name of Tomas, had been involved in the sale of illegal weapons, some of which had been altered with the use of dark arts. PATU had raided one of their strongholds in Texas. The operation was successful, but there had been several casualties on both sides, including the younger DaCosta.

Jaxon took a deep breath as these thoughts converged and began to make up small pieces of a larger puzzle, with Libby at the center of it.

Flashes of her marred skin flew past his mind, and he shuddered as a feeling of helplessness once more began to burn deep in his gut. Was it just a coincidence that the other jaguar clan had attacked him? Gone to all the trouble of hunting him to a cabin out in the middle of nowhere? Were they responsible for the attempt on his life two nights ago as well?

If so, then they definitely had a hand in Libby's resurfacing. He snarled as his thoughts turned toward the frail blond. This meant they had a hand in her disappearance and torture.

He sighed harshly as his thoughts continued to center on Libby, then swore loudly as the crush of emotions continued to batter him relentlessly.

When the hell had it all gone so wrong?

Two weeks ago he'd been the cold, calculating bastard everyone either disliked or avoided. He had spent every waking minute, when not on a mission, tracking down leads, some that had led him to various parts of the globe, all in an effort to find and kill Libby Jamieson.

He'd been focused and deadly.

And now? Now he didn't know what to think.

Was Libby just an innocent victim in this whole mess? Or was she partly responsible?

Did he even care at this point?

He closed his eyes, but that only made things worse. Images of Libby on top of him, moving with him, her body impaled on his hardness, hit him deep in the gut. The ache was intense, and he cursed himself and the weakness that lived in both parts of him.

Often the jaguar was at war with his humanity, the part of his soul that showed restraint and reined in the beast when it scratched too close to the surface. But when it came to Libby, the two halves that made him whole were in perfect harmony.

And that's where things became complicated. It made it hard to fight, to do what he felt was right. Like keep his fucking hands off her until he knew what the hell had happened three years ago and what was in play at the moment.

It's what stopped you from putting a bullet in her brain.

Jaxon winced as that thought slid through his mind, and guilt jumped in, to dance a rhythm inside of him with all the other shit he had going on.

Emotional soup, that's what his insides had become.

It had been so much easier when he had thought of her as the enemy.

But now . . . now everything was upside down, and he'd spent the entire day out in the forest avoiding Libby, hating the fact that he still cared. That his body still craved her touch and smell. That the need to protect had awakened a deeper passion and fury he'd not known existed.

As his thoughts turned back to when he first realized he had enemies in the vicinity, he began to tremble again.

He'd felt ice cold terror at the thought of any harm coming to her. The thought of someone, anyone, touching Libby blinded him with rage.

It was then that he truly came to the realization that she still belonged to him.

She was the one. She completed him. He could either turn her away and live his life as a miserable son of a bitch, or he could fight for her . . . for the both of them.

The jaguar had erupted from him, with such a force and fury his transformation had been painful. Something he'd not experienced in years. Within seconds he'd become a lethal hunter, and killer the likes of which was rarely seen. It hadn't taken him long to track all three jaguars, as none had his warrior strength and cunning. He'd made quick work of them, his powerful canines crushing through their skulls, piercing their brains and killing them instantly. He had left their mangled bodies on display, a macabre testament to his victory.

Once he dispatched them, the cold fear that had clawed at the back of his mind intensified, and he knew in that instant that Libby's life was in danger.

In two days he'd gone from wanting to kill her on sight to a blinding need to protect what was his.

It was the way of his kind. He would claim her as his mate, and deal with the fallout as it came.

Jaxon turned quickly and headed toward the faint light that beckoned through the trees. Hopefully Ana and Declan had been successful in Washington, and had information for him. He needed all the intelligence he could gather before he started to plot his revenge.

It would be far reaching, and deadly. No one attacked a Castille jaguar and his mate without facing repercussions. They would be fast and they would be deadly.

Jaxon growled in anticipation of the fight that lay on the horizon, his ancient warrior blood singing through his veins as he moved quietly through the forest.

The smell of blood remained faint in the air as he silently entered the cabin a few minutes later. He'd sensed a protection ward as he neared the porch, a faint resistance in the air in the form of an invisible shield.

Declan's charms were strong, and he felt better knowing no one would be able to cross unless their body signatures had been woven into the spell.

Once inside, he frowned, not liking the odor that lingered here, among his people. His eyes scanned the room, and all traces of the violence that took place a few hours earlier had been erased.

The great room was empty, and he quickly moved toward the back of the cabin where the bedrooms were located. His eyes fell to the closed door at the end of the hall to his right, and he took a second, letting his senses drift on the air. His acute sense of smell located her scent, and his keen hearing homed in on the unmistakable beat of Libby's heart. Even now it began to beat faster, and he growled softly at the response her body had to his. She knew he was back.

He turned on his heel and grabbed some extra clothes he'd stored in his brother's room, before taking the stairs two at a time down toward the basement.

Declan was leaning over Ana, and they were both staring at a computer screen, but turned when he entered the large open area.

Ana pushed her chair back and they both stood there, uncertain of words or actions. She took a step toward him, but Jaxon spoke first, his voice curt.

"Did you check on Libby?"

"She had a shower, and she's in her room. She wasn't in the mood for conversation, but I think she will be all right." Ana sighed and stretched her limbs as she turned back to the computer. "She's been through a lot, but I think we're all forgetting how strong Libby was, and when push comes to shove, *still is*."

"I have a protection ward in place; she can't leave unless I allow it. Don't worry about her, Jax," Declan cut in. "We have a lot to cover."

Jaxon walked over to the two of them, his eyes scanning the computer screen. "What did you learn in Washington? Was Drake involved?"

Ana shook her head as she settled back into the seat. "I've confirmed he was attending a fund-raising event for some up-and-coming hotshot." She made a face. "A political thing. I have video and a few witness reports that verify."

Declan leaned over Ana's shoulder, pointing out something on the screen before he turned to Jaxon. "Only Drake's retina scan and fingerprints gain access to his office after hours, and we know he was elsewhere."

"That tells me nothing. How many times have we infiltrated high security operations? I need to know who was there." Jaxon's hands raked through the thick hair atop his head as he moved behind the two. "It also means we still don't know if he was involved or not."

"But why would he allow someone access to his computer, knowing it would be traced right back to him?" Declan asked. "He's not stupid. Someone is obviously trying to frame him, or at least lead you to think he's complicit. Maybe kill two birds with one stone?"

"What are you getting at?" Ana leaned back so her head was resting on Declan's midsection as she looked up into his eyes.

"I think someone not only wants Jaxon out of the way, but they're aiming to start an internal war inside of PATU."

"But what does this all have to do with Libby? And why now?" Ana turned to Jaxon, puzzled.

Declan answered, his face dark and resigned.

"That, I can only guess at. What I do know is that I sensed a subtle trace signature of magick in Drake's office. I can't be sure, but it felt the same as what I'd felt in Manhattan. The amount was so minute, it's hard to be one hundred percent sure. But it would make sense to me that the bastard who attacked our base with those commandos was inside Commander Drake's office at some point over the last few weeks. The magick was dark, and powerful. It could have been easily used to manipulate Drake's security defenses."

"The attack in Manhattan is definitely linked to Libby," Ana said. "The chip in her hip is what led them straight to our asses. Whoever's been hiding her for the last three years is deep into all the shit that's been flying." She looked to Declan and back to Jaxon. "I don't like Drake for this. I think he's being used as a scapegoat in case the entire operation falls apart, which I don't mind saying it is."

She jumped up from the chair and crossed to within a few inches of Jaxon, her eyes softening at the tense, wearied look that clung heavily to his eyes.

"We all know what she meant to you, Jax. Don't think for a second that your affair was a secret."

His face hardened at Ana's words, and his eyes flew to Declan's, feeling a twinge of unease as the other man looked away.

"It wouldn't take a good operative long to find that out," Ana said. "The more I think about it, I'm sure that Libby was targeted because someone knew of her connection to you. That she belonged to you."

Jaxon growled a denial, even as he knew deep in his gut that her words were true. From the moment he'd first laid eyes on Libby, no other woman had even come close to captivating his interest, or holding onto his heart.

"Do you think she's remembered who held her?" Declan's concerned words startled him.

"I hope not," he answered, his voice low as his mind turned inward.

A sick feeling in the pit of his stomach took hold as dark thoughts crept through his brain; thoughts of his lady, tortured and beaten, and all because of him. Thoughts of the DaCosta clan touching her made him see red, and he growled savagely as he envisioned all the ways he would make them pay.

Just thinking about it was painful, and he was vaguely aware of the voices dancing around his mind. The last three years had been a blur of hatred toward a woman he'd blamed for the betrayal of his unit, and the death of his cousin. He could acknowledge now that his hatred had been magnified a hundred times, because deep down he was shattered at her betrayal of *him*. It wouldn't have hurt so much if he'd had no feelings for Libby, but they were there all along, he'd just been too damn stubborn to admit to them.

He loved Libby Jamieson.

Had always loved her, in fact. From the first time he'd laid eyes on her at Quantico, he'd been done for.

Jaxon swallowed thickly as the weight of realization hit him in the chest. He'd never once told her that. Never.

He sighed softly and closed his eyes. He'd been willing to put a bullet through her skull because of a betrayal that now seemed to have never happened. It was becoming obvious that she'd been taken away for three years, savagely tortured and beaten, and all because he'd claimed her as his own without even realizing it.

Anguish knifed through his heart, striking deep and hard as he remembered their last conversation. How she'd wanted something more from him than he'd been willing to give. And stupid ass that he was, she'd already had it. He'd just been too blind to see.

And she'd paid for his stupidity tenfold.

Ana's hands on his arm snapped him back, and Jaxon inhaled roughly. He turned away, his shoulders and neck rotating in an effort to bring some semblance of calm to his body and mind. He needed to focus. He needed to make things right.

"It's the DaCostas. It's no coincidence that Alexio attacked Libby here in *my* territory. The arrogant bastard came with only three other jaguars. It was his last mistake."

Jaxon whirled around, a deadly calm now blanketing his features, the darkness that lived inside of the jaguar out there for all to see. His eyes blazed with an intensity that would make most mortal men cringe.

And usually did.

He was beyond anger, fury. As of now, he was in the zone, and nothing would stand between him and the DaCostas. He would exact payment for their crimes, and the cost would be heavy. He would methodically destroy each and every one of them.

"I want intel on the whereabouts of every known member of Jakobi's offspring. I want to know where they sleep, who they sleep with, where they relax, and where they like to torture innocent women."

Jaxon's voice was low, but controlled. "I *will* hunt tomorrow, so let's get our game on and come up with a plan."

Ana grabbed a folder and quickly flipped through several reports until she found the one she needed.

"In addition to the youngest, Tomas, who we've already retired, so to speak, and Alexio, I have five more siblings, four males and a female. All of the men work directly under Jakobi, but the daughter, Jaden, runs two luxury resorts in Mexico. From what I can tell, she has nothing to do with the family business, but that doesn't mean the resorts aren't used to launder all their illegal monies."

Ana grabbed a glass filled to the brim with warm blood and gulped heartily as her eyes ran down the pages before her. "I think we need to focus on Texas and Mexico. They have two large strongholds there, with a lot of property to do whatever the hell they want." She whipped her head back to Declan. "You think you might be able to get some satellite images?"

"That would be a total waste of time."

Jaxon froze as Libby's voice echoed through the cold basement where they were working. His eyes sought hers, but she ignored him and focused on Ana and Declan. His heart began to accelerate and he braced himself as she walked past, wanting to touch her, but afraid of her reaction.

"How the hell did you break through my protection ward?" Declan asked. "You shouldn't have been able to leave your bedroom!" He was aghast, and his question hung in the air between all of them.

Libby laughed softly at that, but her voice dripped ice, and no warmth fell from her lips when she spoke. "Never stopped me in the past, now did it, Dec? Some things you just don't forget."

An uneasy silence followed her statement, broken by Ana. "Why would it be a waste of time, Libby? I know for a fact that two of the brothers are in the United States and at least one was last seen near the family compound in Texas." She looked back to her notes. "Two days ago, in fact."

"Well now, Ana, it wouldn't be a waste of time if those two were in fact the brothers that you want. However, I have *intimate* knowledge as to the whereabouts of Degas and Frank DaCosta."

The lead ball in Jaxon's belly flipped over, and his eyes never left the cool blonde who now stood before them. Her eyes met his briefly, and inwardly he was shocked at the coldness that lay there.

"Libby—"

"I'm not done talking, Castille. Don't interrupt me again." The words were hissed, and Jaxon was taken aback at the depth of anger in them.

She turned to him, the violet of her eyes shaded

dark and full of emotion. Her breathing had become ragged, but she held her head high and took command as she spoke.

"If you want a chance at the bastards who took a shot at you, then you better put aside any notions you have about Texas and Mexico. They're not there."

Libby's voice softened a notch and she put a hand to her head, as if in pain. "I know where they are, where they've been all along." She looked up at them, but avoided Jaxon's direct gaze. "We need to leave for Belize."

Ana moved toward Libby, her voice soft and reassuring. "Libby, we have no intel on Belize, it doesn't make sense to start there."

Libby laughed at that, the sound harsh as it echoed against the cold tile walls. "Doesn't make sense? How the hell would you know what makes sense and what doesn't? It was *me* they took three years ago. You have no idea what I went through. What they did to me—" Her voice broke and she fought back tears, but it was a losing battle. They sprang from her eyes, and she wiped them away impatiently. "I have marks on my body Ana, scars that were *carved* into my skin, and *burned* into my skin, and all because of *him*."

She spat as she waved her fingers toward Jaxon.

"So don't you stand there and tell me I don't know what the fuck I'm talking about. It was me out there in the jungle, with those sick bastards."

She paused, her eyes sweeping the stilled faces that regarded her in silence. Jaxon's eyes had darkened and his mouth was tense, but he remained silent. When she spoke again, the coolly efficient woman from the past had stepped right back into her shoes with no effort at all.

"I'm leaving for Belize in the morning. Personally, I don't give a shit if any of you come, but if you try to stop me . . ." Her eyes latched onto Jaxon's, full of a venom that was barely contained in her next words. "I'll kill you myself and save the DaCosta brothers the trouble."

Chapter 15

Sweat ran down Libby's neck.

She felt small rivers of moisture slowly drip their way over the sharp ridges of her spine and ribs, before sticking to her clammy skin. She fought the shiver that lay beneath the surface, trying to gather the heat that burned hard in her chest.

It hurt.

To be here with *him* less than a foot away hurt like hell.

A wave of nausea wracked her belly, and she clenched her lips, willing it to go away. She had no time to be weak. She was so over that.

Her shattered memory hadn't just fallen into place quick and easy. It had blasted through her brain, bringing with it a bone-jarring agony, the likes of which she'd not had in a very long time. And that was saying something, considering most of the past three years was a blur of nothing but pain, physical and mental.

She'd been through it all.

She kept her eyes focused straight ahead, sensing myriad emotions from Ana and Declan, but more than that, totally aware of the shock that shrouded Jaxon's shoulders. He was confused and angry. She didn't have to look at him to know what he was feeling. It was coming off him in waves.

He moved toward her, and she shot him a venomous look. "Don't." Her single word stopped him cold, and she continued to glare at him until he stepped back.

She had no time to waste on Jaxon. She needed to find her son. She couldn't even explain how or why she knew he lived. She just *knew* that he was alive. She felt it as a truth that was carved deep into her heart and soul. It wasn't just a fanatical wish of a mother. Her little baby was out there.

And she would find him.

He had a name. *Logan.* It slid through her mind quietly, like a secret, and she turned on her heel, leaving stunned faces to stare at her back as she quickly made her way back up the stairs. Her side ached dully, but she isolated and put away the pain, something she was more than used to, and whispered to herself, *"Mommy's on her way."*

Reaching the bedroom, she slammed the door shut behind her, then leaned back against it and inhaled deep gulps of air.

The cold sweat that lingered on her skin swept the flesh in a sea of goose bumps, and she wrapped her arms around her body, trying to find warmth. Her torso was encased in an overlarge T-shirt, the only one she could find after washing the stench of Alexio from her skin.

The only one that didn't hold the scent of Jaxon.

She couldn't bear to have his clothes next to her skin. She felt a flush of anger begin to stain her cheeks as memories of the night before crashed into her.

Even now, her nipples ached and hardened as images of his naked body flashed in little picture frames across her brain. She groaned as her once cold and clammy skin began to burn with something other than the heat she sought.

It was a heat of want, need, and craving that fluttered in her belly, and Libby cursed the weakness of her body as she tried to block the memories from her mind.

She *hated* Jaxon Castille.

It made her sick to think that she'd let him make love to her, to know that her damaged, broken mind had allowed her body to betray her. It stuck in her gut like sour milk. She'd practically begged him for sex. And *he'd* been the one to walk away, as if it was the biggest mistake he'd ever made.

Hard anger washed over her, and she flung herself forward, drawn to the quiet night that lay just beyond the window. She opened it slightly, welcoming the soft breeze that wafted up from the lake below.

The night sky was dark, with few stars blanketing the canopy above.

She inhaled the fresh air. It was cool, and smelled of spring. So very different from where she'd been, from where her child was still.

Libby closed her eyes, picturing the lush jungle that climbed up from the banks of the Macal River, high into the Maya Mountains. The vibrant greens were painted vividly in her mind, and if she tried hard enough, she could feel the moisture, wet against her skin like a blanket. Sometimes the air was so heavy it hurt to breathe.

The ache in her breast sharpened, and she hissed in an effort to control the deluge of emotion that lingered around the edges of her heart.

She had no time for shit like that.

A soft rap at the door made her jump, and she turned as it opened. Ana walked into the room and paused before closing the door quietly behind her.

She seemed uncomfortable and unsure of herself. Interesting.

Ana had always been somewhat detached, and Libby had often wondered what Diego had seen in her. She was beautiful, there was no denying that, but she'd always been so aloof. Like a china doll that could kick your ass.

She sighed. Sadly, Diego had paid the price for being a Castille.

Libby cleared her throat and arched an eyebrow as Ana continued to stare at her in silence.

"What? Not happy with my fashion sense? Sorry to disappoint, but I don't give a shit what your personal preferences are. It's not like I had much to choose from."

She watched as surprise flickered deep inside the vampire's eyes, and feigned indifference as she spoke.

"I just wanted to make sure you were okay, maybe ask a few questions." Ana moved toward the bed and sat down. "If that's all right with you."

"You can ask all you want. Doesn't mean I'll answer."

The vampire was tight-lipped, and cleared her throat softly.

Ana exhaled, her eyes never leaving Libby's as she spoke. "I'm sorry for—"

"Save it. You do not get to go there," Libby exploded, and crossed the room until she was beside the bed, so close to Ana they could touch.

She was filled with such anger, her body began to tremble, and her voice shook as she continued. It had washed over her so quickly, she felt light-headed.

"You do not get to apologize to me. *For anything.* You do not get to feel sorry for me either. I don't need your pity." Her eyes flashed and she felt a rush of blood stain her cheeks as the anger deep in her gut continued to boil.

"I waited months for the three of you to come and get me out of that hellhole. Months, of waiting like the pathetic creature I'd become, for you to save me."

"Libby, you have to understand—"

"I don't have to understand shit. If Jaxon had wanted to find me, he would have. He's a *hunter*. It's in his *blood* . . . it's what he does. Do you truthfully expect me to believe that Jaxon Castille, with all the resources available to him, came up with nothing? That he wasn't able to track down one fucking lead and find me? That's bullshit! He's a goddamn jaguar warrior."

Libby shakily blew out a breath and stepped back from the vampire. Her chest was heaving but she managed to regain some of the control she'd felt earlier in the evening.

"I'm sure he convinced himself that I'd vanished without a trace. It must have made it easier for him to sleep at night." She snorted and shook her head. "He didn't want to find me, Ana. He preferred to believe that I was complicit and responsible for Diego's death. I guess it was much easier than facing the truth. So he left me there, with those animals. For three long years."

The vampire hissed as the skin on her cheeks flushed pink, anger suffusing her normally alabaster complexion. "You don't think I went through hell, Libby? Hmm? I'm sorry you were used by the DaCostas in some kind of war against Jaxon, but at the time, I would have killed you myself if I'd gotten anywhere near you. It was *my* lover who was murdered. Mine."

"*Right*. Diego Castille was a model boyfriend when he wasn't banging anything in a skirt behind your back."

"How dare you!" Ana's fangs began to elongate and her eyes blackened until the whites had disappeared entirely.

"What are you gonna do, Ana? Bite me?"

The vampire hissed, and Libby welcomed the surge of adrenaline that coursed through her veins. She was spoiling for a fight, hoping to alleviate the ache that clung fast to her heart.

"Nothing has changed around here, *nothing*," she snapped. "The three of you live in your little dream world, feeling superior to everything around you, when in fact you're all a mess. You think you loved Diego? You don't know what real love is, Ana. It's been staring you in the face as long as I've been around and you're too much of a coward to grab hold of it."

Libby turned her back on the vampire. "You all make me sick."

She nodded toward the door. "Tell Jaxon the next time he wants to ask me something, he should grow a set of balls and do it himself. We're done."

She waited, tense and on edge until she heard Ana leave. When the door slammed shut, Libby shook her head, suddenly feeling deflated. She'd been awful, absolutely awful. She'd never been close to Ana, and while she knew that Diego's eyes had wandered several times, it had been cruel to throw that in her face.

Libby fell onto the bed and groaned as she caught Jaxon's scent on the bedsheets. The soft cotton weave held fast to his essence, and she hit the pillow, frustrated and weary. She needed to sleep, and clenched her mouth tightly before uttering a curse that would make a sailor proud. She grabbed a throw blanket that had been tossed onto the end of the bed and wrapped it around her shoulders.

But a few moments later she hopped off the bed, crossed over to the window and threw her body down into the corner, against the wall. She pulled her knees up, rested her chin against them and looked up into the sky.

Eventually her mind slowed and weariness infiltrated her muscles, emanating through her body. She didn't fight it. She knew she'd need all the strength she could muster, for the next few days would test her like none in recent memory.

And *that* was saying a lot.

Her eyes closed and she felt the tug of slumber calling her. She snuggled deep into the blanket and relaxed, falling under the sandman's spell less than a minute later.

How long she slept, she couldn't say. The rumble of a large diesel engine woke her from the dead, and the faint scent of its putrid exhaust filtered in through the open window above her head.

Instantly, her senses roared to life and she listened intently, while her eyes took in the shadowed light of dawn.

Two voices crept through the early gloom, and she recognized the deep, husky tones of Jagger Castille as he conversed with someone else. She snorted softly. So, Jaxon had called in the troops. Since Jagger had left with Cracker the other night, she assumed the second male voice was Cracker's.

A soft smile fell across her lips at the thought of the older man, and a genuine feeling of anticipation hit her in the chest. He was a real sweetie underneath the muscular bravado he projected to the world. Cracker was someone who'd seen a lot during his tours of duty, and as far as she could tell, had no family to speak of.

Their particular unit had been his family, and he was loyal to a fault. Obviously, he'd not been pulled under the black cloud of hatred the rest had felt for her, and she was grateful for that.

She stretched out her protesting limbs, the muscles tight and stiff. Once she was on her feet, the ache in her side flared, but she pushed it aside. There was much to be done today.

Hope flared deep in her chest, and she felt light-headed with the enormity of it all. To think that she was on the path to finding her son was incredible. But to know that his father would be there, alongside her, was something she couldn't wrap her brain around.

He didn't even know about Logan.

But he suspected.

The look on his face when he'd seen the long incision low on her belly had spoken volumes.

Two days ago she hadn't understood what the look of loathing and disdain meant. But as the shattered fragments of her mind had slowly fused together, it hadn't taken long for her to figure it out.

That he hadn't asked her outright could be taken two ways: that he didn't give a shit either way, or that he was afraid of what her answer would be.

Libby shrugged and opened the door. She just wouldn't think about it.

Voices drifted down the hall toward her. Everyone was up and ready to go. She looked down at the clothes she wore and grimaced. She needed a change of wardrobe. The overlarge T-shirt wasn't going to cut it.

Determination walked beside her as she entered the great room, hair tousled, sleep vanishing from her eyes and attitude dripping from her pores.

All conversation stopped, and once more she felt like a bug underneath a microscope. Slowly, she scanned the room.

Jaxon and Declan were off to the side, bent over a low-lying table. They were studying what appeared to be a large map; and both men turned toward her as she walked farther in. She took in Declan's wary countenance, and felt the heat of Jaxon's gaze but refused to meet his eyes. She could feel his scowl, and felt a tug of pleasure ripple through her.

Good. Let him stew.

Ana turned away from her and retreated to the kitchen, busying herself with a spot of granite that was apparently dirty, shooting looks of venom her way from half-lowered eyes. A slice of remorse shot through her, but Libby ignored it. She had no time to worry about the vampire.

Cracker and Jagger, however, greeted her with huge smiles, and she was overwhelmed with emotion as the older gentleman swung her into a hug, carefully avoiding the tender area of her ribs.

His voice was rough, and she felt the tickle of his whiskers as he whispered into her ear. "I knew you'd come back to us. I'm sorry to hear about what you went through, but rest assured we will make things right." He squeezed her shoulders gently before releasing her. "*Everything* will be all right."

His double meaning wasn't lost on her, and Libby shook her head sadly. "I don't think anything will ever be the same again, Cracker. But thank you for your kind words."

"Hey, old man, you gonna let me say a proper hello to Blondie here?"

Aware of the dark eyes boring a hole into her back, Libby encircled Jagger in a far more intimate embrace then she normally would have, but the devil was licking at her toes and she answered his call recklessly.

Jaxon's brother was almost a duplicate, when it came to his features, but he was larger both in height and in bulk. She felt the hard muscles tense at her forward greeting, but they quickly softened and she laughed up into the wicked green eyes that regarded her closely. They glinted with both open warmth and something devilish, which manifested itself as his grin widened and he reciprocated, wrapping his long arms around her like a silky net.

She was crushed against him, and he laughed softly against her neck, "I better behave myself or he's going to blow." Gently, she was released, and a genuine feeling of warmth had her pausing. It was tinged with sadness at the realization that it was a reaction she hadn't felt in a long while.

Jagger had never been part of their unit in PATU. He was overseas in Iraq most of the time she'd been with his brother. She'd met him several months after joining Jaxon's unit. He had come home on leave, and they instantly clicked. He was a tough soldier and deadly at his job, and if you were part of his inner circle, he was loyal to the bitter end.

She had always liked that about Jagger. There was no second guessing. He was a no bullshit kinda guy.

Critically, Libby ran her eyes over him. He'd become one hell of a sexy specimen. He had matured. There was no longer any hint of boyishness about him . . . well, until he smiled. The eyes were still devastating, but there was something there; a void, a wariness that she could sense because it was akin to the feelings that coursed deep inside her.

Cupping his face with her hands, she could see the pain that he tried to hide from everyone. It called to her. It was so like her own. "Jagger, you've grown up."

His eyes softened and he chuckled. "Well, you look

exactly as I remember. You're still the same hot little blonde that Jaxon would never leave me alone with."

Libby shook her head. They both knew that was a bald-faced lie, but she appreciated the sentiment.

He was a charmer, for sure, and she wondered if there was anyone in his life. Then she sighed inwardly. He was a jaguar warrior, and in so many ways just like his brother. She wasn't sure it was in their genetic makeup to trust and to love.

"When you're done copping a feel over there, Jagger," Jaxon said, "I'd like to have a few minutes of your time. If it's not too much trouble."

The sarcastic words elicited a wide grin from the younger Castille. He winked down at Libby and whispered as he moved away, "This is gonna be fun. He's already frothing at the mouth, and I haven't even begun to work it."

Libby turned around, her violet eyes flashing as they connected with the Jaxon's. Clearly, he was pissed, and he looked dangerous as all hell. She felt a shiver course through her, and as his eyes dropped to her chest, the tightening of her nipples crested against the thin T-shirt that she wore.

When his eyes met hers again, they were lit with an inner fire that was part madness and most definitely tinged with desire.

She felt her stomach flutter but did not break eye contact, instead following slowly behind Jagger. The large parchment they had spread out was a detailed map of Mexico and several surrounding countries, including Honduras and Belize.

She felt that little flip inside her once more, and nervous tension washed over her in waves. She could see they had red-flagged an area on the south-east side of Mexico, near Cozumel. There were also a series of red-flagged areas in Guatemala, Honduras, and Belize.

Libby felt a slow burn begin as she studied the map. None of the red flags were anywhere near where they needed to be. The burn intensified, and her gut contracted as anger flushed through her veins. Her breathing increased, and the sound of her heart beating fast in her breast was so loud, she was sure everyone in the room heard.

It was obvious what was going on, and she was having none of it. This was her mission. Not his. He thought to leave without her? Christ, he didn't even know where to look.

Her fury burst forth. "What the hell are you doing, Castille?" she demanded, and once more five pairs of eyes landed on her.

She crossed over to him in seconds, and her hand arced out, sweeping the map from the table. Just as quickly, Jaxon's large hand snaked out and he grabbed hold of her arm in a steel grip. She wanted to cry out as pain radiated down from her wrist, but clenched her teeth, her hatred and anger spewing forth from her eyes.

"Leave us," Jaxon growled menacingly, and cast a dark look at the others, who appeared stunned by the ferocity of his order. The cold tone of his voice brooked no arguments, and one by one they cleared the area, leaving the two of them alone. Ana cast a sly look toward Libby on her way out, and Libby fought the urge to stick her tongue out at the vampire as she disappeared into the basement.

"Are you going to let go or are you trying to crush my wrist?"

Jaxon cursed and loosened his grip, drawing a rough hand through the messy crop of hair atop his head. He started to speak, and she watched him slowly gain control of the fierce emotions at war inside him.

"I've made arrangements for you to be taken to a safe place until this is all over. As soon as the transport arrives, we'll head out."

"You will not keep me from going to Belize. You will not."

She was breathing hard, and began to pace as anxiety ravaged her limbs. She was like a junkie coming down from a high, and she sure as hell wasn't ready for it.

"I told you last night I was going. I guess you didn't listen too well, because I also said I would kill anyone that stands in my way. And that includes you, Jaxon. Don't think for one second I would hesitate to put a bullet through your brain if you dared to try and keep me here."

Libby felt a weight settle on her chest. Why the hell did everything have to be so hard? Why couldn't he just let her be?

He regarded her with frozen, black eyes, but remained silent.

"You will not keep me from Belize."

She kicked at the scattered parchments on the floor and snarled, "From the looks of those, you have no clue where to look anyway. I'm willing to lead you straight to Degas and Frank. What more could you ask?"

His face remained closed, and the familiar blankness that he used so successfully when on mission shrouded his features. It dawned on her then exactly what his problem was.

He didn't trust her. Hell, right at this very moment he was most likely thinking that she was part of some nefarious plan to trap both him and his brother deep in DaCosta land. She kicked the maps again as her anger bubbled up. She took a second, not trusting her voice, but thoughts of her baby stolen from her breast overcame her.

"What do you want to know?" Libby asked.

Her voice was soft, halting, and it hung in the air between them as something flickered in the depths of his eyes. It was illusive, gone just as quick as it had arrived.

"Everything."

Chapter 16

Libby continued to stare long and hard at Jaxon. The last thing she wanted to do right now was revisit her not too distant past. One that was so chock full of pain and torment, she could feel her insides tightening, like she'd inhaled a gallon of sour milk.

Her muscles were strung so tight, her teeth clenched so hard, that a dull ache formed along her jawbone. With great effort she forced her body to relax.

Her eyes wandered toward the large window that welcomed the wilderness so intimately into the cabin. Early morning fog shrouded the edges of the forest, and it crept over the grass, lingering along the path beyond the small hill. Birds were chirping away, happily unaware of the darkness that resided so deep in her mind.

She closed her eyes, welcoming the agony that

lanced her heart, thinking that maybe by sharing she'd be able to chase the demons that haunted her still. If anything, he should know what her love for him had cost her.

"They took me an hour after you left, that day. *An hour.*"

Her voice was quiet but she made no effort to speak louder.

"We'd made love, do you remember? Although I suppose we could have called it breakup sex, because I knew then it was over. I'm sure it wasn't hard for them to track me, since my body was drenched in your scent."

Libby moved away from the window and glanced back toward Jaxon. Her face remained closed, tense, but his eyes followed her movements and she could feel the heat of his gaze.

"I still wonder if, maybe if I'd had my wits about me, it would have all turned out differently. Maybe I would have been able to escape. Or not." She shook her head. "I don't know. Either way, when they attacked, it was fast and precise. They used some kind of drug to knock me out, and when I woke up, I was in a crate. My hands were tied and I had a rag stuck in my mouth." She paused, exhaling softly. "It was dark, I was cold, wet. I didn't see the light for a few more hours. Considering what was in store for me, it would have been much better to have remained blind."

Libby's voice wavered and she didn't bother to stop the tears that pricked the edges of her eyes.

"I realized right away who was responsible for my kidnapping. Fat Frank was literally drooling when I wouldn't answer any of his brother's questions. They wanted to know where you and Diego were. They wanted the both of you dead, but like the trained agent that I was, there was no way in hell I was giving it up. Not even after Degas left and Frank moved in with all his torture paraphernalia."

She turned to him then, her eyes full of fire and the need for him to know how hard she'd tried to keep it together. "I didn't say shit to them, not when they stripped me, not when he used a knife to cut into my flesh . . . not even when they used cigarettes to burn me. I held it deep inside of me, but then . . ."

"Then what?" Jaxon's harsh voice cut through her, and Libby turned her tortured eyes away. His voice softened, maybe even trembled a bit. "Did they . . . did they rape you, Libby?"

She laughed outright at that.

The sound was hysterical and tinny, and she caught the grimace that flashed across his face. "No. They never touched me in that way. Frank liked to torture, but Degas made it quite clear that a DaCosta would never lower himself to have sex with someone like me. A Castille whore. I don't think I was called by my name again. And when they found out . . ." Her voice trailed off and she hushed, her eyes falling to the fingers that nervously worried the worn edges of the T-shirt she wore.

"When they found out what?"

"A woman came into the room. She was a jaguar, I could tell. It was in the way her skin shimmered when she moved, and when she looked at me and came so close I could see the veins in her eyeballs, I knew it was over."

Libby's eyes darkened at the memory, and she felt the anger that stuck in her throat, like a heavy dose of bile.

"She took her time sniffing my skin, my mouth, and when she knelt down and touched my belly, I thought I was going to throw up. She knew. She told Frank I was pregnant, and when he aimed a crowbar at my midsection I broke down. I was only a few months along, but already this life inside of me had my heart and my soul and I knew I needed to fight for it."

Libby avoided Jaxon's gaze as she continued. "I gave it up right then and there. They told me that if I cooperated they'd spare my life and the life of my unborn child. I told them everything they wanted to know, praying the entire time that you'd make it through, and a few days later when they told me they'd killed Diego, I felt . . . like Fat Frank *had* gone ahead and slammed that bat into my gut. They told me you and Declan had managed to escape. So they were keeping me . . . biding their time."

She turned eyes full of accusation and anger on him then, and she noticed the sudden whiteness around his mouth and the bleakness that surrounded his dark eyes.

"I know it was my fault the unit was attacked, and that because of me, Diego died. But I had no choice and I would do it again if I had to. Surely you must understand that." Her eyes filled with unshed tears and she looked away as her voice softened with the weight of emotion she was feeling. "I *needed* for you to understand. So I waited for you to come for me. It's the one thing that got me through those dark months. As time passed and my belly grew with the life we'd created, my hope turned to despair. When my time came and they cut our baby from my body, took *Logan* from my breast, my despair turned to hatred. I cursed you and everything that you loved that day, Jaxon."

Jaxon watched as Libby's eyes glazed over, and the tight coil of desperate anguish that pounded in him made it hard to breathe. His sorrow at everything lost was complete. His cousin, Libby, and now a child he'd not known existed. Bitterness washed over him as he thought of the pain and torture imposed upon this woman.

His Libby.

The one that he knew was meant for him, and only him. He just hoped it wasn't too late to make things right. There was a river of hatred, mistrust, and pain between them, and he had no clue if it would ever be bridged. Sorrow washed over him at the thought of the way he'd treated her. Like garbage. Like less than garbage.

But he knew he had to try. Circumstance, fate . . . whatever you wanted to call it had conspired to separate him from his mate, and he would not let it happen again. If it did, he feared the darkness that lived inside his soul would claim the last shred of humanity that still lingered.

And he would be lost forever.

"Libby, I had no idea. Why didn't you tell me about the baby?"

"Are you fucking joking? I tried to! That last day, I tried to tell you everything. All I wanted was one small crumb of commitment, something for me to hold onto. And what did I get? Nothing. Not one goddamn thing."

She crossed to just in front of him, chest heaving. Jaxon mentally shook himself, thinking she was the most amazing thing he'd ever laid eyes on. She poked him hard in the chest and he did nothing to avoid contact. If anything, heat fingered out from her touch, and the cat began to make noise. He clenched his hands in an effort to maintain control over the chaotic blend of emotions that knocked about inside him.

"I let you make love to me one more time because I couldn't stand the thought of never feeling your body against mine again. How pathetic is that? I knew you didn't want me. I knew that you didn't love me enough to claim me as yours, and yet I still craved your body like it was liquid candy. I let you use me, and then you left."

He knew the truth that lived in her words would haunt him till the end of his days. He *had* used her selfishly. He'd not wanted to acknowledge the hold she'd had over him back then. He must have known on some level that she was the only woman for him. And like the coward he'd been, he had abandoned her, and when she disappeared, he'd been quick to believe the worst.

Because it hurt less.

And now they were here, in this time and place with a whole world of hurt and blackness between them.

All because of the DaCosta clan.

He would take his lumps and admit to the mistakes he'd made, but his life—*Libby's life*—had been interrupted, altered and torn all to hell.

For that, he would make every last DaCosta pay with their life.

He felt tendrils of excitement wind along the edges of his mind, down his body, and out to his limbs until he was humming in anticipation of the hunt. He would start there. He would have his revenge on the DaCosta clan, and they would know the fury of a Castille.

He would worry about everything else later.

Libby had turned her back to him, and he reached out his hand, wanting to touch, to comfort . . . to *something.*

"Libby, I . . ." He didn't know how to continue. There were no words to express the pain he felt for her. And he would take to his grave the knowledge that he was responsible for all that had happened.

"Don't bother with an apology, Jaxon. It's way too late for that. I don't want anything from you." She looked directly at him, her violet eyes wet with unshed tears, "except a ride to Belize."

Her body was still so very frail, but he noted the determination and strength in the set of her shoulders. He recognized the signs. There would be no swaying Libby when her mind was set.

Her body hunched inward as if she knew he was hovering.

Jaxon dropped his hands to his sides and turned from her, catching the emerald green eyes of his brother. Jagger nodded, and Jaxon made a decision then that he hoped he'd not live to regret. He was going to Belize, and it looked like he would have more company than he'd wanted along for the hunt.

"We leave in ten minutes. We've chartered a flight

to Texas, where we'll be rendezvousing with Julian. I'll contact him and see about getting you some proper gear."

Jaxon waited for a response, and when there was nothing, turned to leave. A thought struck him then, one that had him pausing mid-stride.

"How did you escape them, and end up in Michigan?"

"I didn't escape, Jaxon." She laughed, a hoarse sound that slid across the room like sandpaper. "Don't you get it? Nothing I did was of my own volition. This is all part of some plan."

He whirled back around, puzzled and not liking it. "I don't understand."

"Well, join the club. Something big is going down. I don't know what it is. The DaCostas are into some heavy shit, and for whatever reason, they felt the need to even the playing field and get rid of your unit at PATU."

He watched as Libby began to pace back and forth, and he tried to shake off the sick feeling of dread forming in the pit of his gut.

"They took me three years ago because they wanted to wipe out the entire unit. They fucked up and it didn't happen. So they kept me. At the time I wasn't sure why, but now I'm thinking they're closer to whatever it is they're looking for. They needed *me* to flush you out, to blindside you."

She crossed the room until she was only a few inches away. Her eyes were heavy with emotion, and his heart ached at the thought of how much she had lost because of him.

"*I didn't escape*. There was this man, his face

is fuzzy but I'm sure he's the one who wiped my memory. He's working with them and *he* left me in Michigan."

She shook her head. "We're just a bunch of puppets, and they're pulling our strings."

She turned from him then, her posture tense but her voice determined. "Personally, I don't give a rat's ass what they're up to. I just want them to pay for what they did to me."

Jaxon's brain went into overdrive. Suddenly everything seemed so much more complicated. What the fuck *were* the DaCostas up to?

His desire to wrap his arms around Libby was so strong it almost hurt. But she'd closed herself off to him, and after a few more moments he quietly left the room. He was filled to the brim with pent-up energy, and it pulsed through him with every heavy beat of his heart.

He needed to clear his mind. He needed to focus.

He snarled bitterly as he felt everything fade away, leaving him quiet, almost serene—yet incredibly deadly.

He had DaCostas to hunt. The cat roared inside at the coming task, and Jaxon welcomed the aggressive nature that lived in him.

Saliva pooled in his mouth, and ignoring the excited tremble that shimmered over his taut skin, he went in search of the rest of his team.

They met the small chartered plane at a local air field close to the Canadian border. It was a somber bunch. Ana was pissed that Libby had been allowed to tag along, but Jaxon ignored her surly attitude. In fact he had briefly considered leaving Ana behind.

Being a vampire, the heat, humidity, and sunlight were more then she could take. But she was a fierce fighter, and once their base was set up in Belize, she could man it while the rest of them hunted the enemy.

A little over three hours later they landed on a private airstrip just east of Houston. It was owned by a group associated with his family's holdings, and Jaxon felt a tug of emotion run through him at the familiar face of his oldest brother, who was there to greet him.

Julian was three years older, and though all three Castille boys were similar in both coloring and physique, he was truly worlds apart from his siblings, just a different animal altogether. He was a jaguar; that was something he couldn't change even if he wanted to. But when Julian's body shifted, he became the spotted creature most associated with the great predators, his rosettes golden. Black cats were rare indeed, and in his race only those bearing the warrior tattoo were covered in a thick black pelt when they shifted into their animal form.

Jaxon and Julian had been very close when they were younger, but when Jaxon matured and warrior tattoos began forming on his body, a distance had crept between them, one that only widened with time. Jaxon had gone the way of the warrior, forging a career for himself in the military, and Jagger had followed in his footsteps.

Julian, however, had followed the path laid out by their father, and as of now was basically running Blue Heaven Industries. The entire operation was an ode to the temple where the ancient jaguar warriors worshiped, one that belonged to their god of war, Huitzilopochtli. Jaxon snorted at that thought. It was ironic, considering how antiwarrior both his father and brother were. It was a bone of contention that the warrior gene was prevalent in his mother's family, something the elder Castille had thought he was avoiding with their union. His father had built the company up from meager beginnings and made it successful, but with Julian at the helm, it had diversified and quadrupled in both size and worth.

But, blood was blood, and he was grateful that his brother had not hesitated when he'd called and asked for the family jet. They needed to fly into Belize under the radar. No government agencies on either side could know their intent. Jaxon needed to attack quickly and with deadly force.

He still had no clue who had broken through their sophisticated defenses in Washington, and that concerned him. No one, not even Commander Drake, could know what he was up to.

Jaxon exited the plane and found himself staring deep into the topaz-colored eyes of his older brother. They were warm with affection, and he bypassed the outstretched hand and enveloped Julian in a hard embrace.

A greeting from behind broke the men apart, and Julian smiled broadly as Jagger, the youngest of his brothers, jumped down.

One after the other his whole team gathered around, Ana swathed from head to toe in protective gear; Libby, quiet, reserved, as she observed everything. Julian tossed him a bag, and he in turn handed it to Libby. She was still avoiding his eyes, but took the bag, clutching it to her midsection protectively.

"Some clean clothes," he murmured, wincing as she jumped at the sound of his voice. Julian elbowed his way into their inner circle, and Jaxon had to urge the beast inside to quiet. He watched as his older brother held out his hand, the long, elegant fingers palm up, a submissive greeting, and one that did not go unnoticed. He was doing his best to alleviate any fear that Libby had, and to let Jaxon know he had no interest whatsoever in the thin blonde who stood so unsure before them all.

"I'm very sorry to hear what you've been through, Libby," he told her. "But rest assured, the DaCostas will pay for their sins, I will personally see to it." Julian's voice was soft, but the underlying steel that clung to his words reassured Jaxon that even though his brother might look the corporate magnate, he was still a jaguar at heart.

And apparently he was going to join in the hunt.

She took his hand, and the two of them led the way toward the Castille corporate jet. Jaxon took a seat in the very back, his eyes never leaving the blonde, who, to him, still appeared too vulnerable for the type of mission that lay in store.

Once they were up to a cruising altitude, he unfastened his seat belt and made his way toward Libby. He felt her stiffen as he sat beside her, his body so very aware of the heat from her skin.

It was approximately two and a half hours until their landing in Belize City, a place he'd not been to in decades. Ironic, that his enemy now made their home in the very jungles he'd once run through as a youngster.

Jaxon pushed that thought aside and concentrated on the task at hand. He needed to know where they were headed. His team had pinpointed three locations, but Libby had indicated back at the cabin that none of them were the right ones.

He cleared his throat, then spoke. "We'll be landing in a couple of hours. I need to know where we're headed. I need numbers, how many civilians, targets, etcetera. And I need to know the *exact* location of the DaCosta residence."

He looked at the long fingers stretched out on her lap. The nails were short, and he was surprised that he'd forgotten how graceful they were. As if they belonged to a musician and not a trained assassin.

Her voice was soft, and he strained his ears in an effort to hear her.

"We'll need to go to San Ignacio. It's southwest of Belize City. From there we'll take the Pine Ridge Road south into the Cayo district. There are some ruins there, in Caracol. They're old and there are people excavating. The DaCostas have a compound to the east, high up into the jungle. It will take the better part of a full day's hike to reach it. It's deep in the heart of the Maya Mountains."

Libby stopped fidgeting and met his eyes fully. "You'll need a lot of firepower. There are no civilians."

"Thank you. That's good."

Silence hung heavy, and it ate at him, the slowly widening space between them. All he wanted to do was close it.

"Libby, we need to talk about a lot of things. I think—"

"Don't think, Jaxon. I can't do this right now, with you." Jaxon felt her sadness and kept quiet as she went on. "I have a lot to figure out, and right now, most of what is on my mind has nothing to do with you. I need you to give me some space, and let me do what I need to do." She raised her eyebrows to him. "Are we clear?"

Libby closed her eyes and rested her head against the headrest, effectively dismissing him. Jaxon took a second to absorb the information, then left her alone with her thoughts as he made his way back to Declan and Ana.

"Declan, call ahead to your contact and let him know we need a base set up near a place called Caracol. There are some Mayan ruins there, should be easy enough to find. It needs to stay under the radar. We'll rendezvous there before heading into the jungle. Tell him to get his hands on as much firepower as possible. We'll be landing in a couple of hours and I want to be at the base by early evening."

"You do know that we're most likely walking into a trap?" Ana replied. "I mean, they seem to know our every move. Maybe we need to take some time and think on this a bit before rushing headlong into the jungle on intel she's fed us." She spoke quietly, but everyone heard her. "I just feel like we're playing into their hands."

Jaxon's face was tense. "Don't think that hasn't crossed any of our minds. But the fact remains that Belize is where we need to start. We need to proceed with caution and be smart." He lowered his voice and looked directly at Ana. "And I need to know that everyone on board is here to fight. Because if not, now's the time to speak up."

Ana was quiet for a few moments, then piped up. "Don't worry about me. I have my own reasons to want to see every single DaCosta dead. But are you sure it's a good idea to take her along?" She kept her tone neutral, but clearly thought of Libby as a hindrance on the mission.

"Nope. Don't think it's a good idea at all."

He ignored her snort and turned toward the porthole of the plane. The sun was shining brilliantly, and he squinted out at the blanket of clouds that dotted the landscape. His gut was nervous, and a cold pressure was pressing into his chest. His heart began to beat heavily.

The jungle called to both his jaguar and the humanity that lived inside of him, yet he couldn't shake the feeling of dread that stuck in his throat.

He didn't have a good feeling about this one.

Not at all.

Chapter 17

They landed amid heat, haze, and a strong breeze that blew across the tarmac, fresh off the Caribbean Sea. The air was thick with moisture, and Jaxon felt it heavy against his cheek as he deplaned. It called to something primal, deep inside his soul, and his spirit lifted even as the coming mission weighed on him. He quickly scanned the area surrounding the plane, and his nostrils flared as he scented the air.

Nothing seemed out of place, and he proceeded, acutely aware of Libby following a few paces behind. Her heart rate had elevated and he sensed the turmoil that ravaged her psyche. He knew that it had to be hard for her to return to this place.

This paradise that hid so many dark dangers.

He cleared all thoughts from his mind save one, and proceeded toward the small building that housed customs. He couldn't afford for his focus to be compromised. His thoughts were centered on the DaCostas and what he would do to them when he had them in his sights.

They were waved through customs, and Jaxon shook his head at how easily a few dollars in the right palms eased their way into the country. Ana drew her share of looks as she walked through the small building, swathed from head to toe in a thick cotton weave with a sun repellant charm courtesy of Declan.

So much for flying under the radar.

Their contact met them outside the airport. John was a tall man, lanky, with strong features that hinted at his Indian heritage. He leaned nonchalantly against a large, older model cargo van that had seen better days, but it blended in perfectly with the odd assortment of battered vehicles parked along the curb.

Drivers were lunging for luggage, trying to outdo each other in a bid to capture a tourist for their next fare. When John saw them approach, he flicked the cigarette he'd been smoking and smiled broadly.

"Welcome to Belize, man."

The drawl was soft, full-bodied, with an island roll that caressed his words. He quickly helped load their gear and stowed it in the back of the van. Once they were all inside, he pulled away and they began the trek to San Ignacio.

They followed the Western Highway as it headed out into the lush tropical countryside. The town was approximately seventy miles away, but the roads were busy, and despite John's aggressive driving style, the ride took almost two hours.

Jaxon's eyes swept along the brush that crept up

to the road and he felt a sliver of excitement as he recalled visiting the Jaguar Wildlife Reserve. He'd accompanied his mother and older brother. Jagger hadn't been born yet, so he knew he must have been a toddler, but it was still clear to him now.

He remembered shifting with his mother, and the three of them running wild for days, intermingling with several wild jaguars that lived on the reserve. They'd made several trips throughout his childhood, but it seemed so long ago. He smiled at the memory, and caught a glance from Julian in the rearview mirror.

He wondered if his brother was thinking the same thoughts. They used to come here, to this wild and untamed place, to mingle freely with true animal jaguars. The mighty predators had once ranged from Belize all the way up past Mexico and beyond, into the southern states. Sadly, with their habitats slowly eroding, there weren't many protected environments for the big cats to live and play in. The Jaguar Reserve in Belize had afforded them the opportunity to do just that.

The sun was high in the sky and crossing over into late afternoon by the time they arrived in San Ignacio. They stopped briefly for food and to pick up a few more supplies. The plan was to continue along and make base before the sun set.

Jaxon tried to keep his distance, but he was concerned about Libby. She had changed on the plane, and a feeling of déjà vu spread through him at the sight of her dressed as if she were part of his unit once more.

She was still favoring her left side, and he looked to Declan as a thought struck him.

"Can't you work some magick to make the pain go away? A charm? Spell? Something?"

Declan looked to Ana and lowered his voice before answering. "It doesn't work that way, Jax. And we don't have the time for me to attempt a healing charm."

Jaxon grimaced, causing Declan to raise an eyebrow.

"Look, none of us thinks she should even be here. I can appreciate her need for closure, and the desire for revenge. Really, I can relate. But she's not in great shape physically or mentally." Declan shook his head and looked away. "She's gonna get us all killed."

"I was just asking a question," Jaxon snapped, "not looking for a lecture."

The mood darkened considerably as they climbed aboard the van and headed south along Mountain Pine Ridge Road. It would eventually dump them deep into the Cayo district. They traveled through a large reserve that was abundant with lush flora and fauna. These forests were famous the world over, full of pine trees that seemed out of place in the middle of its tropical locale. In the distance, large waterfalls could be seen shimmering as they cascaded down, some well over a thousand feet above the ground.

They soon left the reserve behind, continuing along Pine Ridge Road. The journey remained both quiet and tense, until eventually they came upon the Mayan ruins located in Caracol. It was indeed a sight to behold, and Jaxon felt the enormous weight of history beat at him as they parked and slowly stretched their limbs, deep in the shadow of the impressive ruins.

His fingers radiated energy, filled with a new and frenetic excitement that was hard to explain. This . . . *this* is what was real to him: being out in the jungle, deep in the heart of jaguar land with a thousand warrior ghosts urging him on.

He had to use superhuman effort to keep control of his emotions, and as he looked to his brothers, he knew they felt the call of the wild as deeply as he did. Jagger's nostrils were flared and his eyes had darkened until not a speck of green remained.

The sun was beginning to set, and its direct rays no longer affected Ana. She'd dumped the shroud but looked miserable as the heat curled her hair wildly, and her clothes stuck to her body. She quickly pinned her hair back, her arms trim and pale, and Jaxon was startled at the raw emotion that crossed Declan's face as he too watched the vampire.

The man looked haunted, pained even, and Jaxon turned away, not wanting to be privy to such private revelations. Libby was off to the side, her back to him, and he made his way to where his brothers stood.

John returned and confirmed that he'd talked to the person in charge of the site, an archeologist. They would be allowed to leave their vehicle and proceed out into the jungle. Jaxon wasn't sure what he'd told the archeologist and he didn't care. They were here in the heart of the Cayo and would be close to the DaCosta compound in just under twenty-four hours.

They grabbed their gear and Declan radioed his contact. He pointed to the west, and the group hiked nonchalantly around the edges of the ruins before disappearing into the Chiquibul forest that surrounded the ancient Mayan temples and buildings.

They were swallowed up by the jungle immediately, and their eyes adjusted quickly to the dim interior. Howler monkeys trumpeted their advance, and Jaxon felt the eyes of the jungle's inhabitants on him. Cracker led the way, with Libby at his side, with Jaxon content to watch her from several paces back.

Julian fell into step beside him and they carried on for a while in silence.

"Are you all right?" his brother finally asked.

The question surprised Jaxon, and he flashed a quick grin and nodded. "Yeah, once we reach base, I'll have a look at the satellite images we managed to pull . . . not sure if they'll do any good with all this cover, but we'll come up with a plan and they'll never know what hit them."

"That's not what I meant. I'm talking about Libby. Jagger filled me in. I know there was a child."

Jaxon's face whitened and he kept his gaze focused on the slight shoulders that were covered in a tumbled mess of blond waves. He shook his head at Julian, "It's her I'm worried about. She thinks that the child is alive. She even named him. Logan."

He couldn't begin to describe the sorrow that stabbed him as his older brother hiked along beside him.

"Do you think she's right? About the child being alive?"

"No." Jaxon's face turned hard and his bitter eyes darkened at the thought of a child he'd never had the chance to know. "Why would a DaCosta spare the life of my son? It doesn't make any sense."

"None of this makes sense," Julian answered darkly. "I think it's safe to assume that things are not what they seem."

Jaxon shrugged his shoulders and kept his eyes trained ahead, on Libby's frail frame. "Yeah, Cracker and the rest of the team are fairly certain this is not going to go as easy as we'd like. This will not be an operation without consequence." A harsh smile flickered across his handsome face as he turned once more to his brother. "But then, what would the fun be in that?"

Julian shook his head as Jaxon's smile widened, and answered wryly, "Indeed."

Silence fell between the entire group then, and they hiked for just over an hour more before Declan led them to a clearing where his contact had managed to set up a half decent base of operations.

There were four tents in all. One housed equipment and weapons, and the other three were for sleeping. The plan was to get some much needed rest and then leave early in the morning. Hopefully, they'd reach the compound by early evening and attack under the cover of darkness.

Jaxon watched as Ana stowed her gear in the nearest tent, followed by Declan. Cracker and Jagger claimed the second one. Libby stood looking more then a little lost, and he quickly moved toward her, but she turned before he could reach her and disappeared into the remaining tent.

He continued to the larger tent, which held their cache of weapons and a whole host of goodies. Julian was already deep in conversation with Declan's man, and after introducing himself, Jaxon requested the satellite images they'd managed to pull.

Considering the amount of cloud cover he'd observed on the flight over, he was relieved to note that the images were clear, and he quickly made mental notes.

It wasn't a large compound, but there were ten buildings scattered about, and from the looks of the pictures, a fair amount of commandos. He continued to study them, his mind focused and sharp, when a tingle up his spine stopped him cold.

He sensed Libby's presence before she stepped through the tent flaps. Her female scent was enticing hung heavy in the air, drifting lazily through his nasal cavity and making his mouth water with need. His reaction was instant and hard. It slammed into his gut with red hot spikes of desire, and he nearly dropped the pictures.

His head whipped around and he pinned her with his black eyes. Her violet eyes had darkened, and they ignored him as she focused on the photos that he held. Her breathing was ragged, coming in short staccato bursts, but she managed to keep a professional air as she came toward him.

"Let me see those."

The words slipped from between her lips, and the commanding tone surprised him enough that he let her take the satellite photos from him. Her long, graceful fingers avoided his touch as she did so.

Her hair hung down past her shoulders, the flaxen strands curling wildly from the heat. It was all Jaxon could do to keep reaching for her and burying his nose deep in the soft waves.

He couldn't take his eyes from her, and watched as her pale cheeks flushed. Every cell in his body ached for her, and he knew it would not lessen in time. His body had recently tasted her sweetness, and it remembered every detail of their wild coupling two nights ago. He mentally groaned, unable to stop the images of her as she rode his cock, so full of passion atop his body. She'd successfully slithered into the one corner of his heart he'd left vulnerable, and stolen it out from under him.

Again.

He was screwed. There was no other way around it.

She bit her bottom lip as she studied the pictures, and he knew how hard it was for her to be here.

Libby was hurting, and he desperately wanted to comfort her.

Without realizing he'd moved, Jaxon took a step toward her, but stopped as she whispered, avoiding his eyes, "Don't. I need to be strong right now and I *will* fall to pieces if you touch me."

Anguish sliced through him at her words. Reluctantly, he drew back, respecting her wishes. Turning away from her, he noticed that both Julian and Declan's man Bart had left them in privacy.

He cleared his throat. "Where do the DaCostas hang when they're at the compound?"

Libby edged her way to the table just to his right. She was so close he could see the rash of goose bumps that covered her flesh. She drew in a shaky breath, and when she spoke, her voice was strong.

"This large building here is the main gathering place in the compound." He watched as she pointed to the largest of the buildings at one end. "It's where their offices are located and it's also where they like to eat and drink."

"These here," her fingers trailed along several

smaller shelters that lined the eastern side, "are the sleeping quarters for their men. Some are shifters, some aren't." She turned to Jaxon, her lips pursed into a tight line. "But they're all dangerous."

Half of the buildings were hidden beneath the jungle canopy, but as Jaxon stepped closer for a better look, he was able to make them out.

He pointed to two buildings located on the southern perimeter. They were secluded from the rest, which seemed odd. "What are these ones used for?"

Libby tensed but shrugged her shoulders. "They're just storage sheds. I think they use them for extra food and water."

She held the photos for a few seconds more, then placed them carefully on the nearest table. "All the ammunition is kept in the main building at the very back." She looked directly into Jaxon's eyes, and he flinched at the pain that was so clearly present. "Next to Degas's office."

Jaxon nodded, and they stood in silence for a few moments before Libby quietly excused herself. Then he paced the small circumference of the tent, on edge and full of restless energy. His heart pounded out a pagan rhythm, and as the familiar burn began to ease its way up his torso and across his chest, he growled low in his throat.

The jungle was calling to him. To his jaguar.

Tossing the black and whites onto the table, he quickly left the tent. All was quiet.

He could feel energy drifting in the air, and attributed it to the protection wards Declan would have placed in and around their base. Evening had fully enveloped the jungle, and he could hear the nocturnal beings that came alive underneath its spell, deep in the distance. A tingle of awareness raced along his spine, and he whirled, the air cracking around him.

Julian stood there, his deep topaz eyes glowing with a feverish glint, and when he grinned, Jaxon nodded, and the two ran like children toward the foliage that beckoned. His jaguar was chomping at the bit, and his pupils dilated in anticipation as he shed his clothes and called the mist to his body.

He felt incredibly alive. As bones popped and elongated, skin shimmered and disappeared underneath a thick black coat, the animals of the forest were silent. Less than a minute later two large jaguars barked to each other and took off, their powerful legs propelling them forward at breakneck speed. The spotted golden cat led his midnight black companion deep into the underbelly of the jungle.

Jaxon reveled in the savage joy his jaguar experienced, and he let all thoughts of Libby and the DaCostas fade from his mind as the animal took over. In this moment he would feed his need to escape. As he ran to catch up to his older brother, he roared his pleasure, ears perked at the answering call that rang out into the night.

Inside her tent, Libby froze at the sound and shuddered as it brought to mind torturous memories that had haunted her for the last two months. Her fingers kneaded her temple and she wished the dull headache that had plagued her the last three hours would just go away. A plate of food had been left on her bedroll along with a bottle of water, and she smiled, knowing it was either Cracker or Jagger who had provided it for her.

She was so very tired, but forced herself to eat something. She knew she'd need every ounce of energy she could muster, for the coming hours. Once she was done, she lowered her aching limbs to the bedroll, but even though she desperately needed sleep, she was afraid to close her eyes.

She began to tremble as a wave of emotion choked her throat and made it hard to breathe. She was so close to learning the truth about her son. It was almost anticlimactic, really, and on a certain level she wished she was worlds away. Because then she could go on believing that he was happy, healthy, and well cared for.

She could believe that he was alive.

She *had* to believe he was still alive, because if he wasn't, there wasn't any reason for *her* to live.

A thousand thoughts seemed to flutter through her bruised mind, but eventually the pain receded and she relaxed somewhat. She was alone, and while grateful, couldn't help the small snatch of resentment that flashed through her. She was the outsider here and knew she'd never belong again. Even Cracker and Jagger were keeping their distance. She sighed, not surprised.

Eventually she must have drifted off. She wasn't sure how much time had passed, but knew exactly the moment her body became aware of another.

Her insides jerked and she felt her belly skip madly. She bit her lip in an effort to contain the squeak that threatened to spill out, and her breasts began to ache with need, the nipples instantly hard. Her body recognized him even before her mind could. His scent drifted over to her. It was full of male desire and heavy with the remnants of his recent shift. His animal was deeply aroused, and even though she hated him for it, her body screamed for his touch.

He was here.

Jaxon had come for her.

Chapter 18

Libby held her breath, knowing that he was inches from her back. She was fully clothed, having tumbled onto the bedroll in the clothes she'd worn from San Ignacio. But she felt extremely exposed, as if every inch of her body was laid bare to him. Heat suffused her flesh and she broke out into a sweat. Desire radiated in a throbbing rhythm that caressed her skin before settling deep between her legs.

It was a tangible feeling, one that roared to life as she felt a whoosh of air caress the back of her neck. Her eyes were shut tight, and as she fought the exquisite ache that had been sparked deep inside the folds of her sex, she prayed to God that Jaxon would just leave.

Life as she knew it, royally screwed such as it was, would be much better if he'd just turn around and leave her there to suffer. Alone.

But even before a slight groan escaped from his lips, she knew they would be together this night. Her body was turning toward his and she was helpless to stop it. Slowly, she rolled over and felt the heat that burned beneath his skin wash over her cheeks and tingle her nose.

She inhaled raggedly and held his scent deep inside her chest, savoring the richness of it like an illicit aphrodisiac. It made her mouth water, and with a small cry, her eyes flew open, eagerly seeking out the man next to her.

He'd taken something from her, years earlier, and had never returned it.

Jaxon Castille had her heart and her soul. They were lost to her forever, and as her eyes met his, she knew that even though she'd most likely hate herself in the morning, she would give in to him.

He was like a drug habit she would never be able to kick. Even though loving him had brought her nothing but heartache, she could not deny how much she needed his touch. He'd taken her heart and every last scrap of love she was able to scrounge together and pretty much thrown it all away. But in spite of everything they'd been through, or maybe because of it, that invisible bond was once more wrapping itself around the both of them.

It was dim inside the confines of the tent, but as her eyes adjusted she shuddered at the look that lay deep in the recesses of his incredible eyes. It was raw. It was haunted. And as he took that last little step toward her, he growled from deep within his body and the look changed to one of pure hunger.

"Libs . . ."

His rough voice sent shivers down her already taut nerves, and her mouth parted for the words she wanted to say but was unable to utter.

Libby felt a spark of danger and the air seemed to thicken. She began to pant, feeling light-headed. It only worsened as his eyes moved over her body, and the dangerous sensations morphed into a desire that burned hot as his eyes claimed hers. They seemed to glow with a fire that raged from deep within, and she looked away, a small cry torn from her throat at the intensity of the animalistic need they so blatantly projected.

Her nipples, already hard and puckered with desire, chafed against the soft cotton T-shirt, and she felt liquid gathering between her legs as she shook her head in awe of this beautiful body on display.

He had not one scrap of clothing on, and the fine sheen of sweat emphasized the hardness of his corded abs and impressive shoulders. The tattoos appeared to glow, adrift in a sea of iridescent waves that made them seem alive.

Her eyes fell lower, down past his belly, past the soft curls that led to his straining shaft. Jaxon was aroused, and her hands crept toward his hardness. A small smile played around her generous lips when she heard the hiss escape his mouth as her fingers closed around the straining length of him.

He was all hardness, enveloped in a glove of velvet softness. His cock was huge and seemed to swell as her fingers slowly massaged him from base to tip. She looked up at him then, his desire a blatant invitation, saw his hands clench at his sides and sensed his body tighten as she licked her lips.

"You are a beautiful man, Jaxon."

When she bent toward him, she felt him tremble beneath her touch, and when she took him deep into the hot recesses of her mouth, he groaned loudly. She suckled him, teased and tugged. When his hands found their way toward her and his fingers buried themselves deep into her hair, she smiled against him, loving the way he felt.

"Libby. Babe, you gotta stop." His voice was hoarse, yet she continued her ministrations, ignoring his entreaties.

She wanted to pleasure him, to show him what was buried inside her.

She wanted her actions to speak for her, and hoped that he would know what it was she couldn't vocalize.

Jaxon, however, was having none of it. As excitement rippled over his skin, he pulled back and his hands gently pushed her away. She let go of him, her tongue flicking out one last time, eliciting a wicked grin from him as he knelt down.

"Libby, I—"

"Shush. No words. No talking." Their eyes locked as she spoke softly. "Show me what you feel."

Her voice was barely above a whisper, but the need she felt lay heavy in every syllable she'd uttered. His hands reached for her thin T-shirt and her arms were already up in the air, anticipation rocking her to the core. She ignored the twinge in her side as the material was slowly pulled upward. It caressed her skin, and when it dragged across her full, ripe breasts, she couldn't hold back the groan that fell from her lips.

His mouth was upon them immediately, his tongue encircling the soft swollen peaks, and his teeth tugged slightly, spreading sharp pleasure into fragments that went straight down to her belly. His wet mouth was relentless, and her hands crept up into the thickness atop his head, her fingers rough as she urged him on, her breasts straining for his touch, wanting him to taste and torture. The pleasure was so exquisite it hurt.

His mouth continued to rain fire upon her flesh, and while his hands massaged the large globes, he nibbled the base of her neck, sending a plethora of shivers through her. Her head lolled to the side as weakness attacked her knees, and he took full advantage of the soft skin that lay exposed to him.

She could barely breathe, and squeaked softly when his warm tongue lapped at the tender spot just beneath her earlobe. She sighed as she leaned into him. He'd always made a point of touching her there, and she smiled at the way their bodies felt so alive when they were making love.

"Jaxon, don't stop." She barely managed to get the words out, as he kept up his very special brand of torture.

When finally his mouth arrived at her chin, she was a mass of nerves. Her fingers dug into his scalp as she claimed his lips with her own. Her mouth was open and his tongue invaded the velvety recesses without hesitation. He tasted just the way she remembered, and she felt him tremble as her tongue arced into his. The sensations were incredible, and as the throb between her legs reacted to both his tongue and the callused hands that were playing havoc with her breasts, she arched her body.

She began to gyrate her hips, slowly, dancing to

a rhythm older than she cared to imagine. When his lips broke from hers, she caught her breath at the look in the dark recesses of his eyes. His hands slowly encircled her face and his mouth met hers once more. His eyes claimed hers and he refused to break contact as he deepened the kiss.

His dark eyes shone like glistening onyx, and as his mouth slowly caressed every soft crevice of her own, his actions spoke volumes to her soul.

No words were needed.

Jaxon Castille loved her, and God help her, she felt the same insane way about him.

In spite of everything.

Gently, he lowered her back onto the bedroll, his eyes devouring the softness that lay exposed. "You are so beautiful." His voice was hoarse with need. "I want to taste every inch of your body."

His hands caressed her belly, and he smiled as her muscles clenched and her hips bucked up toward him. He followed her hands to the waistband of her pants, and as their eyes met, gentleness was replaced with fervor as she struggled to get out of them.

The need to have him buried deep inside swept over her. She hissed as her legs moved, and the friction that nipped between her thighs drove her to distraction. There, the small nub buried inside the wet folds of her sex began to ache and pulse with an urgency that was relentless. It was almost unbearable.

"I want—" She gasped as pleasure rifled through her body, so intense it was almost painful.

She felt the liquid candy that had flooded her there, and smelled the fruits of her arousal as it lay heavy in the jungle air. Jaxon growled, and she knew her scent was driving him crazy. His hands grabbed the waistband of her pants and he literally ripped them from her limbs.

She'd been given no undergarments, and his black gaze devoured her heated core, his fingers seeking out the blond curls that encircled her secret place. And when they invaded the aching lips, she bucked wildly, her arms reaching for him as her passion reached new heights.

"That feels so good," she groaned softly, still gasping for air.

He continued to watch her as his hands gently caressed and teased, applying just the right pressure where it ached, to elicit even more small groans of delight. When two long fingers found their way deep into her channel, the pressure began to build and spread like a wildfire.

"Please, Jaxon. I need you." Her eyes looked deeply into his as her fingers clawed into the broad shoulders and then down his powerful back until they came to rest on his muscular backside. She urged him forward, her legs spread wide as she opened herself up to him fully.

"I need you inside of me."

Jaxon swore at her brazen words, and she felt a thrill of excitement shoot through her as his knees nudged hers even wider and he settled his large frame between them. He kissed her, his tongue licking her swollen lips and his powerful arms enclosing her in his embrace. His eyes were so dark with desire she was utterly transfixed as he growled and plunged himself into her waiting heat.

Her body stretched to accommodate his size and her muscles clenched against him as he began to move. Slowly at first, each thrust touching off a million spokes of pleasure that coursed through her body, sizzling against nerve endings already heated with desire. Her violet eyes darkened, the pupils fully dilated, and she held his gaze prisoner as they slowly rocked together.

"I've never wanted you more than I do right now." Jaxon's words fell like drops of gold from his lips, and Libby closed her eyes at the joy they brought her.

She urged him on, slowly increasing the rhythm, and murmured, "There has never been anyone else. Only you."

When she sighed, licked her lips, and mewed from the back of her throat, it was too much for Jaxon and his body answered her call. She felt his cock swell, deep inside her warmth, and her fingers dug deep into his muscular ass as he pounded into her. She cried out as the desire rifled through her veins, wanting it harder and faster.

Jaxon's hands cupped her face and he held her there as he increased his rhythm, taking their pleasure to new heights. He growled deeply as the animal that was at the very core of his soul howled in triumph.

"You belong to me, Libby."

The wildness in his face, the black desire that filled his eyes, all of it burned into her brain and Libby melted. She wrapped her legs around his straining body and lifted her hips, meeting his thrusts with such wild abandon, a smile broke across his mouth and she claimed his lips once more.

Their feverish bodies rocked together wildly, and Libby groaned loudly against his lips. "Harder, I need it harder."

She could feel the ache begin to crest, and Jaxon growled again as he strained against her, his thrusts feverish in his urgency to mate. When her orgasm exploded, she screamed loudly into his mouth, and he took from her softness there, his tongue dancing with hers as he gave one final heave and emptied his seed deep inside her body.

How long they lay entwined, satiated, slick with the sweat of their lovemaking, was anyone's guess. It could have been minutes, it could have been hours. Libby didn't care. All she knew, all she felt from the very depths of her heart, was that she wanted to stay that way for as long as she could.

With Jaxon buried inside her body, his heart beating fast and hard. His scent mingled with hers and his jaguar purring roughly against her breast.

Slowly, he slipped from her, and her arms grabbed at him, not wanting any distance between them. He laughed softly and pulled up the thin blanket over their sweat-laden limbs as he turned her onto her side and spooned her smaller frame with his. The jungle was hot, but its night's caress was cool against their feverish skin.

Libby sighed, at a loss for words. She was overcome at such a passionate joining. They'd always had an amazing sex life in the past, but this . . . this had been something else entirely. It had been raw and honest, and hopefully there would be no regrets. She felt his arms tighten around her, and she snuggled into the hard length of him.

"That was . . . incredible," she finally managed to say, and smiled as his arms tightened even more.

His breath was hot on the back of her neck as he gently kissed her there. "Yeah, the bar has been set pretty high." He laughed softly and held her close. "We'll have to work on raising it even more."

Libby snuggled into him and they fell into an easy silence. It was comforting, in a way, as if no more words were necessary. Their bodies had connected on such a level that all of their secrets and desires had been laid bare.

Eventually, Libby felt slumber nibble at the corners of her mind, and for once she welcomed it. Sandman could claim her, no more demons and nightmares could haunt her. A strange feeling overcame her then, as if something foreign had slithered through her brain. She felt a wall go up, but as foggy tendrils of sleep overcame her, it was gone and forgotten.

Her last coherent thought was of her child and revenge on the animals who'd taken him from her.

Libby awoke to such a feeling of contentment that her first inclination was to close her eyes and go back to sleep. She rolled onto her back, her head fuzzy with the remnants of sleep. Slowly, her fingers crept up to her lips, and she blushed as memories from the previous evening flashed through her mind.

As she stretched her legs and the sore muscles in her body protested, her blush deepened at the thought that everyone else in the camp must surely have heard just how animalistic she and Jaxon could be.

Her eyes lazily adjusted as she cleared the cobwebs of slumber, and a small ripple of panic began to seep into her brain as she realized a few things.

First, she was alone.

Second, no sound reached her ears. It was as if the camp itself was abandoned.

And third, it was way too bright inside the tent. There was no way in hell it was predawn.

She rolled out of bed and her arms flew up, clutching her head as the dullness that filled her cranium left her feeling severely light-headed, like she was hung over. She knelt on the floor, fighting to gain some sort of equilibrium, and spied her clothes a few inches away, neatly folded.

"Son of a bitch!"

Her voice was hoarse, full of fury, and she ignored the pain that edged through her brain and across her temple. She grabbed the clothes and hurriedly pulled them over her naked form, noticing the plate and water bottle from the night before. Her heart sank to the very bottom of her toes as she began to piece together why she was here, alone.

With a fuzzy head.

She'd either been drugged or charmed. She didn't know which, but at this point she didn't give a shit.

There was going to be hell to pay, and she didn't care whose ass needed kicking, she was going to oblige with gusto. That Jaxon thought he could screw her and then proceed to really fuck her over was unbelievable. Her eyes flashed coldly as she envisioned all the ways she would make him pay.

She whipped the tent flaps back, her mood growing darker as her eyes swept the empty base camp. There was no one in sight, but she knew Ana had to be there somewhere. There was no way the vampire could handle the intense sun that filtered through the canopy above her head.

She glanced upward and bit her lip in an effort to keep her anger from exploding. It was obviously later in the morning then she would have liked. If she had to guess, she'd say around eight. Shit! That meant that Jaxon and his crew were at least two or three hours ahead of her.

What the hell had he been thinking? Did he really think he could keep her away from the compound?

Libby was so furious she didn't know who she wanted to kill more, the sadistic bastards who'd imprisoned her for the last three years, or the man who'd pleasured her to unheard of heights and then betrayed her, treating her with no respect and a blatant disregard for the consequences.

He better believe there would be consequences. She was done with being thrown aside.

Had she been drugged?

The more she thought about it, she decided it was more likely she'd been charmed. How the hell had Declan managed that without her knowledge?

Because you'd been too distracted with thoughts of your lover.

She stood still for all of two seconds, then quickly crossed to the large tent where all the electronic equipment was set up. She whipped open the flaps, feeling a burst of pleasure run through her at the irritated hiss that greeted her.

Black hair floated in the air as Ana jumped away from the beam of light that now lit the interior of the tent.

"Are you *trying* to fry me?"

The shriek that flew from the vampire's lips would have been comical at any other time, but at that moment, Libby was too angry.

"When the hell did they leave?"

Libby's chest heaved and her eyes pinned Ana with a stare that could have frozen the Amazon. She watched the vampire close herself off, the pale face going blank. She'd seen that look before. There'd be no information forthcoming.

Panic began to beat at her and her eyes scanned the room, searching for weapons of any kind. There was a table to the left of where she stood, and she lunged for it, grabbing a large machete and feeling like she'd hit the jackpot when she spied both a semiautomatic and a rather deadly looking Glock.

"You can't take those! They're for the techie and me!"

Danger scraped along the back of her neck and she warily looked over her shoulder, feeling a pang of victory as she noted the bright ray of sunshine that pretty much had the vampire cornered. There was no way Ana could touch her.

"What are you gonna do? Come over here and bite me?" For the second time, the sarcastic line brought the vampire to a froth.

Libby tucked the guns into her pants, holding the machete in front of her as she shot a look of triumph toward Ana, who let fly a mess of curses, flushing a deep crimson that left uneven splotches across her high cheekbones.

Then Ana began pacing along the edge of darkness, looking wildly for a way to attack. It deflated Libby's own anger. She had no quarrel with the vampire. She just didn't like her very much.

"You should save your energy, Ana. The jungle is a deadly place. There are things that live here that would make your skin crawl. This little corner of the world is haunted by dark magick, and now I have your guns."

Libby turned, her groaning belly attesting to the

fact that it had been far too long since she'd eaten. She decided to raid the other tent quickly to find a few pickings, and after she did, headed into the jungle.

She glanced up one more time and looked to the right, knowing that a few hours earlier Jaxon and the rest had tracked through the jungle on the beaten path that would eventually bring them high up the mountain and close to the DaCosta compound. She looked to her left and felt a spark ignite as she set off. A half mile away was a river that originated near the compound. The going would be tough, but it was more direct and would save her some time.

Hopefully, she'd make it there before the fireworks started. Before someone else got to Fat Frank. Her hand went to the guns tucked safely in the waistband of her pants. She knew that Frank was her last hope of finding out where her child had been taken. She had her own plans for him, and no one, not even Jaxon Castille, was going to stand in her way.

Chapter 19

Jaxon's unit moved deeper into the Maya Mountains, forging their way through the lush underbelly of the jungle until it opened onto a ridge that quickly became permeated with pine, mahogany, and cedar. The trees were taller here, but the vegetation at their feet was healthy, vibrant and deep green.

Heavy moist air filled his lungs and melancholy filled his soul as an array of emotions wove their way into his brain. The cat began to move, burning his skin with a heated shimmer, excited at the hunt and thirsty for revenge. Every cell in his body was wired, crackling with electricity, humming along his limbs like an invisible force field.

He ignored the excitement that hung low in his gut. He needed to be in control. He had to focus and banish thoughts of the previous evening far from his mind.

It was hard . . . *incredibly hard*. Guilt hung heavily around his neck. He couldn't shake the feeling, and felt like a first-class asshole. He hadn't planned on seducing Libby; in fact, he'd hoped a run in the forest would quiet the animal that raged inside him.

Instead it had done the exact opposite, and when he returned to camp after a strenuous hour or so with his brother, her scent lingered in the air, leaving a trail of sweetness that called to him on such a primal level, he'd not been able to resist. He'd made love to Libby. And then left her.

Again.

On top of that, he had gone along with Declan's idea to charm her into a deep sleep.

There would be hell to pay when he next saw her, and not just for him. He looked to the left at Dec and sighed. Libby would kick both of their asses. But he had to admit, he'd rather have her pissed off back at base with Ana to protect her than out here on the hunt facing possible death.

He couldn't lose her. Not ever again.

Jaxon shook himself mentally, calling upon the steel resolve that lay deep at the heart of the jaguar. He took a long swig of water, his hand fisting upward, motioning everyone to stop. They'd been hiking through the mountain range for almost eight hours, and the sun was low in the sky. Soon nightfall would cover the landscape.

The forest was alive with sounds, smells, and activity. Declan had used an invisibility charm to cloak their presence from the animals that lived out here. They didn't want the DaCostas to sense any change in behavior from the creatures that called their territory home. Howler monkeys and a whole host of screeching birds would have been sure to trumpet their presence, but for now the charm was working wonderfully in aiding their silent approach.

And so, their quiet, deadly foray up the mountain had moved quickly, hidden from prying eyes.

Jaxon turned his head to the right, nostrils quivering as he scented the air. They were close.

He motioned to his brothers. "It's time." His dark eyes went from the emerald green of Jagger's to the deep topaz eyes of his older brother, Julian. A flood of emotion cracked through his thick outer shell, and he took a moment to compose his thoughts.

He'd worked with Jagger on several occasions and knew his younger brother was both a skilled warrior and a deadly soldier. But to have Julian there, on the front lines, putting his life at risk, was something he'd not anticipated. It meant a lot.

"Julian, you sure you want to go through with this? I understand if you want to hang back, and—"

His brother hissed at him, "I might not have the warrior tattoos, but I am by no means any less of a threat than either of you. I will do this. No one makes a move against a Castille without facing the consequences."

His eyes had morphed to a deeper amber color, and his mouth slashed into a harsh grin as he began to strip the clothes from his back. "Truthfully, I've not felt so alive in a long while. I've been spending so much time in the boardroom, I neglected the very nature that makes me what I am."

"Yeah, Jaxon, don't worry about us," Jagger growled deep from his gut. "I need to hunt me some DaCosta meat."

"*Nice.*" Declan chuckled. "You boys know the plan?"

Julian and Jagger nodded, and after stripping completely, ran toward the forest as mist formed long tentacles around their bodies, obscuring the change that was taking place. Within a few seconds two distinctly different jaguars glanced back at them, and Jaxon was overcome with pride and love for his brothers. He nodded at them and watched both cats, one golden and one black, disappear into the thick blanket of foliage that laced the forest floor.

Cracker spat from the side of his mouth, coming to a halt beside the others. He opened up a handheld unit and after a few seconds flipped it shut.

"The compound is about two miles dead ahead. Satellite images Ana sent show limited activity." His face darkened as he turned to Declan. "You sense any magick here about? Seems to me they'd have all sorts of wards in place, or whatever the hell it is you people do."

Declan frowned but shook his head, "No, there's nothing out here that I can find. Surprising, actually. I was expecting to at least come across traces of the dark arts used back in Manhattan." He looked around and shrugged his shoulders. "There's nothing."

"I don't like it. Something don't feel right to me." Cracker looked at Jaxon, and made no effort to hide the worry that lined his face.

"This whole situation is fucked, but right now I don't see any other alternative." Jaxon's face was fierce and his voice rough. "This is ground zero. It's the only logical place to start looking for those bastards."

"Yeah, the problem is, they're smart-ass sons of bitches," Cracker said. "They should know we'd be gunning for them after they attacked Jagger's cabin." He shook his head and added, "We gotta play it safe and be alert."

Jaxon nodded. "Agreed. The chances are high that we're walking into a trap." He looked to Declan and Cracker, glad to see the deadly resolve in both of their eyes. "Let's do this."

He started toward the compound, and the two men followed a few steps behind. The three assassins moved quickly, the excitement of the hunt spurring them forward as a deadly calm settled over their bodies.

Ahead, their scouts moved with sinuous grace through the thick underbrush, the animals quivering with the need to hunt as they edged closer to their target.

The great cats' agile bodies and powerful frames allowed them to creep close to the compound well ahead of their team members. The black jaguar veered off to the right, sending a soft bark to his partner as the golden cat went to the left. Their nostrils quivered in excitement as they slowly encircled the encampment, seeking out any of their enemy that might be on point duty.

Julian's heart was near bursting, so intense were his feelings. His spirit was screaming in joy as the animal inside him howled at the thought of the coming hunt. He'd not exaggerated earlier. It *had* been way too long since he gave in to the wild animal that was so much a part of him.

He'd spent too much time ignoring its pleas for

release. He'd actually grown afraid at the thought of letting his jaguar out. But now . . . now his senses were burning with a fire that propelled him forward with a vengeance. He could no longer deny what he was. Nor what he was capable of doing.

The encampment was surrounded by a crude attempt at a fence. Julian rounded the far end of the compound and stopped as a foreign scent made his nostrils quiver in anticipation. The great cat licked his lips slowly, his head bobbing back and forth as he tried to find the source of the smell.

He crouched low on his belly, noticing movement up ahead. Slowly, he made his way forward. When he spied a guard leaning against a tree a few paces to his right, he froze. He began to salivate and his heart trembled. He felt his humanity slipping from him, but didn't care. Savagely, he welcomed the power that surged through his body.

His prey was drawing hard from a cigar, the smoke plumes no more than tiny slivers of white ribbons. They danced just above his head, and if the idiot had been paying attention, he would have realized that the forest had become silent.

Guess there were limits to Declan's charms after all, he thought.

Inside, deep in the hidden recesses of his soul, the cat quieted. He slowly crept closer to the guard, who was unaware of the threat to his life. The man was human. There was no scent of shifter about him as Julian crouched a foot away, ready to pounce. Then, as planned, a large explosion ripped through the early evening.

Startled, the guard dropped his cigar and swore

as he tried to retrieve the little bit of Cuban tobacco hidden amongst the underbrush at his feet.

A second explosion led the guard to straighten and stand upright, but it was too late. With lightning speed and incredible strength, the jaguar leapt up and pounced hard, his paws digging in deep as the man screamed in pain.

His eyes widened and filled with terror at Julian's roar. He tried frantically to move, but the heavy beast had him pinned, and then he was frantically begging for his life.

"Please, I no bad person. I only work for money." Clearly the guard knew that this was no regular animal atop of him. He cringed as the jaguar snarled again, unaffected by the human's attempt to sway him.

The man worked for his enemy. The math was simple—only one of them would leave this patch of paradise alive. With a powerful lunge, his canines pierced the man's skull, and less than a minute later the guard lay dead at his feet.

Smoke from the explosion drifted toward him, and Julian took off like a shot, the euphoric rush of the kill giving him more power, as a black energy inched its way into his essence.

Julian Castille was not a killer. In fact this was his first coup. The scary thing was not only had it come incredibly easy to him, but that he'd enjoyed it.

The jaguar soon lost his human train of thought as more animalistic urges rose to the surface. He quickly faded into the forest, leaving the body there to rot.

* * *

After the first charge went off, Jaxon slipped through the poor excuse for a fence and made his way toward the large building at the far left of the compound. Cracker had gone to the opposite side, and at any minute the second charge would explode.

Several men stumbled out of the small bungalows that lined the main area of the compound, half hidden by a thick overhand of trees. They seemed intoxicated, and Jaxon felt a sliver of unease. Something felt off here, and he signaled silently to Declan to proceed with caution. They each drew their weapons, and as the second explosion rocked the air, quickly made their way to the large outbuilding.

A screech rent the night, and Jaxon glanced back as angry snarls accompanied the shrieks. Jagger and Julian had arrived, and he pushed aside his pride at the ferocity and strength his brothers shared. He needed to focus.

And bag a DaCosta.

He and Declan could hear excited voices coming from inside the building, where it seemed that people had barricaded themselves from attack. The unease he'd felt earlier spiked. These were not seasoned soldiers.

Jaxon snarled savagely. They were fools.

Declan silently crept up the steps that led to a large door. His hand snuck out and he tried to open it, but it wouldn't budge. He signaled to Jaxon, who stood on point while Declan went to work setting a charge at both the top and bottom of the door.

He jumped off the landing and both he and Jaxon had moved when the charges split the door in two, leaving a billowing cloud of smoke and a gaping hole in front of the building. They were joined by Cracker, and all three charged forward, guns raised and adrenaline pumping furiously.

Jaxon was the first inside, and he scanned the dimly lit interior. There was a group of women cowering in the corner, and he swore, but ignored them to continue toward the area where he expected to find the DaCostas.

But there weren't any men to be found there, and he took a second to scent the air, his nostrils telling what his mind already knew. The only people there were the women in the common room. He'd get Declan to find out what they knew.

Something caught his attention then, as a wisp of energy cut the air. He signaled to Declan and quietly made his way past the kitchen area and down toward a narrow hall.

If Libby's details were correct, this was where the offices were located, as well as the weapons room.

There were four doors to choose from, and Jaxon began to check them all. The first two were crudely built storage closets, the second of which had obviously been used as a weapons room at one point. As of now, it was empty of any sort of weaponry other than a few shell casings scattered haphazardly across the floor. The door was open, as if the room had been emptied in a hurry.

He swore under his breath, his feeling of unease now a deafening cascade of warning bells that clamored for his attention.

Something stank, and frustration built in his gut at the thought of being denied the chance to face his enemy. The jaguar wanted to kill. *He* wanted to kill.

He was met at the door by Cracker, who raised his eyebrows, shaking his head in confusion. He signaled that he was going back outside and left as silently as he'd come.

Jaxon paused in front of the last door, which was closed. His senses reached out, searching for that elusive whisper of *something* he'd sensed earlier.

It was gone, and his anger boiled over as his foot made quick work of the door, reducing it into a wreck of splinters, leaving only one large piece hanging by the hinge.

The room was like the others. Empty. Heat burned its way up his forearms as he crossed to an old metal desk and searched through a mess of papers left scattered on top.

Something caught his eyes, and his blood turned to ice as he turned his attention to the wastebasket at his feet. He scooped out several photos and documents that had been thrown into the trash in an attempt to burn them. They were surveillance shots . . . of his brothers, as well as Libby, Declan, Cracker, and Ana.

His fear became more palpable as he pieced together what the photographs meant. All of the photos were recent. Some were from the airport in Texas the day before, and a few others had been taken in San Ignacio.

The anger he felt was immediate, as well as the sinking and empty feeling of a mission not completed. The DaCostas had fled like the cowards that they were. He would not have his revenge.

His com unit began to cackle and he grabbed it. "Jax here."

He waited for the static to clear, but her words only confirmed the worst. "You guys need to get the hell out of there. We've got two blackbirds coming in fast, loaded with explosives."

"God dammit!"

Fear for the safety of his team and all the civilians left in the compound flooded his mind. Adrenaline pumped through his veins at a vicious pace as he ran for Declan, his mind working furiously. He needed to get those women out of the building because he sure as hell wouldn't be party to their innocent deaths.

His com unit was crackling and he could hear Ana fading in and out.

"We've got maybe two minutes before this entire compound is blown to bits," he told Declan, and pointed to the women who were huddled together in a confused and scared circle. "I don't care what you do, just get them the hell away from here. I'm going for my brothers and Cracker."

Declan was moving toward the women before he finished his sentence, and Jaxon sprinted out into the dark night. Smoke was heavy in the air, and his long legs carried him across the compound in seconds. He spied Cracker, who held his com unit high in the air, indicating he was aware of the situation.

Low-lying clouds had converged and helped make an already dark night thick black and deadly. Jaxon spotted a golden jaguar and ran toward it, shouting at the animal as it cornered several men against an outbuilding he'd not noticed before.

"Julian! We're under attack." The cat froze, his long tail flicking back and forth, a testament to his agitated frame of mind. The large golden eyes caught

and held Jaxon's as he signaled for the animal to retreat deep into the bush.

His senses were on full alert, but with the number
of humans present, and their mixed emotions coloring the air, he couldn't lock onto his other brother's
trace signature. Wildly, he looked around, and as he
began to move away, he shouted out into the night
air, "Jagger, retreat!"

Off in the distance his ears picked up on the
speeding aircraft that were locking in on them, and
he turned to follow his older brother out into the
jungle. Cracker was close on his heels, and Jaxon's
lungs felt about to burst as he ran hard and fast.

He hoped Jagger had heeded his warning and
fled.

When the blasts went off, they scorched the earth
in a series of massive explosions that lit the night
and rocked the ground violently. Jaxon was thrown
forward with such force his body hit a stand of
trees. Even though he tried to fight it, he began to
slip away, then lost consciousness.

He wasn't sure how long he'd been out when the
persistent cackling of his com unit brought him
around. His entire body ached. He was pretty sure
he'd bruised a couple of ribs, but all in all he felt extremely lucky to be alive.

Jaxon looked to his left and spied Cracker slowly
gaining his feet, and he pulled the com out from
under him and clicked the receiver.

"—find her?"

"Ana, you're breaking up, what was that?" His
voice was raspy and he hoped she was able to
read him.

"Libby! Have you seen her?"

Jaxon stilled at the vampire's words and felt everything melt away. Every sound that echoed in the jungle, his anger and hatred for the DaCostas . . . all of it ceased to exist.

"What the hell do you mean have I seen Libby? She's with you."

There was a long pause, and Ana's voice broke as it echoed into the night. "No, she's not. She left not long after you did and was heading your way."

Chapter 20

Intense pain wrapped its way around his heart and choked his airway. Jaxon reeled and fell back against the tree, his heart pumping like mad, fueled by a spike of adrenaline. He was dizzy, and fought against the thick blanket of fog that threatened to overcome him.

Libby! Here? Would she have made it this far?

He groaned at the thought of her anywhere near the compound, and as his gaze traveled to the smoking ruins, he turned to the side and heaved, emptying the contents of his stomach onto the moist earth.

It passed, his moment of weakness. And was quickly replaced with a steely determination that blackened his mind to any possibility other than the survival of the woman he loved.

Cracker's feet slowly shuffled toward him, and

he focused on them, waiting as a cool calm began to slip into his bloodstream. He would find her. He would claim her as his once and for all. He would not take no for an answer.

And then he would kill her.

How dare she defy him? And take such a chance with her life? The woman was fucking insane.

And that's what you love about her.

Jaxon pulled his body up from the ground, savagely shaking his head, but the truth was there, buried deep in both his mind and his heart. A lot of things had changed over the last three years, but several things had obviously not.

Libby Jamieson had always irritated the crap out of him, she'd angered him on a daily basis, most times never listened to anything he said, was pigheaded . . . and he wouldn't change one damn thing about her.

He needed to get to her in a way that hurt and cut him sharper than a blade.

His heart was pounding loudly now, and Cracker looked at him, sorrow lining the tired wrinkles around his eyes. He'd heard the conversation with Ana and was awaiting his instructions.

"Do you think she was capable of trekking through this jungle in the shape she was in?" Cracker's voice was soft, but the concern was evident.

Jaxon shook his head ruefully. "Nothing that woman does surprises me anymore, and truthfully, she's been out in this jungle for three years. If there's anyone who can survive and find their way around, it will be Libby."

Jaxon nodded toward the flaming compound.

"I need you to make sure our team is intact. Once you've rounded up everyone, have them start searching for her."

Cracker left immediately, and Jaxon ran toward what was left of the compound, sending his extraordinary senses high into the air, seeking out any trace of his woman that he could find. He passed several charred bodies along the way, but was able to ascertain that they were male and didn't belong to any of his crew.

Poor bastards. The DaCosta carnage continued to pile up.

He sensed movement to his left and whirled around, his stance aggressive. Relief flooded him when he saw it was his brother Julian. "You all right?" He barked the question, not bothering to stop and check himself. The urgency to find Libby was biting at his heels, and he tried to squash the fear that accompanied it.

If something happened to her now, before he was able to make things right, he would never forgive himself.

"Don't worry about me. What the hell happened?"

"The DaCostas knew we were coming. The whole thing was a setup, and now, apparently, Libby might be around here somewhere."

"Libby? I thought Declan sleep-charmed her. Shouldn't that have knocked her out for the entire day?"

"You would think." Jaxon pounded the air with a fist, his frustration and anger exploding as he realized his own stupidity. "How the hell did I let this happen?"

"Don't worry about that now. What do you want me to do?"

Jaxon paused. "See if you can find her scent out in the jungle, and if so, where it leads. For all I know, she's nowhere near here yet."

His brother immediately turned and headed for the jungle, while Jaxon took off toward the burning compound again. His belly was full of knots as his fear for Libby intensified.

The main building was totally engulfed in flames, and he circled it as closely as he could, hoping to catch Libby's scent if she were anywhere nearby. He sensed no trace of her, but bleakly knew that meant nothing.

He began to scan the perimeter, and he jumped over blasted bits of what was left of the main building, as well as remnants of the smaller bungalows that had lined the far side of the compound.

He'd begun to make his way in that direction when a familiar sliver of emotion shivered through his mind. It was incoherent and faint, but it definitely was there. It stopped him cold. It was Libby! He had felt it earlier when he was in the main building, but had been too distracted and bent on revenge to pay attention to it.

Fear began to gnaw at him. She was here! And she was alive.

At least for now.

He needed to find her. The soldier that lived deep inside him quickly took over, and his thoughts turned logical as fear, panic, and the ferocity of the jaguar receded. He could deal with the emotions later. Right now he needed to focus.

He stilled and concentrated, closing his eyes and seeking the energy that lingered along the edge of his mind, elusive but so real to him he wanted to physically wrap his hands around it. The smallest trace of her essence drifted through his nasal passage, and his head turned to the left, where he spied two large buildings, one of which was completely destroyed, the other half standing.

Libby had told him they were used for storage, but now, as his mind wandered back, he realized her nonchalant answer to his questions about the buildings were a little too cut and dried. It was obvious she had not wanted him anywhere near them.

Because she wanted them all to herself!

He flew down the length of the compound, Declan joining him in his mad dash. They reached the two buildings, and the smoke was thick indeed.

"Libby?" Declan's one word question pained the both of them, and Jaxon nodded grimly as her sweetness drifted up at him. She was here, amidst this mess and destruction.

The front of the building had been destroyed and the roof had caved in, pulling the front of the facade and the left side down along with it. The back was still intact, and he savagely began to pull at the smoldering pieces of wood that kept him from ducking inside, frantic to reach the only area that would have provided some shelter from the attack.

He didn't feel the heat of the fire or the toxic smoke he was breathing deep into his lungs. He was numb to everything except his need to find Libby. Inside, the cat howled, wanting its mate, needing to see the face of its woman.

Declan was chanting softly now, his eyes black-
ening as his hands furiously drew a spell into the
air. The wind howled and picked up, bringing with
it heavy moisture that lashed at the flames that had
kept them at bay. Within minutes the heat began to
subside and pull away as the water drenched the
dry wood.

Jaxon made quick work of the debris, and a few
moments later they were able to open up a large
enough hole to allow the two men access.

Libby's scent was so strong it was almost overwhelming, and a new fear began to ride him. He
didn't know if it was because she was indeed there
or because this was where she'd been kept for the
last three years.

She was everywhere and nowhere. Wildly, his
eyes crept over every surface. A bed had been placed
against a wall, with two long chains that were attached to shackles. From the ceiling hung several
more long chains, whose ends held heavy manacles
that swung lazily back and forth. Grimly, his eyes
skimmed over the entire area and he felt a wave of
blackness threaten him; he had to inhale sharply
and steady his mind.

But it did no good. His body began to tremble
violently.

This was a torture chamber. Evidently the one
used to maim and hurt Libby.

Jaxon crossed to the bed, grabbed the chains and
yanked them out of the wall with a huge roar. It did
nothing to abate his fury, but the sadness that now
threatened to overwhelm him was much worse.
How had she survived all of this?

Because of the child . . . their child.

"Jaxon! I think I've found her."

He raced to where Declan was pulling back a huge chunk of debris, and felt his heart literally stop at the sight of a mess of blond hair, intermingled with the unmistakable reddish stain of blood. He fell to his knees, using the strength that only a warrior possessed, and lifted up the remaining slab, his tortured eyes urging Declan to hurry and pull her from the wreckage.

Everything faded to black then. Chaos could be heard from outside, cries lit the night as the wounded huddled out in the jungle, but here, in this tiny enclosed space, all he could see was the matted tangle of blond hair.

He needed her to be alive. He needed her to know he'd never leave her side again.

He grunted with the effort it took to keep the debris from falling back, and watched as Declan gently dislodged Libby from underneath.

There was so much blood. She was covered in it. Thick bile crowded his throat and he felt ill, but still his eyes did not leave her form.

When Declan managed to pull her free, Jaxon released his pent-up breath.

"She's alive and breathing."

He rushed to Declan's side and automatically reached for the limp body, wanting to feel her softness and hold her close.

She was covered in dirt, and so filthy from the black soot that cloaked everything in the immediate vicinity that there was no trace of her milky white skin to be seen.

Jaxon took her from Declan's arms and they quickly exited the ruined building. He drew air deeply into his lungs, then fell to his knees, cuddling her still form close to his heart.

He held her there, close, his nose buried deeply in the side of her neck. And even before the scent clawed its way into his system, he knew. And it killed him.

The woman he held so tenderly in his arms was not his Libby.

Slowly, he held her away from him, taking in the features covered in dirt and ash. The woman was of similar build, but definitely was not the woman he was aching to hold.

Jaxon sat back, feeling crushed. His head swung back toward the wreckage, and the way Declan avoided his burning gaze pissed him off even more.

"She's not in there!" He shouted his words into the chaotic night.

"I know," Declan murmured, before taking the injured woman from his arms and walking away a few paces.

Jaxon's chest felt like it was slowly ripping away from his body, as if someone had taken a large knife, sliced several chunks of his skin and then peeled it away ruthlessly, piece by piece.

He closed his eyes and concentrated, until nothing existed but Libby. He focused, and her image floated in front of him, her large violet eyes so incredibly expressive. So full of mistrust and pain.

His fucking legacy.

That's all he'd ever given her. He clenched his teeth together. He would find her. And he would make it right.

Or it damn well would be the last thing he'd ever do, because he now knew if Libby wasn't in his life, it sure as hell wasn't worth living.

Jaxon's eyes flew open and he sprang to his feet. He threw his shoulders back and calmed the beast inside. He needed to think.

His body screamed at him, wanting to plunge headlong into the jungle and find his mate. But he needed to be smart about this. He couldn't screw this up, not when Libby's life was on the line.

A soft moan grabbed his attention, and his head whipped around, eyes narrowing as the woman in Declan's arms began to pitch forward, her eyes wild with terror. Declan whispered into her ear, and slowly the woman calmed, her limbs going limp once more as she fell against his chest.

He met Declan's eyes and flinched at the knowledge that lay there. The woman had obviously been tortured as well. Bitterly, he thought of Libby out here alone, with no one to help her.

Some warrior he was. How had he not been able to find her these past three years? The bitterness that clogged his mouth made it hard for him to swallow, and his features blackened even more as he watched Cracker and Julian approach. Both men were resigned, and Julian cleared his throat before speaking.

"She was here, Jax," Julian said. "I caught her scent and followed it to a river that's about two miles south of the compound. From there I lost it. I swam to the other side but couldn't pick it up anywhere." He paused before continuing. "There was a man with her."

Jaxon growled long and hard at his brother's words and spat, "Was it the stench of the DaCostas?"

Julian nodded in silence, and they all watched as Jaxon shook his head and moved away from them.

The odd scream echoed eerily on the wind, and the scent of burning wood, vegetation, and bodies filled the air. Darkness blanketed the jungle like a velvety soft sheath of fur, broken only by the glow of fires that would continue to burn for several more hours. The jungle, normally alive with all sorts of nocturnal beings, seemed devoid of life. As if everything with a living, beating heart had been sucked into a vortex and thrown miles from where they were.

Jaxon's voice was raw when he spoke, but the steel that lay at the heart of the jaguar shone through, and there was no mistaking the deadly purpose he held.

"You need to return to base camp. Pack up and get the hell out of here." He turned toward the rest of them suddenly, his face harsh, unyielding. "I'm going to get Libby and I'll join you at the airport."

He began to move away from his team, his eyes meeting each one, realizing he was one member short.

"Where the hell is Jagger?"

His question was fired at Cracker, and he felt frustration claw at him as the soldier hesitated before answering him.

"He's nowhere to be found. I've searched the perimeter. Julian tried to catch his scent in the jungle but it's no use." He shrugged his shoulders, clearly perplexed. "He's gone."

"What do you mean gone? How the hell can he be gone?"

Cracker held Jaxon's eyes, never wavering, his voice steady. "I mean, he's gone. There's not a trace of him around. I don't know what happened to him. He was over by these outbuildings when the planes attacked and now he's not."

"Christ! I don't have time for this shit. I need to find Libby."

Jaxon was so enraged the cat shimmered along his body as mist started to wrap its long fingers around and up the sides of his legs. He moved from them quickly, breathing hard, trying to get his emotions in check.

"Frank DaCosta took Libby."

The soft words hung in the air, coming out of nowhere. Jaxon turned in a rush, nailing the female Declan still held with his black gaze.

"What did you say?"

The woman swallowed hard, obviously scared. But then her eyes widened and her body went rigid. Her piercing gaze ripped through him, and it was full of a dark and extremely malevolent anger.

"You're one of them," she spat, starting to struggle and only relaxing as Declan once more spoke soft words in her ear.

"Who do you think I am?"

"It's not who." The woman's voice was rough and she drew in a ragged breath. "It's what. You're no different than the DaCosta scum. You're all evil."

Jaxon's voice was fierce but soft. "Watch your mouth, little girl. A DaCosta jaguar is but a kitten compared to me."

Her sapphire blue eyes narrowed into twin beams of contempt. Something was off about the woman. Her scent . . . it was different from anything he'd ever encountered. It slapped at some distant memory, but he didn't have patience to sort out the puzzle.

His gaze swung up until he met Declan's. "Take her back to camp." He looked to Julian and Cracker. "I want you two to look for Jagger. He's got to be around someplace . . . maybe he's unconscious; I don't know. You two deal with it and get the hell back to camp."

Then Jaxon peered out into the gloom. He couldn't think about Jagger right now, he had to concentrate on the task at hand. His brother was a warrior and a highly trained soldier. He could survive almost anything. Even though Libby had proved resilient and was tough to the core, he needed to get to her.

The jungle beckoned to him on such a primitive level that his body vibrated with an urgency that could not be denied. He had no choice but to heed its call.

He moved toward the thick foliage that lined the perimeter of the compound, his senses high, his long legs filled with purpose as he broke into a jog. He paused briefly at the edge and turned around.

"I won't return unless I have Libby. I won't leave her out there again."

His eyes washed over the still form of his brother and the remaining members of his team. "If I'm not back by the time the plane is ready to leave . . ."

His voice trailed off, and with a curt nod he turned and disappeared into the thick, silent jungle, his heart black and filled with the need for revenge.

If he wasn't back in time, they could leave without him, because he would not return to the United States alone.

His heart contracted painfully at the thought. If he didn't make it out of the jungle with Libby, then this was where he would die.

He snarled as he silently twisted through the thick, verdant forest floor, and he'd damn well take out as many DaCostas as he could along the way.

Chapter 21

The faint buzzing of an insect whistled close to her ear, and Libby gritted her teeth, flinching as it closed in on her exposed, pale flesh. Her entire arm was already covered in angry looking welts, so one more wouldn't make a difference, but still she winced as the little bastard bit her but good, and it stung for several seconds before becoming as numb as all the other bites.

She cursed silently. Her hair was plastered to her neck and face, scraggly tendrils of blond that tickled even as they annoyed the crap out of her. She wanted so badly to push the mess away and to scratch, and to—her heart took off like a rocket as blackness ran thickly through her veins—*fucking kill* the bastard who stood just a few feet away from her.

But of course she could do none of this, since her hands were tied behind her back. She tried to calm her pulsing heart and slow her adrenaline. She needed to conserve her strength if she wanted to make it out of here alive.

She had to. There was no alternative.

Her eyes slowly trailed along the back of the man she hated more than anyone else. His tubby build was a direct contrast to the fact that he was a jaguar warrior, a piss poor one, but a formidable enemy nonetheless.

She'd been pulled along behind Fat Frank for well over two hours. On top of the almost six hour hike she'd put in just to reach the compound, it had been one hell of a long day, and the next several hours promised to be even more of a challenge.

Her eyes bored into the back of his skull, and all sorts of ways to maim and torture flashed before her. She couldn't remember ever hating this much. Not even when she was at her lowest point over the last few years, and survived on a diet of revenge and hatred, had she felt this all-consumed with such evil thoughts—not even for Jaxon.

Jaxon.

She'd heard the blasts echoing through the night, and another chunk of her heart broke at the thought of him possibly dead or gravely injured. Her eyes closed as she envisioned his face. If she tried hard enough, she could still smell the headiness of their lovemaking from the night before, feel the slickness of his skin as they moved together.

Her body ached, inside and out, so much so that it was almost paralyzing.

"What's got you so down, bitch?"

Frank's harsh words and careless laughter fell

over her head as she looked away from him. She calmed her spirit and turned eyes that were both dull and lifeless toward him. She had to keep up the pretense. There was no way Frank could think of her in any way other than pathetic and weak.

"You told me you were taking me to my son. Where is he?" Libby kept her face devoid of expression, but inside, her heart was pounding madly against her chest.

Frank's dark eyes regarded her in silence. They narrowed, and she felt like spitting in his stupid ass face. He wasn't extremely bright. She had always been able to tell when he was thinking. It took a lot of energy for him to do that sometimes.

"All in good time." He continued to regard her, his eyes shifting and wavering until she felt uncomfortable. Something was up. The silence that stretched between the two of them lasted several minutes before he spoke again.

"I know my brothers don't think I'm very smart, but this time . . ." His voice trailed off as he laughed once more. "This time I'm the one that knows more than they do."

"Yeah? And what's that Frank?"

"Well, wouldn't you like to know? I'm not stupid! I ain't gonna spill." He turned from her. "All in good time."

Libby felt frustration bubble in her gut. "Aren't you afraid Jaxon and his boys are coming for you?"

"Jaxon? You're kidding, right? Did you not hear the big explosions?"

Libby blanched at his words, knowing there was a very real possibility he was right.

"They're all dead. All of 'em. So don't be thinking

any of the big bad Castille jaguars are coming after you. Shit, we had you for three years and they never came. What makes you think this time will be any different?"

Defiantly, Libby held his gaze steady, while her belly took a nosedive and the nausea that roiled inside her gut threatened to spill over. With conscious effort she put all thoughts of Jaxon and the rest of the team to the back of her mind. She had survived out here for three long torturous years, and she was so close to finding out the truth, *to finding her son*, she couldn't blow it now.

The only person she could count on was herself.

She was in charge of her own destiny, and everything that had happened to her since she'd first laid eyes on Jaxon Castille led her to this moment.

Every single act of torture, humiliation, and intimidation that she endured over the past three years had only made her stronger. She could feel it now, sizzling along inside of her, electrifying every cell in her body.

She was meant to be here, and in some insane part of her mind she truly felt more alive than ever before.

Abruptly, Frank broke from her and pulled something from his pocket. It was a phone that must have been on vibrate. He hesitated before answering, and Libby was sure his hands trembled as he nestled the small device against his ear. She tried to calm her nerves while struggling to listen in on his conversation.

She knew that whoever was on the other end was the person in charge, the one pulling his strings. Yanking them would be more accurate. Sweat began to bead along Frank's forehead, and as he continued to listen, small rivers of liquid slid down his bloated face and dripped from the end of his nose.

The man was clearly nervous, and Libby strained harder to hear a voice, something to help her figure out what all of this meant. She had gone to the compound with the express purpose of forcing Frank to give her the necessary information she would need to find her son. She had not been prepared for him to offer to take her directly to Logan.

So she'd agreed to go with him willingly. Really, what other choice did she have? Jaxon and his team were on their way, and if Frank were killed, she would never find her boy. Right now he was the only link she had to Logan, and even if it led nowhere, she had to at least try.

She moved her butt a little to the right and found a modicum of relief from the sharp blade of the knife she'd shoved down her pants, as it eased away from her skin. Her gun was tucked away as well, up high near her left thigh.

She sighed softly to herself. It had seemed a little too easy, but then again, she was dealing with someone who was missing more than a few brain cells. Anyone else would have found her weapons. But Frank was a certifiable moron, who used his bulk and enhanced physical power to intimidate and maim. He was nothing more than a thug.

And his time was coming. How she was going to enjoy exacting her revenge.

Libby watched as his eyes furtively crossed over her, and she resumed her hunched over stance. Was she mistaken or had his color turned gray?

He mumbled a few more words into the phone and then quickly crossed back to where she stood, his breaths coming in quick bursts as they wheezed their way out of his lungs.

She began to feel a growing tingle of concern. The fact that he was obviously scared shitless really didn't bode well for her.

He grabbed the rope he'd tied to her waist, and she raised an eyebrow as he tugged her along behind him once more.

She dug the heels of her boots deep into the moist earth, feeling a sense of glee as he whipped back around to face her, anxious and on edge.

"What the fuck are you trying to pull now? Do you want me to hurt you?"

"I want you to untie me, asshole. I can't keep this pace up with my hands behind my back."

She shook her head, trying to use the whole female in distress thing. It had worked for her many times in the past.

"Look," she said, "I volunteered to come with you. I want my son. I'm not going anywhere other than where you're headed, so untie my hands and we can get there twice as fast."

He studied her, his face harsh and pinched in the waning evening light.

He swore and cursed a blue streak but yanked on the rope, pulling her closer, until she was lodged firmly against his chest. His breath was hot against her cheek, and she felt revulsion as his body odor washed over her.

Libby tried to lean away from him, but his lips found their way to the side of her neck, and as he spoke, a rash of goose bumps spread like fire across her skin.

"You try anything, *anything*, and I will gut you like a pig. You'll never see your son, you hear?"

She nodded her head in silence, biting her lips in an effort to stifle the disgust lodged in the back of her throat. His meaty fingers wove their way between the tight rope and her skin, and with a swift, assured stroke he cut the rope from her waist and turned her around to do the same to the bindings around her wrists.

The relief she felt as the pressure lessened was short-lived. He pushed her along in front of him, barking orders and maneuvering her toward some destination that only he knew. Her wrists were raw, chafed, and coated with dried blood. She did her best to rub some feeling back into them, picking up the pace as an urgent need to see this night end pounded through her.

For surely there would be closure of some sorts. She just hoped she came out on the winning side of this war she'd stepped into.

They hiked through rugged terrain, and she knew if her sense of direction was correct, they were heading away from the Caribbean and west toward the border that divided Belize from Guatemala. A faint buzzing rang in her ears and at first puzzled her, but as she concentrated on the noise, she realized it was Frank's phone. He was pointedly ignoring the summons.

They had just crested a hill when a roaring, thunderous sound reached her. Fine, wet mist caressed her cheeks, and she realized they were near a huge waterfall. Her tongue, swollen from thirst, dryly licked at her chapped lips. Frank was breathing hard as well and stopped for a second, reaching into his pack and grabbing a bottle of water, from which he drank deeply, not caring that a great amount trickled out the corner of his mouth and down his chin.

Libby averted her eyes. She would not beg for a drink. She was close to a water source and would wait until then to quench her thirst. She watched as the large warrior wiped beads of sweat from his face. It had been pouring freely from him since they resumed their march through the jungle, and once more she was struck by how tense he seemed.

An uneasy feeling slithered through her belly as he motioned for her to continue. Her legs carried her forward, and no matter how hard she tried, her pace had slowed significantly. But for whatever reason, Frank seemed content to keep time with her, and she massaged her side, finally acknowledging the sharp pain that had come back with a vengeance.

Her eyes were dark with anger as she shot a glance toward Frank, but he was preoccupied and his own were trained much farther away. Bastard! He was the reason her ribs had been broken in the first place. She remembered it clearly now, and scowled into the darkness as it rushed through her mind, painted fresh and vibrant with color, as if it had happened only yesterday.

He'd been pissed off over something, but with Fat Frank, there always was something. He had come to her prison, his manner loud and aggressive. At that point she had shared her quarters with another woman, a blonde who didn't talk much.

The other woman had instigated a confrontation, and now that she thought of it, Libby was sure she was trying to force a situation that would result in her own escape. Of course that didn't happen, and in a fit of rage Frank lashed out, attacking both of them, kicking Libby in the ribs with all his might, breaking at least two.

She hadn't laid eyes on him again until she walked into her former prison just a few hours earlier. She was surprised to see that the blond woman was still there, defiant and surprisingly still alive.

Libby didn't care. The mystery woman was no concern of hers.

Frank came to a sudden stop, and her mind quickly moved from memories of the past to take in the magnificent falls that cascaded down before her. She cranked her head upward, but the night was thick with a velvety blanket of darkness, and she couldn't see how far up it went. The roar was intense, so she assumed the drop was extremely steep.

Eerie tendrils of fog slithered along the ground, fingering their way outward from the mist that surrounded the fast moving water. Libby took a step back, sensing a darkness that infiltrated the fog as if something, *or someone*, was using it as some sort of conduit to get to them.

It was malevolent. It was evil.

Her mouth went dry as she felt coldness creep into her bones, and her feelings intensified. She held back a yelp as the fog wrapped its long tentacles around her ankles, sliding along her legs and up her body. She took a step back as she sensed a presence, and peered into the gloom, wanting to know, needing to see who her enemy was.

"What is this place?" she whispered, more to herself than to him.

"Shut up and follow me. Keep quiet and for God sakes don't touch anything."

Libby shot Frank a puzzled look, but obediently followed him as he began to pick his way around the large boulders and moved toward the side of the steep cliff. The malevolent feeling continued to follow her, and she shivered with cold. She wasn't sure if it was because she was now soaking wet from the water in the air or because she knew there was something there.

Watching her. Waiting.

Anger surged and rushed from her belly up to her heart, and she began to walk with purpose, her head held high. Her entire frame hummed with repressed energy, and the adrenaline rush warmed her skin.

Frank continued to climb, and she followed suit. They reached a ledge, and now that she was closer she could see an entrance to a cave behind the cascading buckets of water. Frank looked back and motioned her forward.

She snickered silently. *Coward!* Pushing her way past him, she carefully picked a path over an extremely slippery rock face. The spray of mist drenched her even more, but she welcomed the purity of its wetness.

As she moved deeper past the edge, she could see a large opening about ten feet ahead. Within seconds they were both inside the cave. It took a few more moments for her eyes to adjust, but once they did, she had no problem seeing clearly. An eerie glow lit the entire area, which consisted of a smallish entrance with a large passageway beckoning to the right.

Frank pushed her roughly from behind, and Libby gritted her teeth, her fingers itching to pull the gun from her side and put a bullet between his eyes. She stumbled forward and entered the passage, glancing around as she made her way deeper into the cave.

What she saw stunned her.

The rock walls were covered in an intricate series of paintings and pictures that she recognized as N'ahuatl, the language of the Aztecs. She was sure of it. She'd seen many artifacts with similar type etchings in Jaxon's home. She frowned at that, thinking it didn't make sense. The Aztecs had lived and flourished in Mexico, as least according to Jaxon.

Why was there evidence of Aztecs so far south, in Belize? An uneasy lump formed deep in her gut, and as she continued along, she felt as if she were being allowed to witness a small piece of a very large puzzle. One that had fragmented, with certain key elements remaining elusive.

One overwhelming theme was evident. Most of the drawings depicted large black jaguars and equally large, impressive eagles. They seemed to be at war among each other, and at the center of all of it, a large dark disc appeared to be the prize.

Libby's attention to the wall quickly fled as the soft glow sharpened. Up ahead she could see that the narrow passage opened up, widening into a much larger room.

As she stepped into the cavern, she was indeed in awe. To say this room was larger would have been a gross understatement. She looked around, her face incredulous as the sheer size of the cavern rose up in front of her eyes. She cranked her head back and calculated the ceiling at well over five hundred feet.

In the middle of the space a huge well of water rippled smoothly as it slid by and disappeared beneath the ground, most likely joining the rush of water that raced down the side of the cliff. Beneath the liquid glass, a beam of soft green shone through, and the entire area was lit in a hazy, luminescent swath of light.

She noted several passageways that jutted out from the large cavern, going God knows where, and as she continued to study the area, she couldn't help but shiver again. The feeling of blackness that she'd experienced earlier flew at her in a rush, and her eyes frantically tried to find the source. Something evil was here.

And it wanted her.

Frank remained quiet and stood still a few feet away from her, his posture nervous and submissive.

A sound to the right startled them both, and she heard Frank curse behind her as a large bulky man made his way into the cavern. He was tall, his chest bare, the tattoos that proclaimed him a warrior evident as he walked toward them. The man was a wall of muscle, and the sneer that graced his mouth went along with the arrogance that fell from him in waves.

He was not someone to be messed with.

He stopped a few feet from them before Libby recognized him. He had been at the DaCosta compound more than once while she was imprisoned there.

"He's waiting. You are to leave and not return until he contacts you, Frank." The large man had a deep, lifeless voice, and his eyes were cruel, devoid of any feeling. He nodded toward her, indicating that she follow him, but Frank had his own ideas.

"Carlos, that was not the plan and you know it. How do I know you're telling the truth? How do I know you're not trying to take the prize that is mine by right?" Frank's belligerence grew as his confidence began to simmer once more. "You've always wanted to be a true DaCosta, but you'll never be more then what you are. A warrior for hire."

Frank spat at the ground and while his focus remained on the warrior slowly closing the small gap between them, Libby began to inch away toward the nearest passage, Frank's whine echoing along the limestone cavern.

"He asked me to bring him the blonde, and it will be me who delivers the bitch straight into his arms."

The approaching warrior roared his displeasure and suddenly charged. Libby leapt out of the way and watched in disbelief as he began to transform into his jaguar form. Frank began to shift as well, but she wasn't planning on watching the fireworks. She took off at a run and headed straight toward the opening. It was only a few feet away, and she disappeared through it without a glance back.

There, the air felt thick, and it was darker. The sounds of battle ceased as a bloodcurdling scream rent the air. Libby stopped, her chest heaving and heart pounding nearly out of her chest. She found herself drawn back to where she'd just come from, as if an invisible string was pulling at her, and the macabre display there almost brought her to her knees.

She crept forward, not even pretending to have control over her impulses, felt the blood draining from her face at the sight that greeted her.

One of the jaguars was suspended, high in the air, held up by some invisible force. The body turned slowly, and she could see the animal struggling to breathe. Fog crept up from the gentle swell of water far below, weaving its way around the body as the animal writhed in agony. She continued to watch, helpless, as the fog morphed into a darker entity, seeming to pull at the creature, and indeed she realized that's exactly what was happening.

The animal's cries lessened as its very essence was sucked from within, and as the wisps of fog slithered back toward the water, the limp and lifeless body of Frank DaCosta stared back at her, his eyes shot full of black, dead.

Libby held her hand to her mouth as a scream threatened to rip its way through her throat, and she watched in disbelief as his body fell nearly thirty feet and slipped beneath the calm water, leaving not even a ripple in his wake.

Terror clawed at her as she turned and began to run down the passage, her thoughts incoherent and jumbled. She'd come here for her son, but did she honestly think he was here?

Alive?

The passage narrowed and she had to slow her pace, but the need to flee continued to propel her. Something was here, with her. The hair on the back of her neck began to vibrate and tingle, as if reacting to an electrical charge, and sharp edges of pain radiated inside her brain.

The pressure intensified to the point that it brought her to her knees and she was truly afraid her head would burst, so raw and intense were the feelings.

Anguish lit her chest on fire and her hands cupped her cranium. She tried to get up but it was no use.

Everything else dulled, and the ache between her ears was constant. She squeezed her eyes shut and tried to count, and as panic nipped at her, she struggled to breathe. It was then that she became aware of him. She could see two feet planted in front of her, and they belonged to a large man, judging by the size of his boots. Expensive leather boots, from what she could see.

He crouched down in front of her and she flinched as a large, warm hand extended down and cupped her chin, forcing her eyes upward.

He was handsome, of that there was no doubt. Devastatingly so. Dark hair shot through with silver crowned his head. But his eyes were dead, devoid of any emotion. She blinked slowly, feeling her brain liquefy as a myriad of memories rushed through her. They left her breathless, and her chest constricted in an effort to draw air into her lungs. The world shrank away into the rock face at her back, until she was aware of nothing except the man who held her so gently.

A man whose long, well-manicured fingers were strangely familiar. She focused on them, and felt the last part of her shattered memory shift into place. Like the final piece of a puzzle.

He continued to regard her in silence for what seemed ages, and when he finally spoke, his voice washed over her like broken glass.

"Hello, Libby. Been a long time, no?"

Chapter 22

The serene quiet of the jungle was in total contrast to the emotions that ran through Jaxon as he slashed his way deeper into the interior. He had caught Libby's scent on the other side of the river, her sweet musky odor tainted with the stink of the DaCosta bastard who had her.

The thought of his enemy's hands on his woman left him filled with a cold, deadly fury. He fed on it, and right now all of his energy was focused on one thing.

He would bring Libby home, or he would die trying.

He inhaled the heady sweet air that lingered thickly in the extensive range of greenery that surrounded him. The power of the jungle called to his primitive nature, and his senses were electrified, strangely enhanced over and above their already considerable abilities.

Jaxon stood still for a second, his eyes closed as he concentrated on her scent. Satisfied that he was on the right path, he took off at a run, his long legs carrying him forward with great speed as he jumped over rotting logs and an abundance of lush vegetation at his feet. His eyes quickly scanned the path he had chosen, looking for signs that someone had recently passed by. He felt a surge of adrenaline rush through him when he came upon a clearing and noticed two sets of footfalls embedded in the soft earth.

He knelt down, his fingers reaching out to trace the pattern of the smaller of the two. A sound off in the distance stilled him, and he continued to study the ground while sending his senses out on the wind in search of the disturbance he felt.

Someone was here. With him, right now.

His heart began to beat faster and he felt his skin burn as his body heated with anger. His jaw clenched tightly as he continued to hold his position, a position he didn't like, as his back was extremely vulnerable to attack.

Something was off. He knew there was a presence here in the jungle, not far from where he was, but he couldn't tell what it was. Human? No, definitely not. But what the hell was it?

His senses began to scream at him, and he exhaled hard before whirling around and bringing his right leg around in a wide circle. He grunted as it came into contact with something solid, something definitely made of flesh and bone, that toppled from the force of his hit.

Jaxon sprang to his feet as a body fell in front of him, a litany of vile curses following it down.

"Jesus! Fuck, Jax!"

Declan's hoarse shout brought Jaxon up short, and he stood there, heart pounding, body raging with adrenaline. He kicked at the ground and growled deeply from his belly.

"What the hell are you doing? I ordered your ass back to base. I need to know that Ana and Julian make it to the plane."

Declan slowly got to his feet and spat dirt from his mouth. "Ah, last time I looked, Jaxon, I wasn't taking orders from you. I'm along for the ride because I want to be. I need to see this thing through to the end just as much as you do," his eyes narrowed, "and I sure as hell wasn't gonna let you run off into the jungle half cocked, with no backup."

Declan's white teeth slashed through the night as he smiled crookedly. "Besides, I brought a few goodies to help us out."

Jaxon's eyes narrowed as the tall Irishman patted the satchel slung around his shoulder. He snorted, and grudgingly acknowledged to himself that Declan's help would definitely be an asset.

He turned once more and scented the air, indicating they would keep heading west. Declan's long legs fell easily in step with his own, and they kept up a quick pace for several minutes before Jaxon stopped abruptly.

His nostrils quivered as a new scent washed over him. Dread began to pool in his belly and he knelt down, studying the earthen ground, seeking the source of his distress. Over by a thick grouping of trees he spied a long piece of twine amidst the greenery, the ends frayed and raw. His muscles clenched at the unmistakable smell of blood that was heavy in the air.

Libby's blood.

Heart pounding, he ran forward and snatched up two large bits of rope that had been cut. One was much longer than the other, but it was the smaller one that had the beast inside him clawing for vengeance. It had obviously been used to bind her hands, and the rope was covered in her blood from where it had dug into her soft skin.

Jaxon began to pant, and he felt his animal shimmer just below the surface. Blackness coiled its way along the edge of his brain, and he found it hard to maintain his human form. He growled loudly, and when Declan would have grabbed the twine from him, he roared his disapproval and moved away from his friend, needing space and time to quiet the violent rumblings that circulated frenetically through his veins.

He grasped the twine between strong fingers and brought it to his face, inhaling Libby's sweet scent. When he got his hands on Frank DaCosta, he was going to rip him apart, limb by limb, and he would put a hurt on that piece of scum, the likes of which he'd never done before.

It took him a few seconds before Jaxon dimly realized that Declan was speaking, then he let the low, cool tones of his friend bring him back from the edge. He was able to focus, and slowly the red haze receded from his eyes.

"So, Frank just let her loose?"

Jaxon met Declan's gaze, and didn't like what Declan had implied. He didn't answer but his mouth tightened into a frown.

"Hey, I'm just saying it's kinda weird. Don't you think he'd be afraid she would bolt?"

"I don't know what to think, Dec, about any of this." His voice was hoarse and his mind was moving quickly in all sorts of directions. Why the hell *would* he free her from her bindings? It didn't make sense.

"Are they still together? Did she run?"

Jaxon studied the immediate area and moved along a few more feet before crouching low to the ground. After a few moments he spoke quietly. "Yeah, they're still together. She's leading and he's following."

Declan shrugged his shoulders but his face had darkened as he worked through this surprising development. "Maybe she wants to be with him."

Jaxon's head whipped up and he snarled. "What the hell do you mean by that? Why the fuck would she willingly go along with the bastard who tortured her for three years?"

"That, my friend, is the million dollar question, now isn't it? What do we really know about Libby Jamieson?"

The jaguar shattered through the thin coating of control Jaxon still had, and with a fierce growl, he pinned Declan to a tree, his claws ripping through bark. He panted, unsure and extremely agitated, his forearms half shifted into the deadly paws of his jaguar.

Calmly, Declan offered no resistance as Jaxon roared his anguish deep into the night. Jaxon's entire body trembled with the effort it took to tame his animal, and when he was finally able to restore a certain amount of control, Declan gently disengaged himself and moved several feet away, giving his friend a moment to collect himself before he spoke his piece.

"My point is that there isn't a whole hell of a lot we know about her. Her info sheet back at PATU was bare bones. She was adopted at the age of six by a couple of average, ordinary Americans. She was always at the top of her class, blew through her training at Quantico, and somehow managed to get herself attached to our unit, and we don't deal with humans." Declan shook his head. "This whole situation stinks is all. I'm just saying that we're missing a huge part of the puzzle."

Jaxon's face had turned to stone and his voice was low, coated with steel, and so very quiet that Declan had to strain to hear his words.

"I'm going to bring Libby back. You can come along, but so help me God, if you dare to question her integrity or allegiance—we're done."

Declan watched as Jaxon turned abruptly and melted into the trees. He hissed in anger, but without pause followed in the footsteps of the man he'd trust with his very life. He just hoped that Libby was deserving of such devotion and loyalty.

The two men did not speak as they slowly climbed higher. A light rain had begun to mist, and the insects that buzzed around them intensified. The trek became much more arduous as they went on, and Jaxon led them with stealth across small streams and up several sheer rock faces as they climbed higher with a ferocious intensity.

It was now predawn, and Jaxon was beginning to wonder how Libby had managed this trek. The heat and humidity alone was killer, but with the coming rain, the bugs were incessant and their appetite for skin and blood voracious.

Her scent was becoming stronger, and he felt relief as he realized he was closing in on his prey. A distant roar that had been muffled for a while now had become more thunderous and as they crested a small rise, the crescendo of a large waterfall was almost deafening.

She was there, all around him, her sweet scent lingering amidst the earth, the trees, and even across the water that sparkled as it fell from well over five hundred feet above him to several hundred below.

Jaxon sensed that there was more than just his woman here in this jungle paradise. His body began to tingle as his cells reacted to some unseen menace. There was a foul odor that lay like a heavy blanket over the entire area, and he turned his head, nostrils quivering as he scented the breeze that whooshed down from above, riding the fast moving water to the bottom.

He was uneasy, not comfortable with the smells and darkness that emanated from behind the glorious facade of the waterfall.

Declan fell into step beside him, and his curse only deepened the anxiety already riding Jaxon hard. He looked to the tall soldier whose tight-lipped demeanor did nothing to dispel the notion that this place, this small drop of paradise, was to be the final act in the most bizarre week of his life.

"What is it?" Jaxon asked.

He watched as the man of magick took pause, face devoid of emotion as he turned to answer his question. When he spoke, the words were spat from his mouth, as contempt and bitterness washed through him.

"There is some deep shit going on here, Jax. Dark arts, really fucking strong dark arts, are at play. I'm positive it's the same signature from Manhattan, and most likely the same sig that I felt in Drake's office, back in Washington."

Declan's long fingers began to weave a spell in the air, and sparks flew and sizzled as if some unseen force field was in place. He frowned and closed his eyes, to chant in an ancient language that only a fellow mage would have been able to understand.

Jaxon stood beside him, feeling the power his friend was tapping into. The earth began to vibrate beneath his feet, and the energy that surrounded them burned hot. He realized then, for the first time, just how much power Declan was capable of producing. He was no ordinary man of magick, and the wind whipped furiously as fog wound toward them along the ground but stopped just short of where the two men stood.

Abruptly, Declan stopped chanting and turned to Jaxon, his eyes blackened from the source of his magick. "There's an entrance there," he said, pointing up to a steep ledge that ran alongside the waterfall and disappeared behind the cascading wetness. "We'll have the advantage of surprise on our side, but we're sure to be outnumbered."

"Do you know who it is?"

Declan paused before answering, a little too long for Jaxon's liking, but shook his head before murmuring, "No, but he's powerful and stinks to high heaven of depravity, greed, and rotting flesh. He's feeding off souls, both innocent and not. He doesn't care about anything other than himself. He's looking for something, and he's right pissed off that he hasn't found it yet."

Declan grabbed his satchel and opened it quickly. Jaxon grabbed two guns and a knife, feeling the tension that hummed along his friend's body. "Libby is not what he's looking for," Declan added. "I can sense her in there."

At Jaxon's raised eyebrows, he continued harshly, "If Libby were his prize, she'd be dead already."

Jaxon grabbed extra ammo, both anticharm and a shitload of the regular grade, shoving them anywhere there was room. With his weapons loaded and ready, he looked to Declan, suddenly very glad the Irishman had decided to join him in this fight. He had a feeling it was going to get intense, and there wasn't another soldier on the planet he'd rather have covering his back, and he knew Dec felt the same.

"Let's do this."

Jaxon began to pick his way quickly over the slippery boulders that lined the sides of the waterfall. It didn't take them long before they were able to squeeze through a narrow passage that led directly behind the fast moving water and into a long dark tunnel.

There, the air was cool, caressing their cheeks as it was sucked from within and flung outside to tumble alongside the falling water. It was also thick with menace, and Jaxon grasped his gun tightly, his senses on high alert, eyes quickly scanning an interior that while dim, emanated eerily with a faint greenish glow.

He could smell Libby strongly inside the tight

dark passage, and his heart sped up at the thought of being so close to her.

Slowly, they made their way along the narrow entrance. He could smell fear, and along the edges of his mind, recognized the pungent odor of death. It left an intense feeling of distaste in his mouth, and he snarled lightly in reaction to the violence that accompanied it.

Declan motioned toward the walls, and Jaxon noticed a vast array of pictures and etchings that were obviously Aztec. His heart leapt at the unique and magnificent drawings of jaguars and eagles.

He didn't think that the Aztecs had ever foraged this far south. He shook his head and moved on. What the pictures meant was anyone's guess. He had no time to try to decipher it. He needed to find his mate and get her the hell away from there.

Something skirted quickly across his mind, and he held his fist up, both men coming to a silent standstill. He clutched his gun tightly in his right hand as the scent of his enemy drifted down the passage toward them. He looked to Declan, and they began to move again, carefully picking their way forward, eyes and ears on high alert.

There were several warriors up ahead; he could sense them, feel their nervous energy as they lazed about with nothing to do.

Declan had placed an invisibility ward around them, so their enemies would not know they were being hunted, until it was too late.

Jaxon smiled savagely, feeling the power that rippled along his forearms and spread like fire along each and every cell in his body.

They inched their way forward, the greenish light that lit the tunnel growing brighter as they reached the opening that led into a magnificent cavern. At any other time, Jaxon would have appreciated the wild vast area that surrounded him, but his attention was focused solely on five soldiers who were grouped together, talking among themselves in hushed tones.

They were all jaguar warriors, two from the Da-Costa clan, the other three with tattoos he didn't recognize immediately. No matter. They were his enemy, and they would die at his hands.

Declan aimed his gun dead center at the tallest one, who stood in the middle, and Jaxon set his sights on the dark warrior to the far right of the group. They would reduce their numbers by two, but warriors were fast, especially elite jaguars, and they most likely wouldn't have time to fire off another round.

In perfect sync, Jaxon and Declan fired their guns, their targets a blur even as the shots echoed loudly inside the cavern, bouncing off the rock face and slamming back at them. The two intended victims went down as planned, bright red blood seeping from their fatal wounds and leeching into the crystal-like water that flowed quickly by them.

Angry snarls rent the air, and Declan balled energy into his hands, feeding off the black negativity that hung so thick in the air. He flung the red hot balls of crackling energy at the warrior who charged toward him, and he crashed back into the water along with the warrior, before disappearing beneath the glasslike surface.

Jaxon had no time to react, as a warrior in the

process of shifting jumped to the right of him and another ran toward him, eyes blackened in blood lust. He let the large warrior fall into him, taking him down as he plunged his large knife deep into the man's gut. The warrior shouted in rage and his face distorted as the shift started to fall over his features.

Jaxon's animal answered in kind, and he felt his bones elongate and pop as his skin burned away, leaving shiny black fur in its wake. He snarled savagely and twisted his great body as his clothes fell in tatters to his feet.

The wounded jaguar lunged toward him, and the two great beasts rolled end over end, with Jaxon landing hard against a sharp boulder that edged the side of the stream. The smell of blood was heavy in his nostrils, and the rage that overcame him pushed his jaguar forward, his huge paws swiping at the enemy and knocking him off of his body.

Jaxon twisted away and leapt up, meeting the other jaguar in midair, and when he landed on top of him, his jaw clamped down hard on the jugular, his great canines piercing through the soft skin that lay there. He tasted the blood and life essence now seeping uncontrollably from his enemy's neck, and with a mighty roar he struck, his powerful jaw crushing the skull of the great cat and killing him instantly.

His mind felt muddied, awash with the thick haze and adrenaline rush of the kill, and he barked his victory, snarling as he jumped from the lifeless body of his enemy.

He had no time to process his kill, as his body warned him of an attack. He turned, but not in time, as the second jaguar pounced on him from behind. This animal was heavier and fully engaged in the heat of battle. Jaxon pushed his body to the edge as he tried to shake the heavy beast from his back, knowing that the animal's powerful jaw could kill him as easily as he'd just done to its brethren.

He managed to unseat the cat, and had just gained his own feet when a blast of energy rocked the jaguar back several feet, followed by the snap of a gunshot. The animal took another step, then fell into a heap of fur, blood, and flesh as his feet.

Jaxon stood, sides quivering from battle, and glanced back at Declan. He had managed to climb from the water and take out the remaining warrior. They looked at each other in silence, and he followed Declan over to the bodies of the first two warriors they'd killed.

He watched as the sorcerer crouched down, studying the fallen enemy. Slowly, Jaxon began to shift back into his human form, feeling alarmed by Declan's gray complexion as his friend turned back to him.

"Declan? What is it?"

"I don't fucking believe it."

Jaxon wiped the remnants of blood from his hands, not liking his tone, or Declan's tense body language. His friend looked ill, and his concern grew as Declan struggled to speak.

"I just . . . I thought he was—" Declan inhaled sharply and closed his eyes.

"What the hell are you talking about?"

Declan shook his head, and met Jaxon's eyes with a bleakness he wasn't used to seeing. "My father . . .

this is my father. The dead warriors have his mark on their flesh."

"Mark? What kind of mark? What the fuck are you talking about?"

"When a sorcerer binds someone to them, in any way, they leave a mark. It's a symbol of their ownership." Declan's voice was subdued as he continued. "These men have my father's mark on their necks." He pointed to a small crescent-shaped tattoo on the dead warrior's necks.

"But your father is dead, killed years ago. Wasn't he?"

Declan turned from Jaxon, his voice still full of shock, "Apparently not."

Jaxon's steel resolve wavered.

Shit.

That couldn't be good.

He remained silent, watching the myriad emotions affecting Declan.

Energy crackled and sparks flew from his fingers as Declan's face darkened with the realization that his father, whom he'd thought long gone, was somehow involved in all of this craziness. His mouth thinned into a hard line of disgust and he shook his head, clearly not understanding any of it.

"I don't know what to say, Jax."

Declan swore under his breath, and flexed his hands as his anger continued to generate small currents of electricity that hummed and flew about the large cavern.

Jaxon glanced back at the dead bodies and a sense of urgency rippled through him. He quickly crossed over to where his clothes lay in a pile and tossed the completely ruined shirt aside. His pants had fared slightly better, and he grimly pulled them over his long legs before grabbing his boots.

He turned to Declan. "Okay, we need to find Libby. Are you okay with this?"

Declan's eyes met his, and Jaxon clenched his jaw as his old friend paused and then whispered hoarsely, "Let's do this."

He started to move away, then paused. "I deal with my father. Got it?"

Jaxon didn't bother answering, just grabbed his weapons and moved deeper into the large cavern. He closed his eyes and concentrated on isolating Libby's scent. It was there, but elusive.

There were a series of tunnels jutting out into different directions, but he quickly turned to the right and headed toward the last passage. As he stepped into the darkened interior, her unique odor caught at him full tilt.

It punched him straight in the gut, actually. He began to pant as his senses picked up the remnants of her emotions. They hung in the air, mocking him. Pain, confusion, and incredible terror slapped him in the face, and it stung.

Libby was in danger, and he felt like a third fucking tit, less than useless.

He whipped around, and his nose touched on a secondary scent that until then had eluded him.

It was strangely familiar. He closed his eyes and took his time, his mouth watering in agitation as he let the scent wash over his pallet. It was eerily like Declan's, but tinged with a foulness that almost made him gag.

His eyes flew open and he began to run down

the tunnel, Declan hard on his heels. She had been there, but her scent was faint. His heart was pounding hard, and the adrenaline was once more kicking in. Jaxon reveled in the flush of power that lay just under his skin, and his eyes were glowing as he neared the end of the tunnel, only to find . . . absolutely nothing.

He came to a wild halt, his chest heaving as his head whipped around, turning his body with it.

"Where the fuck is she?" The words were ripped from his throat, and sounded harsh as they echoed off the cold stone walls. His eyes traveled along the passage, glancing past the many drawings of jaguars and eagles.

He could sense her. He knew she was just beyond his reach, and it made him furious. Frustration fueled him, working its way to his outer limbs, and he pounded his fists against the stone, not caring about the blood he left on the smooth rock.

The animal inside of him was so close that Jaxon felt faint from the rush of energy and emotions running with chaotic abandon through his veins.

"Jaxon, over here!"

Declan was crouched low to the ground, back several feet along the tunnel.

Jaxon's long legs carried him over quickly, his eyes narrowing as he watched Declan run his hands over the seam of the wall, where it met the floor.

"There's a protection ward here. It's been placed hastily, just give me a second and I'll get us through."

Jaxon stood back, air hissing through his clenched teeth and watched as Declan wove an intricate series of symbols into the air. They glowed from the energy he was producing, dancing along the wall as if resting on a thin band of smoke.

Within a few moments the wall began to glisten and shimmer. Declan stood up quickly and his long fingers once more traced the length of the wall along the seam. He found a small indent and pressed his finger into it hard.

Jaxon watched in amazement as the large piece of rock slowly moved inward until an entrance lay open to them.

Declan grabbed his satchel, and Jaxon slipped past him, lowering his head to allow himself room to enter the secret tunnel.

It was dark, cold, and clammy. He could smell water ahead somewhere, and increased his pace, moving quickly as his nose caught a small bit of Libby in the air.

She was here and he would find her.

Declan grunted from behind him. "Cormac's mine. Do not touch him."

Jaxon continued forward without pausing.

"Cormac's a dead man. If you don't kill him, I will."

Chapter 23

Libby's mouth was bone dry and her tongue swollen. She opened her eyes slowly, wincing as the remnants of a nasty headache wove their way across her skull. Christ! She hadn't had one of those in . . . She shook her head at a bucketful of memories that came to her.

She trembled as the enormity of them weighed her down. *He was here!* The monster from her dreams was here, in the flesh.

Her eyes few open and she looked around wildly. She was in a small room, one that had been carved from the stone inside of the mountain. She shivered as cool moist air moved freely into the room from a passageway to her right, clinging to her damp skin.

The narrow entrance also allowed the strange greenish glow inside, enabling her to see, though it was still dim. Her eyes seemed to be coated with a film that made it hard to focus, and she shook her head, not liking the sensation.

The relief that washed over her when she realized she was alone was palpable. Her heart beat hard against her chest and she didn't think it would slow anytime soon. She reached for the weapons she'd stashed on her body, and felt deflated when she realized they'd been snatched.

She knew she couldn't waste time brooding over that. She needed to get free and find her son, if in fact he was here in this massive mountain cave. For the first time, Libby acknowledged that this whole exercise might have been for nothing.

She shook her head violently. She could not dwell on that now. She needed to get her ass in gear and search for Logan. She had to at least try. To think that her little boy was somehow mixed up with the likes of Cormac was unbelievable.

He was a monster. Quite simply, evil in the flesh. There were no other words for him. He stank of it and he carried it proudly. She'd met him at the Da-Costa compound, on several different occasions. The dislike she'd felt for him was immediate and well deserved.

For it was Cormac who'd wiped her memories from her mind. It was a painful and brutal assault, and she knew that the bastard had enjoyed every single moment of it.

Her thoughts still jumbled, Libby jumped to her feet, calling on her last vestiges of strength and adrenaline to carry her through. She tried to blot out the image of Fat Frank, suspended high in the air, in excruciating pain as his life force was sucked from him.

Cautiously, she edged her way toward the opening to the tiny room where she'd awoken, pausing for a second to warily look around the corner. She held her breath, making not a sound, and exhaled slowly when she saw that the narrow passage was empty.

Her belly was clenched tight, full of worry as anxious energy clawed at her insides. She felt nauseous, and gingerly wiped her hand across the sweat that beaded her forehead. She could feel the fear that lay in wait, and knew that if she gave in to it, she would never see her son. At this thought, standing straight, squaring her shoulders, she stepped out of the room.

There were a series of holes carved deep into the walls here, and she turned to her left, away from where the glow slithered down from the large cavern. Quickly, she began to methodically check all of the tiny rooms that lined the long stone passage.

They were all empty. Some showed signs of recent occupancy, littered with scattered clothes and empty containers of food, but nothing indicated the presence of a little boy.

The ache that cut across her chest was sharp, and Libby fed on it, using the strength of the emotions to propel her forward. She ducked her head into the last tiny room, then turned back toward where she'd come from.

Quickly, she made her way back down the corridor. When she reached the end, she realized that it didn't connect with the large cavern she'd initially emerged from. This was something else entirely.

Water seemed to be everywhere, and once more, along the far side of this particular cavern, a fast tumbling swatch of water beckoned, its surface glittering like diamonds as it rushed away and disappeared underground.

The walls were adorned with a plethora of writings, etchings, and pictures. All of them, from what she could see, were of Aztec origin, and featured jaguars, eagles, and the same strange looking disc she's seen depicted near the entrance to the cave.

Something along the edge of the far wall caught her eyes, and Libby moved quickly toward it, her heart nearly beating from her chest at the sight of a small object protruding from a mess of rocks near the edge of the fast moving water.

Her long fingers reached out, and with a gentle tug she pulled a small toy free. It was a jaguar, carved from limestone, its surface soft and worn from play. She traced the contours of the animal, rubbing its softness against her cheek before clutching it close to her heart. Sorrow nearly undid her as she envisioned a child playing with the toy.

Her child.

"I see you're awake."

His voice cut through her sharply, and Libby closed her eyes, wishing with all her heart that she'd open them and find herself alone. She felt the hairs on her body stand on end and electrify as the air around her vibrated with the power the man possessed.

Her eyes were still closed but she felt his coldness nearby, his presence spilling out and staining everything in his path with his dark aura.

She felt sick to her stomach just being in such close proximity to him, and she swallowed hard, willing her eyes to open so she could face her nemesis once and for all. For surely, her last moments would be spent here, with him, in this strangely marked cave.

"Where is my son?"

The tall man regarded her in silence, obviously enjoying the fact that he held all the power, and dangling it in front of her like the proverbial golden carrot. Libby wanted nothing more than to smash her fist into his arrogant face.

"He's not here."

Surprise, anger, and then blinding rage rushed through Libby, and her body began to shake with the intensity of it.

She took a step forward but was unable to get any closer to him. It was as if an invisible hand had wrapped itself around her body and she was helpless to prevent it. She felt the pressure increase as it worked its way up her body, and she found it harder to breathe.

Her thoughts were chaotic, but one thing rang crystal clear. She would die here, and she was sure it would not be a quick and efficient death. No, the bastard would make her suffer and enjoy every moment of it.

A sadness deeply embedded in her soul broke through and trickled its way along her psyche. So many things lost. Loves that had slipped through her fingers, and a child she'd never had the chance to love and to watch grow.

She began to struggle as her anguish became physical, but it only served to weaken her already spent and tired body.

Cormac clapped slowly, his black eyes seeming to glow with enjoyment as he watched her struggle.

"I always liked your spunk, Libby. Even when you were no more than a whiny toddler, you still had that spark, that will to win. I knew even then that you were special."

Libby froze at his words. Her eyes were wild, the dark violet centers huge in her pale face.

He laughed, deep from his chest, and she wanted to put her hands over her ears to drown out the maniacal sound.

"Oh yes, Libby, I've known you since before you could walk."

He moved toward her then, his long legs gliding across the rocks. "We have a history you and I . . . long ago. So imagine my surprise when I was asked by the DaCostas to place a mind block on a . . . 'Castille whore,' I think they called you."

He grinned up at her, and Libby realized she was slowly rising through the air.

An image of Frank once more slashed through her brain, and she began to struggle again, not understanding his words, but as the need to survive rose in her, not caring.

"When I learned you'd borne a child, and one made with a jaguar warrior, I knew."

Libby shuddered as his smile became even more pronounced and his features seemed distorted, as if there were another person, or thing, inhabiting his body. His voice was barely above a whisper, and he smiled up at her as if they were old friends.

"I had to have him."

"Where is he?" Her words were ripped from her

throat, her muscles left raw and aching as she listened to her voice echo in the still cavern.

Cormac continued to lazily walk around her suspended body. "Oh Libby, he's not here. Silly of you to think that he was. Nope, actually he's far away from here."

His voice changed then, anger coursing through his words, and Libby flinched at the intensity of his anger. "As should you be," he added, then spat, "Frank DaCosta brought me the wrong girl, and for that he paid with his life."

A sound began to build from deep in the belly of the cavern, slicing its way along the passageways until it burst through to where Cormac stood in front of her. Libby's ears perked and her attention momentarily distracted from him to the narrow crevice that led from where they were.

Jaxon!

The roar of a jaguar was tempered by gunshots, and Libby panicked. She struggled and cursed as the invisible bindings kept her securely suspended twenty feet above the ground.

Cormac slowly moved away from her, his eyes black with amusement.

"Seems as if your jaguar has come to call." He shook his head slowly. "Foolish animals they are." His voice was almost a whisper. "They are not like us, Libby."

She looked at him, her expression incredulous. "Not like us? We're nothing alike, you and I." He was a monster, as close to evil as you could get.

Soft laughter fell from Cormac's lips, but his eyes narrowed as he studied her. His voice slithered across her skin as he whispered, "We're more alike than you know."

Abruptly he turned from her, and Libby suddenly felt like crying, so great was the deluge of emotion that filled her body. She began to pant, in short staccato breaths, and they hung loudly in the air between them. She closed her eyes and concentrated, and a few moments later was able to force out a sentence.

"I just want my son back. I'll do anything . . . anything that you want." She knew she sounded desperate, but she didn't care.

The tall sorcerer paused but didn't turn around. His movements were precise and controlled. Everything about the man was cold and calculated, and the hatred that Libby felt as she gazed down upon him nearly choked her.

"Know this, Libby. Your son is alive, because I wish it. *As are you.*"

Time slowed as his words penetrated her brain and their meaning became clear. He had the power. He had her son. A sob escaped her throat, thick with grief, and her eyes were full of tears as she looked at the calm man in front of her.

"What do you want?"

He spoke clearly, his voice low. "I want Skye Knightly."

Confusion rippled over her in waves. Libby shook her head, not understanding his meaning.

"I don't know . . . who is she?"

"Don't play games with me, Libby. I won't hesitate to kill your child, the same way I wouldn't hesitate to crush an annoying little bug."

Her eyes were huge, but the grief was so great

that Libby couldn't answer. All she could do was stare in terror at the man who regarded her with no emotion at all.

"Skye was your roommate at the DaCosta compound." His eyes bored into hers, and as realization dawned on her, his cruel mouth broke into a sinister grin. "You find a way to get her to me, and I will return your son."

"Why should I believe anything that you say?" The words fell from her lips in a hoarse whisper.

Cormac laughed softly and looked directly into her eyes. Libby saw the truth there even as he spoke. "I have no need to lie."

The sounds of battle ceased, and Cormac moved away from her, edging toward escape. His voice was dispassionate and it was raspy, like sandpaper, "Remember what I said, Libby, the woman for your son."

"But how will I . . . How the fuck will I find you?" Her terror and anger burst from her chest as she shouted down to him.

He paused, and though he didn't speak, she heard his words clear as day, echoing deep inside her skull. They whispered through her mind and she shuddered at the creepy sensation. *I'm not going far so don't fail me now. I already told you . . . we are not so different. Pay attention: you will find me, or you will never see your son alive.*

He disappeared, and Libby screamed in frustration. She struggled wildly then, her body breaking out in a heated wash of sweat. There was no way to break through the charm Cormac had used, but still her body railed against the invisible chains.

How long she struggled, she couldn't know. Her

fury was like a black haze that hung in front of her face, and the taste of her salt tears fed the hunger even more. That such evil had a hold on her child made her sick. Most of his words made no sense to her. She'd been adopted as a six-year-old and had no memory of her younger years. Cormac had insinuated he'd known her as a child.

What the hell did all of it mean? How did it all fit together?

Furiously, her brain tried to decipher it all, but Cormac's innuendos and statements just coagulated into a large blob of nothing. None of it made any sense.

Her head lolled back and Libby felt the fight leave as her body began to physically shut down. She tried to wipe all of it from her mind. Everything faded away, and the sound of her own breathing echoed loudly in her ears. She closed her eyes and rested, trying to conserve her strength.

She would need it in the coming days.

When Jaxon burst into the secondary chamber and saw Libby suspended twenty feet in the air, his heart stopped.

Bone-crushing agony shattered his soul and he cried out in anguish at the sight of his woman, lifeless and possibly dead.

Declan was fast on his heels and pushed his way past Jaxon, his hands weaving a pattern quickly in the air. He shouted to the jaguar at his side, and had to repeat himself twice before Jaxon understood.

"Stand beneath her, you'll need to catch her when she falls."

Jaxon rushed forward, his heart beating hard, and when he was in position beneath Libby and she opened her eyes, he almost fell to his knees, so great was the relief that rushed through him.

They were shadowed, full of pain and sorrow. It broke his heart. Rage simmered along with his own pain, but he pushed all of it away. He would find those responsible for this, but first he needed to comfort and care for his woman.

He steadied his trembling limbs and stood waiting, his eyes never breaking contact with hers, and when the charm broke, she slid from the air and deep into his embrace.

"I knew you would come."

Her voice was rough, and his fingers began to feverishly work their way over her body checking for injuries. She was warm, alive, and finally safe in his arms. The joy that he felt at that was unheralded. He hugged her close, inhaling her scent deep into his lungs, holding it there, savoring it slowly. He reveled in the feel of her, the warmth of her, the very weight of her in his arms.

Tenderly, he cupped her face in his hands and gazed down into her eyes. His heart felt about to beat its way from the depths of his chest, and without hesitation he claimed her lips in the most brutally honest kiss he'd ever given. His soul sang as she opened beneath him, and for the first time in a long time he was at peace.

Deep inside, the jaguar purred loudly and barked in triumph at the return of his mate.

"We should go," Declan said. "We need to get to the plane before Belize is overrun with more

DaCostas." His voice sliced through them, and Jaxon wasn't prepared for Libby's violent reaction.

"No!"

She broke away from his kiss and struggled hard against his arms. He fell away from her, shocked at the ferociousness in her tone and the wild look in her eyes.

"We can't leave! Jaxon, our baby is here somewhere in this godforsaken jungle. I need to get to him." Her voice began to shake and her teeth chattered crazily as she rolled away from him and gained her feet. She staggered, but then stood tall, and Jaxon could sense her determination. He stood back and felt an incredible amount of pride as he continued to study his fierce woman.

"Libs, why would you think that our child is out here in the jungle? Why would you even think that he's still alive? I'm their enemy. Why would the DaCostas keep my child alive?" He ran his hands through his hair in agitation. "It doesn't make any sense."

"Jaxon it's not the DaCostas, it's Cormac. You have to believe me. Our little boy is here and he is alive . . . I have to believe that . . . all I have to do is . . ." Libby's voice trailed off and her eyes fell to the ground. Jaxon closed the few feet between them, his strong arms reaching for her, and he was grateful when she didn't pull away from him.

"What do you have to do?" He pressed his lips into the softness of her hair and murmured, "Trust me with this. I can help you."

"Cormac wants the woman who was at the compound." Libby pushed against him, her voice rising. "Did you find her? Is she alive?"

Jaxon looked from Libby to Declan, clearly not liking what he was hearing.

"Well? Is she alive?"

Declan answered as he walked toward them, "Yeah, she's alive, but what the hell does my father want with her?"

"Your father!" Libby shook her head, as she looked to Declan, incredulous. "That son of a bitch is your father?"

Declan's demeanor cooled as he nodded, and when he spoke, it was as if ice had formed in his veins.

"He might have had a hand in creating me, but beyond that he's nothing but garbage. I don't know what he's up to." Declan looked pointedly at Jaxon. "But I can sure as hell tell you one thing, it won't be anything good. And if he's looking to grab the blonde we found, there's no way in hell we can let him have her."

"He has my child, and I'm not leaving Belize until I have him back. How can I leave and never know the truth? I have to finish this, regardless of the outcome." Libby grabbed Jaxon's hand, and the pain that clouded her violet eyes lashed at him. It was as if someone had physically punched him in the gut. It was heartrending, and he felt his heart break a little as he held her.

"Jaxon, I've never even held him. They took him from me as soon as they cut him from my womb." Her voice was thick with emotion, but she forged on, needing to make herself heard, and needing them to know her intentions.

"I know he's alive. I can feel it," Libby pounded her chest hard. "Here." And her expressive eyes told him all he needed to know. There would be no turning back now.

She let him pull her in close once more, and he relished the feel of her trembling form against his chest. He could smell the salt from her tears as they fell from her eyes and moistened his skin. Jaxon's stomach clenched as thoughts of a child alone with Cormac began to take root.

His child.

A son he'd not known about until a few days ago. Tiredly, his mind tried to make sense of it all, but there was just no way he could wrap his brain around it. But what did it matter, really?

As he held his woman so close and tenderly against him, he knew that he would do anything in his power to erase the sadness, pain, and despair that lived inside of her.

Anything. If it meant tearing the jungle apart to find Cormac, then that's exactly what he would do. But he was a warrior, first and foremost. He needed to be smart, calculating. Deadly.

Deep inside his soul, the animal that defined who and what he was stirred, and Jaxon welcomed the rush of power. It burned deep within.

And it wouldn't be denied.

Gently, he pushed Libby away, his eyes never leaving hers, but his words were directed at Declan, who stood a few feet away, tense and on edge. "We need to rendezvous with the others and come up with a plan."

He tore his eyes from Libby long enough to direct them toward one of the best soldiers he'd ever fought with.

"This is going to get nasty. You in?"

Declan gave a harsh laugh, but turned away and began heading toward the passage. "In? Me? Do you honestly think I'd turn down the chance to kick my father's ass all over Belize?" He snorted. "Hell yeah, I'm in. About time I give that bastard as good as he used to give me."

Without another word, Jaxon scooped Libby up into his arms and they followed Declan from the cave. They quickly found their way back to the opening of the large cavern and began the arduous trek back down the mountain.

Once they had cleared the high country and were hiking through the lower forests, Declan grabbed his radio. "Yo, Ana, you guys make it to the airport?"

Static rippled through the air, but the cold voice that shot back at him was clearly not happy.

"No, we're not at the airport. We're still waiting at base camp."

"Miss me much?"

"Yeah, like the plague."

"Now don't go getting all sugary sweet on me, Ana."

"Cut the crap, Declan. Julian has arranged for a helicopter to get us out. He thought the airport wasn't such a great idea, seeing as it's most likely crawling with DaCosta scum. The only problem is that there's a storm brewing out over the water. He's not sure if it's going to develop into something significant, but the chopper was delayed and won't be here until tomorrow morning."

"Good to know. Any news on Jagger?" Declan waited for an answer as static cleared the airwaves.

"That's a negative. Julian picked up his scent, but so far nothing. He's gone back out with Cracker for another pass."

Declan glanced over to Jaxon, noting the clenched jaw, and was about to speak when he was interrupted.

"The girl . . . what about the girl?" Libby's voice was strained, but her hand shot out and grabbed Declan's wrist. He paused before activating the radio once more.

"Ana, how's the girl doing? The one we rescued from the compound."

Ana's sarcastic tone bit through the air, and it was obvious that the newly rescued female had done nothing to ingratiate herself with the vampire.

"She's an ungrateful bitch who attacked Cracker and tried to escape. Julian had to tie her up, just to keep her here." There was a slight pause. "I don't trust her."

Declan nodded. "Good work. Keep her restrained until we get back to camp. We need to question her a little more closely."

The air seemed to thicken and cling to the three of them as they made their way through the heavily forested area that surrounded the jungle. It was thick with pine and mahogany trees. They were descending, and the terrain would soon change into the lush underbelly that made up the Belizean jungle.

It was early dawn, the first streaks of sunlight were beginning to push back the inky black night. They cut through the blackness with arcs of red, orange, and gold, looking like bony fingers.

Libby shivered as she looked up into the waning night sky.

Where are you, Logan?

She sighed softly to herself and drew strength from the man who walked so tall beside her. She was no longer alone, and once she had her little boy, safe and secure in her arms, all of her dreams would finally be realized. She would accept nothing less. It was the least she deserved after all the hell that she'd been through.

She pushed all of her fears to the side and squared her shoulders.

They would win. They would triumph.

There just wasn't any other option.

Think whatever you must, my pet. Just bring me the girl.

Laughter slid through her mind, invading, violating, and Libby nearly stumbled.

Jaxon looked to her, but she nodded, indicating that she was fine, and kept walking.

Keep up the games asshole, she thought, I am so gonna kick your fucking ass.

But there was no answer.

He was gone.

Libby held back the snarl that leapt up from her throat, clenched her hands and looked forward. She would move heaven and hell if she had to, but she was going home with her son.

Off into the distance she heard a low rumble, and it echoed and vibrated across the sky. Something was definitely brewing, the air cracking with energy. Jaxon touched her shoulders reassuringly, and for the first time in a long time, Libby felt hope.

They quickly disappeared into the thick jungle as they continued their way down the mountain, mist and rumbling thunder trailing in their footsteps.

But they were not alone. A lone jaguar watched quietly from high in the canopy above them. It was an impressive animal, long, extending nearly ten feet from nose to tail. It hesitated briefly, its long black tail flicking about in slow, precise movements. Then it stood, stretched, and quietly slid into the jungle after them.

Chapter 24

It was a tired and quiet trio that finally made it back to camp several hours later. The sun had already reached its zenith and was beginning to make its descent once again. The warmth of her rays was oppressive, but the humidity and moisture that cloaked the air and clung to everything was mainly due to the storm that was threatening. Ominous rumblings had echoed over the jungle for hours, and yet it held still, off in the distance.

The wind had answered Mother Nature's call, with gentle gusts giving way to stronger gales. Libby's hair snaked wildly about her face, flying in all directions while still managing to stick to the sweat that coated her skin.

You'd think with a storm brewing, the thick humidity would break, but quite the opposite had happened. Jaxon gently pushed the mass of hair from

Libby's eyes and ran his fingers over her face. Small ripples of pleasure crept over her skin, and in spite of everything, she felt a burst of emotion well up from deep inside her chest.

How she loved this man. Every single cell in her body was screaming for his touch. For his taste. Libby turned toward him and let his strong arms pull her into his hard embrace. She rested her cheek against his chest, loving the sound of his heart beating steadily beneath his flesh.

He belonged to her, and she to him. At the end of the day, that's what it boiled down to. It was that simple. She needed him to breathe, and to live and to love.

"You must be exhausted. Cracker has food for you."

They both turned toward Julian, whose concern was clearly evident. Jaxon embraced his older brother and murmured something into his ear. Libby watched as pain flickered across Julian's face, then she heard Jaxon swear under his breath.

"What?" She looked to each brother and felt her belly tighten as they both shook their heads. "What's happened now?"

Julian paused for a moment, his voice hushed when he finally spoke. "We weren't able to locate Jagger. I did catch his scent, higher up the mountain. But he seems to have vanished." Julian looked at his brother and shrugged his shoulders. "I don't understand why he's not come back to us."

"What do you mean?" Libby asked as both men remained quiet, and was about to protest when she remembered the blasts she'd heard the previous evening. "Is he hurt?" she asked instead. "Captured? What?"

She looked at them and shook her head. Jagger lost? Out here in the jungle?

"Jagger will come to us when he's ready," Jaxon finally said. Though upset, he tried to smile, and gently took her into his embrace as he led her toward the tent. It was the same one they'd shared less than twenty-four hours earlier.

It felt like a lifetime ago.

"I think we're all forgetting that Jagger is a warrior and a highly trained combat soldier," Jaxon said. "He's the best at what he does. Believe me. He's been in worse situations than this. He'll be fine."

Libby hoped he was right. She'd never be able to forgive herself if something happened to his brother.

They entered the tent and she flopped onto the bedroll, wincing as the pain in her side began to throb. It very well could have been there all along, but the adrenaline that had gotten her through the past day was dwindling. She was tired, hungry, and emotionally weak.

Cracker slipped in behind them. She heard more whispering but didn't care what they were saying. The smell of food wafted over to her, and she rolled over, reaching hungrily for the plate that he'd brought with him.

She began to stuff her mouth full of bread, not tasting anything as she wolfed down the nourishment it provided. A warm mug of coffee was given to her, and she closed her eyes, relishing the warm liquid as it slipped down her throat.

"I'm glad to see you made it back in one piece, missy. Don't be doing that again, or you're going to give old Cracker here a heart attack."

Libby's eyes flew open and a tired smile crept over her features as she gazed up at his craggy face. For such a large and fierce-looking man, he'd always had the kindest soul. "Thanks, Cracker."

He nodded and abruptly turned away, and a few seconds later Libby and Jaxon were alone.

He looked down at the frail blonde and shook his head slowly as an overwhelming rush of longing sprang from deep inside his chest. She'd been through so much, and yet here she was, still fighting. She truly was a remarkable woman.

And she was all his.

His dark eyes watched her in silence. There were no words. He waited for her to finish eating and ignored the hunger that gnawed tight at his gut. When she was done, her beautiful violet eyes seemed to shimmer, and he felt his soul move, so great was the emotion that rolled through his body. He would take care of her for the rest of her life.

Starting right now.

He reached for a large basin that had been filled with fresh water. A soft cloth had been draped over the edge, and he dipped it into the bowl, then gently wrung the excess moisture from it.

His eyes never left hers as he knelt down beside her, gently cupping her face with his large hand as he slowly began to wipe every trace of the last few hours from her flesh. Her pale skin glistened with the sheen left behind from the cloth, and she closed her eyes as he methodically ran the cloth along her forehead before moving down to her cheeks, chin, and then to her trembling mouth.

Jaxon took his time, and when he was finished,

he couldn't resist. He began to nibble softly, leaving a trail of small butterfly kisses along the contours of her generous lips. He felt her relax, and smiled against her mouth as she opened herself fully to him. He took a small taste but then pushed himself away, feeling a keen sense of power as her eyes flew open once more and she touched her fingers to her mouth.

She was about to speak, but he hushed her, whispering into her ear, "Not yet."

Libby's eyes darkened and the small catch in her throat tugged hard at his heart. He reached for her top, and her hands went up automatically, enabling him to whisk the dirty garment from her skin. He felt his groin tighten and had to stifle a moan of his own as her breasts sprang free from the cotton and hung provocatively in front of him.

Like candy, ready to be licked. He couldn't help himself, and his tongue darted out quickly, before she even knew his intent, circling an engorged nipple then claiming the ripe bud deep into the hot recesses of his mouth.

Jaxon felt her shudder, and with a mighty effort clamped down on the hot desire that had begun as a slow burn in his belly and was now rifling like wildfire through his veins. This was not about him. It was all about Libby. *His Libby.*

He reluctantly withdrew from the tantalizing flesh, and his hands trailed down her body as she fell back onto the blanket. His fingers grasped the edges of her pants and he pulled them down her legs, hissing sharply at the sight of her sex, exposed and vulnerable. He had to stop and take time to remove her boots, and he felt sweat break out along his limbs as his body raged and the cat began to stir.

He threw her boots to the ground, and the pants quickly followed.

Once more he dipped the cloth into the basin and crouched beside her, gently wiping the grime from her body with slow, precise movements. He started at her neck and shoulders, letting the soothing water wash away all traces of her time with Cormac in the cave.

There was no sound, only their heavy breathing and the soft trickle of water as it fell from the cloth when he wrung the excess from it.

When his hands fell to her breasts, he smiled wickedly at the hard intake of breath and the slow hiss that left her lips. Lovingly, he cupped each globe, taking his time, perhaps too much time, and he reveled in the feel of them as they tightened and filled with pleasure.

He could see her hands clenched at her sides as he slowly worked his way over her ribs, taking special care where she'd been hurt, kissing every one of them as he finished. He moved the cloth down her body while his free hand massaged and kneaded. He felt small shudders underneath her skin as he swept over her belly, each pass with the cloth eliciting small mews from deep in her throat.

Her hips began to slowly gyrate, and Jaxon clenched his teeth together as her knees opened and her soft cleft lay open for him.

He had to pull hard to find the control he needed to continue, but it was important to him to look to her needs first. After rinsing the cloth again, he softly wiped along her inner thigh, inhaling the sweetness of her scent as he continued his ministrations. His eyes were drawn to the soft blond hair that lay there, glistening with the beginnings of her desire. She groaned loudly when he finally touched her heated flesh, gently rolling the cloth over her mound.

She bucked her hips then, and Jaxon chuckled. "In time, sweetness."

He ignored the swelling cock between his legs and reluctantly left her hot core, finishing her body right down to the very tips of her toes. When he was done, he threw the cloth into the bowl and then ran his hands up along both sides of her body, before gently resting them against her hips.

Libby's breaths were coming in short, soft pants, muffled as he turned her over onto her stomach. He felt her still, and then draw away from him. With his hands, he began to caress the scarred, damaged skin that lined her back in a macabre display of artistry.

Jaxon moistened the cloth yet again, to repeat his ministrations, starting from the top of her delectable neck, working his way down along the length of her body. By the time he reached the soles of her feet, he was breathing hard, because of the effort it took to control his need to claim her.

When he was done, he stood, the hard outline of his dick straining against his pants. He looked down at Libby, splayed out, long white limbs relaxed, but her excitement betrayed by the staccato breathing from her lips.

His fingers tore open the waist of his pants and he stripped them from his body, groaning roughly as the heavy material rushed against his aching cock.

In one movement he threw his shirt from his body and reached for the cloth, wanting to clean his own skin before he would allow himself to touch her.

"Don't."

Jaxon paused and hissed sharply as Libby rose in front of him, her breasts swaying teasingly. She moved toward him slowly. "I want you inside of me right now."

He felt his skin begin to burn and itch, and the wash of predatory possession that coursed through him made his breathing even more ragged and rough. She belonged to him.

And he would never let her go.

She knelt in front of him, her beautiful eyes huge and luminous, and when the tips of her nipples caressed the tight abs of his skin, he nearly lost it. He closed his eyes and prayed for control, but it was so hard. The beast in him howled in pleasure as her fingers took a torturous path, tracing the clan tattoos that proudly stood out against his flesh.

Softly, they crept up, and when he opened his eyes once more, he knew by her sharp intake of breath that his own eyes were glowing, full of raging desire. He reached down and cupped her cheeks, lowering himself until they were face-to-face.

For several moments there was no sound other than their harsh breathing as they both inhaled deep gulps of air. For Jaxon, everything faded away and there was only Libby. It was as if a spell had been cast. As if this moment in time mattered more than any other moment they'd ever spent together.

And he guessed that it did. Everything was spelled out. His heart was out there to be shredded to pieces or put back together and healed. She had the power.

And for the first time in his life, Jaxon Castille was willing to surrender to that power.

Her deeply shadowed eyes filled with soft tears, and he kissed them away before claiming the mouth that trembled against his own.

She tasted like home, and when her tongue flicked across his lips and her mouth opened wide beneath his, Jaxon clutched her to him, but then broke away. He needed her to know what was in his heart.

"I love you, Libby." He held her eyes, watching as myriad emotions crossed them and then disappeared. "Do you understand what I'm saying? There will never be another for me. There will never be another for you. I will not live without you in this world. Whatever tomorrow brings doesn't matter," he kissed her gently, "and you'll always have my heart."

He felt her body melt against his, and he caught her, gently laying her back onto the bedroll and pulling his large body up alongside hers.

"Please," she whispered, "Jaxon, I need you to love me."

His body sang with joy and he claimed her lips again, pouring every bit of emotion he had into the kiss as he ravaged the softness beneath them. His fingers dug deep into the thick mass of hair that haloed her head, and the scent of her arousal clung to his nose, sending spikes of hard desire straight to his aching cock.

He wanted to be gentle, but his need was so great and he felt his edge of control begin to slip as her hands encircled his engorged shaft. Softly, her fingers flew over the velvet ridge before running along his straining length. He groaned loudly into her mouth and grabbed her tongue, sucking it hard.

"Christ, Libs, keep that up and the show will be over before we even begin." His voice was ragged and he pulled away, his great chest heaving with the effort it took to control his animal desires.

"Well then, I need you to begin, because I'm aching for you."

Her eyes held his prisoner as she moved and positioned her body, gently gliding his cock to her warm and wet opening. As if the smell of her wasn't enough to drive him crazy, the feel of her slick desire on the head of his cock drew a small curse from him. He watched a satisfied smile race across her face, before a pained one took its place.

"Damn it, Jaxon." She began to rub herself all over him. "I can't wait."

With a growl, Jaxon flipped onto his back, lifting her above his body, barely able to control himself as she placed her legs on either side of him. He looked up at her and marveled that this beauty, this fucking amazing woman, was his, and with a savage snarl he brought her down over him. The feel of her was exquisite, and he felt his balls clench as her slickness slid over his hard length. With a hard thrust, he buried himself deeply within the hot core of her body.

She screamed softly before smiling down at him wantonly, beginning to move and gyrate against him. The pressure he felt was intense. His hands immediately grabbed her hips, slowing the rhythm, wanting the pleasure to last.

But his little hellion was having none of that, her body gliding up and down more forcefully, her channel tightening as she continued to ride him fast and hard. Her breasts jiggled in front of him, and his hands fell away from her hips, letting her have her way, and they found their way to the softness of her generous globes, the long fingers pinching the puckered redness of her engorged nipples.

His right hand left her chest and he held it tight against her belly, loving the feel of her muscles as they clenched and shuddered with each thrust of his cock. He could feel the pressure build deep inside him, and his eyes sought out hers, fastening on the large ovals that stared down at him, misty and luminous with passion.

Her lips were open and her tongue could be seen between her teeth as she began to moan softly. She increased the rhythm even more, and the sounds of flesh slapping hard against flesh reverberated throughout the tent. It only added to the insane pleasure that Jaxon was feeling; for they were the sounds of his body loving the woman that belonged to him.

When he felt her vaginal walls clench even tighter, he knew he couldn't wait much longer, and as she screamed her release, he gave one final thrust and let his body give in to the most incredible orgasm he'd ever had. It pounded through his veins, rough and aggressive, leaving every nerve ending in its wake electrified.

He heard the beast within scream in triumph, or it very well could have been himself. He didn't know and didn't care.

Libby collapsed onto his chest, and he immediately wrapped his arms tightly around her, reveling in the sound and feel of her heart raging deep inside her chest. He wasn't sure how long they lay there, limbs entwined, bodies wet and slick from their lovemaking.

When her head moved and her eyes looked at him, he felt more love than he'd known was imaginable. She gently traced his mouth and kissed him, murmuring against his flesh, "*That* was one hell of a body wash."

Jaxon laughed loudly, and pulled her in close to his body before closing his eyes. A few moments later her even breathing told him that Libby had surrendered and fallen asleep. He kissed the top of her head as his thoughts darkened, and he felt anger once more begin to claw at him.

His thoughts turned to Cormac. They had in their possession something the sorcerer wanted. Badly. There was no way in hell he would just hand over an innocent to a madman like Cormac, but that didn't mean he was above using the woman as bait.

He sighed softly, his breath ruffling the soft blond hair that lay against him. Only time would tell if his son was indeed alive and well. He couldn't dwell on that right now, though. He needed to rest.

Because tomorrow he was going to fucking kill the bastard.

Libby awoke with a start. She wasn't sure what pulled her from the clutches of sleep, but she pushed her hair from her eyes, instantly on edge. She sensed a presence, and it had nothing to do with the warm, muscled form that was flush against her back.

She shook her head and tried to focus. *Something*

was here. She could feel it. Her eyes searched the dim interior of the tent as she tried to locate whatever was making her so jumpy.

The feeling intensified, manifesting itself until she knew beyond doubt that Cormac was calling to her. The urge to run to him was so compelling she found herself moving before she even realized it.

His magick was strong, of that there was no doubt, and her natural instinct was to fight the pull. What kind of power did he have over her? The nagging question flittered through her mind, but Libby pushed it away. She knew it didn't matter. She would follow his crumbs. This was her only chance to get her son back. She had to obey.

Gingerly, she disengaged her limbs from Jaxon, her smile bittersweet as she gazed down at the sleeping man. He was such a fierce warrior, so handsome and strong, yet in repose she could see the young man that he had once been.

That thought alone brought a host of emotions to the surface, and she had to take a moment and compose herself. Quickly, she gathered up the dirty clothes that Jaxon had removed from her the previous evening, wrinkling her nose at the thought of pulling them on. A quick glance around told her there was nothing else available, so she quickly pulled the clothing up over her body.

After dressing, she drank some water and tried her best to untangle the hair that still lay in wild waves, pretty much everywhere. She gave up after a few frustrated moments and gathered the thick mess, securing it with a piece of string from the bag she'd brought with her when she first arrived.

She paused once, her eyes trailing back toward

Jaxon, and then quietly slipped from the tent. She knew she had to do this alone. Jaxon would attack with a vengeance, taking Declan, Cracker, and even Julian along for the ride. There was just too much room for error, and that was something she wasn't willing to take a chance on. Her son's safety was her only concern.

Besides, she knew that Jaxon would never approve of her plan.

It was still dark out, the air heavy with the threat of a storm. The ominous feeling seemed to fall like a second skin over her flesh, and she shivered as her eyes moved about the camp. She'd been so exhausted when they returned that she'd never even inquired about the woman. *Skye Knightly.*

She pursed her lips, then took off without hesitation toward the tech tent. It was the largest and would be the most logical place to stash a prisoner. After moving the flap back, she stepped silently inside, grateful that her eyes had adjusted to the gloom.

"You're up early."

The words sliced through the air and brought Libby up cold. She turned to her left, a small smile playing around her mouth as she spied Cracker.

"I couldn't sleep."

His raised eyebrow brought a blush to her cheeks, but Libby ignored it, her focus shifting to the woman who lay a few feet beyond him. She was bound, and her eyes burned with dark emotions that were evident even through the dim interior of the tent.

"I need to talk to her." Libby nodded toward the prisoner. "Alone."

"Aha." Cracker spat to the side and slowly got to

his feet. "I'm going to give you a few minutes, Libby, but pay attention. She's a slippery piece of work and not to be trusted."

"Don't worry about me. Why don't you try and get a few hours sleep? I'll stay with her."

Cracker's dark eyes bored into her, and Libby hoped he would just leave. She didn't know what she'd be forced to do if the ex-soldier refused and stuck around. Seconds ticked by, and then, with a slight nod, Cracker disappeared and left her alone with the blond woman.

A woman who was the key to her son's survival.

Her face grim, Libby turned and slowly walked toward her. She needed to know why Cormac wanted her so badly. She needed to know what kind of hell she was going to unleash by giving him exactly what he wanted.

Because she *would* sacrifice this woman for her son, if she had to.

Of that there was no doubt.

Libby squatted down in front of the woman that she'd shared a room with for several weeks in the DaCosta compound. They'd hardly spoken then, and the dislike evident on the stranger's face told her she would have to do her dammed best to get her to talk now.

"Skye?" Her voice was soft, silky smooth. As the seconds ticked by, Libby knew with all her heart she was on the right path. *She would do this.*

She would get her little Logan back.

The woman's electric blue eyes were full of anger, but she remained silent.

"Skye, we don't have much time. I need your help."

The woman continued to regard her with eyes

that had turned dark with loathing. "You lay with a jaguar and you expect me to help you? You're fucking crazy."

Libby frowned and shook her head. She was done with games.

"You *will* help me get my son back," she stood quickly, her eyes narrowed as she lowered her voice, "and Cormac will die."

"Cormac? *He* has your son?"

Libby nodded and moved toward a long table, her steps sure and her heart full of many scattered emotions. She grabbed a gun, one that was loaded to the teeth with antimagick bullets, as well as a long serrated knife. The symbols that lined the silver blade proclaimed it as charmed, and she smiled softly as she held the deadly weapon in her hand. She would slice his throat with it, if she had the chance.

Turning back around, she motioned for the woman to get up. Skye hesitated briefly, but then slowly moved her limbs, gingerly gaining her feet with a grace that was surprising considering her arms were bound behind her back. When she was standing and facing Libby, she spoke.

The venom and hatred that poured from her mouth was undeniable.

"I'll help you get your son back, but you will let me kill Cormac. He needs to be stopped."

Libby paused, staring at the other woman suspiciously. "Why does he want you?"

The blond woman grimaced but kept quiet, refusing to answer. A sliver of doubt slid through Libby and was gone as quick as it had arrived. She didn't for one second trust the other woman, but would not change her own course. There was no time. She nodded toward the exit. "All right, let's do this."

She listened intently at the door, and when the coast was clear, pulled back the flap. She let Skye pass and followed suit. Seconds later both women disappeared into the darkness and were enveloped into the arms of the jungle.

Chapter 25

The going was rough.

Libby and Skye had been trudging through the jungle for what seemed hours. The sun was up, but the rays were hampered not only by the thickness of the jungle canopy, but the dark clouds that blanketed the area as well. The occasional rumble of thunder could still be heard in the distance, and as Libby paused for a moment, wiping sweat from her brow, she doubted the darkness that was following her had anything to do with the weather.

Cormac's black magick could be felt in every breath she drew deep into her lungs. It was pungent, thick with the taint of his evil. She tried not to think about the fact that she found the sensation almost familiar. In fact, it seemed as if her legs had a mind of their own and she was just along for the ride.

The two women had spoken barely a word to each

other the entire morning, but the silence that lay between the two of them was not so much one of dislike; rather, it was something akin to slowly gained respect. It had grown as their legs ate up miles of jungle underbelly, and about an hour earlier Libby had finally relented and untied Skye's hands from behind her back.

She was impressed that Skye had no problems keeping up with the relentless pace she set. She was more impressed that the woman hadn't tried to escape. Of course, the gun and knife that she brandished might have had something to do with that, but it also appeared that Skye wanted to destroy Cormac almost as much as she did.

Maybe even more so.

She grabbed some water and took a long draw, letting the liquid slide down her throat as she caught her breath. The stitch in her side had returned, but she'd become so used to ignoring pain that it was no more annoying than a mosquito bite. She rubbed her ribs gently and passed the water to Skye.

The other woman grabbed the bottle and took a long swig. She wiped her hands across her mouth and looked directly into Libby's eyes. "Sorry for that."

Libby looked at her, confused by the comment, but when the woman nodded toward her ribs, she understood. The only reason she'd received the injury was because Skye had initiated a rebellion against Fat Frank.

Libby shrugged and looked away. She was trying to banish the horrific memories that she'd only managed to regain a few days ago.

"You were there when they brought me in." Skye's words were spoken quietly.

Again Libby remained silent, but now Skye had her full attention.

"How long did the DaCostas have you?" the other woman asked.

Libby considered ignoring the question, but for whatever reason, she found an answer slipping from her mouth before she could stop herself. "Three years."

She could tell that Skye was surprised by her answer, and for a moment there was just the familiar silence from before.

"Why did they take you?"

"Why did they take *you*?" Libby shot back.

Skye remained quiet, her deep blue eyes shadowed and pained. Libby exhaled deeply and looked away into the distance. The sadness that encircled her heart was making it difficult to breathe. A plethora of emotions wracked her psyche, but she didn't give into them. She needed to be strong.

For Logan.

"I worked for the government, in an antiterrorist unit. I met Jaxon," her eyes bored into Skye's, "*my jaguar*, at PATU. He was in charge of our unit." A small smile lit the corners of her mouth as she continued. "We became involved, and we've both paid the price for that." She grimaced and glanced at Skye, who was listening quietly. "We are the poster couple for the million reasons *not* to get involved with someone you work with. It *will* come back to bite you in the ass."

Libby sighed harshly, her voice bitter, "The Da-Costas took me, and tortured me to get information on a mission that Jaxon was involved in. They wanted to eliminate him. There was no way in hell I was gonna give up the man that I loved. But then . . ." Her voice trailed off softly.

"Then what?"

"They found out I was pregnant." Libby shook her head as her eyes filled with tears. "Suddenly I had to choose between the man I loved and the child I carried." She shrugged her shoulders. "I chose my child, but at what price? Logan was ripped from my womb two years ago. I didn't even get a chance to hold him."

"I'm so sorry, Libby. I had no idea."

Libby was silent for a moment, as a new thought struck her. "Do you know why Cormac has my child? And what your role in all this madness is?"

She watched as the other woman struggled with something internal. As if she were weighing all of her options.

"I don't know why Cormac has your child, Libby, but nothing he does is random. There's an ulterior motive there, and it's something above and beyond using your son to get to me. He will not hand the boy over."

"And he wants you because . . . ?"

Again Skye hesitated, but then shook her head and answered. "I'm guessing he thinks I'll lead him to an ancient portal that's a direct conduit to the demon underworld."

Libby was stunned at her answer. She opened her mouth to speak but then closed it. She was speechless. All sorts of thoughts ran through her mind. Demons? She'd never dealt with anything like that in PATU, but she'd read reports that had made her skin crawl. If Cormac somehow managed to open his very own portal to the underworld, all hell would literally break loose.

"Can you?" she finally managed to ask.

Libby watched as pain crossed Skye's features. She was a striking woman, but there was also strength there to match the beauty.

"My father died trying to destroy the portal, and I will give my own life to keep it out of that bastard's hands."

Her answer was barely above a whisper, and Libby was still not altogether sure that she trusted her. But at this point she had no other choice. "Okay, then. I'll do whatever I can to help, but my son comes first. Understood?"

Skye nodded, and Libby exhaled slowly. A shrill shriek cascaded across the jungle as a large bird flew overhead. Both women jumped, and afterward Libby tried to calm her nerves.

"We need to get going," she said, stashing the water bottle and standing. "I want to get to Cormac before Jaxon and the rest of the team follow suit. I can't take a chance on everything going to shit. I won't let Logan get hurt in the cross fire."

"Do you even know where we're going?"

The heaviness in her heart turned over, and Libby fought the panic and nausea that roiled in her gut. She nodded and began to move, Skye following her lead. "Cormac has tapped into me somehow. He's leading us right to him."

"That's great to hear," Skye replied sarcastically. "We got a plan?"

"No."

Skye laughed softly. "Good to know." She fell in

step behind Libby, and the two women were once more swallowed whole by the Belizean jungle.

Base camp was quiet, yet the air was thick with anger. It clogged Jaxon's throat, preventing him from articulating the boiling rage that simmered beneath the surface. But maybe that was a good thing.

He could not believe he was about to go after Libby . . . again, the second time in as many days. The woman was certifiable! What the hell was she thinking? Traipsing off into the jungle, going after Cormac alone—taking the only bargaining chip that they had with her.

How the fuck had she managed to sneak out of camp, and take their prisoner along for the ride?

He threw a dark look toward Cracker, but truthfully, he knew he couldn't blame the soldier. They were all exhausted, and there had been no reason to suspect she would pull such an incredibly stupid stunt.

He snarled, angry with himself more than anyone else. He'd had the woman in his bed and still she'd managed to slip away.

Libby was going to get herself killed. And over what? Some fantasy that his enemies had kept his offspring alive? That someone as evil and demented as Cormac would take care of a small jaguar shifter? Out of the goodness of his heart? That even if he had, he would just hand the child over? The man was a monster, and for reasons Jaxon didn't understand, wanted the woman that they'd pulled from the wreckage of the compound.

None of it made sense.

But he was going to get to the bottom of it. And

there would be hell to pay if one hair on Libby's head was harmed.

He clenched his teeth as he heaved his bag across his shoulders. They were full of weapons, Declan specials, and he was ready to use all of it to get back the woman he loved.

"You ready?" Declan asked as he moved toward him, followed closely by Julian and Cracker. The ex-soldier was avoiding his eyes, and Jaxon left it alone. He knew Cracker felt responsible, but he'd come around eventually. No words were necessary.

Jaxon nodded and glanced over to the tech tent. "Ana, we're going silent. Don't contact us unless we've got company." He could see the frustration that lit her eyes. The vampire was damn pissed that she wasn't able to come along.

"I'm coming after you as soon as it gets dark," she replied.

"Ana, we need you here with all the equipment."

"No you don't, Jaxon. Tech boy over here can handle it without my help." Her eyes softened as they passed over the sorcerer, but the familiar bite was still there as she continued, "You better watch your ass, Declan. I don't want to be picking it up off the jungle floor."

"Hell, Ana, is that all I have to do to get your hands on my ass?" Declan smirked and then winked back at the vampire. "Don't worry, darlin', I'll be back, and you can inspect every inch of me for damage. In fact, I'll expect a thorough examination."

"Just be careful." With a whirl of long dark hair and pale limbs, Ana disappeared into the tent. Their tech boy saluted and followed suit.

"All right. Let's head out." Jaxon turned in a

semicircle and inhaled sharply. He felt a rush of emotion threaten to overwhelm him as her scent drifted on the wind and settled deep inside his chest. He could track her easily by smell, but he knew he didn't need to do that any longer. She belonged to him now, and her essence called to him on a primitive level.

His gaze swung west and he began to move quickly, his men following suit. She had at least a two hour head start and they had some rough ground to make up.

The four men moved through the thick trees with deadly precision. Each were consumed with thoughts of their own, and the jungle fell silent as they methodically ate up the terrain. Jaxon could feel Libby's emotions all around him. They were in each breath he took. They ran the gamut from pain, anger, and a touch of hope as well, and surrounded him as if they were hung from the branches of the low lying canopy. Everything that she felt pummeled him with an intensity that left no doubt she belonged to him body and soul.

His long frame hummed with a hunger that ate at him, pushing him forward at a relentless pace.

Julian fell into step beside him, and Jaxon felt grateful for the presence of his brother, although that brought to mind the missing Jagger. He grimaced at the thought and shook his head; one more thing to file away and deal with later. All that he could think about right now was finding Libby and getting the hell out this jungle.

"We have a plan?"

Jaxon stole a glance to his brother and snorted. "We're going to go in with everything we've got, and I'm going to personally rip that fucking bastard to pieces."

Julian nodded. "Not if I get to him first."

"Hey, he's my piece-of-shit father," Declan put in. "If anyone has the right to send him to hell, it's me." He grinned as he pulled up alongside the two brothers. "It's about time we started a pissing contest." He looked back to Cracker. "You in?"

"You young pups are all insane. Cormac O'Hara is one crazy son of a bitch, and he's not going down without a fight." The older man's words sobered them a bit. "Declan, you'd better make sure you're on top of your game, and don't let him mess with your head, or we're all dead."

"Christ, you know how to close a party down but good. Don't worry, Cracker, my old man is in for the surprise of his life." Declan's demeanor changed sharply, and Jaxon looked at him intently. The sorcerer's body crackled with power, and sparks flew from his fingers as he clenched his hands.

Rage, anger, and vengeance were strong emotions indeed. They could prove deadly when mixed with the kind of power Declan possessed. They could also corrupt and eat away at a person until all that was left was poison.

Jaxon forged ahead, filing away that knowledge and knowing he'd have to keep a close eye on his friend.

They hiked through streams, cut their way through verdant greenery, all the while on a direct course toward the Mayan ruins in Caracol.

The thick jungle finally gave way to a vast area that had been cleared. It was early afternoon and they'd been hiking for hours. Jaxon could feel Libby much stronger now, her scent everywhere. It tore at him and he began to breathe hard.

He quickly got hold of his emotions and called for the calm, calculating soldier that was so much a part of him. His eyes scanned the area directly in front of him, but the site was massive, spreading out over thirty square miles into the jungle. He could see humans milling about, but dismissed them as either tourists or members of the archeological team that was slowly rescuing Caracol from the jungle that had laid claim to it centuries before.

The focal point was the large temple that rose well over 140 feet. It was one of the largest Mayan structures ever unearthed, and the largest one in Belize. His eyes narrowed as another flash of anxiety rushed through him.

His body trembled as the cat shimmered and burned beneath his skin. Libby was there. Somewhere deep inside the temple.

He snarled and took off at a run, and the three men followed suit. Declan began to chant a protection ward, his long legs keeping him abreast of the Castille brothers and Cracker as he did so.

They skirted the perimeter of the ruins and slithered into the thick Chiquibul forest that surrounded the area. By the time they reached the back of the stone structure, it seemed that every cell in Jaxon's body was on fire with the need to get to his mate.

A thick ball of dread punched at his gut as a wave of intense fear rolled over him in waves. Libby was in trouble and he knew he didn't have much time. There was a crude opening, and he headed for it, his senses soaring out, trying to locate her exact location.

What he found stopped him cold, and the pain in his gut threatened to bring him to his knees.

Declan nearly crashed into him, and Julian narrowly avoided a collision as well.

"What the fuck?" Declan's eyes were almost feverish as power swelled from deep within his body. "Jax, what's wrong?"

Jaxon couldn't speak at first, and he struggled to clamp down at the beast that was suddenly howling in anguish. "She was right." He shook his head, turning pained eyes to the three men, who stood beside him, their chests heaving from exertion. "Cormac has my son."

Deep inside the belly of the temple, Libby faced her enemy, trying to put on a brave face, but fearing her weakness was pinned to her chest like a large neon button.

About an hour earlier, she and Skye had finally found the temple. Libby had led the way, feeling like a puppet pulled by invisible strings. That weird and creepy sensation had been her constant companion all morning, but though she knew she wasn't in control, she hadn't cared. She knew it was Cormac reeling her in, but that also meant she was on the right path. And that was all that mattered. It was the path to her son, and now as she stood here, facing this demon from her past, she knew it was worth it. All of it.

Because she could feel him. *Logan.* He was here, of that she was sure. She could feel his emotions battering at her brain with a feverish force.

She had no clue whatsoever how she could feel the things that she was feeling. She just did. She knew that her son was scared and hungry. She ached at the very thought, but had to trust that Skye had her back and they would get Logan to safety.

"Libby, how nice to see you again, and just in time for a family reunion."

The tall man smiled down at her from twenty feet above, his voice echoing eerily against the stone walls. She stood still, not saying a word, biding her time. Her violet eyes had darkened and now seemed to shimmer with a fire of vengeance that fueled her body with a flood of strength.

Cormac's lips curled into a cruel smile. "What? Nothing to say? Don't you miss me?"

"Where is my son?" Her voice was low, controlled.

He burst into laughter at her words, but his eyes burned maniacally as he directed the power of his gaze on her. "Don't be rude, Libby. Were you not taught any manners in that pitiful excuse of a house you grew up in?"

"I won't play your game, Cormac."

Cormac jumped down in one fluid movement, and Libby flinched as the weight of his power washed over her. "You'll do whatever I want you to do." His expression changed then as his fingers reached out to touch a stray curl that had fallen loose from her ponytail. She cringed but stood her ground.

"You look so much like her."

"Like who?" A sick feeling began to wind its way through her belly, and sweat broke out on her forehead as dread swirled alongside her already jumbled emotions. She just prayed that Skye was using her time wisely and had found little Logan.

"Your mother, Aislyn."

"My mother's name is Patti. I have—" Under-

standing dawned then, and Libby took a step back,
nearly tripping as she lost her balance.

Cormac's deep laughter reverberated around the
chamber, and she clamped her hands over her ears
as images came and went, crashing through her
brain in a chaotic mess that left her feeling weak.

One constant was threaded throughout every
emotion and memory she was feeling. And it was
the face of the man standing directly in front of her.
Her eyes looked up at him, not wanting to ask, but
she opened her mouth nonetheless.

"Who the hell are you?"

"You haven't figured it out yet?" She watched
warily as Cormac cocked his head to the side, disappointment clouding his cold features. "Libby, try a
little harder. It will come to you."

She shook her head, not wanting to believe what
the bastard was insinuating. She just couldn't go
there. Not now. She pushed his words to the back of
her mind, feeding her anger as she focused on the
reason she had come. She shook her head angrily
and shouted, "Just give me my son and I'll lead you
to the woman."

Cold rage passed over Cormac's features, and
she felt his power billow out as he snarled down at
her. "You really are no different than your mother.
It was her biting tongue and temper that finally got
the best of her, and I had to put a stop to it."

"What the hell are you talking about?"

"Remember what I told you yesterday, Libby?
That it was only because *I* allowed you to live that
you were breathing air?" He laughed harshly. "Your
mother didn't understand the power I wield, and
she pushed me one time too many."

Libby tried to swallow the fear that was rising and spreading like wildfire through her veins, but it was impossible. She watched Cormac's pupils dilate and the whites recede, enveloped by a deep blackness that crept over them. His voice lowered to a strange harmonic timbre that was almost hypnotizing. She resisted the pull, but barely.

"I destroyed her, Libby, and I will not hesitate to destroy you or your child. Tell that eagle bitch to make herself known, or I will blast every trace of you from this earth, and you can join your mother in hell."

"Christ, Cormac! Did no one teach you any manners? Or was that something they didn't bother with at warlock academy?"

Libby's eyes whipped upward and she sucked in air so quickly that she felt faint. Skye was standing about a hundred feet away from them, and cradled in her arms was a small child. Pain lanced across Libby's heart as her eyes feverishly latched onto the small form. But his little head was buried deep within Skye's arms, and the only thing visible was creamy flesh and dark curls.

Cormac turned from her, focusing all of his attention on Skye and the child. Silently, Libby began to back away, her fingers reaching for gun she'd concealed in her pants. She had given the knife to Skye, but now, as she gazed up at the woman who held her son, she wondered if she'd made a terrible mistake.

What the hell was Skye up to? She'd been told to take Logan and run. To make sure that the little boy was returned to Jaxon in case she herself didn't make it out of the temple.

Cormac's laughter sliced through the air, and

it had the same effect as long fingernails running over a chalkboard. Libby's skin broke out in a rash of goose bumps and every hair on her body stood on end.

Cormac's laughter abruptly stopped as he moved closer to where Skye held her child. "I'm impressed," he said to her, his words enunciated carefully. The temperature inside the chamber had dropped considerably, so much that a fine mist shot from his mouth as he continued. "The little bird has grown up. Your father must be so proud. But wait." He paused, and Libby felt him gather more power to himself. "He's not around to witness this, is he? It would be next to impossible, considering I ate his life force and he's nothing but a lost soul."

"You fucking bastard! I will see you dead, Cormac, if it's the last thing that I do."

"Careful for what you wish for, Skye—"

"Cut the crap, Cormac! You will not kill me, the same as you won't harm a hair on the head of this little boy. You need both of us."

Libby caught Skye's eyes for a brief moment as she continued to back away, and her heart constricted painfully as the child in her arms moved slightly, and a pair of eyes as dark as midnight gazed across the room at her. She couldn't help the sob that escaped her lips, and she froze, suddenly unsure of what to do.

"Come with me and the child and his mother can leave unharmed," Cormac said to Skye as his voice dropped even lower. There was no emotion in it, just a coldness that matched the now freezing temperature.

"You are so fucking arrogant. Do you think I would believe anything that leaves your lips? The only expendable person in this room is Libby. You need her son as a sacrifice to open the portal, and you need me to find it for you. I'm an eagle knight, you asshole, and I won't allow you to kill an innocent."

"Enough!"

The room began to tremble as sparks flew from Cormac's hands. "You will come with me or—"

With speed that was preternatural, Skye whisked out the charmed dagger and whipped it at Cormac, shouting to Libby as she did. "Run!"

Libby reacted on pure instinct and began to shoot at Cormac as she ran toward her son. The warlock roared in anger, and the air trembled, seeming to shimmer and darken. A terrific shot of energy consumed the entire area, reverberating around the chamber, and two large boulders came crashing down from the ceiling, landing right where Skye had been standing, holding her son.

Tears poured down Libby's face and everything faded away except the rubble and smoke that covered the area where Skye had been standing only seconds before. Dimly, she heard shouts behind her. On some level she was aware that Jaxon had arrived on the scene, but as chaos erupted and curses were heard, she continued to scramble toward the downed boulders.

She used every last bit of strength she possessed to get her body to the top of the pile, and when she spied Skye, holding her son, she fell to her knees as the enormity of the moment washed over her.

She could do no more than watch in silence as

Skye coughed up smoke and debris from her lungs, a small head barely visible above the safe haven of her arms.

Libby wanted to move, but her body felt glued to the rock that she had collapsed upon, and she could only stare helplessly at the woman who held her son. She moved her lips slowly. No sound came out, yet she knew Skye heard what was in her heart. *Thank you.*

Carefully, Skye disengaged her limbs from the rubble that surrounded her. She murmured softly, and the little boy in her arms relaxed as Skye climbed up toward his mother. And of that, there was no doubt. The child carried the scent of a jaguar, but the magick in him was overwhelming. He would be a force to be reckoned with when he matured into a man.

Skye's eyes narrowed as they settled onto Libby, and she wondered if Libby had realized what Cormac insinuated. That he was her blood father. Obviously, she'd not been born with the strength and scope of his power, but Skye could sense small traces of it present in Libby's aura. The little boy, however, was another story. His blood literally sang with power.

A shout from across the chamber shook Skye out of her thoughts, and she quickly handed the child over to his mother.

Libby felt as if her heart had burst from her chest, and as her arms closed around Logan, she began to weep softly. He was warm, soft, and smelled of the forest. She nuzzled her face against his soft curls and rocked him gently, her eyes shining as she looked up at Skye.

"I don't know what to say . . . how will I ever be able to thank you?"

Skye winked, but when she spoke, her voice was dead serious. "No one can know that I survived this attack."

Libby looked at her, confused. "I don't understand."

"I know that you love your jaguar, but I don't trust them. They've been enemy to the eagle for eons. The eagle knights were created to protect the portal. And because of that my people have been hunted to near extinction." Skye couldn't keep the bitterness and pain from her voice. "Jaguars, magicks . . . all of them played a part, and I will never trust a warrior." She looked away, her voice soft. "I just can't."

"But Jaxon would never—"

"I need to find this portal and seal it before Cormac—or anyone else, for that matter—gets their hands on it. If that happens, my father's death would have been for nothing."

"Skye, we can help you."

"Libby, no one can know about the portal. You have to promise me that you won't tell a soul about it, or that I survived this attack. You owe me."

Libby was about to answer when a shout only a few feet away distracted her. She shook her head and twisted her body around. Jaxon was there, just beyond the large boulders. A feeling of peace flooded her veins, and her only thought was to get to him. She cradled her precious cargo close to her breast and scrambled to her feet, carefully making her way up to the top. At the sight of Jaxon's handsome face, she felt the world slip away until there was only the three of them.

He was speaking to her, but she couldn't understand a thing he was saying. She could barely see him though the haze of tears, the roaring in her ears almost painful. When his mouth claimed hers, the noise stopped.

Everything faded from existence except the three heartbeats that pounded out a rhythm in tandem, together, finally.

She didn't want the kiss to ever end. It was raw and full of need. His hands cupped her face roughly, but then he gently disengaged himself and stared with wonder at the young boy, with eyes that mirrored his own.

"He's . . . beautiful," Jaxon could barely manage to get the words out. He couldn't begin to name the emotions he was feeling.

His long arms wrapped the both of them deep in his protective embrace and he trembled as the jaguar screamed inside, flush from victory. He felt the child still, and when his pudgy hand reached out, to touch his chest, the peace that filled him was indescribable.

The small face looked up to him and smiled, impishly. He spoke one word, but it was clear and strong: "Cat."

"Hey, where'd the girl go?" Declan was breathing hard by the time he reached them, and his eyes glowed with an eerie fire as he looked around the chamber.

Libby looked up, and hoped like hell she was doing the right thing. She spoke softly, and kept her promise to Skye. "She saved Logan, but your father . . ." Her voice trailed off, and Declan swore as her meaning became clear.

"Did you, is he . . ." Libby was afraid to ask, and as Declan's dark gaze swept over her, she knew the answer before he spoke.

"Kill him? That slippery son of a bitch?" Declan took a few steps back, shaking his head as his rage began to boil. "No. But he's given me a reason to look forward to our next meeting." He clenched his hands and muttered under his breath, "Because only one of us will leave it alive."

His ominous announcement was tempered as a rakish smile cut across his handsome face. "And I aim for that to be me, since I plan on living a long and decadent existence, surrounded by beautiful women, good wine, and my favorite Metallica CDs."

"All clear." Cracker's rough voice slid between them, and Libby glanced at the grizzled soldier as Julian joined them as well. "I couldn't find a trace of him, or anyone else for that matter." The wrinkles around Cracker's eyes became more pronounced as he saw Logan for the first time and a wide smile lit up his craggy features. "That is one hell of a handsome kid."

She felt Jaxon's arms slide around her shoulders as he kissed the top of her head. "That he is," he murmured.

Libby inhaled a ragged breath, suddenly desperate to leave. "So what now?" She couldn't keep the tremble from her words as she continued. "Can we just go home?"

She watched as Declan looked hard at Jaxon, afraid of their answer. But it was Julian who spoke up.

"Jaxon will take you home, where you'll be safe with your child."

She felt a rumble from deep within Jaxon's chest

and knew he was torn. Things were very much unfinished. Cormac was still on the loose, the DaCostas were still a part of this whole mess, and Jagger was nowhere to be found. The animal that was his very nature wanted to hunt and destroy.

"Julian, I can't leave this place with that monster on the loose." Jaxon's posture tensed even as his hands remained gentle on her shoulders.

"Jaxon, you have a child to think about. Don't worry about Cormac. That bastard will get his." Declan's voice trembled with suppressed anger.

Cracker spat to the side before chiming in. "We'll find Jagger and bring him back. You look after your woman and little one."

Jaxon hesitated, but when he spoke, there was no doubt as to his intent. "I'll expect to hear daily reports." He hugged Libby again and turned toward the passage that would lead them out of the Mayan ruin. He looked back at Declan, a devilish grin gracing his features. "You know that Ana is going to be pissed you're not returning. She'll kick your ass royally when she finally gets hold of you again."

Declan laughed loudly. "Tell her I'll be looking forward to it."

Then Jaxon bent toward Libby's cheek and whispered, "Let's go home."

They were heading toward the exit when Jaxon realized it was just himself and Libby. He stopped abruptly and whipped around, searching for his brother. "Julian." His voice echoed along the stone walls. "You coming?"

Julian shook his head. "No. Not this time. I need to be here." He flashed white teeth as he smiled. "I need to see this thing through."

The two brothers stared at each other for several long moments, a current of understanding running between them, then Jaxon nodded, before disappearing down the passageway with Libby and his son.

Along the edge of the Mayan ruins, deep within the heart of the Chiquibul forest, a large black jaguar paced back and forth, its long tail twitching, clearly agitated. The beast was confused. But then, it had been confused for a few days now, its thoughts muddled its instincts askew.

It had followed the trio down from the mountain the previous day, and the two women only hours earlier. Something about them had called to his soul. A part of him had wanted to charge into the large structure when they'd all disappeared within its depths.

But he had held back, without knowing why. Back and forth he continued to pace, full of nervous energy. Overhead, a golden eagle soared on the wind, its cry drawing the attention of the great cat.

The jaguar moved toward the edge of the clearing, and watched as the eagle crested against a gust of wind and then slowly circled the large structure before heading south, higher into the mountains. Its curiosity piqued, the animal hesitated and then took off in the same direction, its vibrant green eyes trained on the eagle that was so far out of its reach.

Every step took him farther away from the humans, and eventually the big cat forgot about them entirely. His entire focus had shifted, and the cat picked up speed as it disappeared into the heavily forested stand of pine trees, and in the blink of an eye was gone.

Next month, don't miss these exciting new love stories only from Avon Books

♥ ♥

In Pursuit of a Scandalous Lady by Gayle Callen
Entranced by a portrait and haunted by scandal, Julian Delane, the Earl of Parkhurst, will stop at nothing to learn the truth about the woman he believes to be the mysterious model... even if his quest leads to their utter ruin.

Touching Darkness by Jaime Rush
Nicholas Braden uses his psychic talent to hunt terrorists for a covert government program. Just as he realizes there's something off about the operation, he finds himself under the tempting spell of Olivia, a "good girl" with a wild side and secrets of her own.

The Rogue Prince by Margo Maguire
To the *ton*, the Prince of Sabedoria is a wealthy and powerful royal, but in truth he is a wronged man, hell-bent on revenge. Lady Margaret is chaste, an innocent, but a most tempting seduction ignites a passion she never knew she possessed.

The Notorious Scoundrel by Alexandra Benedict
Like an irresistible siren, orphan Amy Peel lures dukes and earls to London's underworld to see her dance—some say she is a princess, but only one man knows her darkest secret. Edmund Hawkins, pirate turned reluctant gentleman, will not let her out of his sight, especially when a growing threat mounts against the little dancer.

Unforgettable, enthralling love stories,
sparkling with passion and adventure
from Romance's bestselling authors

AVON

Thanks for the Memories
A Novel
CECELIA AHERN
NEW YORK TIMES BESTSELLING AUTHOR OF P.S. I LOVE YOU AND THE GIFT

978-0-06-170624-0

kitchen chinese
A Novel About Food, Family, and Finding Yourself
ANN MAH

978-0-06-177127-9

marian keyes
this charming man

978-0-06-112404-4

CARRIE ADAMS
the stepmother
A Novel

978-0-06-123266-4

How to Knit a Love Song
Rachael Herron

978-0-06-184129-3

BEVERLY JENKINS
A Second Helping

978-0-06-154781-2

Visit www.AuthorTracker.com for exclusive
information on your favorite HarperCollins authors.

Available wherever books are sold, or call 1-800-331-3761 to order.
ATP 0410

At Avon Books, we know your passion for romance—once you finish one of our novels, you find yourself wanting more.

May we tempt you with . . .

- **Excerpts** from our upcoming releases.
- Entertaining **extras**, including authors' personal photo albums and book lists.
- Behind-the-scenes **scoop** on your favorite characters and series.
- **Sweepstakes** for the chance to win free books, romantic getaways, and other fun prizes.
- Writing **tips** from our authors and editors.
- **Blog** with our authors and find out why they love to write romance.
- **Exclusive content** that's not contained within the pages of our novels.

Join us at
www.avonbooks.com